Praise for *Sparrow H*... e:

"Hitchhiking ghosts, the unquiet dead, the gods of the old American roads—McGuire enters the company of Lindskold and Gaiman with this book, creating a wistful, funny, fascinating new mythology of diners, corn fields, and proms in this all-in-one-sitting read!"

—Tamora Pierce, *New York Times*-bestselling author of *Battle Magic* and *Bloodhound*

"Seanan McGuire doesn't write stories, she gifts us with Myth—new Myths for a layered America that guide us off the twilight roads and lend us a pretty little dead girl to show us the way home."

—Tanya Huff, bestselling author of *An Ancient Peace*

"The best ghost story I've read in a very long while."

—The Green Man Review

"An evocative and profoundly creative work that instantly wraps around readers' imaginations . . . this emotional, consistently surprising collection of adventures is also a striking testament to the power of American myths and memories."

—*RT Book Reviews* (top pick)

"McGuire brings empathy, complexity, and a shivering excitement to this well-developed campfire tale. . . . A powerful blend of ghost story, love story, and murder mystery, wrapped in a perfectly neat package."

—*Publishers Weekly* (starred)

"McGuire's twilight America contains some strikingly strong mythic resonances."

—Tor.com

"Unusual, sometimes dark, but rather lovely and even poignant."

—My Bookish Ways

DAW Books presents the finest in urban fantasy from Seanan McGuire:

InCryptid Novels
DISCOUNT ARMAGEDDON
MIDNIGHT BLUE-LIGHT SPECIAL
HALF-OFF RAGNAROK
POCKET APOCALYPSE
CHAOS CHOREOGRAPHY
MAGIC FOR NOTHING
TRICKS FOR FREE
THAT AIN'T WITCHCRAFT*

The Ghost Roads
SPARROW HILL ROAD
THE GIRL IN THE GREEN SILK GOWN

October Daye Novels
ROSEMARY AND RUE
A LOCAL HABITATION
AN ARTIFICIAL NIGHT
LATE ECLIPSES
ONE SALT SEA
ASHES OF HONOR
CHIMES AT MIDNIGHT
THE WINTER LONG
A RED ROSE CHAIN
ONCE BROKEN FAITH
THE BRIGHTEST FELL
NIGHT AND SILENCE*

*Coming soon from DAW Books

SEANAN McGUIRE

Book One of *The Ghost Roads*

DAW BOOKS, INC.
DONALD A. WOLLHEIM, FOUNDER
375 Hudson Street, New York, NY 10014
ELIZABETH R. WOLLHEIM
SHEILA E. GILBERT
PUBLISHERS
www.dawbooks.com

Portions of this volume were originally published, in a modified form, in *The Edge of Propinquity*.

Cover art and design by Amber Whitney.

Additional cover design by G-Force Design.

Interior dingbats created by Tara O'Shea.

DAW Book Collectors No. 1650.

Published by DAW Books, Inc.
375 Hudson Street, New York, NY 10014.

First New Edition Printing, June 2018

1 2 3 4 5 6 7 8 9

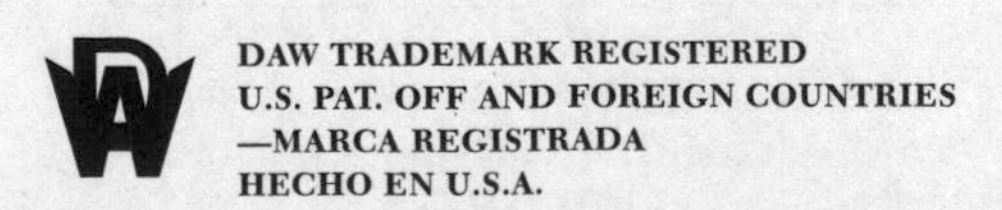

DAW TRADEMARK REGISTERED
U.S. PAT. OFF AND FOREIGN COUNTRIES
—MARCA REGISTRADA
HECHO EN U.S.A.

PRINTED IN THE U.S.A.

For the original Rosettes: Amy, Alyssa, Erica, Meg, and Vixy.
And for Jennifer.

Thank you all for letting me tell you about Rose Marshall.

INTRODUCTION

LET ME TELL YOU ABOUT ROSE MARSHALL.

She's a ghost story wrapped in a series of urban legends; she's an idea that got away from me and decided to hitchhike for the coast before I could stop her. She's a song, she's a story, she's a novel, and in some ways, she's one of the most "real" characters I've ever created. And, as befits a character whose story is as tangled as hers is, she didn't start as any of these things.

She started in a game.

My friend Phil was running a campaign and asked me to come in and play an NPC (non-player character) who was related to one of the main characters. Specifically, he wanted me to play a hitchhiking ghost. He knew I liked them, that I'd been interested in them since I was a kid, and thought I'd do a good job. Rose Marshall was born. She showed up for a few sessions, complicating an already complicated situation, and stole my heart. I needed to do something else with her.

So I wrote a song.

The first Rose Marshall song, "Pretty Little Dead Girl," was intentionally filled with inaccuracies, things that the "real" Rose would never do. I was already starting to think of her as an urban legend, you see, and urban legends are always told in a dozen different ways. That song went on to become the title track of my first album, and I kept writing more, presenting different aspects of Rose, different ways the story could have gone.

While this was going on, my friend Jennifer Brozek was editing an online magazine called *The Edge of Propinquity*. One of the things that set it apart from its peers was the use of what she called "universe authors," authors who had been commissioned to write twelve stories—one per month—set in the same world. It was an exercise in serialized fiction that was unlike anything else happening at the time, and I was incredibly flattered and excited when Jennifer asked me to be her 2010 universe author. But what to write?

"You keep saying you want to tell me about Rose Marshall," she said. "So tell me."

Twelve months; twelve stories. Twelve opportunities to let Rose tell *her* side of the story, the side where she wasn't a killer or a temptress or anything like that, but was just a teenage girl who'd lost control of her car and found herself on the other side of the grave, still trying to figure out her existence. We came up with the title "Sparrow Hill Road" for the world, and I had a crackerjack time writing them. Bit by bit, Rose was becoming real.

When I approached Sheila Gilbert at DAW to ask whether she'd consider reprinting the Rose stories as what's called a "fix-up novel," she was open to the idea, and eventually eleven of those original twelve, plus a few new tales, became the book you're holding. She helped me to refine and focus Rose's story into something tight and bright and worthy of the scared teenager from Buckley Township, Michigan who went over the side of the hill and became so much more.

I'm still telling people about Rose Marshall.

I hope I never have to stop.

Editor's Note

Most of what we know about the life and death of Rose Marshall, often referred to as "the Girl at the Diner" or "the Ghost of Sparrow Hill Road," is circumstantial and unclear. We have verified the dates in this document to the best of our ability, but as most of the participants are deceased, we are unable to swear that all dates are accurate.

Of this much, we are sure: Rose Marshall lived. Rose Marshall died. And as of the time of this writing, Rose Marshall does not yet rest in peace.

—Kevin and Evelyn Price, eds.

Book One

Campfire Stories

And when the night hails down and you're afraid
That you'll never get what you're owed,
Go and talk to the girl in the green silk gown
Who died on Sparrow Hill Road.

And when you see her face in the truck-stop light,
When the final cock has crowed,
Then you'll go with the girl in the green silk gown
Who died on Sparrow Hill Road.

—excerpt from "The Ghost of Sparrow Hill Road," author unknown.

There is nothing more human than the ghost story. Every culture in the world creates hauntings for itself, things that lurk in the shadows and wait for the unwary. Yet, at the same time, there are certain ghost stories and certain forms of haunting that seem to be quintessentially American. This leads us to the story of the Phantom Prom Date. Her story is considered an example of the Hitchhiking Ghost sub-type (see Appendix A for further details on the base legend), but has been expanded into a cautionary tale for teenagers about the dangers of driving recklessly. It is perhaps no coincidence that the Phantom Prom Date first began to walk the roads of America in the early 1950s, when concern for teen driving was at a national high.

The most interesting thing about this legend is that it presents a hitchhiking ghost with no specific geographical ties. Unlike Chicago's White Mary or New Hampshire's Lonely John, the Phantom Prom Date can be seen anywhere in North America, and has made appearances in locations as diverse as Florida, Ontario, and the Pacific Northwest. The only American state with no recorded sightings is Hawaii, which fits with the legend—how would a ghost whose only means of travel is the highway reach a state surrounded entirely by water?

The physical appearance of the Phantom Prom Date may also be relevant. One would expect a legend this far-ranging to present with a dozen different descriptions, but all recorded sightings have included the same details. She is in her mid-teens, with shoulder-length, light brown or dark blonde hair, Caucasian, attractive enough to be noticed without being strikingly beautiful, and wearing a green silk prom dress with matching dress flats. Neither the style of her hair nor the style of her dress changes from report to report; she seems to be caught in the era where she died, forever roaming the highways of America, forever looking for someone who can help her find the way home . . .

—*On the Trail of the Phantom Prom Date*, Professor Laura Moorhead, University of Colorado.

1973
The Dead Girl in the Diner

THERE'S THIS VOCABULARY WORD—"linear." It means things that happen in a straight line, like highways and essays about what you did on your summer vacation. It means A comes before B, and B comes before C, all the way to the end of the alphabet, end of the road . . . end of the line. That's linear.

The living are real fond of linear. The dead . . . not so much. It's harder to make everything fall into a straight line when nothing begins until you die. The dead begin our "lives" as newborns with heads full of memories, and it can make even the most straightforward story a little difficult to follow. I'll do my best.

My name is Rose Marshall. This is not a story about my life, although my life will occasionally intrude on the proceedings. It's messy and unfortunate. It's also unavoidable. Sorry about that. Only not really, because like I said, the dead aren't all that invested in "linear," and I've been dead for a long damn time.

I was born in 1936. The country was just starting to come out of the Great Depression. Skirts were tight, movies were big business, and everyone was trying to put their best foot forward. Of course, it wasn't sunshine and roses for everybody. My parents were still tightening their belts and pulling up their bootlaces when little Rosie Marshall made the scene, just one more mouth to feed and one more untried heart to break. They wouldn't be feeding me for long. Daddy split when I was eight years old. Me, I made it all the way to 1952, sixteen short years of chances and choices and opportunities. And then it was over.

I died on a hot summer night in my junior year of high school, driven off the road by a man who should never have been there. My body was battered almost past recognition by the accident. My spirit fared a little better, sweet sixteen for the rest of time, missing the warm coat of life's embrace.

I was alive, and then I wasn't. Someday, they'll say the same thing about everyone. Someday, they'll say the same thing about you.

There are a lot of names for people like me, the ones who can't let go, even when the movie's over and the credits finish rolling. Specter, haunt, phantom . . . and my personal favorite, the sweet and simple "ghost." "Ghost" is a lot like "linear": it's a word that doesn't fuck around pretending to be something it's not. There are even a lot of names for me in specific, names that try to dance around the word "Rose." I'm the phantom prom date, the woman at the diner, the girl in the green silk gown, and the walking girl of Route 42. But most of all, I'm the ghost of Sparrow Hill Road. Rosie Marshall. Just one more girl who raced and lost in the hand of the forest, the shade of the hill, on the hairpin curves of that damned deadly hill.

People call me a lot of things these days. You can call me Rose.

Now come with me.

The truck stop air has that magical twang that you only ever find in roadside dives that have had time to fully merge with their environment. It's a mixture of baked asphalt, diesel fumes, hot exhaust, and hotter exhaustion. The smell of grease and lard-based piecrusts join the symphony as I get closer to the obligatory diner, the charmingly named FORK YOU GRILL. The smell of ashes and lilies runs under it all, cold and enticing as the grave, and I know that I am where I am supposed to be.

My fingers are cold. My fingers are always cold, and the coat I'm wearing is too thin to really warm them up. I got it from a twenty-something on his way to California to be a rock musician. He said it belonged to his little sister. From the smell of the perfume permanently bonded to the denim, she was only his little sister if his little sister was moonlighting as a prostitute. But who am I to judge? I traded the coat for a backseat quickie, and now my hands are cold no matter how far I shove them into my hooker's-coat pockets, and I can taste the truck stop air. Being dead is one of those things that really teaches you how to be glad to be alive.

The distant drone of cars on the highway accompanies me across the parking lot, my shoes crunching on the glass and gravel. The sound of the jukebox slithers out to meet me as I open the diner door, Top 40 country hits with all the passion of a dead dog on the side of the highway. I keep on going. I'm not here for the music.

The air inside the diner is hot and dry and sweet with coffee and apple pie and the distant ghosts of greasy breakfasts past. Half a dozen truckers sit belly-up to the counter on stools twice the size of standard; this is a place that stays alive on the trucker trade, and isn't ashamed of that reality. Another half-dozen patrons are sprinkled around the place, seated haphazardly at booths and tables. That tells me what the deal is even before I see the hand-written sign inviting me to "PLZ SEAT YOURSELF, B RIGHT WITH U."

From the expressions of the folks who aren't too tired to enjoy their food, the staff here cooks better than they spell. That's for the best. Killing your customers with food poisoning isn't a good way to stay in business.

There's something not-quite-right about one of the truckers, a barrel-chested man with a neat little goatee and the hands of an artist. He has those artist's hands wrapped tight around a coffee mug, stealing heat through the porcelain like a small child stealing cookies from the cookie jar. Most of the eyes in the diner skitter right off me, frightened mice catching the scent of a cat, but not him. He doesn't look at me for long, but when he does, he *sees* me.

That, even more than the scent of ash and lilies lingering in the air around him, tells me he's the one I've come here for; he's the one that called me, made me give up a perfectly good westward ride to come to this middle-of-nowhere dive with nothing but the coat on my back and the frostbite on my fingers. I can't save him, but I know him.

At least, I know his kind. He's in the process of sliding into the space between two Americas. This one, where the air tastes like apple pie and the jukebox plays the Top 40, and a quieter, colder America, one where the kisses pretty girls sometimes give never taste of anything but empty rooms and broken promises. He's falling into my America, and there's not a damn thing to be done about it. It's not the sort of trip that you recover from. If the scent around him were rosemary and sugary perfume, maybe, but ashes and lilies . . .

There's nothing to be done. The record on the jukebox changes as I walk toward the counter. The Country Gentlemen, "Bringing Mary Home."

I hate it when the inanimate pretends to have a sense of humor.

He looks up when I sit down, a flicker of interest showing in his eyes. They're the color of sun-faded denim, all their darkness bleached out by the road. The blue-eyed boys have always been my weakness. I meet that brief look with a smile that's more sincere than I intended, flashing white teeth between candy-apple-red lips.

It's hard to dress for the truck stop circuit. Can't be too wholesome or they're afraid to even talk to you; there's too much of a chance that you're some sort of lure set out by the local cops. Sandra Dee doesn't play with the long-haul boys. Neither does her evil twin: going too far the other way makes you look like you're just another lot lizard, worth the price of a blow job, but not worth the cost of conversation. So here I am in flannel shirt under denim jacket over too-tight wife-beater tank top, faded jeans worn as thin as paper, hiking boots, and makeup that would verge on slutty if it wasn't so inexpertly applied.

I know my audience. I've had a lot of time to study it.

"Hi," I say, with a questioning lilt that blurs the remnants of my accent, blotting out the route signs that might lead back to my origins. "My name's Rose. Do you, um, come here often?"

He looks my way again. His eyes are kind. That makes it a little easier. We're about to get to know each other real well, and it's better when their eyes are kind. "Let me stop you right there, honey. You're way too young for me. Hell, you're way too young to be out here at all. Don't you have a home to go to?"

"Not for a long time."

"I see." Disapproval overtakes the kindness like the sun going down—but the disapproval isn't directed at me, and that makes what has to happen next easier still. "When's the last time you ate?"

This time I don't have to force myself to smile. "Too long ago." It's the truth. I'm always hungry—one more consequence of being what I am—and I have to follow certain rules. If the living choose to feed me while I'm material, the food has flavor and substance. If I try to feed myself, it's only air and ashes, like chewing on nothing.

"Would you mind if I bought you a burger?"

"Not at all." I slide over a little on my stool, trying to make myself comfortable. "If you're going to buy me a burger, can you tell me your name, maybe? I like to know who I'm thanking."

"It's Larry. Larry Vibber."

"Pleased to meet you, Larry."

"Pleased to meet you, too, Rose," he says, and laughs as he waves for the waitress to come over to our little stretch of counter. I'd feel guilty, if I had anything to feel guilty about. There are worse ways to spend your last night on Earth than buying dinner for a stranger in a diner, and if I wasn't here, he'd be spending this time alone.

The burger tastes like Heaven on a sesame seed bun, assuming that Heaven comes with ketchup and raw onions. If Larry wonders why I ask him to pass me the condiments before I dump them on, he doesn't say anything about it. The coffee is even better than the burger, and the apple pie is so damn good I could cry. The living don't know how lucky they are.

Larry finishes his food well before I do. After that, he just watches me demolishing my meal, until I'm chasing crumbs with the tip of my index finger and wishing I'd thought to chew a little slower. I wish that every time. I never do it.

Then Larry clears his throat, and I turn to look at him again. He smiles, weakly. "I was thinking, Rose . . ."

"Yeah?"

"A girl your age shouldn't be alone in a place like this. Now, I know you don't have much reason to trust me, and I'll understand if you don't think it's a good idea, but I'm rolling for Detroit tonight. I'd be happy to take you along, get you to a place where maybe . . . you could find somewhere to stay."

Oh, Larry. He won't be getting anywhere near Detroit tonight. I know that, I've known it since I saw him across the diner, but that doesn't matter, because this is what happens; this is what I came here for. I push my plate away, and if he sees that my smile is painted on over sorrow, he's polite enough not to say anything. He's trying to help. Most truckers are essentially good people, living one of the few vagabond lifestyles that's survived into this changing world, where it gets harder every year to keep from putting down roots. They help each other when they can, and they like to be seen as shining knights riding dragons instead of snow-white chargers.

"Thank you." I tug my borrowed coat tighter, smelling old perfume, old sex, old lies. My lies are some of the oldest of them all, but I tell them for the very best of reasons. "I'd really appreciate a ride." Rides are what I don't live for, after all.

The waitress who takes Larry's money looks at me a little too hard, a little too intently. She knows me. She's deep enough into the twilight Americas to know me, but she's still in the shallows. She's still too close to the daylight layers to understand *why* she knows, or what, exactly, it is that she's seeing. I flash her a smile. She steps backward, counts Larry's change wrong twice, and finally—once she has the register closed again—flees into the back.

She won't be here much longer. She'll go back to the daylight, leave this blacktop twilight to the people who can breathe its air and not worry about suffocating. That's good. People like her should get out while they still can, to make up for all the people who never get the chance.

Then Larry leads me out of the diner, out into the night, and the waitress doesn't matter anymore. We're on the road again, and there's nothing that can save us now.

Most truckers have permanent addresses, places they can sleep when they're not rolling down the midnight miles, eating distance and turning it into dreams. Very few truckers consider those addresses to be anything resembling a home. They live and breathe for their steel darlings, those eighteen-wheeled wives who carry them so faithfully, and understand what it is to be one half of a marriage that goes deeper than passion, all the way down into true, undying love.

Larry's truck shines like a beacon through the outside dark, glittering with a light he's never seen. If I asked him, if I had a way to frame the question, I bet he'd tell me he's felt it. That he feels it every time he crawls into his little wandering-man's bedroll and closes his eyes: the arms and the protections of his lover, soothing him into sleep.

He sees me staring at her, rapt, and reads the message on my face for what it is, even if he doesn't see the reasons for it. "Isn't she a beauty?" She shivers when he puts his hand against her door, a loving bride welcoming her husband home. She's missed him so. If only he could see how much she loves him.

"She is," I say solemnly, and he opens the door for me, and I step into the open arms of his lover.

She knows me, like the waitress knew me, like the routewitches and the ambulomancers know me. She knows what's coming as soon as the door closes behind me, and the question hangs heavy in the cabin air: *Is there another way?*

I press my palm flat against the worn leather of her dashboard. It's warm, like a beating heart. The heat spreads through me, wiping away the frost. I'm riding. Even if the truck isn't rolling yet, I'm doing what a hitchhiker is supposed to do. I'm riding, and I'm wearing a stranger's coat, and my belly is full of diner food eaten alongside a good man's last supper. That's enough to bring around the thaw.

Some accidents can be avoided; some drivers can be saved. Some . . . can't. *No*, I tell her, and she sighs. It's a deep, shuddering sigh, one that even Larry feels as he's getting in on the driver's side.

"Now, don't you be that way," he says, patting the steering wheel. "I just had your shocks looked at."

"You talk to your truck?" My hand stays warm after I pull it away from the dash. I try to sound curious and amused at the same time, like the idea strikes me as funny somehow. All I really manage is wistful.

"I spend more time with her than I do with anybody else," he says, and slides his key into her ignition. The engine comes alive with a muted roar, like a lioness ready to defend her mate from the wilderness that surrounds them. Larry pats the wheel again, the gesture seeming to come automatically. "She's a good girl. She's always done her best by me."

"She always will." I lean back into my seat, pretending not to see the curious look Larry sends in my direction. I just keep my eyes on the distant freeway lights. The headlights come on, and then we're away, and it's too late for anything beyond the open road.

The night closes in around us on every side. Larry guides the truck around a gentle curve, and says, "So, Rose, what were you doing back there? A girl like you, in a place like that, well . . . it's just not safe. Not everyone is out to help. You're old enough, you should know that."

"I do." The road is unspooling all around us, and the air tastes like lilies and ashes and miles that flicker out and die like candles. Not long now. We're almost there. I wish like hell that this could have been different, but I know the hopeless cases, and I know the ones I never could have fought for. "I just . . . I'd been hitching a ride, and the guy I was driving with decided he wanted to go in a different direction. So I thought I'd stop in and see if I could find anybody who was going my way."

I don't need to see his frown. I can hear it. "You never asked which way I was going."

"You told me Detroit."

"Yes, but . . ."

"I left home when I was sixteen. I didn't have a choice." I let the sentence sit there to be examined, letting him fill in all the spaces between the words, letting him realize that I still look sixteen. He doesn't know that I'll always look this way. The story he tells himself will be terrible, because the stories we tell ourselves always are, but it won't come anywhere close to the truth. It never does. Until they finish their falls onto the ghostroads, into the twilight, they never start those stories with "How did you die?"

"Oh." His voice is soft. Silence closes in around us for a while. Not long enough. "Don't you have any family you could go to?"

Family. There's an interesting thought. Show up on the doorstep of some woman twice my age who has my older brother's eyes, and try to explain who I am, where I've been, and why I went away. I shake my head.

"Not really. We were never a very close family, and there's no one I could go to."

"I'm sorry."

"Don't worry about me." I offer a smile across the darkened cabin. Something flickers in his expression, something old and sad and scared. We're getting close to the border; close to the final fall. He's starting to feel the wind from the onrushing ending, and he still can't see it clear enough to do a damn thing about it. They never can. "I've been on the road a long time. I can take care of myself."

The truck rattles on beneath us, eating the road, turning distance into dreams. I have to try. I always have to try. It might hurt less if I stopped, and I think that's why I do it.

"Have you ever heard the story of the woman at the diner?" Such an innocent question. Such a guilty answer.

Larry laughs. "Now we're telling ghost stories? I guess that's one way to get me to stop asking personal questions. Yes, I've heard of her."

"How does the story go? The way you heard it for the first time, I mean. It's different everywhere you go."

"Road stories always are." He clears his throat. "Uh, the story goes that she was a cheerleader."

That's a variation I haven't heard before. "A *cheerleader?*"

"Yeah. She went to some middle-of-nowhere school, and all she wanted was to get to Hollywood. So she and her boyfriend saved their pennies until they thought they had enough, and then they hit the road. Only he lost control of his car less than three hours outside of town. It flipped over, and he was killed instantly. She managed to pull herself from the wreck and went staggering off, looking for help. She found a truck stop. The truckers said they'd help her. They put her in the diner with a cup of coffee while they went down the road to find her boyfriend. They wanted to see if maybe she was wrong and he was still breathing."

"He wasn't, was he." He never is. In the versions where I have a boyfriend in the car, he's always dead on impact. Guess it would screw up the story if their little wandering lady wasn't doing her wandering alone.

"No. So they covered up his face and said they were sorry, and one of them stayed to wait for the police while the others went back to the diner. But by the time they got there, the girl was already dead. Her throat had been slit. The short-order cook was gone. He left a note saying their meals were all free, and thanking them for the tip."

I shudder. Murder. Also new.

Larry doesn't see, or maybe Larry just thinks it's the sort of delicious fear that comes with a good ghost story. Either way, he keeps on going. "The one trucker they'd left back on the road, see, he doesn't know she's dead. So when she comes walking down the road a few minutes after the police take her boy away, he just thinks she got tired of waiting. He tells her that her boyfriend's dead, and she cries so hard. She cries like her heart's been broken. The trucker, he's a good guy, and he asks if there's anything he can do."

"So she asks him to take her home," I whisper.

"Yeah," says Larry. "She's cold, so he gives her his coat, and he drives her all the way back to where she started from. Drops her off in front of her very own house. It's not until the next day that he realizes she didn't give back his coat, and so next time he's driving that route, he stops by. Figures he'll see how she's been doing. Only the police are waiting. The police have *been* waiting ever since her body was found, tucked into her own bed, with her throat cut ear to ear, wearing a stranger's coat."

"God." The ways the story twists and changes never fail to surprise me. People are nothing if not inventive in the lies they tell.

"He tries to say that he's innocent, but nobody believes him. He gets the death penalty, of course, and when they bury him, this pretty little teenage girl comes up to his wife. Walks up to her right next to the trucker's grave. She says she's sorry. She says she didn't mean for that to happen. She just wanted to go home. Then she walks away. The wife realizes who she was and runs after her, but she's already gone, like she'd never been there at all . . . except for the coat. The trucker's coat, hanging on a tombstone."

"That's a new version," I say, trying to break the silence that the story leaves behind. "I haven't heard that one before."

"Really? How many variations do you suppose there are?"

"Hundreds." The weariness in my voice could be used to veil every star in the twilight. The smell of lilies is strong now. Not much longer.

"I guess that little ghost-girl gets around."

"You have no idea," I say, and Larry laughs, and that's it: no more warnings. We're in this till the end.

The road signs flicker and blur in the dark outside the cab, Larry's headlights cutting a bright banner through the night. He chatters about inconsequential things, all of them mingling and blurring like the signs, until they're nothing but the final solo in the symphony of a man's life. Would things have gone differently if I hadn't been here? I used to think so, but I know better now. He's tired. It comes off him in waves, under the lilies and the ashes and the growing scent of empty rooms. If I hadn't been here for him to talk to, he would have just dozed off at the wheel.

I don't condemn them, no matter what some people say, and I can't always save them. That I can save any of them at all is a miracle. Most of the time, all I can do is get them home.

The other truck looms out of the darkness like a demon, whipping around a blind curve at the sort of speed that's never safe, not even when the sun is up. Larry swears and grabs the wheel, hauls it hard to the side, fights to dodge and then fights even harder to keep the truck under control. There's a crash behind us, the sound of metal tearing into metal, and all the stars go out overhead.

Larry doesn't notice. Larry is too busy clinging white-knuckled to the steering wheel, eyes wide and terrified, breath coming in panting hitches. "That was . . . oh, Jesus. Rose, are you all right? Are you hurt?"

One more thing he hasn't noticed: my coat is gone. It's an artifact of the daylight, and I left it on the road when we dropped down. It'll be found among the wreckage. The man who gave it to me may have a few questions to answer, if they can find him. "I'm fine, Larry. I'm not hurt." It's the honest truth. I'm not the one he should be asking.

"That was—that was way too close. We have to go back. Did you hear that crash? I think he tipped over. We have to go back."

I lean over, putting one cold hand against his arm. The ghostroad is smoother than the real one, and the highway signs are easier to read, glowing like lanterns against the starless night. "We have to keep going, Larry. We have to get you home."

"But—"

"Please."

Maybe it's my tone, maybe it's his own fear, or maybe it's just the twilight already starting to dig its claws into him, already getting under his skin. Finally, slowly, Larry nods. "All right, Rose. We'll keep going."

"Thank you." I touch the dashboard again. It's cool now, as cool as my skin. I wonder when he'll notice. "I think it's time for me to tell you my version of the woman at the diner."

"She wasn't a cheerleader—she didn't have the money to buy herself a spot on the team—but she was a high school student. She liked to drive. She liked to watch other people drive. And she liked her boyfriend, who came to visit her behind the auto shop, and who let her fix his car so that it ran like a fairy tale. The cheerleaders would never have let her get anywhere near them. She might have gotten them dirty. But that was a long time ago.

"After the crash, after she . . . died . . . she liked to hitchhike. She was walking down the side of the road one night when a man pulled up next to her and asked if she needed a ride anywhere. She said yes, and that she'd really like to go get something to eat, so he drove her to the nearest truck stop with a diner. Only when they got there, she thanked him for the ride, and then she went and sat with somebody else. A trucker. And after he bought her a burger, she asked him for a ride. Or maybe he offered. It doesn't really matter in this version of the story."

Larry is watching me more than he's watching the road at this point, watching with the sort of terrified understanding that only comes on by inches, only comes when you're not looking for it. He's starting to realize that something—that everything—is wrong.

"So he let her into his cab, and they drove off together. But there was a crash. A terrible crash. He was killed. The body of his passenger was never found."

"Rose . . ."

"Only a year later, a year to the *day*, that first trucker saw her walking down the median again. Same place, same stretch of road. He pulled over. He told her he'd been afraid she was dead. She just smiled, and asked for a ride. And when he asked her if she'd stay in his truck this time, she said no; said she was meeting somebody. Same thing happened. Accident, dead trucker, missing girl. And again, two years later, she showed up again. By then the first trucker was starting to realize that there was something wrong. So he pulled off the road when he saw her, and he demanded to know what she was doing. 'Are you killing these boys?' he asked. 'Are you doing this to them?' "

"Rose—"

"And she looked at him, and she said, so sadly that it just about broke his heart, 'No. I've never killed anyone. I just want to make sure that somebody's there to see that they make it all the way home.'"

This time his voice is just a whisper; this time, he understands. "Rose."

I offer him a smile as sad as a Sunday in September. "I came to you for a reason, Larry. I'm just here to make sure you find the right roads. I'm only here to get you home."

Driving on the ghostroads is easy, and Larry's rig knows the way. She travels light and faster than she ever did in life, finally free to corner on her own, to compensate for her driver when he can't focus through his tears. He only cries for a while. Not as long as some, longer than others. That's fine. There's nothing wrong with crying when someone dies, not even when it's you. If you can't cry at your own funeral, when can you cry?

The road gets simpler, turns and curves fading into straight lines and dark exits. Finally, the bright neon oasis of the Last Dance Diner appears ahead of us. I reach over and squeeze Larry's wrist.

"This is my stop."

"Rose . . ."

"It's okay. Yours is just ahead." The danger is past. Once they reach the Last Dance, they can find the rest of the way on their own, and I don't dare go any farther—for me, the Last Dance is where the danger really begins, because that's where I have to face the fact that my future is a story not yet told. I don't know where that road ends, and until I'm finished with everything I have to do, I don't want to find out. Besides, the Last Dance makes damn good malteds.

He pulls off the road, letting the engine idle, and turns to look at me. His face is younger than it was when we met. The twilight is easing the years away. "Why me?"

"Because the crash was coming whether I was here or not, and sometimes people get lost on this stretch of road. They need someone to tell them which exits to take." I lean over to kiss his forehead—cool lips brushing cooling skin—before opening my door. "Good luck, Larry."

Larry looks at me in silence for a long while before he nods and turns back to the road. I slam my door and the truck pulls away, driving down that long, straight stretch of highway. And then it's gone like a piece of tissue whipped away by the wind, and overhead, the stars start blinking back on. The wind picks up and I'm cold again, falling out of the midnight back into the twilight, where the air still tastes like apple pie and dreams.

Hunching my shoulders against the cold, I start for the Last Dance Diner. Maybe they won't be too busy tonight, and I'll be able to sweet-talk Emma into sliding a malted or two down the counter. There are worse ways for a dead girl to spend the night that never ends.

Trust me.

1956
Three Rescues and a Funeral

EVERYONE IS BORN BASICALLY THE SAME WAY: bloody and screaming. We come out of our mothers, shriek with our first breath, and find ourselves lost in a world that we don't understand. But we're hungry for understanding, hungry for *life*, and so we learn. We grow. We wrap the world around our shoulders like a blanket or a coat, and we wear it proudly every day of our lives, for however long those lives may last. We are temporary creatures, and we know it—that's why we fear the dark, after all, that's why we build walls and light candles to keep it out.

Even if everyone is born the same way, every death is different. Even two people who died in the same car crash will experience different deaths, one by crushing, one by short, sharp impact to the head; one as a driver, one as a passenger. Those final experiences shape them as much as anything they knew in life. Still, for most people, that sort of thing is a temporary concern. They're born, they die, and they pass through the ghostroads like shooting stars, leaving only contrails and broken hearts behind them. For some, it's not that simple. For some, death is a wound that will not heal, and it refuses to let them move on. So they build a new life for themselves, one distinct from the old in that, well . . . they're not actually living anymore.

The lands of the living have a thousand different mythologies and storytelling traditions. They keep them segregated, carefully split along whatever boundary lines are in vogue this year, and any story older than the country that it's told in is pinned like a butterfly under glass, refused the capacity to grow or change. Urban legends can still warp themselves to fit the times, but everything else is expected to stay the same forever. Sleeping Beauty sleeps over and over again; Snow White never learns not to eat the apple, and her spiritual sister in fruit-based stupidity, Persephone, does the same with her new husband's pomegranate tree. Over and over, again and again, forever and for always.

I don't know about you, but that sounds sort of like the definition of insanity to me.

Things are less clear-cut in the lands of the dead, where no one has the authority to say which stories can be told in which places, or when. No one gets to say "You can't be here" when one tradition bleeds over into another, and everything mixes and mingles and blends, until every death is a cocktail of a hundred different faiths, a thousand different stories. That's how you get urban legends like hitchhiking ghosts sitting in diners managed by Irish *beán sidhe*, arguing about who owes who when the sky goes black as bruises. People like me are only possible when life's blinders have been pulled aside, revealing the truth that hides behind them in the dark: that boundaries are what we make them, and that the only power they have is what we give them.

Still, there are fairy tales of a kind in the lands of the dead, stories that have power over us because they're ours, and because we want, so badly, for them to be the truth. We already know that there's an afterlife, and so we whisper stories of redemption and reincarnation, rebirth and resurrection. They're a lot like the stories told by the living, in at least one respect.

They all begin with once upon a time.

Madison, Wisconsin, 1956.

I drop off the ghostroads to find myself standing in the middle of a blasted field, the skeletal remains of winter wheat jutting up from the ground like claws. Wisconsin doesn't look kindly on the weeks that slip in between the death of cold and the birth of warmth; Persephone may have left her husband, but she isn't home yet, and this is one state that'll be damned before it lets anyone forget it. The air is cold enough that I feel it even through the endless chill of death. It works under the illusion of my skin, seeming to sink all the way down to the bones that I don't technically have anymore.

There are times when being dead sucks more than usual. Any time that involves going to Wisconsin when the weather's bad counts as one of those times.

This used to be a road, this place where I'm standing; carriages used to travel here, horse-drawn and loaded down with produce or baled hay. Time flowed on, and they were replaced by cars, but not for long, because the highway cut through these fields—but not through this spot—and this good old road was forgotten, turned back into open land and longing. That's what dropped me here. The highway is a good one, but the cry of this old road was stronger, at least on the ghostroads, where anything that dies can live forever.

It's a little sad, and a little just plain the way things work in this world, and it's a whole lot the reason I'm standing in this damn field, rather than safely tucked onto the highway shoulder, waiting for a ride to somewhere else. I mutter under my breath as I wrap my arms around myself, trying to hug some warmth back into my bones. It doesn't work. It never works. The only thing that clears away the cold is a living human's coat, freely given, and that's not something I'm going to find out here.

"I hate my afterlife," I complain, and begin wading through the blasted winter wheat.

The road isn't as far as it seemed when I first appeared. I've barely walked a quarter of a mile when I start hearing cars in the distance, their hissing wheels and roaring engines sweeter than any song that Buddy Holly ever sang. I pick up the pace a little, not even pretending to hold my skirt away from the grasping ground. The habit of pretending to be alive is strong, partially because it's always easier to catch a ride when the driver hasn't seen me walking through solid objects just before flagging him down. At the moment, I care less about looking like the living than I do reaching that liminal holy land known only as the highway shoulder.

I'm almost there when I hear a sound even more pressing than the siren song of the passing cars—maybe the *only* sound that could be more pressing in the here and now, with the wind blowing cold across the blasted fields. The sound of a little girl, crying.

My feet make no sound as I walk. That bothers me sometimes, but not right now. Right now, I don't want anything getting between me and that little girl, who's sobbing like she thinks her heart's been broken for good. She sounds . . . it's hard to define the quality that I'm hearing in her voice, but she sounds *alive*. The dead can cry. The dead cry all the time. Only the living can cry like that.

I find her huddled in a ditch near the edge of the field, dirty skirts hitched high around her scabby knees, her legs hugged tightly to her chest. She doesn't look up at my approach, maybe because she can't hear me. And she's wearing a jacket and a sweater both.

"Hey, kid," I say. Her head jerks up like a startled jack-in-the-box, big blue eyes wide. Her cheeks are red from cold and crying. "You lost?"

Words are too hard for her to manage, and so she doesn't; she just nods, chest still hitching and fat tears still rolling down her face.

"I'm sorry. I'm Rose. What's your name?"

It takes her a moment, but finally she manages to say, voice softer than her sobs had been, "A-Amy."

"It's nice to meet you, Amy. Do you live around here?"

She shakes her head.

"Well, if you don't live around here, how did you get here?"

"Do *you* live around here?" she asks, looking briefly too curious to be sad.

It's a valid question. "No," I say, "but I'm not the one who's lost."

She's willing to accept that, thankfully. She sniffles, wiping her cheeks with the back of one grimy hand before she says, "We stopped for the rest stop. I just wanted . . . I was tired of being in the car, we've been driving for *hours*."

Ah. "You went for a little walk, and you couldn't find your way back, am I right?"

Amy nods solemnly.

She can't be more than seven years old, little girl lost in a field where distance doesn't have much meaning. She could freeze to death out here. She'd probably be a road ghost, maybe a hitcher like me, maybe a homecomer, or even a little white lady, so sweet, so cold, so deadly. That's what the night intends for her, I can taste it now, phantom breath of ashes and honeysuckle on the wind—honeysuckle, not lilies, because her death is of the road, not on it.

Fuck that. Honeysuckle is negotiable. I reach out with the part of me that knows the road the way a swallow knows the sky, feeling the heartbeat of the highway until it whispers rest stop, half a mile from where we're standing. "I think I can get you back there, Amy," I say, "but I need you to do something for me, first."

Her eyes go wide with sudden hope. "Anything you want," she says. "I'll do anything you want."

I feel like a heel for even thinking what I'm about to ask, but I have to do it. How much worse would it be if she tried to take my hand—a natural thing for a little girl to do—and found herself holding nothing but the air? "Can I borrow your coat?" She has a sweater. She won't freeze. Not in half a mile.

Amy looks at me like I'm insane, but she shrugs off her coat and hands it to me, the fabric carrying flesh and life and the sudden smell of the frost-shattered wheat that's standing all around us. I tie it around my neck like a cape, and she giggles, somehow reassured by what has to look like an adult playing silly to make her feel better. She does take my hand, her fingers almost as cold as mine, and together we walk down to the edge of the highway, where the gravel makes the going a little easier. She holds my hand all the way back to the rest stop. Her parents are there, shouting her name, clearly frantic.

"Mommy!" Amy's hand is out of mine almost before I know she's moving, and she's running, running, running to fling herself into the arms of a woman with her wide blue eyes and dark chestnut-colored hair. I untie the coat from around my neck, letting it flutter to the ground as I step just deep enough into the ghostroads to shut myself from sight. Amy might be willing to accept my convenient presence in the field; her parents would be rather more suspicious.

She looks startled when she turns and I'm not there. I watch as her parents bundle her into the car, ignoring her protests that her friend had been *right there*, she *swears*. Then I let go of the daylight entirely, tumbling back down into the twilight. It's only in the instant before the rest stop falls away that I realize I'm not alone; a redheaded woman is watching me from the shadows of the weathered old brick building. And she's smiling.

Then Wisconsin, and the woman, are gone, and it's just me and the twilight and the ghosts of winters past, alone again together.

Madison, Wisconsin, 1958.

There's a county fair raging in this flat-mown field, carnival lights and carousel music turning the night into a fairy tale. I'm walking toward it almost before I register that I've crossed into the daylight levels—a name that shouldn't apply this long after the sun goes down, but is accurate, all the same. It's lighter here at night than it ever is in the twilight, come night or day or something in-between. The part of me that's forever sweet sixteen says the carnival's the place to be, especially on a night like this one, where the hay's been cut but the winter hasn't come yet, and we're all prepared to bid farewell to the summer.

Carnivals are good places for someone like me. A lot of the carniefolk are routewitches, or know one. A few of them are even ambulomancers. They understand that sometimes a road ghost needs a little solid one-on-one time with a carousel pony, and they can almost always be counted on for a flannel coat and a funnel cake.

I can't smell the funnel cake, but I can almost taste it as I hurry to the carnival's edge, where the light bleeds through into the darkened fields. Getting a coat is as easy as I hoped it was going to be. I don't even have to ask—I just turn around and there's a man with blacktop eyes and a half-quirked grin holding it out to me, like a boyfriend offering his best girl a corsage. He doesn't wait around for me to thank him. He just hands it to me and disappears, and when I tuck my hands into the pockets, I find them full of tickets and vouchers for the concession stands.

This is one of those nights where it's good to be alive, even if you're dead. Vouchers count as food freely given, even though money doesn't, and I can taste everything the concession stands give me. I eat cotton candy and funnel cake and hot dogs dripping ketchup and mustard and fresh-chopped raw onion. I ride the Ferris wheel and the merry-go-round and the bumper cars, and just when the tickets are about to run out, my black-eyed carnie-boy appears again, shoving another strip into my hand and fading back into the crowd. It's magical. It's wonderful. It's exactly what I needed.

At least until I'm riding their rickety home-brew roller coaster around its looping track for the third time, and the sudden scent of ashes invades my nostrils. Not ashes and lilies; not a road death. This is ashes and red cherry syrup, death at the carnival, and I don't even know what kind of ghost that death would make. I look around, searching for the source of the scent, which is getting stronger by the second. There; the little girl in the next car, the one with the dark wheat hair and the joyful scream rising from her throat. Her harness isn't fastened right. She's going to fall out on the next curve, and the impact with the ground will break her spine. I can see it, if I look at her the right way.

I'm barely aware that I'm unfastening my own belt. Then we hit the curve, and she's falling, and I'm leaping after her, dead girl arrowing after living girl, dead girl catching living girl around the waist as the first startled scream breaks from her lips. We hit the ground hard, with her landing hard on top of me, and I feel something essential as it snaps.

Then she's crying, staggering to her feet and screaming for help. It's the sound of her scream that does it, sharp and terrified, like a child's sobs by the side of a road. She must be twelve now, but I know her by her screams.

"Hello, Amy," I murmur, and close my eyes, and the land of the living falls away.

I'm already on the ghostroads when I realize who was sitting next to me on the roller coaster, the redheaded woman with the green, green eyes, and the bright, bright smile. But she's in the land of the living, with Amy, and I'm back among the dead. My night at the carnival was fun while it lasted.

Madison, Wisconsin, 1965.

"Wisconsin *again*?" I want to stamp my foot and scream. I settle for glaring at the street sign, like it's somehow to blame for my situation. I was aiming for Minnesota, where the college boys will be driving into the Twin Cities in their shiny new roadsters, their eyes bright with dreams and their hair dripping with pomade. Lots of easy pickings for a girl like me on the Minnesota road on a night like tonight. But this isn't Minnesota, and these streets are empty, twilight bleeding over the horizon like grenadine bleeding into a cocktail.

There's nothing to be done for it now. I could drop back down to the twilight, but I'm tired; it's been too long since I put on a young girl's skin and danced for a few hours among the living. Hitchers live on life the way some ghosts live on tears or terror. If we go without it for too long, we start to go fuzzy around the edges, drifting toward a total fade. The only difference between a truly old hitcher and a really young homecomer is sometimes intent: faded hitchers kill the same way homecomers do. We just don't mean to do it. I need a coat. I need to touch the living.

Madison has changed since the last time I was here. It's still a Midwestern city, and the streets still sing their songs of winter snow and summer sweat, but the houses are closer together, and the buildings have started to get taller. The last time I was here, there was a county fair—I ate a funnel cake and saved a little girl and broke my spine. I got better. She wouldn't have. The field where the carousel turned is a bank now, squat and solid and looking like it grew up out of the ground without any human aid. The times, they are a'changing.

What hasn't changed is the sound of a girl, somewhere close by, crying. I turn toward it, catching the barest scent of ashes on the wind, and sigh. Why does Wisconsin always seem to mean trying to avert the inevitable? "I think this state hates me," I say, to no one in particular, and start walking.

She's sitting on the edge of a marble fountain that contains no water, her head in her hands, crying so hard that her ponytail bobs up and down with the force of her sobbing. She's grown into the perfect little Miss Teenage USA, with her hair flipped just so and her patterned blouse and her calf-length trousers. Her hair is darker than it used to be, chestnut brown instead of winter wheat gold, but I still recognize her. How could I not recognize someone I've already saved twice?

"Hello, Amy." I sit down next to her—a gesture, mind you, that a younger, less experienced ghost would be incapable of making; a younger, less experienced ghost would plummet right through that marble fountain if they even tried: I am getting better at this—and smooth my skirt across my knees, watching her out of the corner of my eye. "It's been a while."

Her head jerks up, same startled little girl motion as in that long-ago field, and she stares at me, no recognition in those wide blue eyes. "Do I know you?" she asks.

I want to tell her no. I want to get up and walk away and let her go back to crying without me to make it any better, or any worse. But the scent of ashes still coils around her like a snake, twisting and twining and not giving me anything to grab onto. I can't smell lilies, or honeysuckle, or anything to tell me what the danger is. There's an accident coming for this girl, who may not be a medium and talks to ghosts anyway—talks to *a* ghost, at least. Once is chance. Twice is coincidence. Three times is something that *matters*.

"My name's Rose," I say, mildly. "I helped you find your parents once, when you wandered away in a field. It was pretty cold out there. You could have frozen to death. So I guess you're lucky that I came along."

She keeps staring at me. Maybe I'm the only ghost she's ever seen. Maybe she doesn't know what to say. Maybe she thinks I'm crazy. I don't know until she opens her mouth, and when she finally does, what comes out is, "I thought I dreamed you."

"I get that a lot," I say. "I'm not a dream."

Slowly, like she's afraid I'm going to disappear, Amy reaches for my arm. I hate being touched by the living when I don't have a coat on. It itches. Her hand sinks through the place where my skin ought to be, fingers disappearing into what her eyes are telling her is my flesh. Her eyes get even wider, whites showing all the way around her irises. She looks like she's just seen a ghost. Oh, wait. She has.

"I'm not a dream, but I'm not alive, either," I say, fighting the urge to yank myself away, to get her out of the space that only I should be occupying. "I died a long time before we met in that field, and I've saved your life twice, so it would be nice if you'd pull your hand out of my arm, and maybe let me borrow your coat. I'm cold."

She opens her mouth like she's about to ask me how that can even work. Then she clearly reconsiders, maybe remembering the times I've touched her in the past—the barren field, the carnival. "Rose," she whispers, pulling her hand away from me. For a moment, I think she's going to run. The moment passes, and she shrugs out of her coat, holding it out. Again, she says, "I thought I dreamed you."

"Well, fortunately, your sanity isn't that questionable." Solidity settles over my bones as I take the coat from her, and I'm wonderfully, blessedly breathing again, back among the living for at least a little while. The fabric settles warm and comforting across my shoulders as I slip it on. "I'm as real as you are. Just a little deader."

"But how . . ."

"That's a question, and a concept, for someone a lot smarter than me. Dead doesn't mean getting a free pass on the secrets of the universe. Sorry." I shrug expansively, sniffing the air as I do. The smell of ashes is still there, and there's a new scent underneath it, rich and rotting, like a body that's been left to decay in a sealed-off room. It's enough to make me choke, and it's while I'm taking that second, shallower breath that I catch the final note in her personal perfume of catastrophe.

Wormwood. She smells like wormwood and ashes and decay, and that particular combination only ever means one thing in this world—in *my* world.

Bobby Cross is coming.

"We have to get out of here." My voice is barely loud enough to qualify as a whisper. I clear my throat, pushing the panic down, and try again: "We have to get out of here, Amy. What are you doing out here, anyway? Why aren't you safe at home?"

"I can't go back there!" She swallows a sob that threatens to turn into a wail before burying her face in her hands. "You're dead. You wouldn't understand."

Pretty little teenage girl sitting alone and crying after sundown. I'm not as clueless as she seems to think I am. I'm almost insulted. "Your parents don't like your boyfriend, do they? They either think you're too good for him, or they think he's no good for you, or maybe a little bit of both."

She raises her head to stare at me again. Apparently, having a clue about what it's like to be a teenage girl is even more amazing than being dead. "How did you know?"

"I've been sixteen for almost as long as you've been alive, and my boyfriend's parents used to feel that way about me," I reply. "I guess they were right. I went and died on the boy I loved, and that can't have been good for him." I stand, grabbing her arm. "Come on. We're getting out of here."

"I can't go back there!"

The wormwood is getting stronger. Bobby's coming, and maybe it makes me a bad person, but I'm not strong enough for this, not when I didn't pick the fight, not when I didn't pick the battleground. I yank Amy to her feet, shouting, "You don't have to go back, but you have to go *somewhere*, or you're going to die! Right here, right now, tonight, and when your death catches you, you're not going to get a normal afterlife. You're going to get pain and screaming and something you don't deserve to suffer through. Now we. Are getting. Out. Of. Here."

Every time that I have saved her, every time the accidents in her path have called to me, it's been because of this night. Because one day, she'd be in the path of Bobby Cross—assuming she lived that long, which she wouldn't have done without me; cause and effect don't really work very well on the ghostroads—and if I wasn't there to save her, she'd be burned to ash and memory in his hands. "I don't understand."

"Is this boy—"

"Will."

"Fine, whatever. Is Will worth dying over? Or is he worth growing old with?"

She looks uncertain. The taste of wormwood is getting stronger. I give her one more solid pull, and she stumbles forward a few feet, not quite braced.

"Amy, dying sucks," I say, as softly as I dare. "Trust me on this one. You don't want to do it if you have another choice, and right now, you have another choice. You can run."

I've been saving her since she was a little girl, even if it took a while for her to realize it. Her eyes widen briefly, and she nods, her hand seeking mine. I lace our fingers together, and then we're running, dead girl and endangered girl, running so fast that our feet barely seem to touch the pavement. Half the time I'm pulling her, and half the time she's pulling me—more than half the time, once we really start moving, because I don't know our destination and she does. She knows this town, this is *her* town, and I'm only passing through.

An engine roars somewhere in the dark behind us, and that old dark feeling uncurls in the hollow of my stomach as the taste of wormwood washes everything else away. He's here. Bobby Cross is close enough to end my world forever. And then, ahead of us, like sweet salvation, I see it. The diner, lights still on, neon sign still glowing. I clasp my fingers tighter around Amy's, shouting, "This way!" and haul her toward that bright cathedral of the milkshake and the cheeseburger and the ice cream soda.

His car roars one more time in the dark as we hit the diner door, the bell above it jingling too merrily for the situation. Panting, I drop Amy's hand. "You're safe here," I say. "You can't be on the streets. Not until dawn. Tomorrow, you go see your boyfriend. Tell him you love him. Tell him he's worth the risk." Bobby only takes the chaste girls, the ones who've never been caught. I didn't know that when he came after me. I never had the chance to fix things.

"W-what?" Amy stares at me, as baffled as the waitress who's turning in our direction, trying to figure out why two teenage girls just came running in hellbent for leather at an hour that's usually seen only by grave-shift workers and drunks looking for one last pause before the serious boozing begins. "You can't leave me here. Not if there's someone out there who's going to hurt me. You *can't*—"

"I can, and I have to." Bobby is still outside, frustrated by the disappearance of his prey. I can feel him, and that means he can feel me. If I step outside this oasis of the road, he'll know beyond the shadow of a doubt that I'm in range, and he'll forget all about Amy. Given a choice between us . . . I'm the one who got away. He'll never choose her over me. "You need to stay inside until the sun comes up. Promise me."

"Rose, I—"

"Promise me!"

"All right! I promise, I promise!" She looks scared out of her mind. Good. That means she may live to see the morning.

"Don't let her leave," I command the waitress, who nods, fear worming through the confusion in her eyes. No one works the night shift in a diner for long without learning that the world is bigger, and bleaker, than they ever dreamed. "Good. Thank you." And I turn, Amy's coat still wrapped around me, and step out into the warm Wisconsin night.

Everything is silence, no sign of Bobby Cross or his demon car. I don't need to see him to know that he's here. I can taste him in the wind. I can always taste him. Murderer, monster, man who made me. He's still here.

"Come on, asshole," I say. "Come on." I shrug out of Amy's jacket, feeling warmth and solidity and finally life itself peel away with the fabric, until my ghostly fingers can no longer hold it; it falls to the ground, and my hair is wild around my shoulders, lemon-bleached blonde, and my sweater and long skirt are gone, replaced by a green silk gown meant for a Michigan June, not a Wisconsin night in March. I would be chilly if I were alive. Instead, I'm freezing, because I'm dead. *"Come on!"*

In the dark, his engine roars. I take a step backward, all too aware of the diner at my back, that sweet sanctuary that has already opened its arms to me once tonight.

I've saved Amy twice before. They say the third time's the charm. I twist around, feet seeking purchase on the sidewalk that I can't even really feel, and I run. I run.

I run.

It takes the better part of an hour for me to race and dodge and evade Bobby all the way out of the city limits. Amy's still safe inside the diner. I have to believe that, and I have to believe that he would have turned back if she'd been available to him. That's the only thing that makes the close calls of the past hour worthwhile.

I dive into a field of new corn, hearing his engine scream frustration on the road behind me, and I keep on diving, driving myself down from the daylight into the comforting dimness of the twilight. The corn is taller here, almost harvest-ready, even though the season has barely begun. It towers above my head, broad leaves blocking out the moon, and everything smells of loam and greenness and safety. I drop to my knees, more tired than I should be. Exhaustion after death just isn't fair.

The corn rustles to my right, and a woman's shoe appears in my field of vision, sensible brown walking shoe, the sort of thing worn by farmer's daughters the whole world over. I lift my head, following it up to a knee-length pleated skirt in plaid wool, a white cotton shirt, and finally, the smiling face of a green-eyed, redheaded woman who I've seen twice before, both times in Wisconsin, both times when I was in the process of inexplicably saving Amy.

"There you are," she says, and smiles, showing straight white teeth with the slightest of overbites. "I was hoping you'd stick around long enough for me to catch up with you." There's a slight strangeness in her accent, like another country that's been worn away to almost nothing. A ghost of a beginning.

A ghost. The other times I've seen her, she's been in the world of the living, and she'd never shown any signs of crossing into the twilight. I stagger to my feet, glad to realize that I'm back in the clothes I chose for myself, rather than in the clothes my death chose for me. "You," I say. "Who *are* you?"

"We're starting with the tough philosophical questions tonight, I see." She keeps on smiling. "My name is Emma. I . . . look after the girl you've been saving. Amy."

Oh, great. "You're a guardian angel?"

Her laughter is startled and joyful and tells me what her accent doesn't. Ireland. My mystery woman comes from Ireland, or did, so long ago that it's almost washed away from her. "Do I *look* like a guardian angel?" she asks. "If you asked Amy, I think she'd be like to give you the job, since you're the one who's come sweeping in to save her. Three times, even, and that has to be something of a record. No. I'm no guardian angel."

"What are you, then?" She's a little bit shorter than I am, even though she looks like an adult woman, and I look, as always, sweet sixteen. "And don't tell me you're a friend. Nothing that identifies itself as 'a friend' ever really is."

She sighs. "What I am is Emma. I'm Amy's family *beán sidhe*."

I stop at that, blinking at her. She blinks calmly back at me, waiting. Finally, unsure of how else I should be responding, I say, "Okay, that's new."

"Since I've been their family *beán sidhe* for about fifteen generations now, no, it's not. But I can see where it would be new to you." She grins again, another flash of those so-white teeth. "I wanted to thank you for what you've done for Amy. I'm not allowed to intervene with members of the family, and I would have hated to see her die so far ahead of her time."

"People have times?"

The words are out before I can really think them through. Emma's smile dims a little. "Yes," she says. "People have times. The trouble is, the world doesn't always stick to the timetable. She's been in serious danger three times in her life, and you've stopped her from getting hurt all three times. I owe you for that."

I don't understand any of this. I'm a road ghost. We live in the twilight, and we don't go any deeper when we have a choice in the matter. *Beán sidhe* are creatures of the Irish underworld, and my experience with them is minimal, which really means I don't have any experience with them at all. I've been pretty happy keeping it that way. "Why didn't you step in, if she's your charge?"

"That's not what *beán sidhe* do," says Emma, and her smile is back, if a little thinner than before. Her teeth still seem too white against the dark, and something about them doesn't read quite human to me. Not all things in the twilight started out as human beings. "I'm not allowed to interfere like that. If I were, well. Some *beán sidhe* would keep their families alive at the expense of everyone around them. Others would kill their families off in order to win their freedom. It would get very ugly, very quickly. So we're not allowed to step in until the people we watch are too far gone to be saved."

Most of the time, when I interfere, the people I'm trying to rescue wind up dying anyway. Most of the time, but not always. I can't imagine what it would be like if I could never save anyone, if I had to keep standing by and watching as they died. I shudder, trying to push the thought away. "I'm sorry."

"I'm used to it." Emma's smile softens. "Amy's the only member of her generation, and when she marries, her children won't be O'Malleys. Not the way she is. My duty is done when Amy dies . . . but I've had to bury a lot of people to get this far, and I've wept for every single one of them."

"What happens to a *beán sidhe* without a family?"

"Depends on the *beán sidhe*. Some adopt new families. Some go poltergeist and spend some time breaking things. Others take over diners and learn how to make ice cream sodas." Emma grins again, and this time there's nothing inhuman in the expression. "I understand that I make a pretty darn good ice cream soda, if I do say so myself. And in case you were wondering, I count as the living when it comes to giving food to hungry ghosts who have themselves a little credit. Have you ever heard of a place called the Last Dance?"

Everyone's heard of the Last Dance Diner. It's a hitcher legend, a place everyone swears exists and no one knows how to reach. "Sure," I say.

"Great." Emma offers me her hand. "Come on. I think I owe you dinner."

I don't have a coat, but her fingers are solid all the same, and I hold onto them as she leads me out of the corn, out onto the moon-washed surface of the ghostroad. There's neon gleaming in the distance, and we walk toward it, hand in hand.

Madison, Wisconsin, 2008.

It was a stupid accident. The car—a 1992 Ford—needed maintenance, the brakes were just a little squishier than they should have been, and when Amy needed them most, they weren't there for her. The other vehicle was a pickup truck with a driver who'd had three beers more than he should have before getting behind the wheel—which is to say, he'd had three beers. Amy didn't have a chance to scream. It was over in seconds. There was no smell of ashes, no oracle of impending doom; this time, the fourth time, there was nothing I could have done.

Emma's hand bears down on mine so hard that it hurts. It shouldn't be possible, not with her solid and me intangible, but the rules don't apply to her, not here, not now, not with the last member of her family taking her last breath some twenty yards away.

We both know when it ends. Emma closes her eyes, looking so young and so old at the same time, and she starts to sing. I don't know the words, but the tune is familiar, like something I used to hear when I was dreaming. I pull my hand free and walk over to the car, dropping from daylight down to the twilight when I'm halfway there. Emma is in the twilight, too, still singing, still apparently solid. Emma, and someone else.

Amy stands beside the wreckage of her car, expression one of utter bewilderment. Her hair, light when she was a little girl, darkening as she became an adult woman, is light again; she's lived a lot longer than I did. She looks up at the sound of my footsteps, and her eyes widen, making her look like the teenage girl who ran with me through the Wisconsin night. I stop, and smile.

"Hello, Amy," I say.

Her smile is like streetlights coming on in the middle of a winter night. The years melt away as she steps toward me, now almost seventy, now in her thirties, and finally seventeen years old, little Miss Teenage USA from a decade as dead as the both of us. "Hello, Rose," she says. She looks past me to Emma, and there's recognition in her eyes, but her gaze returns inevitably to my face. "Is Will . . . ?"

He died two years ago. Cancer. She held his hand the whole time. He's been waiting for her at the Last Dance ever since.

"I'll take you to him," I say, and offer her my hand. She takes it, trusting me to save her one last time, and we walk toward Emma, away from the ending of a life, and into the beginning of something so very much more.

1998
Hitchers and Homecomers

THERE ARE PEOPLE who will try to tell you that there are two Americas: the bright and shining daylight country where normal people live their normal lives and count their normal blessings, and a second, darker nighttime country. A country where men with hooks instead of hands haunt Lover's Lane, and scarecrows walk when the moon is full.

Those people are full of shit.

There are a lot more than just two Americas. Every inch of ground on this planet is a palimpsest, scraped clean and overwritten a million times, leaving behind just as many ghosts. That daylight America exists, alongside a thousand other Americas just like it, but the twilight Americas outnumber them a thousand-fold, and beneath them, the midnight Americas lurk, hungry and waiting. People who aren't careful . . . well, people who aren't careful run the risk of slipping through the cracks between the countries. They run the risk of falling off the map, and in the spaces where the map doesn't extend . . .

In those places, there be monsters.

You can learn to read the pattern of those cracks. There's a secret language written across the length and breadth of North America, etched out in highways and embellished in side roads. It sweeps from the top of Canada all the way to the bottom of Mexico, telling a story too big and too old for any living soul who isn't an ambulomancer to understand. There just isn't room in a mortal lifetime. You'd need to ride those roads for fifty years or more, just listening, just learning, before you'd start to have a clue. Even then, you wouldn't really *know*. You'd just be a little bit less ignorant. I've been running these roads since 1952, and I'm still not sure what some of the side roads and interchanges are trying to tell me.

I do know enough to understand that every story starts in more than one place, driving anchors into the flesh of the world, digging in its claws and screaming for the right to live. My story started at a desert crossroads, and at the hairpin curve near the top of Sparrow Hill Road in Buckley Township, Michigan. The roads are still there, if you'd like to go and find them. They'll tell you everything they know, and all you have to do is ask them the right way.

Of course, you have to *listen* the right way, too, and for most people, that's the hardest challenge of all. That's what keeps the routewitches in business—they already know how to listen, and it's usually easier to pay somebody else than it is to take the time to learn. I don't have that problem. I've got nothing *but* time.

It's everyone else whose time keeps running out.

The accident that's coming is a bad one; bad enough that it's been sending ripples through the ghostroads for days now, bruising the skies with the inky streaks of pain to come. There are a hundred accidents every hour, and most don't announce themselves like this—if they did, no one would ever get any work done around here.

I put down my malt on the smooth Formica counter of the Last Dance Diner, kicking the base of my stool to spin me around until I can look out at the blackened sky. "That's going to be one pisser of a storm," I say, shaking my head. "I pity anyone who has to go out there."

Emma's silence from behind me is better than any comment could have been.

"No." I spin myself with more force this time, slapping my palms down on the counter before momentum can carry me into a full turn. This way looks tough and determined, like I should be listened to. If I kept spinning, I'd just wind up looking like a little kid. There are downsides to being a teenage girl for eternity. "I don't care what's going on out there. Whoever's up the creek isn't one of mine, and I'm not running toward an accident this bad if I don't have to. I'm going to sit right here and drink my malt, like a sensible dead girl."

"There are a great many ways to belong to someone, Rosie," says Emma calmly. The redheaded *beán sidhe* picks up my half-empty glass, pulling it out of my reach. "An accident bad enough to storm like this is no good for anyone. Do you really want to take the risk that the victim might belong to someone worse than the likes of you?"

I glare at her. Emma smiles sympathetically back. Out of everyone I've met since I died, she's the one who seems to understand how much I hate doing the psychopomp's duty, which should never have been mine in the first place. I'm a hitcher, not a reaper or a gathergrim. I should have a carefree existence, all coffee and pie and anonymous sex with truckers who need to feel like they're getting some value for the rides they give me. "I'm not the only hitcher in this state."

Now she raises an eyebrow, an amused smile appearing on her lips. "Is that so?" she asks. "And what state are we in then, Rosie-my-dear? Denial? Transition? Oh, could we be in a state of grace? I'm really quite fond of that one, grace."

I glare harder. It won't do any good; Emma owns the Last Dance, inasmuch as anyone can own the Last Dance, and she's right about my having no idea where we technically are. The diner moves around to suit its own wishes, and no one, not even Emma, seems to have any real say in its position from day to day. I can always find it when I need to. Sometimes I just need to travel a little farther before I get there.

Emma doesn't say anything. Emma doesn't *have* to say anything. All she has to do is wait me out, and if I think a half a century in the grave has refined my glaring skills, that's nothing compared to what several centuries in the twilight has done for her ability to wait. *Beán sidhe* are neither alive nor dead, but what they are, above all else, is patient.

Finally, I throw my hands up in disgust. "Fine. Fine. You want me to check it out? Fine. But I'm going to need a ride."

"Oh, that shouldn't be any trouble at all," says Emma. She looks down the counter, suddenly all smiles, to the booth where a lanky phantom rider is busy eating cheese sandwiches and vegetable soup. "Tommy? Rose needs a ride. Think you can give her one?"

He looks up, and smiles, and for a moment I see the boy he was before he died, headstrong and hopeful and not listening to a damn thing I said when I told him not to get behind the wheel. Tommy never did learn to listen to me. "I'd be happy to, Miss Emma."

I sigh, trying to make it clear just how put-upon I am. "Can I at least get a burger to go?"

Tommy isn't much for conversation. He drives like he's making love to the road, hands gripping the wheel, eyes fixed on the black ribbon of the asphalt stretching out in front of us, reaching toward forever. In the ghostroads, you really can just drive and never turn back. As long as Tommy wants this road, it will be there for him, long and straight and eager for the kiss of his wheels against its surface. Everything leaves ghosts, even roads, and what could the ghost of a road want more than a man who drives like there is nothing else?

Normally, I'm pretty chatty, but when I'm on my way to an accident I haven't been personally called to, all I want to do is focus. With an accident that can't be avoided that I'm intended to be at, there's warning. I taste ashes and lilies, sometimes for days ahead of time, sometimes only for instants. I know the people I'm looking for, even if I've never seen them before. Here and now, with this fool's errand of an accident, all I know is that someone's about to die, and it's going to be bad. So I focus, and I stretch myself as far as I can go, until I'm a wire vibrating across the twilight, and I search for the taste of ashes.

I feel like I'm on the verge of snapping when I find it, a pale bloom of empty hallways and dust-covered bridal bouquets. "East," I gasp, falling back down into myself. "Turn east."

Tommy gives me an appraising look before he hauls hard on the wheel, turning us. He doesn't reduce speed at all, and the brief glimpse I have of the landscape tells me that there's no road waiting for us—we're about to drive into the badlands that surround every throughway in the twilight. I'm not too thrilled about that. There are . . . *things* . . . in the badlands, and not all of them are well-inclined toward human-form spirits.

But the road reaches up to meet Tommy's wheels, and we zoom on without so much as a shudder. The ghostroads love him like they've never loved me—like they've never loved any hitcher. All that, and his car, too. Phantom riders get all the luck.

I huddle in my seat, wishing for the warm safety of a borrowed coat, to drape me in skin and bones and take me away from all of this, into a world where the sky never turns black with the bruises of an impending death, and pushy *beán sidhe* rarely send anyone off on a fool's errand. The only comfort I have is that the air still tastes like, well, air. When I'm not struggling for the distant flavor of ashes and lilies, all I taste is the sterile nothingness of the dead. I'm not a big fan of the flavor, but it's better than the alternatives. Wormwood and gasoline would signal Bobby Cross ahead of us on the road, and if there's one thing I'm not ready to do yet, it's go up against the man who killed me. Maybe I'll never be ready.

Look at me: dead for almost fifty years, and still a coward too interested in continuing to exist to get anything done. On the other hand, cowards have time to change their minds. Heroes who decide to get heroic too soon wind up not having time for anything, ever again.

I'm finally starting to relax, soothed by the familiar feeling of the car vibrating around me, when the sky goes black above us. Not bruised, but black from side to side, like someone had pulled a hood over the head of the world. I barely have time to consider what this might mean when the taste of ashes and lilies crashes down over me, a cold wave of accident-coming, accident-*here* that blocks out everything but the need to go, go, go, to see the twisted metal and the broken glass and the birth of a new ghost.

"Here!" I shout, and Tommy, bless him, doesn't hesitate. He grabs the stick and shifts gears, carrying us up out of the twilight, away from the ghostroads, and onto the cold, cruel daylight roads of the living.

"Daylight" is a misnomer at the moment: we emerge from the twilight into the dead of night, suddenly racing down a highway I've never seen before. Road signs tell me that we're thirty miles outside of Birmingham, Alabama. If I had a coat on, I'd be drowning in the humidity of the Southern summer. Without it, I'm just another dead girl, and the night is so cold.

The smell of ashes and lilies is pulling me on toward the accident, but even without it, we'd have no trouble finding our destination. Flames have lit up the hills ahead of us like it's the Fourth of July, painting them in orange striped with smoky shadows. Tommy hits the gas a little harder and his car eats up the last of the road, bringing the wreckage into view. The portents in the twilight were right: this was a bad one. A yellow school bus lies on its side, still smoking, and a tanker truck is off the road not far away, the cab crushed in from its collision with the cliff wall. A scattering of smaller vehicles surrounds the two behemoths. None of those drivers had a chance.

There are ghosts who could look at a scene like that and tell you exactly what went wrong, painting you a picture of the accident so accurate that you'd almost believe they'd been there all along, watching as the cars collided. That's not part of my skill set. What I *can* do, though, is spot the newly dead. And an accident like this was going to make ghosts.

"Here," I say. Tommy stops the car on a dime, and there's no jerk as inertia kicks in, because we're in the daylight now, and not even the for-your-convenience physics of the ghostroads can touch us here. I blow him a kiss and then I'm out of the car, running toward the accident.

Broken glass and twisted metal litter the ground, but that doesn't slow me down, because none of it can touch me. The pieces I step on pass right through my sneaker-clad feet, and I leave no footprints behind. If I look back, I know that Tommy will be gone, so I don't look back. I just keep on running.

I got here fast, thanks to Tommy, thanks to Emma and her not-so-subtle prodding; the first responders aren't even here yet. For the moment, the only things that move are me and the flames. That will change soon. Waking up always takes time.

The first bodies I find are a man and a woman in one of the smaller cars. He died when he was crushed against the steering wheel, and she wasn't wearing a seat belt; she's halfway through the windshield, a chunk of glass sticking out of her throat like a blade. I check them both, running my fingers through their shoulders without finding any resistance. They died painfully and without warning, but they didn't leave ghosts behind. They've already moved on to whatever waits for the living on the other side of death.

All the cars are like that, holding only slowly-cooling bodies whose residents have already vacated the premises. So is the tanker truck. I turn my eyes toward the thing I was hoping to avoid: the bus. Which came, according to the lettering on its side, from Centerville High School.

God, I hate dealing with dead kids.

There aren't many hard and fast rules about who will or won't leave a ghost behind when they go. You can game the system sometimes, die the right way to really get the universe's attention, but for the most part, unless you're a routewitch or an ambulomancer, you don't get a say in whether or not you move on when you die. One of the ways to stack the deck in your favor, though, is to die violently, unexpectedly, and in your teens. Trust me. I'm practically the poster child for "die young, leave a hideously burnt corpse, wander the world forever as an unquiet spirit." Maybe it's because all teenagers consider themselves immortal. We just can't accept the idea that we've actually died, and so we can't move on.

An entire bus full of dead high school students would definitely explain why the twilight was vibrating with the pre-echoes of this accident. Something like this could spawn twenty new road ghosts, easy, and not all—or even most—of them would be the friendly kind. Ghosts like me and Tommy are essentially the minority. It's just that we all hang out together, because the alternative is a little horrifying.

The remains of a homecoming banner wave gently in the breeze generated by the fire. I don't know how it hasn't burned yet, but I'm grateful for its survival, because it tells me that the school colors are purple and gray. I change my clothes as I approach the bus, keeping my jeans, turning my comfortable old mechanic's shirt into layered tank tops in the school colors. I even streak my hair: the ultimate modern expression of school spirit. We wore ribbons in my day, but those would mark me as an outsider in the here and now.

All this takes less time than it takes me to cross the short remaining distance. The dead are malleable. The only thing I can't manipulate is the dress I died in, and I'm not wearing it now. That means things aren't as bad as they could be.

The smell of ashes and lilies is still lingering. The accident is over, but it hasn't ended yet. I reach the bus, standing beside it and trying to decide what to do next. I could walk through it and see what I can see, but if there's anyone inside awake enough to see me, all I'll do is freak them out. Not a good way to make an introduction, especially since so few of the newly dead really understand what's happened to them. Understanding takes time.

I settle for the easy route. Cupping my hands around my mouth like a cheerleader at a pep rally, I shout, "Hey, is anyone awake in there? Johnny? Heather?" One thing that hasn't changed in the last fifty years: give me a bus full of high schoolers, and I'll show you at least one Johnny—probably more than one—and the corresponding Heather. The odds were in my favor.

Minutes tick by. The police will be here any second, and with them, the crowd of living bodies that inevitably clogs an accident scene like this one. That's good, because any survivors will be able to get the help they need. It's also bad, because it will alert the dead that they're not going to get better. The last thing I need right now is a newly dead teenage poltergeist kicking my ass because they're going to miss prom. I try again: "Hello?"

"Oh, God, I thought I was the only one. What happened?"

The voice comes from behind me. That's not a shock. The newly dead have a tendency to wander. I turn to see a pretty brunette in a purple-and-gray cheerleading uniform standing behind me, shivering uncontrollably. She hasn't adjusted to the temperature change yet. The dead are always cold.

"I didn't see," I say truthfully. "I wasn't paying attention."

She's never seen me before, and in this moment, that doesn't matter. I'm wearing school colors and standing next to their bus, and that's all that matters. She may not even realize that I'm not injured. "Is anyone else . . . ?"

"Not that I've seen." Not yet. The others will rise soon, if they're going to rise at all.

Her eyes roll toward the bus, and she shudders, the sort of full-body shake that never presages anything good. For a moment, she seems to flicker, and her cheerleading uniform is replaced by jeans and a plain purple T-shirt. Then the uniform is back, like it had been there all along, but that doesn't matter, because I know what she is, and I know why I'm here.

She's a homecomer. And I get the privilege of explaining to her why she can never, ever go home.

Sometimes being dead really sucks.

There's no hierarchy among the ghosts of the road. We all died in transit, one way or another, and we all kept going after our bodies let us down. Some of us are harmless, or close enough to harmless to be safe to deal with if you don't have a choice. Hitchers, for example. My clan. All we need is a coat and a ride. Anything else you want to give us is extra, and we give as good as we get. One in three hitchhikers on the North American road died long before anyone offered them a ride, and for the most part, we're pretty friendly.

We're not the only dead people who sometimes go looking for rides, and that's where the homecomers come in. They die the same way hitchers do, but they die with just one thought in their minds: I can't stay here. I have to get home. So when they rise, all they do, forever, is try to find the car that can get them where they're going. It can take them years to realize that no living driver will ever be able to take them to the past—it can take them years to start killing. Their need to make it home is so strong that almost all of them inevitably do start to kill, and once they start, nothing stops them but an exorcism.

Homecomers are like the dark mirror of the hitchers, even down to their appearance. We're stuck, to some degree, in the clothes that we died in. We can change them, but if we're not paying attention—or if the danger is too great—they'll reassert themselves, returning like a rash. Homecomers discard the clothes they died in when they rise, dressing themselves instead in the clothes they wish they'd been wearing. They're the girls by the side of the road in the pretty dresses and the Halloween costumes, the cheerleading outfits and the club wear. Hitchers never forget the accidents that killed us. Homecomers forget almost immediately, becoming convinced that they were on their way to homecoming, or to a costume party, or to anything but the grave. Once that forgetfulness sets in, they can't be reasoned with anymore. All they want is to go home.

My heart aches for her, for this poor cheerleader the age that I seem to be. But that doesn't matter—that can't matter—because I can't let her leave here. I can't let her start to walk. That's why I still taste lilies and ashes, even though the accident itself is over. This girl is an accident walking, and as long as she's on the loose, others will die.

"What's your name?" I ask.

She looks at me like I've just said something crazy—and if she's still dazed enough to think that I go to her school, I probably have. Everyone knows the cheerleaders, especially the ones as pretty as she is. She'll have no trouble finding rides if I let her walk away from here.

Sirens are ringing in the distance, still far off, but getting closer. Any one of the people who shows up here could be—*will* be—a target.

"Mackenzie," she says.

"Huh." I give the bus another look. No one is stirring, not even a mouse. Could be none of them will rise. Could be they're all going to rise as soon as my back is turned. Better to focus on the problem at hand. I turn back to her, and offer, "I'm Rose."

Her expression changes, turning suspicious as she studies me. "You don't go to our school, do you?"

"Nope. I just thought the school colors would make you feel a little better about talking to me." I stop focusing on my clothes, and am unsurprised when jeans and tank top melt and flow into the ankle-length green silk gown that I've been wearing off and on for the last fifty years. It's welcome for once, because it means she's really the reason that I'm here: she's really what made Emma send me.

Mackenzie's eyes go wide and round. "What . . . what are you?"

"Ever hear the story of the phantom prom date?" I ask.

Apparently, that's the wrong question, because her eyes get even wider and rounder, and she practically trips over her own feet backing away from me. "That—that's just a story! There's no such person!"

How right she is. The phantom prom date is just one of the many urban legends I've played accidental midwife to: Gary and I never made it to the prom, and I sure as hell didn't kill him. He was the first boy I ever loved. There are many people who could have moved me to murder, but Gary wasn't one of them. "You're right. It's just a story. But it's a story with a grain of truth at the middle of it, because it's about a ghost. It's a ghost story. I'm a ghost story, Mackenzie, and now so are you. I'm sorry."

I hate this part, I *hate* this part, telling the newly dead that they're no longer among the living. It's so easy not to notice. Death is a trauma, and so we block it out, trying to convince ourselves that it didn't happen, until someone—some busybody in a green silk gown that went out of style decades ago—shows up and starts saying otherwise.

"You can't be serious," she whispers.

"Mackenzie—" I take a step forward.

"Get away from me!" she howls, and the wind howls with her, lashing out at me like a fist. I'm not braced—this isn't something I was expecting when I started trying to talk to a newly dead homecomer—and so it sends me flying backward, through the bus. I'm treated to the unpleasant sight of several dead teenagers as I pass through them, and then I'm hitting the pavement on the other side, rolling to a stop half-in and half-out of one of the smoking cars.

"Oh, great," I mutter. "All this, and a fucking poltergeist, too. *Great.*"

I pick myself up, a little more slowly than I would if I actually wanted to deal with this, dust myself off, and go running back toward where I left Mackenzie. It's just become a lot more important that I handle her fast . . . and it's just become even clearer that I have no idea how I'm going to do it.

There may be no hierarchy among road ghosts, but we're not the only ghosts out there, and some traits can show up regardless of what else you may be. Poltergeists, for example. Throwing shit around in the real world and beating the crap out of your fellow dead people isn't what I'd call a common trait among the ghosts of the road—it's more common in lost children, and they're strictly house-haunters—but that doesn't mean we don't get poltergeists. And since poltergeists pretty much require violent, horrible, traumatic deaths, the ones we *do* get are just as unhinged as the normal kind.

A homecomer poltergeist is just about the worst scenario I can think of. She'd be able to crash the cars that refused to pick her up, and that sort of death could very well create more ghosts, stranding innocent people who had no business on the ghostroads until a reaper or a gather-grim could come and sweep them up. Not to mention all the damage a normal homecomer does. Mackenzie might be confused, but she was also the spiritual equivalent of a nuclear bomb, and I did *not* want her on my roads.

Luckily for me, she's still a teenage girl in mind as well as in appearance. I walk back through the bus to find her standing there with her hands clutched under her chin, obviously praying. I don't have the heart to tell her that no one's listening.

"Mackenzie . . ."

"Stay away from me," she says dully. "I need to be here when Kyle wakes up. I need him to see that I'm okay."

Kyle's not going to wake up. He might rise, or he might not, but waking up is no longer on the table for anyone in that bus. The glimpse I had as I went flying through has made that very clear. "Mackenzie, you need to come with me, or more people are going to get hurt. I'm sorry I don't have time to do this nicely. I don't have a choice."

"People are going to get hurt?" She turns to face me, the poltergeist fire kindling in her eyes again. It's all I can do not to take a big step backward. "You're telling me that I'm *dead*, and you expect me to worry about people getting *hurt?*"

"Well, yeah, I kind of do. You and me, we're dead. There's not much left that can hurt us. But people like them," I wave a hand toward the distant sound of sirens, "they're still alive, and they deserve to stay that way. Accidents happen, Mackenzie. I'm so sorry, and believe me, I know what you're going through right now. That doesn't mean we get to take our anger out on the living."

Mackenzie hesitates. "You went *through* the bus just now."

I consider the value of telling her that she threw me through the bus, and decide that for once, I should keep my stupid mouth shut. "Yeah, I did. I'm a ghost. I do that sort of thing."

"You're a ghost."

"Yeah."

"So am I." The change in her expression is abrupt, confusion and misery becoming determination. I don't have time to shout or tell her not to do what she's about to do, and I'm not sure it would have done me any good; she's too far away. Before I can react, Mackenzie turns and dives, vanishing into the metal undercarriage of the bus.

Her screams begin an instant later, ringing across the night with a volume she shouldn't be able to reach, much less sustain.

"Oh, you owe me *so* many malts, Emma," I mutter, and run toward the bus, diving in after my wayward homecomer. What's she going to do? Kill me?

I'm reflecting on the fact that the joke I just made was in poor taste, even if I only made it inside my own head, and then I'm through the undercarriage into the bus itself, where Mackenzie is trying frantically to wrap her arms around a dead boy. She doesn't understand yet what her limitations are; that as a poltergeist, she can smash things, and as a homecomer, she can borrow flesh and bone from the living, but that either way, she's still a ghost, and no corpse has anything to give her. She doesn't seem to have noticed her own broken body, lying half-folded over the back of a nearby seat. Small mercy. She'll notice soon enough, and with my luck, that's when all hell is going to break loose.

"Kyle-Kyle-Kyle," she's saying, almost like it's a chant, a benediction meant to be spoken in the church formed by their bodies. My heart breaks for her a little bit more.

Heartbreak never woke the dead. "He's gone, Mackenzie. *You're* gone, and so you need to come with me, before things get any worse."

"No," she says, as sullen as only sweet sixteen can be. "He's taking me to prom. He promised. I bought my dress—"

The mention of prom brings inappropriate laughter bubbling to my lips, where I have to swallow, hard, to keep it from breaking loose. Wasn't a teenage poltergeist upset about missing prom exactly what I'd been hoping to avoid? "I didn't get to go to prom either. Sometimes the world's not fair. And we have to go now."

"What if I won't?" She shoots me a venomous glare over Kyle's shoulder. "What if I want to stay here with him?"

"You won't stay," I say, quietly. "You'll get distracted when the firemen get here. The living will draw you, because that's what the living *do*, and then you'll ask one of them for a ride home. That's where it will start. With one ride. You'll forget that you're dead; you'll forget about Kyle; you'll think that all you have to do is get home and everything will be perfect. Only eventually, the truth will come back to you, and you'll start killing the people who pick you up. You'll fill a graveyard before you're done, and no one will remember the sweet little cheerleader who died too young. They'll remember some horrible *thing*, some monster out of a campfire story." I allow myself to smile, small and bitter and honest. "They forgot Rose Marshall, but they'll remember the phantom prom date forever. Do you want that to be you?"

"How can you be so calm?" Her voice is a betrayed whisper.

I shrug. "I've been dead for a long, long time, Mackenzie. Now come on. Let me take you away from here, before someone else gets hurt. Please."

She looks down at Kyle's face, still handsome, despite the blood streaking his cheek. Then she nods. Just once, as sharp and short as the bell for the end of class.

When she kisses his forehead, her lips dip down below the surface of the skin. I don't say anything. I'm not sure she even noticed.

Mackenzie's cheerleading uniform is perfect when she straightens up and turns toward me. She's still a homecomer; her death dictated that for her. She's just a homecomer who found somewhere else to go. "Okay," she says.

"Okay," I echo, and offer her my hands. She steps forward, and as she takes them, I smile, and ask, "How do you feel about milkshakes?"

A poltergeist wind follows us down into the ghostroads. The emergency personnel will be confused when they find the school bus back on its wheels, each student in their proper seat, but they won't question it too much; no one who works on the road questions anything like that *too* much. They might not like the answers. And none of them will notice the football player and the cheerleader, both of them out of uniform, with their fingers twined together as they wait for the end of eternity.

Book Two

Ghost Stories

I drove her to the limits of a town not far away,
And she vanished like a fable at the breaking of the day.
As she slipped away, she kissed my cheek and said, "We'll meet again,"
And I find that I'm not worried 'bout the how, or 'bout the when.

For there's beauty on the open road a man can learn to find;
Flowers blossom on the median, and fate is sometimes kind.
When it's time to make the final drive, I won't be scared at all,
Rose will be right here beside me, all along that final haul.

And she's never been a good ghost, not for one day in her death;
She stopped playing by the rules the day that she gave up on breath.
She's the angel of the truck stops; it's the afterlife she chose.
She's the flower of the graveyard, she's our ageless roadside Rose.

She's the blossom of the median; she's the place a lost man goes.
She's the flower of the graveyard, she's our ageless roadside Rose.

—excerpt from "Graveyard Rose," as performed by
William Davis and the Billy Davis Band.

. . . "The first time I saw her, I was nineteen." So begins the eyewitness account of sixty-three-year–old Patrick Swenson of Billings, Montana. Mr. Swenson has been the head librarian of the Downtown Billings Library for the past twenty years. In that time, the library's selection of local history and American ghost stories has swelled to become one of the premiere public collections in the nation. "I was driving home from a concert one weekend. It was late, and I was tired, and I was probably more than a little drunk, but I wasn't thinking about that at the time. I was just thinking about how nice it was going to be to get home and sleep in my own bed."

He pauses, expression distant. It's difficult to look at him like this and not see a man who truly believes every word he says. "I pulled off at this sleazy little diner to get a cup of coffee, and she was there. Standing in the parking lot, like some kind of angel. 'You don't want to go in there,' she said. 'The coffee's terrible, and besides, the fry cook just shot somebody.' That's when I heard the screaming coming from inside. She didn't have any blood on her, and she looked so young—younger than me, anyway—that I told her that she shouldn't be out alone. She asked if I could give her a ride home. I said sure." He looks toward me, hope and anxiety in his eyes. "That was the right thing to say, wasn't it? That I could get her home?"

I allow that it was the gentlemanly thing to say. Right and wrong don't come into it.

Relieved, Mr. Swenson resumes his account. "She got into the car. Told me her name was Rose. And then she told me she knew a shortcut. We talked all the way back to Billings, and then—right about when I crossed the city limits—she stopped talking. I looked over at her side of the car, and she was gone. Just gone.

"I went home, and got into my own bed. Woke up the next day with a killer hangover. It got worse when I saw the front page of the newspaper. 'Ten car pile-up at the city limits,' that's what it said. If it hadn't been for Rose and her shortcut, I would've driven straight into that accident. With my reflexes dulled, and as tired as I was, there's no way I would have lived." He chuckles a little, half-wry, half-sad. "So now I look for her on every road I can find. I just want the chance to say thank you to her face, you know? Maybe that means that I'll find her the day I die, but I'm all right with that. I've never had a better driving companion than Rose."

—from *American Ghosts*, Michael Hayes, Ghost Ship Press.

2010
Bullets and Bad Coffee

THERE ARE AS MANY KINDS OF GHOST as there are ways to die, but death starts the same way for everyone. One moment we're alive, and the next, we're not. It's that simple. The blink of an eye, the final beat of a broken heart, and everything changes.

Everything changes forever.

There are a thousand types of the newly dead, each with their own destinations in the twilight or the midnight. Those who died running tumble out of the daylight and find themselves on the ghostroads, the narrow veins of dark asphalt that run through the body of the twilight like veins through the thighs of an aging hooker. The trainspotters say new arrivals used to find themselves standing in railway stations or next to remote stretches of track, and the routewitches say that before that, the new-dead wound up on dirt roads or narrow horse-trails. They're all the ghostroads, and they've all got one thing in common: they're all physical evidence of the scars mankind leaves on the world.

We created the ghostroads through our lives and through our deaths, and they provide a home and haven to our wandering souls . . . at least until the wandering is over. No one knows exactly where the terminus of the ghostroads can be found, although everyone knows that it exists. It has to. No one can ride the ghostroads forever, after all; eventually, every journey comes to an end, and those of us who serve as psychopomps have seen more than our fair share of wandering souls to their rest. But while the journey is still going on . . .

It doesn't matter whether you're alive or dead—either way, the ghostroads are the best way to move through the twilight. They dependably exist, which gives them a definite advantage over the roads that sink down from the daylight or rise up from the midnight. They aren't exactly safe, but nothing in the twilight really is, and the ghostroads generally don't go out of their way to kill people. They're content to strew themselves with hidden dangers and wait, instead of going hunting like some of the routes that can get you through the midnight.

The ghostroads are less direct than the roads on most other levels, and that's part of what gives them their stability. As long as there's a hidden turn to take or an intersection yet uncrossed, the ghostroads will retain their reason to exist.

The most important thing to remember about the ghostroads is this: every road that's ever been is a part of them, and the twilight is just as stretched and painted-over as the daylight. If you want to find a road that isn't there anymore, all you have to do is close your eyes, plant your feet, and let go. Stop trying to be anchored; stop trying to convince yourself that anything ever ends. The ghostroads know the way, and they'll take you if you'll let them. It's not the sort of thing people do without good reason—even the routewitches are careful when it comes to surfing the palimpsest atlas of the ghostroads' memory—but it can get you where you want to go, if you're willing to trust the path you're on.

I only have one piece of advice to give about the ghostroads: don't get lost. Maybe you won't always know where you are. Maybe that's for the best, but there's a big difference between not knowing where you are and truly being lost. Before you try to pull any fancy tricks or turn the road to your own advantage, learn to believe—to truly *know*—that you're never, not for a second, lost. Because people who get lost out there . . . those people are never found again, not by anyone, and what the ghostroads claim, they don't give up easily. Living or dead, the ghostroads don't care. We're all travelers when we're with them, and we all owe the roads a traveler's respect.

Most of all and most importantly, when you tell the ghostroads that you want to go somewhere, be sure you really mean it. They don't take kindly to being toyed with, and they don't give second chances. Every trip you take in the twilight, you take for keeps.

Happy trails.

The air outside the rust-colored Chevy tastes like diesel fuel and shadows. It's bitter when I breathe in, burning the back of my throat. The urge to get back in the car and tell the driver—I think his name is Josh; he told me who he was when he picked me up, but he was just a short-time driver, and it didn't matter enough to stick—borders on unbearable. Every inch of me wants to be out of here, wants to be *miles* from here. To be anywhere but this narrow strip of asphalt outside yet another roadside dive. Something's wrong.

"Rose? Are you sure this is where you wanted to be dropped off?" The glow of the diner's neon marquee glints off Josh's glasses as he leans across the passenger seat to look out at me. He's in his early thirties. I've been sixteen for fifty years, and it's hard to think of anything except how goddamn young he looks. He's dipped deeper into the twilight than he ever had before during this drive, and he did it because of me. "I can take you somewhere else if you'd prefer."

So damn *young*. "It's fine. This is where I want to be." His sweatshirt is too big for me, generic red department store cotton washed pale and worn feather-soft. I wrap my arms around myself, trying to stay warm, trying to look pathetic enough that he won't ask for the sweatshirt back. I've had a lot of practice with that particular expression. "Don't you need to get on the road? I don't want to make you late."

"I'm ahead of schedule, thanks to your little shortcuts." His smile is sincere. I hope mine looks as real as his.

We took those shortcuts, even though they meant dipping down into the twilight, because if we hadn't, we would have been on the highway when a group of drunk college kids lost control of their car and flipped it over the center divider. They'd been in the parking lot where I first found him, and they smelled like ashes and lilies. They were already over the edge, too far gone to save. But Josh . . . Josh could drive away clean, if he could hit the gas and floor it out of the twilight before the ghostroads claimed their own.

"Get out of here." I nod toward the road. "Highway's calling. I'll be fine."

He's in too deep, and part of him knows that, because he nods, says, "Take care of yourself, Rose," and then he's gone, peeling out into the night, leaving me in the parking lot with the taste of diesel fuel and shadows filling my mouth like cheap wine. I wish I could go with him. I wish I could leave the twilight like he can.

I wish I knew where I was.

I turn toward the taste of diesel fuel and shadows, toward the rainbow gleam of neon struggling to paint the night in something more than darkness. Then I stop, frowning, because I know this place—I've seen this sign. The Starbright Diner, one more little piece of Americana struggling to stay alive in the evolving maze of the highways, old enough to echo into the twilight . . . but never this deep. I've been here a thousand times. It's never looked like this before. Something is very wrong, and whatever it is, it's not something I'm familiar with.

That smell that lingers in the air is starting to worry me. A lot is done by smell in the twilight, maybe because it's one of the few senses that ghosts reliably retain. For me, ash and lilies means an accident ahead that can't be avoided, while rosemary and my grandmother's sugary perfume means the chance to turn things a different way. Josh smelled like rosemary and perfume when I found him. That's how I knew he wasn't too far gone to save. But this mix of diesel fuel and shadows . . .

This is something new. I don't like new. I haven't liked new since the days when I was sixteen for real, a frightened little phantom running rabbit down the ghostroads for the very first time.

Half the moths fluttering in the glow of the streetlights are translucent, and as dead as I am. The ghost insects overlay the living ones for a second at a time, and that's not right, either. That sort of melding only happens when the ghostroads are bleeding through, and I haven't been here long enough for that to start happening. I watch them as I walk toward the diner, trying to count the ghosts and figure out how bad the bleed is. They move too fast for me to get an exact number, but what I do get is enough to tell me that there's trouble. The kind of trouble that makes me glad you can't die twice—not under normal circumstances, anyway.

Death doesn't smell like anything, not like an accident does. Death is more of a feeling, like a woman's razor-sharp fingernails being dragged slowly along the skin just above your spine. It's hard to feel death until you're right on top of it. That's why I don't realize what's wrong until it's too late, when the diner door swings open at the touch of my hand and sets the bell above it ringing wildly.

There are a dozen people clustered around the counter. They all have wide, terrified eyes. The left side of the night waitress' pink-and-white uniform is stained a deep berry-red by her own spreading blood. I freeze just inside the door, feeling the nails along my spine, and realize why I tasted diesel fuel and shadows, understanding, too late, what the ghostroads were trying to tell me. It was a warning.

"Looks like we have another guest for our little party," says a voice behind me. It's whiskey-rough and a little shaky, like even the speaker isn't sure how things are going to end. The gun barrel he digs into the back of my neck is a lot surer of itself. It's cold, and it's solid, and I can't stop myself from cringing. Maybe that's the right response, because the speaker sounds pleased when he says, "Well, little party crasher? Go on ahead and join the others."

He plants a hand between my shoulder blades and shoves me forward. I'm almost glad to go staggering away from him, away from the gun in his hand. One of the people at the counter catches my arm before I can fall. "You shouldn't have come," he whispers harshly, a middle-aged man in a white apron and a fry cook's paper hat.

There's no recognition in his eyes; he doesn't know me. He's a daylighter, plain and simple, and I start hoping that maybe this is a daylight problem; maybe the smell of death is just the natural result of what's happening here. The blood on the waitress' uniform isn't enough to account for the blood on the floor. Someone has already died in this room—maybe more than one someone—and that happens in every America. Death is not the exclusive province of the darker levels.

"Hey. Look at me."

The man guarding the door sounds completely at ease. That's enough to slice through my fear and turn it into anger. Anger that he's managed to scare me. *Me.* I've been dead longer than anyone in this room has been alive, and here I am, held captive with the rest of them. I turn, ready to give the man with the gun a piece of my mind, and I see him for the first time.

He's in his early twenties, older than I look, but still so damn young. He's dressed like a thousand other roadside runaways, in ripped jeans and combat boots, with a beat-up old leather jacket over his stained red flannel shirt. It's the jacket that gives him away. It should have been the eyes, but it's the jacket, because after fifty years of following the rules that bind the hitchers to the road, I know my outerwear. I can only take jackets from the living. And the man in the doorway, the man with the gun, the man holding this entire diner of terrified, living human beings hostage?

Yeah. He's real damn dead.

His eyes skip up and down the length of me with forced hunger, a leer twisting one corner of his mouth into an angle that's more pathetic than predatory. He's trying to make me uncomfortable. He's succeeding, but not because I'm afraid he'll take advantage of the fact that I'm female, smaller than him, unarmed. No; it's the gun in his hand that's making me uncomfortable, because it looks as solid as I do. It's clearly solid enough to wound the living—the bleeding waitress and the body or bodies I haven't seen are proof enough of that—and I don't know what a gun like that could do to me. I've never encountered anything like this before.

"Aren't you a pretty one?" he asks, rhetorical question with a sneer underneath it. There's a quaver in his voice that all his painted-on confidence can't quite conceal. "So, you here for a cup of coffee, or for a cup of cock?"

The people behind me are silent, all the fire frightened out of them. The waitress in the bloody uniform is close enough that I can feel her shaking. Terror is coming off her skin in waves. None of them will raise a hand to save me. That realization cuts through my own fear, turning it into fury. How dare he? This is the *daylight*. He has no business here.

"Coffee," I say, canting my chin up so that he can see the challenge in my eyes. "You the fry cook on duty?"

His snort of derision is too quick, too tight with his own terror. I'm not the only frightened ghost in the Starbright Diner tonight. "Do I *look* like a fry cook, lady? Maybe you should think about being nice to me. I have enough bullets for everybody."

At least he knows how to share. I'm running down the encyclopedia of the dead in the back of my mind, trying to find the round hole that connects to this square peg. He's not a hitcher; that coat's his own, and has no heat to loan, no solid skin to clothe a shadow in. He's not a pelesit, either; if he had a master, they'd know me, and they wouldn't be letting us talk. They don't like letting their slaves get too close to the free dead.

Too bad that leaves a couple of hundred options open for what he might be, how he might have died, how he can be laid to rest and get the fuck out of my face.

Hitchers like me aren't the only ghosts of the twilight, too well-lit for the midnight Americas, but too dark for the daylight levels. There are other types of ghost that walk here, and every one of them follows different rules. Some of them don't understand that they're not in charge anymore. When that happens, somebody has to teach them what they're doing wrong. And sometimes, when I'm less than lucky, on nights like this one, somebody winds up being me.

"No, you don't look like a fry cook." I cross my arms, cock my hip, and level a flat stare at him. "You look like an idiot. Is this any way to take a diner hostage? I mean, *really*. The door isn't even locked. I just waltzed in here like it was no big deal, situation normal. Do you have enough bullets for the entire highway? Because that's what it's going to take if you keep on this way."

Disquiet flashes across his face, there and gone like a cloud sliding past the moon. "You really think it's a good idea to sass me?"

"You really think it's a good idea to leave those doors unlocked?"

One of the hostages grabs me—a white-faced college boy with eyes the color of day-old coffee. There's blood splattered across the front of his University of Michigan sweatshirt. None of it's his. "Shut *up*," he hisses. "You're making it worse."

"Really? I wasn't aware that there *was* anything worse than this." I pull my arm away, still watching the man with the gun, still running silently through the lists of the dead. He's not a bela da meia-noite; they only come in one flavor, female, and they don't take hostages. He's not a toyol; they're always the ghosts of children, and they never seem this solid. Most of them can't even be seen by the living. "So what do you say? Can we lock the doors?"

I'm not needling him for nothing, no matter what this looks like. He postures like a living man, but he's not one, and I need to know how far his mimicry of the human condition goes. A pissed-off ghost won't care how many people stumble into this diner; whatever grudge he has will spread to cover as many of the living as he can catch. A confused one, on the other hand, a ghost who doesn't know what's going on . . .

"Yeah." He licks his lips before jutting out his jaw in a display of exaggerated machismo. "I think this is all the guests we're gonna need if we want to have a real kick-ass party, huh? A major blast."

The other hostages look to me as he turns to lock the door. Some of them are glaring, while others just look lost. The air is heavy and cloying with the taste of diesel fuel and shadows, joined now by the funereal scent of lilies and the sharp-spice smell of rosemary. There's an accident ahead, one that could go either way, lilies *or* rosemary. For the sake of these people—for the sake of this *place*—I have to hope that it's an accident I can find a way to steer us clear of.

The clock on the wall says it's just past ten. The night is young. So are these people, and they deserve to live longer than this night. "So," I say, a little too loudly. "How about that coffee?"

The waitress with the bloody uniform is named Dinah. He shot her about ten minutes before I walked through the door. She was trying to sneak out through the back door. She's lucky he only shot her in the shoulder. Two other members of the staff—the other waitress and the busboy, a teenage kid who only took the job to pay for repairs on his death trap of a pickup truck—were already dead when she tried to make a break for it.

I learn this while she walks me through the process of making coffee on a machine so old I could probably operate it in my sleep. That's fine. I'm happy to let our rogue gunman think I'm a few sandwiches short of a picnic, especially if it gets Dinah off her feet for a little while. If she faints, I think he'll shoot her again—and this time, he won't be shooting to wound.

"He came in here a few minutes after sunset," she says dully. That's the shock speaking, the timeless voice of a witness at the scene of an accident. "Josie went to take his order. He put a bullet right between her eyes. Right . . . right between her eyes." A wondering note overcomes the shock. She sounds almost childlike as she finishes: "Bang."

"That's charming." The coffee is thick and hot and doesn't smell like anything as I pour it into an industrial white diner mug. I made it, I poured it; nobody gave it to me, and that means I have no right to it. Coffee is reserved for the living. "Where do you keep the cream and sugar?"

"Counter," says Dinah, voice still soft and sweetly childish. I can't be angry with her, although I try to be. I could have been her, if my own life had gone just a little differently.

"Thanks. I'll try to get him to let us take a look at your shoulder." I offer her a thin sliver of a smile. It's not as encouraging as I'd like it to be. It's still better than nothing. I pour a second mug of coffee, place them both on a tray, and then I'm gone, heading for the door by way of the counter.

The dead man with the gun is standing next to the closed door, one eye trained on the room while the other keeps watch through the front window. He stiffens at my approach, but tries to look relaxed as he turns to face me. He's thinking now. He sees how big a risk he's taken by taking this diner—and I still don't know why he's done it, or what he's hoping to achieve.

"Coffee's ready." I hold up the tray, showing him. "I didn't know how you take it, so I brought cream and sugar."

He eyes the second cup and sneers. "So what, you think you get whatever I get? Is that how this works in your empty little head?"

"No. I just thought you'd want to make sure it wasn't poisoned before you drank any." I shrug a little, trying to look unconcerned. If he were alive, I wouldn't be worried at all. No living man has scared me since the night I died. Dead men, on the other hand . . . "If you want to drink them both, that's fine, too."

". . . right." Another flicker of disquiet crosses his face. Maybe *he* doesn't know why he's doing this. "Fix them both, bitch. Three sugars, two creams."

"Got it." I put the tray on the nearest table, start doctoring the coffee, keep running through lists of the dead in my head. He's not einherjar; they like to fight, but they don't take hostages, and they don't abuse the innocent. He's not deogen. They can turn visible when they want to make their presence known, but they can't touch the living, and they don't like to interact when they can just watch. He could be working for the deogen . . . but it's a clear night. There would be a heavy fog blanketing everything if there was a deogen near here, and there's nothing.

"Hurry up."

"I'm done." I lift the tray, tilting it slightly toward him. "You get first pick."

His jaw juts out with pride that barely masks his fear. "You're damn right I do." He grabs a mug, jerking his chin toward the other. "Better enjoy that, bitch. It could be your last cup."

Enjoy it? Not likely. I put down the tray and wrap my hands around the second mug, stealing what little heat it's willing to give me. The liquid inside tastes like nothing but ashes. It doesn't even burn my lips or tongue. It isn't mine.

The man with the gun watches me, eyes narrowed, until I finish my third sip. Then he thrusts his untouched mug toward me, commanding, "Trade."

"What do you mean?" I make doe's-eyes at him, looking as confused as I can.

"What are you, stupid? Gimme your coffee. I know that one's clean."

No, you don't. All you know is that I'm willing to drink poison if it takes you out. The thought barely has time to finish forming before I realize something a lot more important. I hold out my mug, asking slowly, "Does that mean you're giving me yours?"

"Damn right." Coffee slops over the side of the cup and onto my hand as he jerks my mug away, replacing it with his. The scalding sting is almost sweet, because it comes with the smell of sugared coffee and the knowledge that when I take my next sip, I'll taste it. "You got a problem with that?"

"No." He can't give me a coat, but he can give me coffee. The list of the dead has stopped running. I know something he doesn't. I know what he is. *He doesn't know. How is it that he doesn't know? How do you not* notice *something like that?* He's looking at me sidelong, suspicion in his eyes. I take a sip of coffee flavored with cream, sugar, and paradise. That confirms my suspicions. Only a fully incarnate spirit can give me food that tastes like anything but ashes. "No problem."

"Good." He runs his eyes over my breasts again, trying to make me uncomfortable. It isn't working. All I have left for him is pity, poor little ghost who doesn't even realize that he's dead and gone. "So you've got your cup of coffee. Are you ready for your cup of cock?"

The other hostages are staring at us with silent trepidation, mice caught in a cat's cage and watching the one mouse too stupid to stay out of reach of the cat's claws. As long as I'm making myself a target, he's not focusing on them. Two of them are dead already, and one is wounded. I'm the last one to the party. As far as they're concerned, I'm the expendable one.

I'd be offended if it weren't for the fact that they're right.

"Sure," I say, and watch his eyes widen. That wasn't the answer he was expecting. "But can I ask you for a favor first?"

He blinks, surprise hardening almost instantly into irritation. "Oh, yeah? What's that?"

"Let them patch her up." I take another sip of coffee before nodding toward Dinah of the serious bullet wound. "Dead bodies are depressing, and she's bleeding bad enough to gross me out. I'll do whatever you want if you let them give her a little first aid. Deal?"

Suspicion sits at the front of his expression as he considers my proposal from every angle, searching for the double cross. He doesn't find it, because it isn't there. "Sure," he says, finally. "Whatever."

Strigoi. Some people say that they're a kind of vampire, and maybe they are in some places, on some layers. Up in the daylight, maybe, where people fight monsters instead of turning into them. Here on the ghostroads, the strigoi are just one more breed of the unquiet dead: angry spirits tethered to the world of the living by something they didn't get to finish doing before they passed into the twilight. They're normally intangible, as trapped on the ghostroads as most of the dead, but once in a while . . . once in a while . . .

Once in a while they can fight their way back into the daylight levels, dragging the twilight in their wake. Only on special occasions, nights like Halloween, Epiphany—and the anniversary of their deaths. I look over Dinah's shoulder as I help the fry cook and the college boy clean out her wound, assessing the cut of the strigoi's clothes, the style of his jeans. Now that I'm looking, I can see how far out of fashion he is. Not as far as I would be, if I dressed myself in the green silk gown I died in, but far enough. He's a traveler from another country, a country called "yesterday," and I don't think he knows it.

Poor little ghost. He's in over his head.

I pitch my voice low, ask the fry cook the question I most need to have answered: "How long ago was the accident?"

There's a momentary confusion in his face, like I just asked him when water became wet, or when the first "r" in "February" turned silent. Then the confusion clears, and he gives the answer I was hoping for, the one that comes as a question: "How do you know about—?"

"Just tell me what happened."

His gaze stutters toward the strigoi, who still stands guard at the diner's locked front door. "It doesn't have anything to do with . . . with anything."

"Humor me." The college boy casts a sharp look in my direction, narrowing his coffee-colored eyes. I smile and keep binding Dinah's wounds. Right now, a suspicious bystander is the least of my problems. "How long ago?"

"It was back in '89. I didn't work here yet. Tom—he owns the place. He only works days now, since he doesn't have to do overnights if he doesn't want to—Tom told me about it." The fry cook worries his lip between his teeth, abandoning his watch over the strigoi in favor of squinting at me, like I'm a blurred image he can somehow make come clear. If he's been working here long enough, that idea isn't too far off. All diners touch on the twilight. People who work in them tend to stumble into shadows whether they mean to or not. "It was pretty bad."

I look at him calmly, my fingers busy taping gauze over Dinah's gunshot wound. Her skin has gone clay-cold, and feels like ashes. With the amount of blood she's lost, she may not see the morning, no matter how things go from here. "What happened?"

"This guy and his girlfriend came busting in and tried to hold up the place. They wanted the contents of the register. It could have gone peaceful, if the guy who was working the kitchen hadn't freaked out the way he did. He started screaming about demons or something, and they started shooting. One of the bullets hit the propane tank." The fry cook shudders, eyes closing momentarily, as if against a bright flash of light. "Tom said it took two years and all the insurance money to clean the place up enough to open again. He doesn't like to talk about it. The folks who've been here longer than I have say that's when he stopped working nights."

Twenty-one years ago. I don't need to ask for the exact date of the accident; I can see the awareness stirring in the fry cook's eyes, slowly waking and making itself known. He'll be lucky to pull free of the twilight after this. He's falling deeper with every second that passes. They all are, but thanks to the push I gave him—the one I *had* to give him in order to get the information I needed—he's falling faster than the rest of them. Damn.

"Finish patching her up," I say, and pass the rest of the gauze to the fry cook. The college boy's eyes are still fixed on me, filled with suspicion and with fear. Out of everyone here, he's the one who least belongs, the one most likely to break loose when everything is over. Lucky bastard. I've hated men for less.

The cook takes the gauze with something like gratitude, Dinah still a dumb doll sitting placid between us. "What are you going to do?"

My attention drifts to the strigoi, lost ghost on a road he doesn't recognize. He's just like my drivers. He just needs someone to make sure he gets home. The answer comes easy. This particular answer always does.

"I'm going to keep my word."

No matter what form your soul takes when it hits the ghostroads, it has rules it has to follow. I can borrow flesh and blood from the living for the span of a night by putting on the coats and sweaters that they put aside, stealing breath and skin and all the trappings of mortality. Ghost hunters can't see what I am, and spirit eaters can't consume me. Those who walk the twilight will know me as one of them, but not exactly what that entails—only a routewitch can recognize a hitcher when she's wearing human skin, because only a routewitch can see all the roads that we've walked stretching out behind us, like ripples on water. When I'm physical, I'm generally protected from the twilight.

Generally. The trouble is, when I'm playing dress-up dolly in a living girl's skin, I'm stuck with the same rules as everyone else. Drop the coat and I'm no more substantial than a sigh. Until then, I can bleed, and I can break, and I can walk across a diner feeling my pulse hammer in my veins like an overcharged engine.

The strigoi who doesn't know he's a strigoi watches my approach with hooded eyes, taking in the blood caked on my fingers and the coffee stains on the wrists of my oversized sweatshirt. "She gonna live?" he asks, curt and unconcerned.

I nod, trying to look timid—trying to look anything but angry. He's the one with the gun. I'm the one whose bag of tricks consists almost entirely of taking off her clothes and disappearing. "I . . . I think so. It'd be better if we could get her to a hospital—" His snort answers the question I wasn't planning to ask. "But I guess we can worry about all that later."

"You *guess*."

"Yeah." I shrug, doe-eyed and frightened. "I mean . . . you want something, right? That's why you're here? Because you want something."

"Everybody wants something." He reaches out with one hard-fingered hand and takes hold of my chin, twisting my face a little to the side as he studies me. His skin is rough and smells like motor oil. I'd never know he wasn't among the living if it weren't for that coat of his. "Do you remember what I want, bitch?"

"Rose."

That seems to startle him. His grip falters, almost losing hold of me, before he tightens up and barks, "What?"

"My name is Rose." I search his face for a flicker of recognition, for anything that says he knows who—or what—I am. There's nothing. Just that anger, anger like a wound, anger deep enough to raise the dead. "Um. R-Rose Marshall. What's yours?"

"You think I'm an idiot, *Rose?* You think I'm going to leave you with a name you can give the cops when they show up tomorrow?" He taps the muzzle of his gun against my temple, the hand that holds my chin in place not letting up. "Nice try."

"No! No. I don't think you're an idiot. I just thought . . ." I shrug helplessly, fighting the urge to rip myself from his grasp. "I said . . . I said I'd do whatever you wanted if you'd just let us take care of her. I thought it might be nice to know your name. That's all."

Confusion overwhelms the anger for a moment, longer this time than it did before. He really doesn't know what he's doing here. Poor little strigoi, just as lost as his captives, without half as much reason. Expression hardening, he taps my temple with the gun again, like he's trying to ring a bell for service. "You just want me to get distracted so you can give the rest of these assholes a chance to get away."

I don't know who my laughter startles more, me or him. He lets go of my chin, taking a half step backward, and stares at me like a man who's just seen a ghost.

"What are you laughing at?"

"Like I'd do anything for *them*?" I wave a hand, indicating the rest of the people in the diner. "I mean, sure, I said I'd do you if it meant we could bandage up the girl you shot before I got here, but that's because I don't want to be stuck in this hole with a dead body. That's unsanitary."

He keeps staring at me. "Are you crazy?"

"I've been called worse." I shrug. "Look, I don't want to die in here. You don't really want to kill me, or you would've already put a bullet in my head, and somebody would be mopping my brain off the wall. I don't know why you've decided you want a diner of your very own, and frankly, I don't *care*. If sex is going to keep you calm enough to not shoot me, I'll do you right here, right now."

Now he slowly nods, some private question answered by my reply. "Yeah," he says. "You're crazy."

"You're the one who took a whole stupid *diner* hostage." I plant my hands on my hips, looking down my nose at him and trying to look like I don't give a damn what he does. Several of the other hostages are muttering, sending a nervous ringing through the diner walls. At least they're buying my cocky idiot act. "What do you want it for, anyway? Convenience stores have more money."

"I'm not here for the money." He rubs his forehead with his free hand, confusion flashing in his eyes like a neon sign. Poor little strigoi. "I'm here because . . . I'm here . . ."

Careful, now; don't push too hard, or it's back to square one, if not worse. I still don't want to know what happens if he decides to shoot me. "I mean, at least a Denny's would have those really greasy four-dollar breakfast plates with the stupid names."

"Trina wanted to stop here." He frowns, confusion flickering into anger and back again as he looks around the diner. It seems like he's really seeing it for the first time. "Where the fuck is Trina?"

The hostages exchange anxious glances and draw closer together, confirming with their silence what I suspected all along: Trina, whoever she was, didn't rise with her boyfriend. Maybe she survived the original accident. Maybe she's living somewhere miles away from here, scarred and sorry, but still breathing. Maybe she just found peace after she died, while he missed it by a country mile. Whatever her story is, it's not the same as his anymore, if it ever was.

"Trina isn't here," I say quietly. Ashes and lilies. The air smells like ashes and lilies, and the smell of rosemary and sweet grandmotherly perfume is almost gone. I'm not holding back the accident that's heading our way, and I can't see this road clearly enough to know if it's even possible. I drop my hands, look the strigoi in the eye, and continue, just as quietly, "I don't think Trina's going to come tonight. I don't think you understand what you're really doing here."

"I'm doing whatever I fucking well want to do," he snarls. Familiar ground, a beaten dog that wants to bite.

"You're holding a room full of strangers hostage like it's going to change anything!" I step toward him, the weight of lilies and ashes crashing down on me. My mouth is filled with the burning taste of propane—I mistook it for diesel fuel, I didn't know any better, and I died on impact, I was dead before I could burn. I jab my finger at his chest. "You can't change anything. Don't you get that? Don't you get that *yet?* Trina isn't here because she isn't coming. She *left* you. After the explosion, she *left* you, and you're too busy being wrapped up in the drama of your own death to let yourself see it. You—"

The gun goes off with a bark like one of those big blast firecrackers my brothers used to let off down by the train tracks. The pain comes half a second later, and I look down to see the blood spreading out from the center of my chest, staining the sweatshirt Josh gave me. It hurts like nothing's hurt since the day I died.

"You asshole," I say wonderingly, and I touch the wound with one shaking hand, and I fall to the floor. My eyes are closed before I hit the ground, and for a little while, the rest is silence.

Ghosts can die. That may sound like a paradox, but it's not. Everything that's conscious and aware is alive in its own way, and anything that's alive can die. Only it turns out that ghosts *can't* die from being shot in the chest by other ghosts, which is pretty nice to know.

My eyes snap open after what feels like only a few minutes, and I sit up, half-relieved, half-furious. My fury grows as I see my hands, the nails buffed and polished just *so*, the bracelet of jade beads around one wrist. I'm back in my stupid prom dress, *again*, back in the clothes I was wearing the night my car went off the curve at the top of Sparrow Hill Road. There is no such thing as fashionable forgetfulness among the hitchhiking dead.

I climb to my feet and look down, ignoring the gasps and muffled shrieks behind me. There, peeping out from under the hem of my green silk gown, is the sleeve of the sweatshirt I got from Josh. I step back. The bloodstain is gone. The bullet hole isn't.

The sound of the gun going off isn't even enough to make me flinch this time. Without a coat, without a borrowed skin to tear away, there's nothing a strigoi can do to me. As long as he's shooting, I don't even have to look to know where he's standing. So I look to the clock instead. The big hand is on the five, and the little hand is on the three. It's been hours. I was on the ground for *hours* before my borrowed body figured out that it had to let me go.

I wonder how many others he's shot since then. So I ignore the third gunshot as I turn and survey the hostages, trying to count. At least two of them are missing, Dinah with her bandaged arm, the college boy with his coffee-colored eyes. The rest are still ciphers to me, frightened shadows whose only role in this little drama is to watch, and live, or die. I should feel bad about reducing them this way. I can't. I've been shot, which isn't exactly an experience I was hoping to have, and I'm in a pretty shitty mood.

"I killed you!" shouts the strigoi, sounding strangled. At least the hostages aren't the only ones frightened now. That's something, anyway. "You can't be walking around, you stupid bitch. I *killed* you!"

"God, get with the program, will you?" I spin to face him, angry avenging spirit in green silk and second-hand dancing shoes. He takes a step backward, fear written big and bright across his face. "You can't kill me, you asshole. I've been dead for years. Now what is your *name?*"

He's too startled to lie to me. "D-Dmitri," he stammers. Catching himself, he brings the gun up, pointing it at the center of my chest—the spot where he shot me the first time. Some people just never learn. "Don't come any closer!"

"Or what? You'll shoot me again? The same way you shot poor Dinah? Like you shot the propane tank?" I don't have any bullets of my own. He still winces like he's the one who just got shot. I take a step toward him, ignoring the gun, focusing on his eyes. "You're *dead*, Dmitri. Trina's gone. Maybe she's dead and maybe she's not, but she's *gone*. She's not coming back for you. You can hold this place hostage a thousand times, a million times, and she's still not going to come back. You're in the twilight now. You're too far away for her to reach."

"I don't know what you're talking about," he whispers. His words drop into the silence like stones into a lake, sinking fast, ripples spreading. "You're lying."

"It's one or the other, Dmitri." Another step forward, another set of ripples. "You died here. You shot the propane tank, and it blew sky high, and you *died*."

"Shut up."

"The fire ripped down the walls and melted the skin off your body and ate the flesh off your bones, and you died here. The insurance money paid for new paint and a new kitchen and everyone forgot your name, even the people who had to watch you burn, and you *died* here."

"SHUT UP!"

The bullet passes through the center of my chest without finding any resistance. There's a yelp of pain from behind me. I don't look back. I just keep walking toward Dmitri. "Maybe there was a funeral. That's assuming they could find your next of kin, and that there was enough left of you to identify. Maybe they just cremated you and stuck your ashes in a box in the police station for somebody to come claim, someday. Either way, you *died* here, and you have no right—"

"Please," he moans. There's no gunshot this time. Just the pleading, just the prayer that maybe if he asks me nicely enough, I'll stop.

"No, Dmitri, *no*, because you have no right to take these people's lives away from them." I'm in front of him now, and so I reach out and take the gun. I reach out with my ghost fingers that shouldn't be able to touch or take anything, but they wrap around the metal all the same, and when I tug, he lets go. Poor little strigoi. More gently, I say, "You're dead, Dmitri. I'm sorry."

His eyes fill with tears, and he looks past me to the huddled hostages clinging to each other in the shadows of this suddenly haunted diner. Two dead people for the price of one. Welcome to the ghostroads.

"How long?" he whispers.

"Twenty-one years."

Those words seem to take all the strength out of him. He hits his knees as the smell of ashes and lilies fades into memory, replaced by the normal scents of a living diner, apple pie and bubble gum and scrambled eggs and coffee. I put the gun down on the nearest table, where it wisps into nothingness before any of the hostages can make a grab for it. That's good. I don't have time to worry about a hero right now; I'm too busy worrying about a dead man.

"No no no no," Dmitri moans, rocking back and forth.

"Yes." I crouch and grab his wrists, pulling him halfway back to upright. "*Yes*. It was a long time ago, and yes. It happened."

"We were—we were pulling into the driveway. Then there was this flash, and the sun was going down, and Trina and the bike were gone." He lifts his head, studying my face like he thinks he'll find the answers he's looking for in me. Best of luck to him. I've been looking for the answers for fifty years, and I haven't found them yet. "I still . . . I had the gun, and I came in here, and it was all *wrong*, it was just so damn wrong, and it made me so damn *mad . . .*"

I want to be angry with him. I want to be furious. He shot me. He killed people.

He died here. Poor little strigoi, who didn't know what he was doing, just that he was alone; who didn't even know that he'd already left the daylight twenty-one years behind him. He died in fire. Maybe that's punishment enough for what he's done tonight. Maybe not. Either way, it's not my place to judge. I tug him to his feet, keeping hold of his wrists, not letting him go.

"You're coming with me," I tell him. "But first, you're going to wait here."

A flash of arrogance in those eyes. "And what if I don't?"

All I have to do is smile and the arrogance crumbles, replaced by confusion, fear . . . and relief. No one wants to haunt the living forever, not once they realize that they're dead. At least I'm offering him another way. "You will," I say, and let him go, turning my back.

He waits.

There have been five casualties all told, five lives ended by a dead man. Dinah comes the quickest, towing a mousy-looking girl by one wrist. The mouse wears a uniform just like Dinah's. Her name is Josie, and she has a lovely smile. A teenage boy fades out of the woodwork as Josie and I finish making introductions. He has acne on his forehead, and the kind of hands that were meant for cupping a woman's hips long into the night. He says his name is Michael. I say it's nice to meet him, and he looks away, mumbles something about better circumstances. I can't blame him for that one.

The college boy's name is Anthony, and even when he comes to me, he stays so faded that I can see the walls right through him. The last one to emerge is an old man whose cane has crossed to the ghostroads with him, a sturdy piece of oak for him to lean on until he realizes that he doesn't need it anymore. I gather them all to me, five little pieces of the twilight, and we turn and walk back to the doorway where Dmitri is waiting.

"It's time to go," I tell him, and he nods, resignation radiating from his face like sunlight. Poor little strigoi. Looking back over my shoulder, I meet the eyes of the fry cook, and say, "Don't unlock the doors until we're gone."

"I won't," he says, in a voice that barely qualifies as a whisper. Poor *everyone*. Half these people will never leave the twilight. The other half may fight their way back into the daylight, but they'll never dream without crying again. That's the penalty for this sort of deathday party; that's what happens when things overlap this completely.

I turn away, stepping through the glass of the door without opening it. The others follow me, phantom parade out into the parking lot, and the line dividing the daylight from the twilight fades with every step we take, until there's only the dark, and still we walk on, out of the twilight, into the midnight, where the ghostroads are the only route to anywhere.

We walk on, going home.

"What happens now?"

"You all wait here. Someone will come along to get you soon enough."

"But—"

"I don't know who will come, and I don't know where they'll take you. You're not road ghosts, and that means you're outside my jurisdiction." I look at the crowd, tattered little spirits, frightened and lost here in the midnight before their time. Even Dmitri isn't really prepared, and he's the only one who's been dead for any time at all. Finally, I sigh, and say, "If you're not sure—if you're not ready to take the final exit off the highway and see what's on the other side—ask whoever it is to drop you off at the Last Dance. They usually need staff."

Dinah, Josie, and Michael can probably find work there; Anthony and the old man can at least get a good cup of coffee before they continue on.

Dmitri looks at me levelly, and asks, "Think they'd take me?"

I meet his eyes, and answer: "No. But I've been wrong before."

He nods, and that's the end. I turn and walk away, leaving the six of them standing beneath the bus stop sign at the edge of the ghostroad highway that runs between here and there. They'll find their way soon enough; the dead always do. My prom dress dissolves into jeans and a white T-shirt that can't keep out the cold, my hair shedding its careful curls in favor of the short-cropped bob I favor these days. Changing with the times is sometimes the best I can do.

Shoving my hands into the pockets of my jeans, I walk on, down the cold line of midnight, moving toward the distant glow of dawn.

2012
True Love Dies Like Everything Else

I SPENT MY FIRST YEAR on the ghostroads trying to find a way off them and back into the lands of the living. I walked the frontage roads that run closest to the surface of the twilight, scaring the living crap out of countless fraternity boys and high school seniors as I flagged them down, begged them to take me home, and then disappeared on them. The first stage of grief is denial, even among the dead.

I spent my second year trying to find someone I could argue with, someone who'd have the authority to take back what had happened to me. Angels, demons, rumors, I chased them all. I got luckier than I deserved to be: I didn't catch any of them. Instead, I walked the sorrow off my shoes, and walked myself deeper down into the twilight, where I could start to learn the realities of my new existence. It took a lot of years and a lot of walking to work my way deep enough to come back into the light, and maybe that's the biggest secret that the ghostside has to offer; that if you work long enough to reach the darkness, you're almost inevitably going to find your way to the light. They're the same thing, viewed from two different directions, and they can both get you lost, and they can both bring you home.

The danger in walking your way to freedom is the way things change depending on your point of view. What's dark to me is light to you; what's true to you is lies to me. I leave the philosophy to the umbramancers and the routewitches, and I try to keep myself focused on the things that matter in the here and now: following the whispers of the running road, following the signs that lead me between the layers of America, and learning to read the palimpsest etchings that dig deep as bruises and unchanging as scars into the flesh of the ghostside. I've been in the dark a lot longer than I was in the light, and while I still regret the way that I died, I've given up on trying to fight my way back. All I want to do now is find a way to stop the man who condemned me to this twilight wandering—the one who would have done a lot worse, if I'd given him the chance.

I guess you can call me an angel of vengeance, these days. That and a quarter used to be enough to buy a cup of coffee. Still is, at the Last Dance. Everywhere else . . . not so much.

The trouble with truth is that it's subjective, depending entirely on where you were standing when you saw the accident happen. Maybe you saw the first car veer to avoid hitting a cat, and maybe you didn't. Maybe you saw the second car try to hit the brakes, and maybe you only saw them go careening into the vehicle ahead of them, making no attempt to slow in the moments before impact. Maybe all you saw was the shadow of the cat as it darted through the underbrush, running away from a tearing roar that sounded like the end of the world. Every splinter of the broken glass of the moment is a genuine part of the whole, but none of them is the whole in and of itself. We carry our own truths tucked away inside us, bright bits of glass blunted by our living flesh, and when they come into the light, we bleed.

No one saw the accident that killed me. No one but me and Bobby Cross, and I'm sure the version he'd give you is very different from mine.

Honesty is in the eye of the beholder. It can be hard as hell to tell the truth from broken lies even when all the pieces of the puzzle happen in the daylight. When half the story is buried in shallow graves along the ghostroads, it can turn impossible to tell what's real from what's not . . . and sometimes, without that knowledge, there's no way to move past grieving into acceptance. Sometimes, the dead aren't the only casualties, especially here. Especially in the dark.

Jackson, Maine, 1992.

It's a beautiful night, all big white moon and the distant gold-silver glitter of too many stars to count, scattered across this desert sky like dime store confetti. This is the middle of nowhere, one of those places that manages to exist half a mile outside of every jurisdiction, half an hour away from any sort of safety, real or not. The man—the boy, fuck, he's barely twenty-two, he's too young to be here—behind the wheel of this aging Toyota is practically vibrating as he gazes toward the stretch of road ahead of us. He'd be handsome, if he didn't look so scared, if he wasn't so damn close to tumbling into twilight, leaving this road and all the roads like it behind him forever. We've been parked here for ten minutes now, while he tried to talk himself into something irrevocable, and I tried to talk him out of it.

"That's the raceway," he says, and he means the empty expanse of nothing he can't stop looking at, that little slice of nowhere-road that stretches smooth and deserted through the night. He's breathing too fast, just this side of panting, tension filling the car like smoke. He doesn't want to be here. He thinks he does, but he's wrong. "You'll be able to find another ride from here. There's lots of guys here every night. One of them will be going your way."

I seriously doubt that. This is pure daylight road, for all that the sun's gone down, and the only piece that edges into the twilight is the driver himself, boy who thinks he's a man, boy teasing things he should know enough to leave alone. I've been trying to steer him away from this place since I asked him for a ride two hours ago, and he didn't listen then, and he isn't listening now. The smell of ashes and lilies is gathering around him, accident preparing to happen, coming on stronger with every minute that ticks past.

"I don't think this is a good idea, Tommy." He isn't listening. I still have to try. I always have to try, because that's part of how this story goes: part of what keeps me on the edge I walk along. If I start walking away from the ones who might be saved, I'll lose my grasp on the narrow line of the twilight, sink deeper down into the dark, and never find my way back to the levels where the living play spin-the-bottle with the dead. I've seen it happen. I have to try. "We should go back. We should—"

"My girl deserves better than some crackerjack ring from a grease monkey." There's a set to his jaw that I know. Gary used to look like that, late nights in the diner when he was telling me how we were going to get out of town someday, how we'd be together forever, and he wouldn't be just a mechanic, and I wouldn't be just the mechanic's girl. I bite my knuckles. The pain helps, a little. Not enough, but it keeps the tears out of my eyes, and right here, right now, I'll settle for what I can get. "You understand, don't you, Rose?"

I understand the way poverty can turn solid in the middle of the night, pressing down on your chest until it steals your breath away, the way they used to say cats stole the breath from babies in their cradles. I understand watching your father work until all he can do when he gets home is drink to forget how much work's still waiting, until the day he doesn't come home at all, and watching your mother clip coupons and count her pennies, skirting a little closer to the edge every day. I understand hand-me-down skirts and triple-darned socks, cabbage soup and homemade shampoo. I understand better than he thinks I do.

Most of all, I understand that this is not the way.

"Turn back," I whisper, and Tommy starts the engine, and we roll onward, toward the raceway, toward the future, toward the place where the road he's on now comes to its inevitable end.

We roll on.

Jackson, Maine, 2012.

March has slammed down on the American coast with the force of a hurricane, washing out bridges and turning the roads into something closer to an obstacle course. Rides are always harder to get during March and April; it's warm enough that you lose the wintertime "poor thing, come in out of the cold," but it's wet and nasty enough that no one wants to slow and stop for a stranger. Springtime is the worst time of year for hitching. I keep walking along the edge of the pavement, thumb thrust jauntily upward. Either I'll find a ride or I'll find a rest stop; that's how this works. In the meanwhile, if I want to stay on this level of America, I'll keep following the rules, and the rules say that hitchhiking ghosts, well, hitch.

The rules will change if I can get someone to give me a coat. Even the definition of "coat" is a generous one, since I've been able to accept jackets, sweaters, lab coats, smocks, even once—at a carnival in Alabama, where the ground was the color of dried blood and the rain came down so hard it seemed like the sky was falling—a yellow plastic rain slicker. Any of them is enough to shift me off the ghostroads and back into the light. I'm not quite the living and not quite the dead when I have a coat to steal substance from, and in that in-between state, a lot of rules don't apply. They can't catch hold for long enough to bind me.

Staying wet was one of the hardest things to learn about hitching in the rain. You can recognize young hitchers easily when it rains; they're the ones walking in a downpour and staying completely dry, because the water doesn't even know they're there. Never open your doors to a dry stranger in a rainstorm, not unless you're sure of your protection against possessions. Older hitchers understand that being able to change your clothing with a thought means being able to change dry clothes into wet clothes, even if it's only ghost-water, even if it only dampens the ghostside. Most people don't look closely enough to catch that little distinction, and once one of us has a coat in our hands, well, it's like I said. All the rules change.

It won't be the end of the world if I can't catch a ride on this stretch of deserted Maine highway, hemmed in by the creeping undergrowth and ringed with ditches full of muddy runoff. I've gone without rides before, and with the way the rain keeps pounding down, I'd be cold even with a living person's coat to loan me warmth. That's the worst thing about being dead: the cold that never ends. Only way to beat it back is to join the living for a little while, but on a night like this, I'm not sure I want to be warm quite that badly.

There's a truck stop ahead. I remember it from the last time I walked this way, and the road may be worn-down and lonely, but it isn't singing the songs of the completely abandoned. Even if the stop is limping on its last legs, the doors are open, the coffee is hot, and the neon is still sending out its lighthouse prayers to the sailors of the inland American sea. "Come to me, come to me, and I will grant you warmth, and I will be your home until the tide rolls out."

Roads don't sing the same when the stops close down. They turn lonely, and then they turn bitter, and then they turn dangerous. If you're lucky, they die after that. If you're not, a lot of people die before the road does. I helped to kill a highway once, one that tried to keep on going after the *beán sidhe* keened its termination and the ambulomancers read its future in the potholes on the blacktop and the pebbles on the median. That's an experience I'd be happy never to have again.

The sky rolls white with lightning, and the rain starts falling harder, pounding straight through me like it wants to wash the world away. I keep my thumb out—follow the rules, always follow the rules, it's breaking the rules that gets you in trouble—and walk a little faster, following the lighthouse song of safety through the night.

Too much focus can be a dangerous thing. The condition of the truck stop parking lot barely registers with me when I finally get there, head down, walking to escape the rain. Potholes and broken pavement are a consequence of use as much as neglect, and the truck stop is singing. That should be enough. I'm halfway across the parking lot when the song cuts off, abrupt as a razor blade in candyfloss, and I lift my eyes to the shattered shell of a sanctuary. The bones of the truck stop are standing almost naked in the night, the skeletal pumps, the broken shell of the garage, the crumbling diner with its neon sign, unlit, still almost intact on the edge of the roof. This is no lighthouse. This is a tomb.

This isn't right. This can't be right. The songs of this road are not the songs of a road in the process of dying, but they should be; this is the heart of the highway, and a heart that's been broken keeps nothing alive.

I take a step forward, frightened little ghost-girl in the rain, and that step is all it takes to tip the balance, because once I start, I can't stop. I know I should turn back, that I'm acting like one of those stupid girls in the drive-in horror movies, but I can't stop. My feet keep pulling me onward, through the parking lot, into the broken diner, where everything is darkness.

Jackson, Maine, 1992.

We're the first ones at the raceway, Tommy too eager and too stupid to be anything but early, even with me in the seat beside him begging him to find another way. His heart is set. "I don't know anyone who's ever gotten out of here," he said earlier, eyes wide and earnest and too young to understand what he was getting into. "People say they will, but they don't. We all wind up working for our daddies, if our daddies are still alive. We drink in the bars where they drank, we sit on the porches where they sat, and we get old swearing we're going to get out one day. Meanwhile, our sons grow up just like us, and the cycle never gets broken. I don't want that. I want roads I've never seen before, and a house where the walls don't always smell like grease and old butter, and I want my girl to be proud of me. I want her to say 'that's my man,' and have it be pride speaking, not shame."

"You want more." That's what I said to him then, and if I could take those words back, I would, because he took them as permission to do what he'd been planning anyway. He took them as permission to drive out here to this empty road that sunset turned into a raceway, and all the while, the smell of ashes and lilies gathered deeper and deeper around him. I'd take them back if I could.

The world doesn't work that way.

Tommy's car is beautiful, a 1985 Toyota he's rebuilt so many times that even the air inside the cabin feels custom. She trusts him, this blue-black beauty with her wheels set solid on the pavement. She *believes* in him. The love of a car for its owner may be the truest love there is, save maybe for the love of a dog for its person—and even there, there's a divide, because the love of a car proves that the car has been loved. A dog loves because dogs exist to love man. A car loves because man exists to love the car.

I touch her hood as I slide out of the passenger seat. My fingertips are only slightly warmer than her engine-heated metal, and I want to tell her that everything is going to be all right, and I can't do it. Everything isn't going to be all right. Everything will never be all right again.

"Tommy, I got a bad feeling about this. Let's just go. You can find the money some other way. I know people, people who maybe could help you. I—"

"If you know people, why were you standing off the Interstate with your thumb up in the air, Rose?" Tommy's face is challenging and cold. "You're wearing my jacket, and you ate that grilled cheese like nobody'd fed you in a month of Sundays. If you can find the kind of money I need, what are you doing here?"

There's not an answer for that question in the whole world, because he's standing in the daylight, and in the daylight, "I'm here because I'm dead" isn't an answer, it's a joke. I swallow, shift, look toward the horizon, and pray for a miracle, even though I don't believe in miracles anymore, if I ever believed in them to begin with. The age of miracles has been over for a long time, and the final nail went into that coffin in February of 1959, when the world asked for a Valentine and got the death of Buddy Holly in its place.

"Tommy—"

"No, Rose. *No.* I don't want to get old in this ten-cent town, and there's no way I can marry my girl if that's what I'm sentencing her to. She deserves better, and I'm going to get it for her."

"Or you're going to die trying. Did you ever think of that, Tommy? How proud of you is she going to be when you're six feet underground?"

Tommy shakes his head and steps away, moving toward the rear of the car, where he can watch for the other racers. They'll be coming soon. The road is singing so loudly of their arrival that even I can hear it, and I'm no routewitch. "You don't understand."

He's right; I don't understand. I may understand poor, and I may understand frightened, but if someone had begged me to stay home the night I died, I would have listened. I know I would have listened. I would have locked the door and waited until Gary came to apologize, and if I'd missed the prom, so what? I would have so many other opportunities to dance. I would have listened.

I hope.

But he won't listen to me, not here, not now, not with the race singing so close. The night has fallen, the stars are shining, and Tommy's going to die tonight. And there's not a damn thing I can do.

Jackson, Maine, 2012.

Stepping through the door of the diner is like sticking my entire body into a swarm of biting ants. The pain is brief and intense, and shocking enough that I finish my step, stumbling forward, hitting the ground on my knees. It doesn't hurt as much as dying, or even as much as being shot in the chest by a crazy strigoi who doesn't know he's dead, but it hurts enough to make my vision go blurry. The broken linoleum covering the old diner floor cuts my knees through the denim of my jeans as I fall, and I have to catch myself on my hands to keep from scraping my face across the floor.

With everything else that's going on, I don't notice that my heart has started beating until I'm pushing myself back to my feet. The scrapes on my hands and knees burn dully, a familiar childhood feeling that calls forth the memory of parental kisses and Mercurochrome. My hands leave trails of blood behind when I wipe them on the front of my shirt, and my breath plumes slightly in the chilly springtime air.

"What the . . . ?"

It's breaking the rules that gets you in trouble, and whatever this is, it's sure as shit breaking the rules. My heart hammers with almost-living fear as I turn and run for the door. I need to get out of here. Something about this place is breaking all the rules of the road, and that means I can't stay any longer than I already have. I need to get out.

The air turns solid and stops me almost a foot and a half from safety. The door is still open; I can see the outside, see the rain sheeting down, but I can't get there. All I can do is bounce off the air. I back up, run for the invisible wall, and throw myself against it, to no avail; it's too solid, and I can't break through. Panting, I step back, and feel every drop of blood in my suddenly-living veins go cold as my gaze falls on the floor beneath the unseen barrier.

"Shit," I whisper, feeling very small, and very vulnerable. I've been careless. I let myself be led astray. I'm about to pay for it.

The edges of the vast Seal of Solomon painted on the diner floor are clearly visible near the open door. It's no wonder that I didn't see it when I was coming in—I was walking away from the light, not into it—and the lines are done in red-and-black paint, detailed with what looks like silver Sharpie. Only the metallic parts would have been at all visible, and even if I'd seen them, I would have just dismissed them as broken bits of glass or metal. I sure as hell wasn't expecting a trap. Not here, not now . . . and not for me. Traps are for the dangerous things, the strigoi and the goryo and the shadow people. They're not for hitchers. We're harmless.

"Fine. So some genius ghost hunters caught me by mistake. Great. Okay." I rake my fingers through my hair—dry still, since the rain is outside and I wasn't solid until the trap made me that way—as I squint to follow the outline of the Seal in its path around the room. Whoever did this knew their demonology. It's not the most intricate Seal I've ever seen, but intricacy doesn't always equate to strength, and this one is made to be strong. There's gold ink as well as silver in the pattern, marking the cardinal points, and there's a second ring around the first, this one of pure salt. The salt ring is only open at the diner door, to allow the spirits foolish enough to get caught to make their way inside. I rake my hair back again. This isn't some teenage routewitch prank. This is serious hoodoo.

After an hour of throwing myself against the Seal, I give up and sit down at the center of the circle, cross-legged, propping one elbow on my knee and resting my chin atop my knuckles. Whoever set this trap has to come along eventually to see what they might have caught. Part of me keeps screaming that it's Bobby, it's Bobby, he's changed his ways and he's coming for me, but I'm still calm enough to know that for the nonsense that it is. Bobby Cross could no more draw a Seal of Solomon than he could walk past Saint Peter and through the pearly gates of Heaven. This isn't him. This is something else.

The rain outside keeps falling as the hours trickle by, adding an element of psychological torture to a situation that really doesn't need help scaring the crap out of me. I know what happens if I'm wearing a coat when the sun comes up: the coat loses its power and I fade back onto the ghostroads, dead as always. But what happens if the sun comes up while I'm trapped in a Seal of Solomon that's somehow doing what only a coat's supposed to do to me? Do I go free? Or do I get sucked into a bottle like some fairy-tale djinn, Barbara Eden with a bad attitude and better fashion sense?

"I would kill for a routewitch about now," I mutter, and go back to waiting.

Enough time has passed by the time the door swings all the way open that I almost don't notice; I'm staring off into space, thinking about how much I'd be willing to do for a cup of coffee. It's the sound of footsteps on the linoleum that makes me realize I'm not alone anymore. I scramble to my feet, the scrapes on my hands and knees complaining at the rough treatment. I don't care. I don't want my captor to see me looking that defenseless.

The woman who's just stepped into the diner doesn't even look at me as she pulls a canister of salt from her pocket and closes the break in the circle. This accomplished, she starts walking around the edges of the Seal, lighting candles I didn't notice in the gloom. Each one beats back the darkness just a little; nowhere near enough. I turn, watching her, but I don't say anything. I'm not going to be the first one to speak.

I see her more and more clearly as the candles flicker to life. She's in her late thirties, with long, straight hair that shade of dirty blonde that means she's been blonde all her life, too proud to start dyeing when it started to darken. Her glasses glitter in the candlelight, making it impossible to tell the color of her eyes. She's pretty, in the dark, in the candlelight, but it's hard to focus on anything but the book she's holding under one arm, the thick, leather-bound book with the Seal stamped on its cover.

That sort of book never means anything good to twilighters like me, especially not in the hands of someone like her, someone who carries the twilight with her like a sour perfume. She was born a daylight girl, but she's burrowed her way down, I can taste it. I just don't know *why*. I just know that I've never seen her before in my life, or in my death. I've been trapped by a stranger, ghost rat in a ghost cage. That makes it all the worse when the last candle is lit and she closes the diner door, finally turning to study me. She runs her eyes over every inch of my body, measuring what she's caught. Finally, horribly, she smiles.

"Hello, Rose," she says.

Shit.

Jackson, Maine, 1992.

I could never have prevented this accident from happening. It was too late before Tommy met me. Maybe it was too late before I got within a hundred miles of this town. I don't know. All I know is that I tried as hard as I could, and that it wasn't enough.

I'm glad I don't need sleep anymore. After this, I'd be awake for a week at least.

The racers came just like Tommy swore they would, rolling over the horizon in cars that were ten times more expensive and half as alive as Tommy's. Some of them were good men, and some of them were bad men, but they were all of them hard men, because they'd chosen a hard aspect of the highway to receive their worship. A few of them tried to tell Tommy not to race, and those are the ones I'll remember to the Atlantic Highway the next time that I venture near her borders. Some just laughed. The boy wanted to put down his pink slip and his pride on a race he couldn't possibly win? Well, he'd learn a lesson from the losing. Only there are no more lessons for Tommy on this road, or on any other.

The wheels of his car are still spinning as I run across the blacktop toward him, my breath harsh in my ears, my feet striking hard against the pavement. He's still alive, and so I run to him. Once he dies, slips onto the ghostroads and leaves the daylight forever, the coat he gave me will lose its power to hold me to the laws of the living. That's in the rules. Only live people have substance to share, and you can't steal life from the dead.

The men who raced against Tommy have realized that something is very wrong; that this isn't the sort of accident someone laughs at and walks away from. Their cars have stopped, and the men are getting out, looking back toward where Tommy's car lies shattered on the road. None of them are moving to help him—to help *us*, since every one of them thinks I'm his townie girlfriend, the one he's doing this stupid, suicidal thing for. They just let me run, my throat raw with screaming, tears running down my cheeks as I reach for another soul I failed to save.

They were going too fast and the road seemed smooth, but there are cracks in the cleanest pavement, slick spots, potholes, rocks. I may never know which one hit the wheels of the car ahead of Tommy, and it doesn't really matter; the driver spun out, adjusted, caught himself and drove on. In the process, he clipped Tommy, and something about that collision was enough—just enough—to send the smaller, lighter Toyota into a spin she never pulled out of. Tommy's car rolled three times before she stopped, twisted metal and smoking engine, a broken body on the road.

Her death is faster than his: she's already gone when I get there. All that's left is cooling death, and a young man cut almost in half by his own steering column. There's blood everywhere. I don't let that stop me. If there's one thing I've learned since the night I died, it's that blood washes off, but no one—no one—deserves to die alone.

"Tommy? Tommy, can you hear me?" I beat my fists against the glass of the passenger window, trying to catch his attention. I could take off the coat, slide through this door like it was smoke, but then I'd be on the ghostroads again, and I wouldn't be able to hold his hand until the dying finished. He's a fool, yes, and he still deserves to have someone holding his hand while the lights go out. "Tommy!"

Three of the racers come running up, big men, muscling their way past me to wrench the door open. Then they stop, hands dangling uselessly, as they try to figure out what else they can do for him. Maybe someone's called an ambulance, and maybe nobody will; this sort of race is illegal, after all, and they have to be measuring their own lives yet to come against the death of one boy barely out of his teens and too stupid to know when to find another way. They can't take him out of the car, that much is clear; the way it's wrapped around him is like a lover's embrace, and there's no way of breaking it without breaking him even further.

If Tommy can't come to us, I'll go to him. It's the only thing left that I can do. I squeeze my way between the racers (and if any of them notice the sudden give to my flesh, the way I seem to be losing substance by the second, they don't say anything; the ones who'd notice are the ones who know the twilight well enough to know me) and kneel next to the driver's-side door, gravel biting into my knees. My hands are bloody even before I realize that his blood is on the seat, and it doesn't matter, it doesn't matter, blood can't hurt me.

"Tommy? Tommy, can you hear me?" My fingers almost pass through his cheek the first time I reach out to him. I pull back, concentrate, and try again. This time I can feel my fingers graze his skin, and I don't know if that's because I'm closer to living, or because he's closer to dead. "Come on, Tommy, stay with me. Open your eyes, and stay with me."

It's too late now. It's all over except for the dying. But I'm still here, and he's still here, and as long as that's the case, I'm going to be here for him. I owe him that much. I owe all of them that much.

Tommy swallows with obvious difficulty, and opens his eyes. They aren't quite focusing anymore. He won't really see the other racers, or the road, or the blood that's dripping over everything, like the red flag signaling that it's time to leave the starting line. But he'll still see me. We're in the same place right now, he and I. "R-Rose?"

"I'm here. I'm right here, Tommy."

"I think I messed up, Rose."

It's a beautiful night, big white moon and too many stars and the desert around us like an ocean of gold. It's a beautiful night, and Tommy—a boy whose last name I never learned, a boy who did this for a girl I've never met, and maybe never will—is bleeding to death with my hand against his cheek. "Yeah," I say, not looking away from him. "I think you're right."

Jackson, Maine, 2012.

"You don't know how long it's taken me to track you down." She pulls a rusted chair with a ripped green vinyl cover from one of the nearby tables, moving it to the edge of the salt circle and sitting primly. Resting the book on her knees, she smiles at me. "I mean, at first I wasn't even sure you were real. It took me years just to find someone who could really prove to me that you existed. I appreciated that day. It told me that I wasn't crazy. I spent three years chasing truckers and visiting psychics and going into every diner I saw to ask if anyone in there knew who you were or had seen you or knew where I might find you." She leans forward and smiles at me, smiles like a rattlesnake getting ready to strike. "You have a lot of friends, Rose. A lot of people looked me in the eye and lied for you. I was impressed by that."

"Who the hell *are* you?" I step toward her, as far as the Seal will let me go. She doesn't flinch back, just keeps smiling that rattlesnake smile. She knows she has me pinned. "I don't know why you want me, lady, but I'm not a good house pet."

"Oh, I'm not going to *keep* you. Don't be silly." She looks genuinely amused as she settles in her seat. "Keep you. What a ridiculous idea."

"Then what—"

"I'm going to exorcise you. I'm going to read aloud the words of a thousand ancients, and I'm going to rip you from this world one thin thread at a time, until you're nothing but a thin scream clinging to the memory of pain. And then I'm going to call you back, and I'm going to do it again. And again. And again. Until, when the sun rises, I finish the exorcism and send you to the hell you deserve, you murdering little slut."

Her expression doesn't change once as she speaks. That may be the most terrifying thing of all. She's talking about murder, about killing me for the second time in my existence, and she isn't batting an eye. I'm not a person to her. I'm a thing to be exterminated.

"What-what . . . what are you talking about?" My heart is hammering and my mouth is dry as cotton. That's the worst thing about this damn Seal—all the downsides of being alive, and none of the benefits, no sex or coffee or cheeseburgers. Just raw terror and every nerve in my body sounding the alarm. "I don't know who you are, or who you think I am, but I assure you, I am *not* your girl."

"Your name is Rose Marshall. You were born in Buckley Township, Michigan, in 1936—that was a hard one to confirm, by the way. There was no birth certificate on file for you at any of the local hospitals. There was an announcement in the paper, though. I suppose it was a slow news week."

"I was born at home," I whisper.

"Ah! Well, that explains it, then. You made the news again in 1952 when you decided to drive yourself to the senior prom and confront your boyfriend, who had failed to pick you up. It's not really surprising. You were only a junior. He probably didn't want to be seen with you." This time, her smile is cruel as well as venomous, human snake that knows exactly what she's doing. "Poor little Rose. I suppose you didn't know he'd broken down on the way to your house—and by the time he got back on the road, you were so much cooling meat."

"Lady, why are you doing this? What do you want from me?"

She keeps going like she hasn't heard me—and maybe she hasn't, not in any meaningful way. You don't learn to draw a Seal like this on a whim, or in a weekend. You don't track down the dead for nothing. Whatever strange engine drove her here, she's not letting it go that easily. "Only you couldn't stay dead, could you, Rose? You couldn't rest in peace. That would have been too easy for a spoiled bitch like you."

I've been called a lot of things, and some of them I even deserved, but "spoiled" has never made the list. My eyes narrow, and I speak before I think, spitting out my words: "You don't know anything about me."

"I know you killed the only man I ever loved." The accusation is casual, almost offhanded; there's no heat behind it. She's just reciting a fact. I still freeze, rooted to the spot as she continues, "For a while, I thought I was chasing a myth, looking for you, but once I had a name, you got a lot easier to follow. Legends and ghost stories scattered across a country—you've been a busy little girl, Rose. How many innocent men have you killed? How many have died for your vanity, all because you couldn't bear to be the one left standing home alone?"

I've heard this accusation before. It doesn't get any easier to bear. "I've never killed anyone. You have the wrong girl."

Candlelight glints off her glasses as she lifts her head and looks at me, smile fading into memory, replaced by terrifying emptiness. "His name was Tommy," she says, in a voice like a crypt door slamming shut. "His name was Tommy, and he was going to marry me, and you killed him. And now I'm going to kill you."

Jackson, Maine, 1992.

Tommy is bleeding out fast, red blood mingling with the black oil that drips from the car's shattered engine. At least they're not both suffering. She's already gone to the ghostroads. She loves him enough to wait for him there, and that's better than many men will have. Still, he's alone in the here and now. I keep my hand against his cheek, feeling my solidity waver a little more with every breath he struggles to take, and I wonder when, if ever, the moments like this will stop hurting so damn bad.

"I can't see."

"It's all right, Tommy. Just keep on breathing. Help is on the way." That's a lie, that's a goddamn lie—help isn't coming, help won't get here for hours, not until the raceway is a road again and there's nothing left of Tommy but an empty shell cradled in a steel-and-chrome coffin. I don't regret lying to him. Sometimes lies are the only thing I have to give them.

"Will you find my girl?" His voice is fading, losing strength. He'll find it again on the other side, when he doesn't have to fight against failing lungs and a broken spine. Somehow, that's cold comfort, even to me.

"Yeah, Tommy, yeah. I'll find her." More lies, but they're the lies he needs to hear. How could I find her, dead man's living lover? I'd have no way to even start the search. "What do you want me to tell her?"

The question seems to puzzle him for a moment, leave him fumbling for words. Only the fact that the gravel still digs into my knees tells me that he's still holding onto life; I'm slipping, but I haven't slipped, not all the way, not yet. Finally, he says, "Tell her I love her. Tell her I did this because I love her." A smile twists his lips upward, heartbreaking snapshot of a lover on his way out the door. "I was going to marry her."

"I know."

"Just tell Laura . . ." His voice falters and fades in the middle of the sentence, leaving him silent. One more hitching breath, two, three, and then no more; his chest is still, his struggling heart finally finishing its fight. The race is over at last.

His blood falls through my fingers, leaving them clean and pale as I rise. His jacket falls at the same time, hitting the concrete with a soft, anticlimactic rustle. I turn to face the racers still standing clustered behind me. The ones who let me through before—the ones who've touched the twilight, or been touched by it—take a step backward, faces going pale. They know what they're seeing, they know what the fall of the jacket has to mean. The rest only look at me, puzzled and afraid, boys mixed with men in almost equal numbers.

"This race is over," I say, my tone leaving no room for argument.

"If you must race, do it somewhere else. No more stupid kids who don't know the risks. Understand? If you let this happen again, I'll know, and I'll find you." It's an empty threat. But they don't know that.

"Yeah?" asks one of the ones who doesn't look frightened enough to understand who I am, what I am, what he's seen. "Who the fuck are you?"

The living are difficult to convince and easy to impress. I fix him with a stare, smile, and say, "I'm Rose." Then I release my hold on the daylight, and the racers are gone, left in another America, while I step onto the ghostroads where I belong.

Tommy is there, unbroken, unbloodied, standing next to his car and staring blankly up into a sky the color of ink. There are no stars. Not here; not in the midnight. We're on the deepest level now, the one where ghosts are the natives, and the living are the strange invasions. He looks toward the sound of my feet scuffling on the surface of the road, eyes wide in his young man's face. "Rose? What's going on?"

"You died, Tommy." There's no point in candy-coating it. I step forward, offer him my hand, offer him a smile that almost balances the sorrow in my eyes. I could never have saved him. I have to keep telling myself that until I start believing. "Now come on."

"Where?"

"That's up to you." I cast a glance toward his car, which has never looked this good, and never could have, not in the daylight, where metal is constrained by the limits of construction, and not the limits of love. "But I can make a few suggestions."

Jackson, Maine, 2012.

"Oh, fuck." I never saw a picture of Laura, and Tommy never called her anything but beautiful. Still, she's the right age to be the girlfriend of the boy I helped through the painful process of dying, and I wasn't exactly subtle when I told those racers to shut their deathtrap down. "You're Laura."

"Finally." She shakes her head, stands, moves to relight a candle that's blown out. "I thought you'd be smarter than this. You've been at it for a long time. I suppose I didn't think dumb luck could carry you this far." She rakes another look along my body, and adds, "I also thought you'd be better-looking, or at least have bigger breasts. I guess being pretty isn't required in a dead whore."

"I didn't kill him! God, what is it going to take to make you believe me? I tried to keep him *away* from that stupid race!" I stayed with him while he bled to death; I guided him down the ghostroads like he was an old friend, and not just some kid too dumb to listen when I told him to be careful. "I did everything I could to save him."

"Well, you didn't do enough." She blows out her match and drops it to the linoleum, grinding it into dust with the toe of one foot. "I hope you're happy with all the lives you've ruined."

"Laura—"

"You won't be ruining any more." She opens the book, standing outlined in the candlelight like some avenging angel, and she begins to read.

Her words are ice and fire and acid and the bitter needles of pounding rain turned into a weapon by the driving wind. Her words are the bite of locusts and the sting of wasps, rust consuming steel, poison corroding silver. They blister my skin and rip the screams from my lips, writhing like living things as they flay me open and display my inadequacy to the universe. I don't know how long she reads; I don't *care* how long she reads, because every word is murder, and I die a thousand times before she quiets. There is only the sound of rain and the harsh rasp of my breathing as I pitch forward, sprawling on the diner floor.

"Oh, I'm sorry, Rose, didn't you like that? Wasn't that *fun* for you?"

I want to say something nasty, want to match the malicious joy in her tone with the acid in my own, but I can't seem to force my lips to form the words. Everything hurts too badly.

"Well, I hope you're recovered enough to continue, because we're just getting started, and I'm not ready to put you back together again. I thought you'd be sturdier than the ghosts I killed getting to you. Don't disappoint me."

She starts to read again. This time, somehow, I find the strength to scream.

True to her word, Laura takes me to the very edge of truly gone before pulling me back, changing her wasp-words for milk and honey and the soothing promise of peace. It's almost worse than the pain, because it means the pain can start all over again, flaying off the layers of my existence until I barely remember who I am. I'm not sure how long she can do this before I lose my mind. I'm even less sure that she cares.

She stops once the restoration is complete, watching impassively as I struggle to breathe. Then she puts the book down on her chair and begins to walk the edge of the Seal, relighting candles, checking her line of salt. "I bet you're wondering if I know how much this hurts you. If I've considered how cruel I'm being." She glances my way and smiles, rattlesnake again. "Believe me, I've considered it. I just wish I had a way of making it go on for longer."

"Yeah, well, forgive me if you're alone in that," I whisper. "I didn't kill him."

"You didn't save him."

"I tried."

"He's still dead."

There's nothing I can say to that. I sag into the floor, trying to gather what strength I can from this brief respite. There's still no escape route presenting itself, no golden "Get Out of Jail Free" card suddenly appearing to tell me which way to run. The Seal is close enough to perfect that I can't worm out of it, the line of salt clean and unbroken, the candles lined up in triplicate so that even when one blows out, the light endures. I am well and truly fucked.

"You know, I'll be sorry when the sun rises. I've been looking for you for so long, and I've worked so hard for this night . . . I suppose I'll have to find something else to do with myself after this. Maybe I'll go into the exorcism business. It's surprisingly satisfying, when you know what you're doing."

"Go to hell."

"No, Rose. That's where you're going." She walks back to the chair, collects her book, opens it. I take a breath, preparing for the pain to start.

Instead, I hear the sound of tires on broken blacktop, an engine drawing closer and stopping, a car door being slammed. Laura tenses and looks up, light glinting off her glasses. I consider screaming, and decide against it. Most people won't believe me if I say that I'm a ghost, not right now, when I can't prove it; they'll think we're playing some sort of fucked-up sex game and leave me here, and then Laura will just be angrier. It's not worth the risk.

The footsteps start a few seconds after the car door slams, drawing closer with every heartbeat. Laura puts down the book and reaches into the belt of her jeans, producing a Bowie knife which she holds loosely behind her back. I guess when you've decided to commit one murder, the second one gets easier, even if that first victim was already dead.

The diner door swings open, and a dead man steps across the threshold, stopping just shy of the circle of salt. "You okay, Rose?" he asks. His voice is young, but the tone is much older, the voice of a man who's spent a decade running the roads in the midnight, where young is forever and innocence is over in an instant.

"Not really," I say, pushing myself unsteadily back to my feet. The world is reeling. I feel like I'm going to throw up. "Hi, Tommy."

Laura drops the knife.

Her shock only lasts for a few seconds. Then she takes a step toward him. "You—you can't be here," she says. Her eyes are wide behind her glasses, shock and terror and amazement mingling in her expression. "You're dead. We buried you. I cried at your funeral. You're *dead.*"

"So is Rose, but that hasn't stopped you locking an innocent hitchhiking ghost in your little cage." He glances toward the salt line, his lip curling in unconscious disgust. "I thought a lot better of you, Laura. I knew you were out there looking for her, but I never thought you'd do anything like this."

"Wait," I say. "You knew she was looking for me? Could you maybe have shared that information?"

I might as well have held my tongue. Laura only has eyes for Tommy, and he's just as focused on her. "Why didn't you come to me?" she demands. "I prayed every night for you to come. To haunt me. I needed you so much."

"Dead is dead, and living is living, and I'm not the kind of ghost Rose is; I don't move between the levels as easy. I'd have been haunting you like you were an empty house, and it wouldn't have been fair. You'd never have been willing to be filled if I were there."

"I was never anyone's home without you," she whispers.

Tommy looks at her calmly, an infinity of love and disappointment in his eyes, and says, "That's not my fault, and my death wasn't hers. Now open the circle, Laura. Let Rose go."

Her eyes stay on him as she crosses back to the Seal, kicks a break in the salt, and bends to slash a Sharpie across the delicate lines of the outer ring. My substance goes the second the binding breaks, leaving me as weightless as fog. I have never in my life been so glad to be dead.

"Rose?" says Tommy.

"I'm okay." I step out of the circle without looking at Laura, and keep my shoulders steady as I walk out the door, to the parking lot, where the rain falls straight through me. Tommy's car flashes her lights as I approach, offering a warm welcome. The passenger-side door swings open. I slip inside, leaning back into the warm seat, closing my eyes.

The sky is turning light when Tommy finally comes to join me. The engine starts without him turning a key. "Where to?" he asks me.

"Take me down, Tommy; take me all the way down." I shake my head. "The living are too damn dangerous for me."

The rain starts to clear as he pulls out, and we drive down through the levels of the world, away from the living and their pains, back into the world where we belong. Back down to the ghostroads, and the dead.

2013
The Pretty Little Girl in the Green Silk Gown

THERE HAVE ALWAYS been way stations on the roads of the dead, places where the spirits and psychopomps can stop and rest a little while before continuing to their final destinations. They're necessary, especially given that so many psychopomps are dead themselves. If they follow the ghostroads too far into the dark, they lose the ability to turn back. So taverns and temples spring up along the most common routes into whatever lies beyond the ghostroads; boarding houses and hotels, cathedrals and cloisters . . . and in this modern age, truck stops, diners, and seedy little bars with sawdust on their floors. They teeter on the edges of here and there, and even the living can find their way into those in-between places, if they get lost enough, if they need it badly enough.

Everyone's way station is different, determined by what we were in life. Most of the souls I shepherd along were drivers, with a spattering of vagabonds, hitchhikers, and people who were just walking home—people, in other words, who were traveling under their own power. I only get passengers when they come with a driver. I guess that's because, as a hitcher, I don't relate well to people who let someone else make the decisions about where they'd be when the journey was finished. It may not seem like hitchers have much agency, but we do, really; we decide which cars to get into, we decide which destinations to name. It's not the same degree of agency that goes to the drivers, but it's enough for us.

My way station is a little diner that looks like it was built in the early fifties, all chrome and cherry leather and the sound of the jukebox that never runs out of tunes. The music changes sometimes, updating itself to the tastes of the patrons, but the jukebox itself is always the same, sweet and clean and retro-futuristic in design, the sort of thing we used to pretend was all the rage on Mars. It would be a museum piece in the daylight. For me, it's like a snapshot of home in the days before I died.

The Last Dance wasn't made for me, but it might as well have been. It doesn't matter that I'm not the only psychopomp who uses it. If I have a home anymore, it's there; everything circles back to the Last Dance. It's the snake that eats its own tail and the story I can't escape. That's okay. I like it there, no matter how complicated it gets. And trust me, once the dead get involved, things can get *very* complicated.

The way stations exist for the dead, *belong* to the dead, but they aren't owned by the dead. Too many of us are only passing through, psychopomps because of circumstance, making a few runs along the road before we give in to the call of taking that last exit, riding the midnight train to whatever's waiting on the other side. The natives of the twilight tend the way stations, using them to provide themselves with a purpose, something to keep themselves from sliding down into the midnight. They work for everyone, in a way.

When you die on the road, if you're lucky, a phantom rider or a hitchhiking ghost will be there, waiting, to offer you directions to the Last Dance Diner. Best malts this side of the 1950s, pie to die for, and best of all, a chance to rest, for just a little while, before moving on . . . and everyone moves on, in the end.

Everyone goes.

The clock was striking midnight when Tommy dropped me off in the parking lot of the Last Dance Diner, leaving me alone as he dwindled into taillights and memory down that endless road to morning. I've been here for hours now, and it's still midnight at the Last Dance.

That's not as strange as it seems: it's always midnight here, or close to it, the hands on the clock locked in perpetual embrace above the window that cuts through to the kitchen. Heating lights shine down on the clean surface of the counter there, warming stacks of pancakes and cheeseburgers with their accompanying heaps of fries. Nothing ever stays on the counter long—Emma's staff is too well-trained, the diner running like a well-oiled machine whenever someone actually comes through looking for a meal—but its presence is reassuring, granting glimpses of other people's meals as you wait for your own. Normally, anyway. That's how it's supposed to work.

Not tonight.

Tonight, the kitchen is dark, the cook and busboy and even the dishwasher gone to attend to some accident down the road, an accident bad enough that when it happened, they sat up like hunting dogs hearing their master call and were out the door almost before Emma gave them permission. I'd only been here for an hour when it happened. I stayed behind. I didn't taste ashes, I didn't smell lilies . . . I wasn't involved. There's no point in rushing to an accident that I have no part in. It wouldn't have me if I tried, and those who die in its embrace will have other psychopomps to lead them home.

For a little while—not long, but a little while—it was just me and Emma, her in her cotton candy-colored uniform and sensible shoes, me in the faded jeans and white tank top that are practically *my* uniform, these days. I change my clothes to suit the people who pick me up, but when I'm left to my own devices, I always seem to wind up back in the jeans I wasn't supposed to wear, in the shirt I borrowed from Gary, once upon a time and once upon a life ago.

Then there were tires crunching on the gravel of the parking lot, and headlights shining through the window until they clicked abruptly off. "Go toward the light," they tell the dead, but in my experience, the light has always been an oncoming car.

Emma pushed herself away from the counter, offered me a small, apologetic smile, said, "The Last Dance is open for business, even when the kitchen's closed," and went to greet her customers. That was an hour ago. They're still here. Busload of cheerleaders in school colors, red and gold, frilled skirts that would have been suitable only for porn stars and pin-up girls when I was their age—*really* their age, not just a shade who'll be sixteen until the stars blow out at last. The logo on their sweaters marks them as the Oxville Knights, and their laughter—loud and gleeful and ringing from the rafters—marks them as the living.

Maybe. Because they're here, in the Last Dance, and we get the living sometimes, but not normally for this long, and not normally this many of them at one time. It's possible that they just took the wrong series of exits from the highway, turned on the wrong frontage roads and followed the wrong signs, but . . . I don't know. Something's wrong. Emma brings them malteds and pie a la mode, things that don't require an understanding of the grill and the fryer, and something's wrong, and I just don't know what it *is*.

Thunder rolls outside the diner, and the long-threatened rain begins to fall. It showers down lightly at first, but a sprinkle becomes a deluge in a matter of minutes, leaving us all looking out the windows at a world wiped away by water. Emma walks to the door, opens it, and sticks her head outside. Only for a few seconds; long enough to douse her hair, leaving her dripping when she steps back, letting the door swing shut again.

"Looks like we're going to be here for a while, ladies," she says, drawing theatrical groans punctuated with giggling from the cheerleaders, who seem incapable of taking anything seriously for more than a few minutes. I can barely remember ever being that young. "Since the kitchen's closed and the rain's likely to knock out the power any minute now, I'm going to go grab some candles—and the ice cream. No sense letting it all melt."

This earns her a round of applause from the cheerleaders. Everyone likes free ice cream, even girls who probably spend half their lives on diets. Emma winks my way as she walks toward the kitchen. "Rose, you're in charge until I get back," she says, and then she's gone, leaving me with a dozen cheerleaders staring at me like wolves staring at a wounded deer.

This is going to be a long night. I can already tell.

The hours tick by like seasons, endlessly long and strange. The cheerleaders fall on the ice cream with terrifying enthusiasm, leaving nothing but smears at the bottom of their bowls and smug smiles on their faces, like they've somehow managed to get away with something. Emma and I have barely finished clearing away the dishes when lightning illuminates the sky, turning the world brilliantly white for a few seconds before fading away and leaving us in darkness.

"Right on cue," says Emma cheerfully, and strikes a match. The tiny flame is a signal flare in the gloom, one that spreads from candle to candle as she makes her way around the diner. "Chuck will get the generator on when he comes back from his errands. Until then, who's up for ghost stories?"

I hate ghost stories. Too many of them are autobiographical. That's why I'm still sitting at the counter, nursing a glass of flat, warm Coke, watching as the circle of stories goes around and around the room. The call comes from inside the house, the hook is left on the door handle, the roommate was dead all along. The beautiful dress in the thrift store came from the funeral home, the husband who stole the golden arm is punished for his sins . . . the girl in the pretty green prom dress is just looking for someone to drive her home.

She only ever wanted to go home.

I stare off into space, trying not to listen, trying to focus on the rain. Then Emma's voice cuts through my self-imposed haze, saying, "Your turn, Rosie-my-girl. It's time to pay off a few of those milkshakes and tell us a ghost story."

"What?" I snap back into the present, blinking at her. Emma only smiles, cat-green eyes reflecting the dim light the way that human eyes just never do. *Beán sidhe* bitch. "I don't know any ghost stories."

"Oh, I think you do," she says. "Come on, Rose. Tell us a story."

The cheerleaders pick up the request, catcalling it across the room like I would be somehow susceptible to peer pressure; like the opinion of a bunch of teenage girls I've never seen before and never will again somehow matters. But the candlelight turns their red-and-gold uniforms black and yellow, blurs the outlines of their mascot until the Oxville Knights become the Buckley Buccaneers. I can feel their eyes on me, the tension in the room making it impossible not to move.

So I move. I slide down from my stool and walk over to the circle of cheerleaders and Emma, taking a seat in the space that opens up for me. The air seems too thick, smells like candle wax and ice cream . . . feels like summer in Michigan, when the sky presses down like a blanket, and the trees are almost too green to believe in. I take a breath. It rasps against the back of my throat, so I take another one, close my eyes, and begin.

"This is a true story, and it happened in the summer of 1952, in a place called Buckley Township, in the state of Michigan. Rose Marshall was sixteen years old that summer . . ."

Buckley Township, Michigan, 1952.

Rose Marshall was sixteen years old the summer that she died.

It had been an unusually hot year in Buckley Township. The leaves were already starting to brown from the want of water, and while the lawns in the nicer parts of town were still lush and green, the scrubby grass outside the house Rose shared with her mother and brothers had long since died, leaving the yard embarrassed by its own nakedness. The skeleton hedges seemed to huddle in, like the house was trying to cover itself against the shame. Rose didn't mind. The less of the house that was visible to the casual onlooker, the happier she'd be. They weren't the only poor folks in Buckley—not by a long shot, not when it seemed that everyone who lived along the Mill Road was just this side of starvation more than half the time—but she didn't have to live in all those other houses. She only had to live in her own.

Rose Marshall was sixteen years old the summer that she died, and she wanted out of her mother's house, out of Buckley, out of her entire *life*, more than she wanted anything else in the world.

"Rose! Are you still lolling about in there?"

"I'll be out in a minute, Ma!" she shouted, dropping her hairbrush onto the dresser. It wasn't making a bit of difference one way or the other. All that lemon juice she'd used to lighten up her normally brown hair had left it brittle and dry, like straw that was somehow being forced into a parody of a wave. If they'd been better-off—if they'd been rich enough to make her like all those other girls at school, the ones with new shoes every September and bag lunches every day—she could have bought real peroxide, and done her hair up proper without as much damage. But done was done, and wishing wouldn't make her hair lie smooth and pretty, no matter how much she wanted it to.

Rose grabbed a ribbon off the top of the mirror and tied her hair back into a half-ponytail, hiding the bulk of the damage while leaving the carefully-acquired gold as visible as possible. She was an expert at tying bows to hide tattered edges, just like she'd learned how to scrub out stains before they could set and mend clothes from the church cast-off boxes, darning and patching until they were just about as good as new. That didn't make wearing them to school any easier—not with girls who'd laugh behind their hands when they saw her wearing a sweater they'd donated to charity two seasons back, not when they saw her with her patched hems and her scuffed-up too-big shoes—but it made pretending pride a little less hard.

"*Rose!*"

"I'm coming, Ma!" she shouted, and jumped to her feet, running to the door. Her books were on the dresser just inside the door, stacked helter-skelter with her pencil case and the notebooks she diligently filled with her semi-intelligible scrawl. She grabbed them, tucking them up under one arm as she made her way down the hall to the living room. Her mother was still wearing her bathrobe, sitting at the scuffed old kitchen table her brothers dragged home one night (and she'd never been able to bring herself to ask where they'd found it; there was too much chance they'd tell her if she did) with a cup of coffee steaming in front of her. Her eyes swept along Rose's body from head to toe in a matter of seconds, assessing, calculating, measuring everything she saw against some secret scale where her only daughter was always found wanting, and always would be.

"You're late," she said. "That boy won't be waiting for you if you don't haul your pretty little ass out to the curb."

"His name's Gary, Ma. He'll be waiting."

"If you say so," she replied, and picked up her coffee. "Don't you dawdle after school today. You've got chores to do, and I want to see you before I head for work."

"All right, Ma," said Rose, and walked—decorously, always decorously; better a little lost time than another lecture on how boys viewed girls who reached high school without learning to be ladylike—to the front door. Her mother didn't say good-bye. Neither did she.

Ruth Marshall waited at the table for the sound of the horn honking twice at the front of the house. Then she stood, faster than her daughter would have given her credit for, and crossed to the kitchen window, where she watched Rose get into the passenger seat of Gary Daniels' car. She didn't hate her only daughter, no matter what Rose would have said if asked; she just knew what it was to be sixteen and poor and have the boys looking at you with those falsely sweet eyes, the ones that said, "I would never leave you." They could get you to do anything, when you were sixteen years old, and when they looked at you with those eyes. And in the end, they always lied.

Ruth didn't know it, but she didn't need to worry about Rose and Gary going farther than a good girl would go; didn't need to worry about them doing much of anything she wouldn't approve of. There wasn't enough time for that. But she didn't know that, *couldn't* know that, and so she stood and worried as she watched the car pull away from the curb. Only when it was gone did she turn from the window, walking slowly back to the kitchen table.

It was the summer of 1952, and Rose Marshall had less than three days left to live.

The Last Dance Diner, 2013.

The cheerleaders shift and squirm on the vinyl seats of the diner, some frowning, some yawning, others just looking bored. One flips her hair and asks, "So, like, what the hell is this? Some Hallmark special about the Great Depression?"

I don't have the patience for a history lesson right now, and none of these girls would be likely to care if I tried. I narrow my eyes instead, and say, "This is after the Depression, and it's the only ghost story I know. Do you want to hear it or not?"

I'm not lying, I'm *not*, because this is *my* story, my ghost story, and it contains every other story I've ever come across. There isn't room for another ghost story in my world. Not until the first one is finished, and it won't be over until Bobby Cross is in his grave, and the ghostroads are free of him forever.

"We want to hear it," says Emma, her *beán sidhe* voice carrying the weight of a commandment. She doesn't use her powers on the patrons often, but when she does, she sounds like that. She isn't forcing me to speak—I'd know it, if she were—but she may be forcing the cheerleaders to listen. I'll have to thank her for that, later. I'm starting to realize that I *want* to tell this story; that it's been waiting long enough to be told. Something about tonight makes me feel like this is the right time to tell it.

I clear my throat, shifting on my seat, and begin to speak again. "Rose and Gary weren't the sort of couple that most people expected to find in Buckley . . ."

Buckley Township, Michigan, 1952.

Rose and Gary weren't the sort of couple that most people expected to find in Buckley . . . or the sort of couple that most people approved of. It was generally accepted that Gary had prospects. He was a member of the football team, and not the least skilled, either; his family had money enough that college wasn't out of the question, scholarship or no. They'd come out of lumber, like most of the old families in Buckley, but now they were in the business of real estate and land rentals, and there wasn't a speck of dirt on their hands. If Gary liked to mess around with cars, well, boys will be boys, and he'd grow out of that soon enough. If he liked to mess around with girls like Rose, on the other hand . . .

Gary's father swore the little tramp was just trying to get herself pregnant and land a husband who could take care of her and the screaming brats she'd be happy to weigh him down with. Gary's mother tended to think of Rose a little more charitably—she'd gone to school with Robert Marshall, before they both went on to the lives their place in society defined for them, and she remembered him as a kind boy, friendly, sweet, and willing enough to do what needed doing—but agreed with her husband on one thing, at the very least: their son could do better.

As for Gary himself, he listened patiently to the things his parents told him, met the girls his mother brought home for him, and then returned to the things he cared about: auto shop, hanging out at Bronson's Diner, and dating the daughter of the night-shift waitress. Rose Marshall might not have money, and she might not come from the best family, but she had eyes he could look into for the rest of his life, and she knew how to fix a transmission, and he was pretty sure that he was a lot more than halfway to being in love with her.

Best of all, he was pretty sure she was halfway to being in love with him, too. Being with Rose made him happy in a way that almost nothing else did, or could. He was seventeen, and she was sixteen; in another six months, he'd be eighteen, and he could ask her to marry him. It didn't matter what his parents thought, or what her mother thought. He wanted to spend the rest of his life with Rose Marshall. He knew that, and that was all that he needed to know.

"Your radio's broken again."

Gary glanced toward Rose. The sun was glinting off her lemon-bleached hair like a halo, making her look even more like an angel than she usually did. (That was an image that would haunt him in the days and nights ahead, making sleep an impossible fantasy. But that was the future, and the future was another country.) "Just give it a thump. It'll start working again."

"I'm not sure I can handle all those big technical words," said Rose, and smacked the radio with the heel of her hand. Rock and roll blared into the car, turned up just a little too loud for the safety of their eardrums. She twisted the volume quickly down, and smiled. "Much better."

"I swear my car likes you better than it likes me."

"She just likes that I know how to fix her better than you do, that's all." Rose ran her fingers along the dashboard, smiling almost maternally at the machine. "You should take better care of her."

"What's the fun of something that works every time you try to turn it on?"

"I guess that could be a kind of fun," allowed Rose, who had been on the receiving end of too many broken things to really share that point of view. Some of them didn't start up again when you hit them. Some of them required begging and tears and giving six months of saved-up babysitting money to your brother to pay off the electric bill. "So, tomorrow . . ."

"Tomorrow, huh? I was thinking I'd go see a movie. Maybe drive up to Ann Arbor for the afternoon." Rose made a face at him. Gary laughed. "Or I could pick you up at six for dinner, and we can go from there to the prom. If that's okay with you?"

"That'll have me on cloud nine for sure," said Rose solemnly. She was smart enough to know what it was *really* costing Gary to take her to the prom, and still innocent enough to hope that his intentions were honorable ones. They might not be—no girl with two older brothers and no father to look out for her could be quite that blind—but as long as she could hope . . .

If this ended with the school year, if he said, "It's been fun" and drove off to college in some big city like Detroit or Columbus, well, it would still have been worth it, every minute of it. Because he'd been good to her, and she liked it when he laughed, and there wasn't enough in Buckley that made her happy. If everything he'd been to her was a lie, well. She'd run that road when she came to it.

Gary pulled in the lot behind the auto-shop classes, scattering greasers and smokers like quail before he killed the engine, and gave her a little grin, that little grin she always thought of as existing just for her. “See you after school?”

Rose grinned back. “It’s a date.”

The Last Dance Diner, 2013.

“But when are we going to get to the ghost story part?” asks a cheerleader, sounding plaintive and bored at the same time. I blink at her in confusion. The Last Dance seems almost like a mirage somehow, blurry and unreal in the flickering candlelight. This can’t be the real world, can it? This cold, wet, twilight world, where the sun never rises and the dead live on forever? This can’t be where I’m spending eternity—not after the hot, clean heat of a Michigan summer, not after Gary’s smile . . .

“Rose?” says Emma.

I blink again, clearing the candlelight from my eyes, and nod in her direction. “I’ve got it,” I say, and take a breath. “The ghost story part is coming. Now listen. The school day inched by like a thousand days before it; like a thousand more would inch after it. One minute at a time, counting down to the freedom of the final bell . . .”

Buckley Township, Michigan, 1952.

The final bell rang like Gabriel’s trumpet, and students poured out of classrooms like angels answering the call to war. Rose stayed seated at her desk, counting slowly backward from twenty. She’d learned the hard way that it was best for her not to hurry. Let the popular girls—the ones who couldn’t understand how someone like *her* could ever be competition for people like *them*—make their way out of the halls and off campus. Once that was done, it would be safe to move.

"Rose?"

"Yes, Mrs. Jackson?" Rose raised her head from the book she'd been pretending to read, flashing an appropriately respectful smile at the anxious looking teacher in front of her. Irene Jackson had only been teaching in Buckley for a year; hadn't learned the rules yet, the signals that meant it was time to look the other way, the patterns that meant something was too big for a single person to stop. She was young. She'd learn. If she had time.

Irene Jackson was a good woman, and she'd gone into teaching because of girls like Rose—girls like the girl she'd been, once upon a time. The ones who didn't think they had any options, because their families couldn't buy those options for them. "Are you all right? You looked . . ."

"I'm fine, Mrs. Jackson." Rose stood hurriedly, grabbing her books from the rack beneath her desk and clutching them against her chest. "I just have so much to get done before prom that I guess I was letting my thoughts run away with me."

"Gary Daniels is taking you to his Senior Prom, isn't he?"

"Yes, ma'am."

"He seems like a very nice young man."

Rose's smile was brilliant enough to shame the sun, if only for a few seconds before it faded back into her normal low-caste wariness. "He is, Mrs. Jackson. A very nice young man. Thank you, ma'am." And then she was gone, heading for the door at the brisk walk-half-skip that all the female students used when they were trying to escape their teachers without being rude about it.

Irene Jackson—who would never forget the way Rose had smiled; who would later write her memorial page for the school yearbook, and would weep without shame over every word—watched her go, a frown pulling down the corners of her mouth. That night, she sat on the edge of the bed with her husband brushing out her hair, sighed, and said, "It was like she was weighing the rest of her life, right there in my classroom, and she was finding every bit of it wanting. How am I supposed to help these kids? They don't want my help. They don't want anything but to be left alone."

David Jackson was a smart man, and knew that sometimes, his wife worried about things she had no business worrying about, like teenage girls from the bad side of town. He pressed a kiss to the top of her head, and said, "She'll be *fine*. Girls like that can surprise you sometimes, if you give them the chance. Just be there if she needs you."

"I'm there for all the kids," said Irene, with the conviction of a true believer. "All they have to do is ask."

"There, you see?" He put the brush aside, reaching for her. "Now come here. It's time to forget about other people's children for a while."

The Last Dance Diner, 2013.

I'm filling space, relating events that I wasn't there to witness . . . but I know that they happened, because the people involved told me about them. They told me when I went back to Buckley to offer them a guide into the dark places, playing psychopomp for the people who'd known me and cared for me when I was alive—the only people who were mine to shepherd, even though they didn't die on the road. The ones who mattered in life can matter in death, if you want them to, and I've guided everyone I cared about who's died since I did.

Everyone who'd go with me, anyway. I ran for Michigan when I felt my mother dying, but she was long gone by the time I got there, and the shades of the streets told me she'd known I was on the way, but chose not to wait for me. I guess some things don't change, not even among the dead.

Maybe especially not among the dead.

I take another breath, smiling gratefully as Emma slides another dish of ice cream in front of me, and continue. "The next night, with her mother off to work the diner's night shift and her brothers off doing whatever it was they spent their evenings doing, Rose walked to her closet . . ."

Buckley Township, Michigan, 1952.

Rose walked to her closet the way she imagined a bride would walk on the evening of her wedding. She'd worked all year to save her pennies for a prom dress, putting up with endless hours of babysitting and doing more odd jobs than she cared to count. Every cent she got went toward the dress. She'd been hiding her money under the bottom drawer of her dresser, where her mother wouldn't think to look. Her brothers wouldn't steal from her, although it was best not to tempt them; the Marshall boys were still looking for their own roads out of Buckley. Still, they knew what the money was for, and they wouldn't deny her the chance to get away. A prom night might not change the world . . . but then again, it might. If she was lucky, it just might.

The dress she'd purchased from the department store downtown was green silk, almost daring in the way it hugged her hips and waist, almost demure in the way it circled her chest and shoulders. The perfect dress. The color was right for her, whether her hair was lemon-bleached or its darker natural brown, and she'd even been able to find matching shoes at the secondhand shop downtown. That was the final straw, the thing that decided her, even if it meant she had to work another month of Saturday nights while her perfect dress sat on layaway, waiting for her to come and claim it. Even the store manager had smiled when she came to pick it up, paying her last five dollars with hands that were very nearly shaking. It was the perfect dress for prom. It was the perfect dress for *everything*.

It was the perfect dress to die in.

But thoughts like that were a million miles from Rose's mind as she stepped out of her coarse cotton skirt and slid the silk up around her waist, feeling the fabric cupping her the way Gary sometimes did, when he was feeling daring and she was feeling wild. She pulled it up a little bit, letting the heavy fabric whisper against her legs, tiny silk kisses on her skin. But draw it out as she might, she couldn't make the process last forever. All too soon, she was looking at herself in the mirror, at the green silk bodice, at the matching ribbons tied oh-so-carefully through the tamed and tempered straw of her hair.

"If he asks me to go to the top of Dead Man's Hill tonight, I will," she whispered, the words wicked on her tongue, and watched the wanton blush spreading up her cheeks. She was going to get out of Buckley, she *was*, and one way or another, this was going to be the night that started her escape.

One way or another.

The hours ticked by as slowly as shadows creeping across the street at sunset, and Gary didn't come. Rose sat on the porch, keeping her back carefully lifted away from the wide slats of the porch swing, and watched the road with eyes that had gone from anticipatory into worried, and were now making the transition into angry. He hadn't come because he wasn't coming. Someone—his mother, maybe, or those pretty girls in school who didn't think a boy like him should go anywhere near a girl like her—had finally talked some of their brand of sense into him, and he wasn't coming.

She'd been a fool to think a night like this was ever intended for a girl like her. Rose stood, blinking back tears as she turned to storm back into the house, away from the summer air and the hope of something more.

Then she paused, hand stretched toward the doorknob. Paused, and thought.

The umbramancers say that every choice we make can change the future, and that every future exists, somewhere. If anyone would know, it would be them, with their wild, mad eyes that see past the highway's end, off into forever.

If what they say is true—if every choice we make creates a future—then this story has a happy ending. In a thousand, thousand futures, Rose Marshall went back into the house, took off the green silk gown, chose another path. Maybe she sold the dress back to the department store and used the money she'd worked so hard for to leave Buckley forever. Maybe she confronted Gary at school on Monday morning, found peace, found closure. Maybe she just decided to wait a little bit longer before she turned off all the lights, and was still awake when her prom date arrived, greasy-handed from changing his tire, with a half-dead corsage clutched in one hand. Maybe. But those are other stories, about other Roses, and that isn't how this story chose to go.

The frown bloomed on Rose's face like the flower she was named for, starting small, but opening swiftly. By the time she wrenched the door open and stormed into her brothers' room, it was in full display, petaled in anger, disappointment, and shame. Arthur and Morty were gone for the night, off on some mysterious errand, and they'd taken Arthur's truck, leaving Morty's clapped-out old car behind. He always left his keys in the dish beside his bed when he wasn't going to need them. Rose snatched them up and turned to go, not looking back, not pausing to change her clothes.

If any of the neighbors had chosen that moment to look out the window, they would have seen a small, pale-haired figure dressed in green silk go stalking across the yard to the car parked beside the curb. They might have said "There goes that Marshall girl," might even have commented on what a strange thing that was to wear on an evening drive. But no one saw her go. No one said a word.

Rose Marshall shoved the key into the ignition, turned it, and was gone.

The Last Dance Diner, 2013.

I pause for a moment, struggling to find the words that come next; struggling to find the next breath. I don't have to breathe, not really, but here and now and wearing the coat that Emma gave me when the cheerleaders arrived—wouldn't do to have them realize they could see right through me when the lightning flashed—it helps me think. I don't want to tell them the parts that come next. I don't want to remember them. I want to lie, say things worked out, say that somehow, this was never a ghost story at all. It was just another high school romance, long ago and far away, once upon a time in Michigan.

I take that next breath, sigh, and say, "The fastest way to Gary's house was by way of a narrow, winding road that ran the length of the closest thing in town to a mountain. They called it Sparrow Hill Road . . ."

Buckley Township, Michigan, 1952.

Rose slowed as she took the turnoff onto Sparrow Hill Road, a sudden chill making the skin on her arms lump up into hard knots of goose-flesh. Something was wrong. Something was very wrong. Every instinct she had was telling her to turn around, to take the long way, or to just go home; this wasn't worth it. People had *died* on Sparrow Hill Road. A girl from her high school had been killed there just last year. It wasn't *worth* it.

Rose Marshall was nothing if not stubborn. Tightening her hands on the wheel, she hit the gas and drove forward into the shadows lurking underneath the trees that covered the hill. It only took a few moments for the light to disappear completely.

No one in Buckley ever saw Rose alive again.

Sparrow Hill Road was a little over three miles long from end to end, following a winding route around the outside of the hill it was named for. Rose had traveled nearly a mile and a half when headlights flashed on behind her, sudden and almost blinding as they reflected off her rearview mirror. "Ah!" she exclaimed, throwing up an arm to block the glare. "Jerk."

Adjusting the mirror didn't help; it was almost like the car behind her was aiming to kill her night vision. Rose muttered something unladylike under her breath and sped up. She'd been driving Sparrow Hill Road since long before she was legally allowed behind the wheel of a car. If she had to drive it halfway-blind, then so be it. It wasn't like she had another choice. The road was too narrow where they were, and she couldn't turn around, or pull off to the side to let the bastard pass.

Another half-mile slunk by, sliding away into the night. The headlights faded from her rearview, and Rose dropped her hand from her eyes, putting it back on the wheel. She had time, barely, to grip the wheel before the car that had been driving behind her lunged forward and slammed into her rear bumper.

The impact was hard and unexpected, throwing Rose forward. She cried out as she caught herself against the wheel, more in surprise than pain, and was in the process of straightening when the car was hit again, harder this time, knocking her almost onto the dash.

"What are you trying to do, kill me?" she shouted, even though she knew full well that there was no way the other driver could hear her. Then she paled. There were always stories about girls foolish enough to drive alone on spooky deserted roads in the middle of nowhere—and then there was that girl, what was her name, Mary or Martha or something . . .

Rose slammed her foot down on the gas hard enough to hurt, sending Morty's car leaping forward at a speed it hadn't seen since it was new. "Come on, come on, *please*," she whispered, shifting as she urged the car to go even faster, to break whatever mechanical laws were holding it back. It said something about the car's love for her that it tried, oh, how it tried to do as she was asking. Just a little farther. If she could make it just a little farther, she could get off the hill, and then—

She didn't dare slow for the curve in the road. She twisted the wheel sharply left, trying to swing the car around. She would have made it—her reflexes were good, as the reflexes of the young and afraid so very often are—if the strange car hadn't slammed into her bumper one final time just as she began her turn, sending her, and her brother's car, plummeting down into the darkness on the side of Sparrow Hill Road.

There was time to scream. There was time to think *Oh God, oh God, I'm going to die, this is it, I'm going to die, oh God . . .*

And then there was nothing.

The Last Dance Diner, 2013.

Silence reigns in the Last Dance Diner. Silence, and the sound of the rain. The cheerleaders stare at me in open-mouthed silence, waiting for the story to continue. I take a breath.

"If Rose was awake when her car hit the ground, that night granted her a single mercy; she didn't remember it when she came to. The woods were silent all around her . . ."

Buckley Township, Michigan, 1952.

Rose opened her eyes on darkness.

She was sprawled next to the road at the base of Sparrow Hill, her head pillowed on a clump of fallen leaves. She pushed herself slowly up, eyes wide as she stared, disbelieving, at the woods. She'd been falling; she remembered that. After that was nothing but darkness. "There was an accident . . ." she whispered, to no one, to the night. "The car . . ."

But there was no car. Only the road, and the night, and Rose, standing lonely and confused in her green silk gown. Standing? She remembered sitting up, but when did she stand—? She looked down at herself; the dress was intact, no tatters or even stains from the ground where she'd been lying. She brushed her hands against her skirt, disoriented and confused. "I don't understand."

"Rose?"

The question came from the left. Rose turned, eyes wide, to see Gary Daniels—her prom date, the one she'd been coming to find—walking toward her with his tuxedo jacket tied around his waist and oil coating his hands. "God, Rose, what are you doing out here? I was going to call just as soon as I got back to a place with a phone—how did you get here?" He paused. "Rose, what's wrong? You're shivering."

"I'm cold." It was the first thing to come to mind. It shouldn't have been true, not on a hot June night in the hottest summer of her short life, but it was. It felt like her bones had been replaced with ice, freezing her from the inside out.

"Here." Gary untied his tuxedo jacket and offered it to her, saying, "I took it off before I started working on the tire. It shouldn't . . . it shouldn't stain your dress."

"Thank you." She slipped the jacket on, the cold fleeing almost instantly. Tears welled up in her eyes, and she threw herself at him, almost without thinking. "I want to get out of here, Gary, Gary, please, please, get me out of here. Please."

"Sure, honey, sure." He hesitated, finally stroking the back of the jacket as soothingly as he could. It was his coat; if he wanted to get it greasy, he could. "I've got the tire back on. We can go anywhere you want. We can even head for the prom, if that's what you want to do. I'm pretty sure they'll still let us in."

"No. Not the prom." Rose pulled away, wiping at her eyes with the back of her hand. "Let's just drive, Gary. Can we do that tonight? Can we just drive?"

Gary Daniels looked into her eyes, and realized two things all the way down into the bottom of his heart. He would go anywhere this girl asked him to . . . and he loved her. He wasn't halfway there. He loved her.

"Sure, Rose," he said, and smiled. "Anywhere you want to go."

They stopped at a service station, where he washed the grease from his hands and filled the tank to the very top with gas. Enough to go just about anywhere, especially for two kids with nowhere else to be. They were together, and it was a beautiful night, and that was enough. That was enough for the both of them.

It was one of those nights that every summer should have, especially for a girl who's sweet sixteen and very much in love. The roads were clear, and every star in the sky was shining just for them. He kissed her down by the old river bridge, and she let him. She kissed him behind the drive-in theater, where the flickering light from the soundless screens turned the sidewalk into something barely this side of a dance floor. It was perfect. That was how Gary would describe it later, when people called him crazy. "Perfect," he'd say, and look away. Sometimes, if they pressed, he'd add four more words—four more words that silenced everyone who heard them.

"It was worth it."

Only two things tainted the perfection of that night. The first was the sleek black car that followed them, once, twice, three times, tracking them for a few miles and then sliding into the shadows. Rose wouldn't get out when that car was there. She clung to Gary's hand, staring out the windshield, and refused to let him go and start a scene. "Just drive," she said, all three times, and because he loved her, and because the night was perfect, Gary did.

The second was a commotion on Sparrow Hill Road. They saw it when they drove past; what looked like every police car and fire truck in the county, all flashing their lights and lighting up that hill like a beacon.

Gary slowed, squinting up at the center of the fuss. "What do you think happened up there?"

"I don't know," said Rose, who was becoming slowly, dreadfully afraid that she *did* know; that she knew all too well. But for the moment, she could still lie to herself, and so lie to herself she did. "Let's not bother them, okay? I bet they're pretty busy."

"Yeah, okay," said Gary, and kept on driving.

They drove the night away, measuring it in kisses and parking places, miles and moments. The sky was getting light when Gary pulled up in front of her house, stopped the car, and got out to walk around and open the passenger-side door.

"Thank you for bringing me home," said Rose, and smiled—a sweet, heartbreaking smile, the sweetest he'd ever seen from her. She ducked her head forward, pressing a kiss to the corner of his mouth, and whispered, "I love you, Gary Daniels. Always remember that."

Then she was gone, heading up the narrow pathway toward the door. Gary stared after her, one hand going to touch the place where she'd kissed him. He closed his eyes, reliving the moment for just a few seconds more.

When he opened them again, Rose was gone . . . and when he got home, the police were there, waiting to tell him what had happened.

Waiting to tell him what had happened on Sparrow Hill Road.

The Last Dance Diner, 2013.

"Wait—I know this one," says one of the cheerleaders, breaking the trance I was close to falling into. "Doesn't he go back to her house to be all, dude, what the hell, and then there's his coat, folded on her pillow?"

"I thought it was on her tombstone," says another cheerleader.

"And their initials are there, written in lipstick," contributes a third.

"She doesn't *have* a tombstone, dummy, she, like, just died the night before. So it has to be on her bed." The cheerleaders look to me, waiting for me to answer them, to choose a winner in this strange little contest.

Most of me is still on a hot summer night in Michigan, Gary's arms around me and the truth of my own death still something I can deny. "I don't know," I say, simply. "That isn't part of the story. Rose walked back up the pathway wearing his coat, and somewhere between the car and the door, she was just . . . gone. She was gone for a long time after that. But eventually, people started seeing her again. Standing on Sparrow Hill Road. Looking for a ride home."

It took me the best part of a year to learn that I didn't have to make that loop over and over again, that I could go elsewhere if I wanted to. Hitchers are only bound by geography when they want to be. And all I ever wanted was to get out of Buckley.

"That's not much of a story," says a cheerleader dubiously.

"It's the only one I have."

"It would be better if, like, the man who ran Rose off the road sold his soul at the crossroads so he could live forever," says yet another cheerleader. The others murmur agreement. "Only he didn't catch her ghost before she woke up and caught a ride, because he was still pretty new at the harvesting business, and she got lucky. If her boyfriend hadn't been there, and she hadn't been so in love with him that she manifested before she knew what she was, that driver would have had her."

I feel myself go cold. Not the crushing chill of the ghostroads, but the simple, freezing cold of utter terror. "That . . . might be a good story," I force myself to say.

"Yeah, only because he didn't get her, she's stuck," says the first cheerleader, jubilantly. She sounds like she's won some sort of a prize. "'Cause she can't make herself move on while that guy's still out there, killing people and feeding them into his car."

"She's still out there. Hitching around the country, looking for a way to stop him."

"Maybe she's finally found it. But she's not sure yet. She's still too scared."

"Poor little ghost."

"Doomed to walk the Earth as a restless shade, hunting for Bobby Cross."

All the cheerleaders are looking at me now, their uniform gazes calm and interested, like I'm a cat toy—the best one they've had to play with in a long time. The lightning flashes outside, and for a moment, the shadows they throw against the walls have winged helmets instead of artfully tousled hair, hold spears instead of ice cream spoons. The shadows fade, and they're cheerleaders again, just looking at me, waiting.

"But Gary—poor Gary—he has to be pretty old now, doesn't he?" asks a cheerleader. "I mean, she died so long ago. Maybe that's her out, if she wants to take it. When her true love dies, she won't have anything else to tie her to this world. She can take him to the last exit, and go through by his side. It would be *so* romantic, don't you think? If she went with him?"

I stand abruptly. "I'm sorry, Emma. I'm going to go."

Her eyes flash cat-green in the dark, and she says, "No, you're not." There's no command in her words, only fact, calm and simple as anything. She raises her hand, snaps her fingers, and the lights come back on.

The cheerleaders' uniforms have changed again, going from Buckley Buccaneer black and yellow to silver and red, with "Valhalla Valkyries" written across their sweatshirts and blazoned on their gym bags. They smile at the look on my face, starting to gather their things, starting to get ready to go.

"It was nice to finally meet you, Rose," says one of the cheerleaders. Her smile is sweet as summer, but I can see a thousand years of warfare in her eyes. "It's always nice to meet someone who knows that you can't win if you let yourself stop fighting. You have our blessing, for what it's worth. Bobby Cross has denied us our duty too many times." If her smile was terrifying, her frown is a thousand times worse. How can he cross these girls? They look like they could pick their teeth with souls.

But they also look sweet and soft and sugar-candy careless. That's the face they wear as they hug Emma, thank her for the ice cream, offer their farewells, and head out the diner door. The rain stops as soon as the first one steps outside. No surprise there. If the stories are right, they have the storms on their side.

"Thanks for stopping by," says Emma, escorting the last of them out the door. Then she turns and smiles at me. If I didn't know her so well, I wouldn't be able to see her anxiety. "How are you feeling?"

"Tricked," I spit at her. "I thought better of you."

"Better of me than what? Better than me arranging for you to have the chance to tell your story to the Valkyries on neutral ground? Their blessing is a good and important thing to have, especially with what you're planning. And don't you tell me you're not planning to go after him. I know you better than that." Emma frowns, eyes flashing again. "I've been dreaming about you, Rose. They're not all good dreams. If you start down this road . . ."

"I've already passed the exit." I sigh, walking back to my stool and sitting. The air smells like ozone in the wake of the Valkyries. "Start the grill back up."

"Am I paying for deception with cheeseburgers?" I nod, and Emma smiles. "Okay. That's fair enough. I'll call Tommy back after you eat."

"Why? Am I going somewhere?"

"Yes. You're going to the Ocean Lady. You just told your story. It's time that you heard his." This time, when she snaps her fingers, the jukebox spins to life. Tom Petty sings about a girl taking her last dance, and I sit at the counter of the Last Dance, listening to Emma moving through the kitchen, listening to the minutes ticking by. One more time to kill the pain . . .

. . . and the dancing never ends.

2013
The Ocean Lady

YOU START TO LEARN things after you've been walking the ghostroads for long enough. There are no formal schools in the twilight; the old schoolyard chant of "no more pencils, no more books, no more teachers' dirty looks" applies more completely than most people can possibly imagine before they slid between the cracks. Things look different in the twilight. Things *are* different in the twilight. The rules aren't the same here. The old patterns won't protect you.

The twilight is another country, a layered series of Americas where the sun never rises, and the people who wind up here have two choices: adapt or die. Some chase a mythical third choice, and spend their time on the ghostroads trying to claw their way back into the light. I sometimes think they're the saddest ones of all, because they never let themselves accept the reality of their situation. There's no way to escape once you're fully in the twilight. Get out while you're in the shallows, or never get out at all. That's just the way the ghostroads run.

It seems like everyone who walks the twilight has something else they're looking to learn. The routewitches are seeking the stories of the highways and the byways, the hidden riddles worked into frontage roads and ghost towns where the tumbleweeds hold dominion over all. They practice their little magics, they speak to strangers, they give rides to hitchhikers both living and long dead, and they learn. Even they have their divisions, their strange allegiances, their legends and their laws. The Queen of the Routewitches keeps her court on the old Atlantic Highway, the oldest major artery in North America. Most of it's gone in the daylight levels, replaced first by Route 1 and later by Interstate 95, but the twilight has a longer memory than the light does, and the old Atlantic is the strongest and the cleanest of the ghostroads. If you cross her palm with silver, she can tell you things not even the highway commission remembers, like why Route 1 cut so far inland when the Atlantic Highway ran through Savannah, Georgia, and what really funded the construction of the Waldo-Hancock Bridge. They're just stories in the light, but down here, they're the things that can keep you breathing.

If you were breathing when you arrived, that is.

I didn't find the ghostroads; the ghostroads found me, looming up out of the dark like the iceberg that felled the *Titanic*. Everyone in the twilight is looking for something, and I'm no different; I went looking for ghosts, a phantom chasing phantoms through the night that never quite begins or ends. I had to find them. It was the only way to know for sure what I'd become. They were tangled in a thousand half-stitched seams across the fabric of reality, waiting to be found, and I found them. The ghosts of the twilight taught me what I am—a hitcher, a ghost tied not to a physical place or a specific person, but to an unfinished task. We have our rules, just like every other kind of ghost, but we run closer to the skin than most, closer to the daylight, because we got lost by mistake. We were never meant to be here.

The Last Dance moves around. It's located in one of Maine's unincorporated townships when Tommy picks me up, a crumbling, dying little settlement that must have been alive and vibrant once, before the heart and the hope leaked out of it like water through a broken vase. From there, we drive the ghostroads to Calais, just on the edge of the Canadian border. This is the edge of his territory, and the closer we get to Canada, the slower he drives, until it's like we're moving through molasses. We're still three miles from where I need to be when he stops the car, shamefaced and sweating, and says, "This is as far as I go, Rose. I'm sorry."

He's got nothing to be sorry for, and this is farther than I expected him to take me. I want to tell him that, I really do, but the words slip away when I look into his eyes. There's something in them that speaks of exits, of road signs that lead to final destinations, and I can't bear the sight of it. I knew this night was coming—this night always comes. It still hits me like a blow. Tommy is coming close to realizing that the road isn't forever, that he can drive beyond it, and the knowledge burns.

How many will that make? How many racers and riders and hitchers and ferrymen who've fallen onto the ghostroads, and then found their own way off them, while I'm still here? Too many. And Tommy—sweet, stupid Tommy—isn't going to be the last of them.

"I'm good," I say, and slip out of his car, back into the cool, sweet air of the everlasting twilight. The feel of asphalt beneath my feet is centering, a benediction directed only toward the road. "I can walk from here. You can find your own way back?"

It's a fool's question, and I want to take it back almost before I finish asking it. Tommy's a phantom rider, a man who died behind the wheel and carried his car into the twilight with him. He's tied to the stretch of road where he crashed. His presence makes the road safer than it would have been without him, makes the drunks think twice before they stagger out of the bars, makes the teenage hotheads lighten up on the gas and take the turns a little more slowly.

Phantom riders have their place in the way of things, and they do more than just make good ghost stories. I envy the shit out of them; always have, always will. They have something no hitcher gets to have. They have homes.

Tommy frowns a little, confusion blocking out the exits in his eyes. "Yeah, Rose, I can find my way." The car's engine growls, a little roar from a captive lion. We may be old friends, but she doesn't like me messing with her driver.

I step back, ceding the point. "Good. Now get out of here." That doesn't seem like enough, not with the exits so close, and so I add, "Thanks for the ride."

"It wasn't anything," says Tommy, and smiles awkwardly. "Good night, Rose."

"Good night, Tommy," I say, and then he's gone, roaring down the road at the sort of speed that's only safe on the ghostroads, and even here, only barely. He'll be back on his own stretch before morning, wheels gripping familiar asphalt, phantom rider riding hard where he belongs.

I have another road ahead of me. Tucking my hands into my pockets to show that I'm not looking for a ride, I turn and start walking toward the border, and the beginning of the old Atlantic Highway. I'm a long way from home. I'll go a lot farther before this night is done.

The first routewitch I ever met was named Eloise. She had sun-chapped skin the color of old pennies, curly brown hair, and the sharpest eyes I've ever seen. I was hitching my way toward Michigan when she picked me up; she drove a rattling old pickup truck in those days, the bed fenced in with wooden slats and piled high with potatoes. "Get in," she said. That was all. None of the pleasantries, none of the pretenses. "Get in," and that was all.

She handed me a heavy wool sweater and a paper bag once I was in the truck, not even waiting for me to start my usual routine. "I made the sandwiches myself," she said. "The cookies are crap, and the coffee in the thermos ain't much better, but I figure it'll do you well enough, considering your circumstances. What's your name, girl?"

"Rose," I said, shrugging into the sweater. The wool settled across my shoulders, and my heart began to beat, steady internal drumbeat keeping me anchored to the world that I was once more a part of. I took a breath, and saw that she was watching me, a small smile on her lips.

"Rose, huh? Would that be White Rose out of Tennessee, or Rose Marshall out of Michigan?"

I almost stripped the sweater off and ran. But the way she was looking at me didn't seem hostile, just curious, and so I stayed where I was, and we started talking. I'd heard of routewitches before—everyone hears about the routewitches, if they stay in the twilight long enough—but I'd never seen one. She wasn't what I'd been expecting, more Dorothy Gale than Glinda the Good Witch, and when I told her that, she laughed so hard she nearly ran us off the road.

"Now you listen to me, Rose Marshall out of Michigan, and you listen close, because there's not much in this world going to help you more than what I've got to say. The routewitches, and the trainspotters—hell, even the ambulomancers, a'though you don't ever want to tell one of them I said this—we're just folks like anybody else. It's only that we listen different than most people do. The road talks to us, and we know how to talk back. Thing is, the road knows a secret or two. Like how to spot a hitcher when it comes strolling along, looking for a life to share."

Eloise died years ago; her ghost rides the California coast in a battered old pickup truck a decade younger than the one she was driving on the night she picked me up. I see her, from time to time—I've even ridden with her. She's a good person. Most routewitches are, even the dead ones.

She's also the one who taught me about the Atlantic Highway. "The daylight was afraid of the power in that road, so they banished Her to the deeper levels as soon as they could. Route 1 claimed to be the old Atlantic, but they folded it farther inland than the Ocean Lady, pulled it away from Her places of power. Even that wasn't enough for them. They broke the back of Route 1, carved it into a dozen tributaries and threw it away. Guess no one ever told them that you can't kill something that's written that deeply into the land. You ever need to see the Queen, Rose Marshall out of Michigan, you follow the Ocean Lady. She'll take you where it is you need to go."

The Atlantic Highway isn't a safe place for the dead. There are too many ghosts packed onto its slow-spooling miles, and once you start, it can be all but impossible to stop. The Ocean Lady runs from Calais, Maine to Key West down in Florida, and the Queen of the Routewitches keeps her court somewhere in the Lady's asphalt embrace. That's where I need to go. If anyone can tell me what to do from here—what I *have* to do, what I've been putting off for too damn long—it's the routewitch Queen.

I take a breath I don't need, close my eyes, and step from the ghostroads onto the old Atlantic Highway. The Ocean Lady stretches out beneath my feet, and there's nothing to do from here but walk on, and pray.

I don't know how long I've been walking. Long enough, that's for sure. My feet ache, which strikes me as singularly unfair. I'm not among the living here, walking the spine of the Ocean Lady from Maine to God-knows-where; I'm freezing through, which is my normal state of being, and I'd kill for a cheeseburger. All the normal trials and tribulations of my death are weighing on me, and normally, the one good thing about being dead is knowing that I can walk forever without getting tired.

"This sucks," I mutter, and keep walking.

I haven't seen another soul, living or dead, since I started down the old Atlantic Highway. The scenery on either side is blurred and indistinct, world viewed through a veil of cotton candy fog. I can feel the ghostroads running through the levels nearby, but I don't know that I could reach them if I tried. The Ocean Lady has her own ideas about shortcuts like that, and she isn't always a fan of the dead.

One thing's for sure: I've been walking longer than the stretch of a single night, and the sky hasn't lightened in the least. It's always dark in the twilight, but there's normally a sort of gloaming when the sun rises and sets in the daylight—something to keep us in tune with the passage of time. This is just . . . darkness. Darkness that doesn't end, not until the old Atlantic Highway does.

This is starting to seem like it might not have been such a good idea after all. I still can't think of anything better, and so I keep on walking, into the dark.

I have never wanted to punch a highway in the face as badly as I do right now.

I'm on the verge of abandoning this idiotic quest, clawing my way back to the daylight and flagging down the first car I see, when the Ocean

Lady starts singing under my feet, and the song that she's singing is "truck stop ahead." That's a new one on me. I start to walk a little faster, forgetting how sore my feet are as I move toward this new mystery.

Then I walk around a curve in the road, and there it is ahead of me: the mother of all truck stops, the truck stop on which all the pumps and service garages and five-dollar showers were modeled. Its neon burns the fog away like a searchlight, until the whole thing is illuminated and holy, the chapel on the hill remade in the image of America. I stop where I am, breath hitching in my chest, pain and cold and hunger all forgotten as I gape like a tourist on her first day in New York City. This is my destination, the heart of the Ocean Lady, the chapel of the routewitches . . . and if this whole adventure was a bad idea, it's officially too late to turn back now.

A routewitch apprentice I vaguely recognize meets me at the truck stop turnoff, his sneakers crunching in the gravel that encroaches from the shoulder, looking to betray careless drivers. Acne scars dot his cheeks, and his lips are wind-chapped. He's cute enough, and he'd be handsome if he took the time to comb his hair, straighten his shirt, and dig the oil from underneath his nails. "What is your name and your business, traveler?" he asks, words running together until they're almost like a song.

I'm Rose Marshall out of Michigan. I'm the Girl in the Diner, I'm the Lady in Green, I'm the Phantom Prom Date, I'm the Shadow of Sparrow Hill Road. All those names—all those stories—flash through my mind as my mouth opens, and I answer, "My name is Rose Marshall. I've walked the Ocean Lady down from Calais to visit the Queen, if she'll see me. I have a question for her to ask the roads for me."

He reaches up to scratch at the scabbed-over pimples at one temple, frowning. He probably doesn't even know he's doing it. "Be you of the living, or be you of the dead?" More ritual, and stupid ritual at that—he knows I'm dead. Routewitches always know.

Or maybe not. This is the Ocean Lady, after all, and she makes her own rules. "I died on Sparrow Hill Road, in the fall of 1952. How about you?"

Oh, he's young, this routewitch, and more, he's new to the twilight;

he isn't used to dead girls talking back to him. He'll learn. Almost all the dead are a little mouthy. I think it comes from knowing that most of the things you'll run into simply don't have the equipment it would take to actually hurt you. He frowns for a moment, trying to remember the words of the ritual, and then continues, "The dead should be at peace, and resting. Why are you not at peace, little ghost?"

I fold my arms across my chest and glare. "Maybe because I'm standing outside in the wind, being harassed by an apprentice who doesn't know his ass from an eight-foot hole in the ground with a body at the bottom. I have walked the goddamn Ocean Lady to visit the Queen, and you're rapidly burning off my pretty shallow reserves of patience. Are you going to let me in or not?"

"I—" He stops, looking at me helplessly. "I don't know."

Lady Persephone and her sacred midnight preserve me from routewitches who don't know their own traditions. "How about I wait here while you run back to your trail guide and find out?"

His eyes light up. "You'd do that?"

Of course I won't do that. There's no level, daylight on down, where I'd stand out here alone while I waited for some idiot to figure out how to handle me. I don't say anything one way or the other. I just watch him.

"Wait here," he says, making a staying motion with his hands, and turns to run down across the truck stop parking lot, toward the diner. The neon seems to brighten as he approaches, like a loving wife welcoming her husband home from the war.

I follow him, the gravel crunching under my feet. My skirt swirls around my legs, and I realize I'm back in my prom dress. Changing my clothes should take less than a second—having a wardrobe defined only by the limits of my imagination has been one of the few benefits of death—but no matter how hard I concentrate, the green silk remains. Suddenly, the reason for the apprentice's confusion makes a lot more sense. The Ocean Lady is somewhere between ghost and goddess, and on her ground, there is no difference between the living and the dead.

I shake my head, and follow the apprentice routewitch inside.

Every diner, roadhouse, and saloon is a tiny miracle, a piece of comfort and safety carved out of the wild frontier of the road. I died in the age of diners, when chrome and red leather and the sweet song of the jukebox were the trappings of the road's religion. From the outside, that's what this stop on the Ocean Lady looks like to me. The perfect diner, a place where the malteds would be sweet and gritty on the tongue, the fries would be crisp, and the coffee would be strong enough to wake the dead. As the apprentice reaches the door, some ten feet ahead of me, I catch a glimpse of what he sees; his hand ripples the facade, and for a moment, it's a roadhouse, tall and solid and hewn from barely-worked trees. Then he's inside, and the diner is back again.

The diner remains as I finish my trek across the parking lot, and the burnished metal door handle is cool and solid as I curl my fingers around it. I can hear music from inside, Johnnie Ray singing about walking his baby back home. That song got a lot of radio play in the weeks before I died, hit of the early summer, soundtrack of Gary's hands cupping the curve of my waist and his breath coming hot and sweet against my neck.

I open the door, and step inside.

The diner melts away—as I more than half-expected that it would, carnival illusion meant to call the faithful and the faithless alike—and I am standing in a saloon pulled straight from the American West, miles and centuries away from the time and place that I came walking from. There are easily two dozen routewitches here, talking, laughing, eating. One pair is making out in a corner, randy as teenagers. I've never seen this many routewitches in one place before, and the miles they carry have an almost physical presence. The sheer weight of all that mapped-out road distorts the fabric of the room, dragging it into a shape that I don't know.

"Told you she wouldn't stay on the curb, Paul," calls one of the routewitches, a middle-aged Hispanic man with a bristling mustache. "You owe me a cup of coffee."

The apprentice who met me at the gate scowls and kicks the bar, refusing to look at me. Every society has its hazing rituals. I'm not sure I like being part of this one. "Excuse me," I say, looking around the saloon, studying the routewitches. The oldest I see must be in his nineties; the youngest, no more than eight. The road isn't picky about who she calls, or when she calls them. "I've walked the Ocean Lady to see the Queen. You think that could happen today, maybe?"

"That depends," says the mustached routewitch. He stands, walking toward me. "What are you here about? This isn't a place for ghosts, little one, not even those who've died on the road. You have your own cathedrals."

"The Queen of the Routewitches doesn't visit our cathedrals." And neither do I. Hitchers are spirits of the running road, the diners and the dead ends. The cathedrals of the dead are built in frozen places, moments sealed in ice and locked away forever. Road-spirits can't last in places like that for long, not without curdling and going sour, turning into nothing but sickness and rage. I avoid the cathedrals of the dead whenever I can. Stay in them too long, and I wouldn't be Rose Marshall anymore. I'd be what the stories make me out to be. "My mama taught me that when you can't get the mountain to come to you, you'd better be prepared to go to the mountain."

"So you hopped onto the Ocean Lady like She was just another road, and thought our Queen would see you, is that it? Seems a bit arrogant for a long-dead thing like you."

"Yeah, well, your attitude seems a bit asshole-ish for a guardian of the American road, but you don't see me judging, do you? Oh, wait. I just did. Sorry." I cross my arms, glare, try to look like I'm not a reject from a 1950s prom night that ended more than half a century ago. "I'm here to see the Queen. A routewitch named Eloise told me how to get here, if I ever had the need."

His mustache curls upward at the corners, his grin spilling out across his face like it's too big to be contained. "Shit, girl, why didn't you say? How *is* that old *carretera bruja*? She running hard?"

"She's a phantom rider driving the length of California, giving rides, giving advice, and picking oranges, last time I saw her. She said it was more fun than the alternatives." I continue glaring. "Was this some sort of trick question to get me to prove that I didn't know her? Because math would be better if you wanted me to give you a wrong answer. I suck at math."

"You're Rose Marshall, the Shadow of Sparrow Hill Road," says one of the other routewitches. She puts down her sandwich and stands, stretching languidly before she walks toward me. Her expression is lively with undisguised curiosity. She's a tiny thing, a whisper somehow stretched into a slight sigh of a girl, Japanese by blood, American by accent, dressed in jeans and a road-worn wool sweater at least three sizes too big for her. "The Ocean Lady let you through?"

"That, or this is the single most irritating hallucination I've ever had," I answer, watching her carefully. She's clean, this little routewitch with her close-clipped fingernails and her fountain-fall of black silk hair. Most routewitches don't bother with that sort of thing. The road dresses them in dust, and they wear it proudly, carrying the maps of where they've been in the creases of their skin. But a routewitch who doesn't swear allegiance to any single route, to any single road . . . she'd need to be clean. I quirk an eyebrow up, and take a guess: "Am I addressing the Queen?"

"I guess that's up to you, isn't it?" she asks.

Stupid routewitches and their stupid rituals. I take a breath, and say, as I said to the man at the gate, "My name is Rose Marshall, once of Buckley Township in Michigan. I died on Sparrow Hill Road on a night of great importance, and have wandered the roads ever since. I've walked the Ocean Lady down from Calais to visit the Queen, if she'll see me. I have a question for her to ask the roads for me."

She raises her eyebrows, looks at me thoughtfully, and asks, "Is that all?"

My patience is anything but infinite. Scowling, I say, "Who does a girl gotta blow to get herself a beer in this place?"

And the Queen of the North American Routewitches smiles.

They have good beer here, these routewitches do, and their grill is properly aged, old grease caught in the corners, the drippings of a hundred thousand steaks and bacon breakfasts and cheeseburgers scraped from a can and used to slick it down before anything starts cooking. The plate they bring me groans under a triple-decker cheeseburger and a pile of golden fries that smell like summer nights and stolen kisses—and they *smell*, even before the platter hits the table. I look to the routewitch Queen, silent question in my eyes.

"Eat up," she says, reaching for her own plate. "The Ocean Lady doesn't feel the need to withhold the simple joys from anyone who's brave enough to walk this far along Her spine."

"I may have to take back a few of the things I said while I was walking." The fries taste better than they smell, which may be a miracle all by itself. The Queen is already eating, ignoring me completely now that she has a meal in front of her. I don't know much about routewitch etiquette, but I've learned to go with the flow of things. If she wanted to eat before we talked, well, at least contact had been made.

The other routewitches settle all over the room, some of them sitting at tables, some perching on the bar. A few even sit on the floor. They break out decks of cards and tattered paperbacks, fall into hushed conversations, down shots of whiskey, but they're watching us. Every eye in the place is on the Queen, and on the uninvited guest who's come to try her patience.

The Queen looks up, sees me watching them watching us, and laughs. "Don't worry," she says, fingers grazing my wrist at the point where my resurrected pulse beats strong and steady. The half-life of the hitcher extends here, it seems, and I didn't even have to swipe a coat. "They get protective of me sometimes, and your reputation is a little . . . mixed."

I bite back a groan, grinding it to silence between my teeth. When I'm sure it's gone, I say, "I thought you, of all people, would know that I'm not like that."

"We know what the road tells us, Rose, and what the road tells us is that your story is still being written." She dips a fry in the smooth white surface of her vanilla milkshake and raises it, glistening, to her lips. "The Lady in Green is just as real as the Phantom Prom Date, on the right stretches of highway. They watch to be sure the right one has come to visit."

This isn't a new concept—the idea that stories change things, rewrite the past and rewrite reality at the same time—but it's jarring all the same, hearing the routewitch Queen suggest that I could be something other than what I am. I swallow a mouthful of fries that somehow fail to taste as good as they did a moment ago, and ask, "So am I the right one?"

"I think so. I guess we'll know I was wrong if you try to kill me, now, won't we?" The Queen picks up another fry. "Eat. We'll talk when the meal is through."

For the first time in fifty years, I don't *want* to eat, I don't *want* to put something off until the meal, however delicious, is finished. The Queen is ignoring me again, her own attention returning to her fries and shake and grilled cheese sandwich. It's clear that arguing won't do me a bit of good, and so I pick up my burger, and I take a bite.

There's always someone eager to tell the living what the worst thing about being dead will be. Those speeches usually start with the lakes of fire and the eternal damnation, and get nasty from there. I used to believe them, when I cared enough to listen, which wasn't often. Then I died, and I learned that the worst thing about being dead has nothing whatsoever to do with fire.

The worst thing about being dead is the cold. The way it creeps in through every remembered cell of your phantom body, wraps itself around you, and refuses to ever, ever let you go. The worst thing about being dead is the fog, the one that clings to everything, blocking out the taste of coffee, the smell of flowers, the joy in laughter and the terror in a scream. On the living levels, ghosts are shadows wrapped in cotton, held apart from everything around them. Hitchers like me are lucky, because we have a way to claw ourselves back out of the grave, filling the world with substance and with joy. We're also unlucky as hell, because it means we never forget how bright and vivid life is for the living. We don't get to move on. Not until we let someone drive us to the exit past the Last Dance Diner; not until we move on completely.

All hitchers are addicts, and our drugs of choice are diner coffee, cheeseburgers, and the feeling of hands against our skin, the feeling of lips crushing down on ours and making us forget, even for a moment, that we've already paid the ferryman his fee. The taste of the cheeseburger fried for me in the kitchen of the Ocean Lady's stronghold is all those things and more; it's life in a bun, and I could easily forget everything I came here for. All I'd have to do is keep on eating, keep on tasting *life*.

I choke on that first bite, overwhelmed by the taste of it. Then I spit it out and shove the plate aside, sending it shattering to the floor. I grab for my napkin, wiping the last traces of temptation from my tongue.

The room has gone silent. I look up, still gasping a little. The napkin isn't helping; the taste of life is still harsh and heavy in my mouth. The Queen of the Routewitches is watching me, the fountain-fall of her hair covering one eye, the other filled with quiet thoughtfulness.

"So you're not that easy to tempt," she says. "I like that. Devi, Matthew, you have the floor. Let anyone who arrives know that I'm in consultation, and I'm not to be disturbed." She stands, leaving me behind as she starts across the floor toward a door at the back of the bar.

I'm still trying to catch my breath when she stops, turns, looks back toward me. Looking at her, I realize that we have at least one thing in common: we're both of us a great deal older than we seem. "Well?" she asks.

Just that, and nothing more. That's all she needs. I stand, forbidding myself to look at the bloodstain-splash of ketchup on the floor, and I follow the Queen of the Routewitches out of the main room, into the shadows of the unfamiliar.

The door at the back of the bar opens onto a hallway, which opens, in turn, onto the back parking lot. The Queen doesn't look back once as she walks toward a double-wide trailer parked near the side of the building. No matter how fast I walk, she stays an easy six feet ahead, her steps eating ground with quiet, unflagging speed.

She stops when she reaches the trailer, resting her hand on the latch as she says, "Once we're inside, Rose Marshall, daughter of Michigan, daughter of the road, once we're inside, then my Court is called to order. Are you sure? Are you truly sure that this is the route the roads intend for you?"

"Fuck, no," I say, before my brain can catch up with my tongue. "But I don't have a better map, so I guess it's gonna have to be you."

"Good answer." I can hear the smile in her voice as she opens the latch. The trailer door swings open, and she says, with the calm cadence of ritual, "Now we begin the descent. Enter freely, Rose Marshall, daughter of Michigan."

"Aren't you supposed to add 'and be not afraid' or something like that?" I ask, moving to enter the trailer.

The Queen of the Routewitches gives me a small, faintly amused smile, and asks, "Why would I do something like that? I'm here to answer your questions. I'm not here to lie to you."

Somehow, that fails to reassure me in the slightest. Still, in for a penny, in for a pound, as my grandmother always used to say, and I've come too far to turn back now. I shrug, green silk sleeves moving against my shoulders. "Okay, then. Let's rock."

The trailer of the Queen of the Routewitches is decorated in Early Vagabond, with a few exciting traces of Thrift Store Chic. Not the sort of thing I'd expect to see from royalty, but the more I think about it, the more sense it makes. Routewitches don't like to buy anything new when they have a choice in the matter. Things get stronger the farther they've traveled, and the more hearts they've had calling them "mine." As the Queen, she had to have her choice of the best the country's flea markets and antique shops have to offer, and if that means things never quite matched, well, I don't think that was necessarily going to be a factor in her decorating choices.

She motions me to a seat at a battered card table with a slightly stained lace tablecloth spread across it. "I'll be right with you," she says.

I sit.

She has a red glass wine bottle in one hand and a deck of cards in the other when she returns. "Now, what is it that I can do for you tonight?"

My throat is dry. The words are harder to say than I expected them to be. "Bobby Cross," I say, finally.

"I thought as much. I asked myself, 'what could bring the Phantom Prom Date to walk the Ocean Lady, even knowing how dangerous it is for someone like her,' and the only answer I could come up with was 'revenge.'" She places the bottle between us as she sits, watching me with faint amusement. "People are really pretty simple. Even the dead ones."

"It's not about revenge," I protest, but I'm lying. It's been about revenge for decades. It's been about revenge since the day I understood just what was really going on. "It's about stopping him. He *needs* to be stopped."

"I didn't say he didn't need to be stopped. I only said that this was about revenge—and it is. Lie to me, if you like, but take care not to lie to yourself. That won't make things better when the cards are down, and you've done what you feel needed doing." The Queen begins to shuffle the cards, sliding them through her hands with quick, practiced ease. "Sin applies even after death, Rose Marshall, and if he's what's held you here all this time, disposing of him could very easily send you to your eternal rest. Were you in a state of grace when you died? Do you think you're in a state of grace now?"

"I don't know." There's something about the cards that pulls my eyes to them, making it difficult to look away. "I don't think it matters, really. He has to stop. It's gone on for too long now."

"Longer than you think; you weren't the first. You weren't even the first from Buckley." She stops shuffling, sets the cards between us, and looks at me. "Ask your questions, Rose Marshall, and we'll see what we can see."

I swallow hard, and ask her, "How do I stop Bobby Cross?"

"Some men don't need introductions, do they?" The first card is flipped, revealing a picture of a sleek black muscle car with red headlights racing along a midnight road. I can't tell the make or model, and I don't need to; I know what this represents.

"The Chariot," she says, voice sweet as dandelion wine. "Robert Cross loved to drive. He loved the speed, and the thrill of the chase, even when all he chased was the wind. He chased that wind all the way to Hollywood, all the way to the silver screen. They called him Diamond Bobby. Some people say James Dean died the way he did because he was chasing the ghost of Bobby Cross, trying to catch up with a legend." Her eyes dart up toward me, gaze piercing and cold. "You know the truth in that, don't you?"

I don't speak. I don't need to. The Queen quirks the smallest of smiles and flips a second card. This one shows a little girl with hair the color of late-summer wheat standing in front of an old-fashioned movie theater. "The roles came fast and the lines came easy, and still he kept racing to catch up with the next big thing, the next thing that could prove to be worth chasing. They said he'd be one of the greats. But he was getting older, and he was afraid."

"Everybody gets older," I say. Everybody who lives to have the chance. I've watched my family grow old and die, leaving me alone in the world, and I'm still sixteen, and I'm still here, and it's all because of Bobby Cross.

"Age may come for us all, but there are ways to beg indulgence." She turns a third card, and there's the truck stop on the Ocean Lady, neon bright and seeming to glow even when it's only ink on paper. Her fingers caress the image ever so lightly, like they might caress a lover. "He came to the King of the Routewitches in the summer of 1950, a living, breathing man whose need and desire burned bright enough to set him on the path of the Atlantic Highway. He was no routewitch, no ambulomancer or trainspotter. He was just a man. That's why, when he walked this far and begged for audience, his request was granted."

My stomach lurches with the sudden need to lose what little I'd managed to eat in the bar. "Bobby Cross made his bargain with the routewitches?"

"No." Her answer is sharp, silk circling steel, and she raises her head to glare at me. "Not only ghosts are allowed to come to us for answers, and the road answers the questions it decides deserve response. Bobby Cross asked the King how he could live forever, and the King sent him to the crossroads, where bargains can be made, if you're willing to pay them. He made his own choice, and he made his own deal. The King did only as the road bid him, and he paid for that obedience. When next the time that the crown might be passed came around, our King removed himself from the throne, and passed his regency on to me. Place no blame without the knowledge to support it."

"But Bobby—"

"Routewitches are born in the daylight and live in the twilight. We die in the midnight, and the ghostroads are the closest thing we have to a true home. Without them, the Ocean Lady will not open Her arms or Her heart to us, and we wither and die. Who has once worn the crown and sets it aside is no longer welcome on the ghostroads." The Queen's gaze remains coldly challenging. "When our King realized what he'd allowed by answering Bobby's question, he exiled himself by passing the crown along. He died in the daylight. He died alone. He has been more than punished for his sins."

I want to argue with her. I want to list off the names of Bobby's victims. My own name would be at the head of that list. I don't say a word.

The Queen gives a small, sharp nod and turns another card, two roads crossing in the desert night. "Have you been to the crossroads?"

"Yes," I whisper. I wish that weren't true. But I made no bargains there; I sold no souls. Not even my own.

"Then you understand. When you go to the crossroads, you take your chances with the bargain you'll be offered. There's no backing out once you begin. Bobby Cross requested eternal youth, time to race every road he could, and something came up out of the deepest levels of the midnight and granted him his heart's desire."

Bobby Cross rode out into the desert one night, following another successful movie premiere in a string that seemed like it would go on forever, and he was never seen again. There was no body, no wreck, nothing but some skid marks cutting across the pavement, and the disappearance of the greatest star of an age. Had he managed to drive into the twilight, where the cameras couldn't find him, after making his bargain?

I was starting to believe that he had. I swallow, and ask, "So what was the catch? Nothing's free. Not when it comes from the midnight. Not when it comes from the crossroads."

"Clever little ghost." She turns another card, and my stomach lurches again, dinner demanding the right to make a return appearance. The likeness is so exact that it could have been painted from a photograph, sixteen-year-old girl with her wheat-colored hair lightened by lemon juice, wearing a green silk gown that was risqué once, and now seems almost hopelessly old-fashioned. Sixteen-year-old girl with wide, trusting brown eyes, and all her life ahead of her.

If only I'd stayed home that night. If only I'd waited for Gary to call, to tell me why he was so late. If I could take it back I would, all of it, every second of that night and all the nights since, all the time that slipped away since the night that I looked in the mirror and saw the girl whose face is painted on the card.

"Eternal life is an easy thing to grant. All it takes is convincing the ghostroads that a person is already dead, while leaving them among the living. I could do it, if I had time enough, and reason, and wanted to anger the Ocean Lady. But eternal youth . . . now that's a harder race to run." She turns another card. This time the image shows a broken mirror, with blood staining the cobweb maze of shards at its center. "If Bobby wants to stay young enough to enjoy his side of the bargain, he has to do things. Things that might not seem so pleasant."

"You mean he has to kill people."

The Queen of the Routewitches smiles as she takes her hands away from the cards and opens the bottle of wine. The sharp, overly-sweet smell of cheap port fills the trailer. "I mean that it's time we discussed the topic of payment."

Nothing's free in the twilight; everything's an exchange. Sweet-talking someone out of their jacket for a few hours of stolen-back life. Preventing one accident at the cost of causing another. I don't know why I thought for half a heartbeat that dealing with the Queen would be different. "I think I left my wallet in my other coffin," I say, as drily as I can.

"We don't deal in money here." The Queen offers the wine bottle across the table, eyes fixed unwaveringly on mine. "A favor, Rose Marshall. That's all I'll charge you for your answers. One day, one of mine will come to you, and ask you to do something. Refuse, and the hands of my people will be set against you until such time as you run these roads no longer. Agree, and your debt is paid."

"I can't agree to every single thing I'm asked to do just because the person asking might be 'one of yours,'" I protest.

"The one who comes to claim the favor will bring proof that they speak for me," she replies, smooth and calm. "All you have to do is what you're asked."

"I won't kill anyone."

"Pretty little ideals for a ghost with nowhere else to turn. Do your scruples extend to Bobby, or has he forfeited his right to live?" The Queen smirks, utterly amused, utterly patient. She knows she has the upper hand here. God help me, so do I. "Agreed. You won't be asked to kill anyone, or deliver anyone to any fate they have not earned through their own actions. If these requests are made of you, our bargain is done, and you owe me nothing."

If there's a catch here, I can't see it. I'm tired. I really don't know where else to turn. It was a whim that set me on the Ocean Lady . . . but it was a whim that's been a long damn time coming, and it's time that this was done. "A favor for my answers," I agree. "I'll do it."

"I thought you might." She continues to hold out the bottle, clearly waiting for me to take it. "Go ahead. Have a drink."

The wine is sweet enough to be cloying; it burns the back of my throat, setting my head spinning in an instant. The Queen pulls the bottle away, taking a drink of her own before she sets it aside, and says, "So we have bargained and so we are bound, Rose Marshall of Michigan, Shadow of Sparrow Hill Road. May the Ocean Lady keep our words in safety."

"That and a buck-fifty will get me half a cup of coffee," I gasp, trying to swallow away the burning in my throat. "How do I stop Bobby Cross?"

"The eternal life is his, to do with as he chooses, but the eternal youth is centered somewhere closer to the road." This time, the card she turns shows an odometer, with the mileage set at zero. "As long as his car is fed and tended, he stays young and strong—strong enough to keep racing, keep running, and keep his part of the bargain."

My skin is living-warm, and the Queen's trailer is well-heated, but I shiver all the same. I can't help it. I've been chasing Bobby for years, and running from him for even longer, and I know all about the bastard's car. I know what he feeds the damned thing.

Bobby Cross' car runs on the souls of those who die in his vicinity.

"He doesn't actually have to kill them himself, as long as they're fresh; the bodies can't be in the ground more than a day before he reaches them. And he doesn't exactly need to run them off the road, although he enjoys that part. What he does need to do is harvest those souls from a very specific class of the dead. Ghosts are common. Specific *types* of ghost are rare. There are so many of you out there, dying so many kinds of death, that sometimes catching the ghost you want can border on impossible. Bobby's car needs ghosts of the road to keep running, and to keep him young."

"And death on the road is the best way to get us," I say, very softly.

"Unless you're a routewitch, yes," she says, and the look she gives me is level and calm. "Routewitch ghosts are always road ghosts. It's the last gift the road can give to us. So he picks his victims carefully, and he runs them off the road when they seem most likely to leave a shade behind. After that—"

I hold up my hand. "I know what happens after that." I'm not always fast enough, that's what happens after that. I don't always see the accident coming in time, I'm not always in the right place, they don't always believe me before the time runs out and I have to turn and run. Bobby's still out there, because I'm not always good enough to save them, even after they're dead. "How do I *stop* him?"

"You have to take his car from him." The Queen of the Routewitches looks at me calmly. "Separate the two of them, and age will catch up with him. He'll live, but he won't be able to stalk the ghostroads any longer. Not without his car to carry him."

"Is that all?"

"It's harder than it sounds."

"I'll believe that. If it were easy, I'd have done it by now." I rub my arms, trying to warm myself back up. "Just take his car away, huh?"

"Yes. As for the how, well . . ." She smiles again. "I think we can help you with that."

Tattoos and piercings are the only things I can't fake when I change my clothes and shift my hair around to suit the places that my travels take me. I can do clip-on jewelry, magnetic nose studs, fake belly button rings, but nothing that actually changes the body that I died with. That sort of thing was a lot less common when I was still among the living. My mother told me once that she'd die before she saw any daughter of hers scribbled on like a carnival hoochie dancer.

Good thing she's been dead for a long time.

The room the Queen leads me to has been turned into a makeshift tattoo parlor, with white sheets on the walls and a pillow on the narrow wooden table. One of the younger routewitches—a boy who looks no more than ten—stands next to it with a tattoo artist's full kit spread out on a folding TV tray next to him.

"This is Rose, Mikey," she says. "She's the one we were talking about."

He nods earnestly. "Evening, ma'am," he says, and his accent is Midwestern, and out of date by at least thirty years. No one here is what they seem to be. "It's a pleasure to finally meet you."

"Same here, Mikey," I say. I look to the Queen, unsure what the etiquette is here.

She smiles. "Get up on the table, Rose, and let Mikey work. He knows what you need to have done. The Ocean Lady's agreed to let you carry your protection with you when you leave here." She must see the hesitation in my face, because she puts her hands against my cheeks and says firmly, "Trust me. We know we're to blame. We want Bobby stopped as much as you do."

So I get onto the table and stretch out on my stomach, eyes turned steadfastly toward the wall. The boy Mikey pulls up my dress, begins wiping something cool across my back. This is not what I expected when I set out to walk the Atlantic Highway.

The Queen of the Routewitches circles the table, crouches down next to me, and says softly, "The one who comes to claim the favor will tell you that I sent her, and give you my name."

"What is it?"

"Apple," she says, and I know where the shadows in her eyes came from—a town whose name means "Apple Orchard," a place where the whole damn country fed ghosts into the darkness—and then the needle bites my skin, and like Sleeping Beauty with the spindle, I don't know anything anymore.

The Old Atlantic Highway ran from Calais, Maine to Key West, Florida. I wake up at the Key West end of the road, sprawled in a truck stop parking lot, back in the jeans and tank top that I wore when I started walking the Ocean Lady in the first place. I'm chilled to the bone, back among the dead, but the small of my back aches like it hasn't caught on to that fact just yet. It hurts like I'm still among the living.

I climb to my feet and start for the diner, making small adjustments in my appearance as I go, fitting my looks to my environment. Time to see if I can't talk someone out of a sweater and a plate of bacon, and maybe see if I can't get a fry cook on his way off-shift to strip me down and tell me what the Queen of the Routewitches ordered written on my skin.

Look out, Bobby Cross. Your diamond days are coming to an end, and I'm coming for you at last.

Book Three

Scary Stories

Now she's a pretty little dead girl in a coup de ville,
And she's looking for a drag race up on Dead Man's Hill,
And if you've got a brain, boy, you'd better drive on by (bye-bye, bye-bye!).
Because she looks real sweet and she smiles real nice,
But you'd better take some well meant good advice:
If you race with Rose, then you're probably gonna die.

—excerpt from "Pretty Little Dead Girl," as recorded by the Rosettes.

. . . It was a hot summer night, and these two teenagers, see, they were parked up on Dead Man's Hill. Now, everyone in town knew you didn't want to park on Dead Man's Hill if you didn't have to, because the place was haunted. Only this girl was new in town, and she said she didn't believe in ghosts, and any boy who wanted to take her out should be man enough not to be afraid of some little urban legend. Maybe he would have said thanks but no thanks, only she was totally hot, right, and everyone said she put out. So he told her he didn't believe in ghosts either, and she was like, prove it, and he was like, how, and she was like, take me to Dead Man's Hill.

Yeah, she was a real idiot.

Anyway, right around midnight, they're, like, getting real hot and heavy—if you know what I mean—and he's thinking, score, I'm going to get all the way tonight. And then there's this noise out in the woods. Not like, screaming, or chains, or anything, but like, music. This real old-timey big band stuff, like they used to play at school dances back in the olden days. The chick, she's like, what the hell? And the dude, he looks out the window, and there's this girl, right, this gorgeous stacked blonde in like, a tight little green dress, and she was all, come on, let's dance, and he got out of the car, and she led him into the trees.

They found the chick's body still in the car, only it was all burned up and gross, like she'd been in a wreck or something, even though the car was parked the whole time.

The dude's body was never found.

Don't go up on Dead Man's Hill, man. The Phantom Prom Date's real. And she will really fuck you up.

—transcribed from a recording of Chris Hauser,
Buckley High Class of '12.

2013
The Devil in the Wind

THE SECRET OF the palimpsest skin of America is that every place is different, and every place is the same. I guess that's probably the true secret of the entire world, but I don't have access to the world. All I have is North America, where the coyotes sing the moon down every night and the rattlesnakes whisper warnings through the canyons. Here the daylight, the twilight, and the midnight are divided and divided again into thousands upon thousands of realities that never seem to touch—barely even seem to exist in parallel—while secretly they're like horny teenage lovers who can't keep their hands off of each other. They're stealing kisses at the drive-in, the midnight girls with their daylight boys; they're slipping love notes to their twilight sweethearts, they're telling lies to keep their friends from ever figuring out. They're ripping holes in the world every day, every hour, every *second*, and they're doing it because people are just people, no matter what onion-skin level of the world they think of as their home. People are just people, and people don't like being fenced in.

The true secret of the skin of America is that it's barely covered by the legends and lies it clothes itself in, sitting otherwise naked and exposed. It's a fragile thing, this country and this world of ours, and the only thing it can do to protect itself from us is lie.

Things that happen in the daylight echo all the way down to the midnight. It works the other way, too. What happens in the midnight will inevitably make itself known in the daylight, given enough time to echo through the layers, to pass hand to hand down all those chains of secret lovers. What happens in the dark always shines through into the light.

There are times when I wish we weren't all so good at forgetting that everything is connected to everything else. Because those are the times when people get hurt.

The itching at the small of my back is a low, constant burn, the sort of thing that hasn't been a problem since that hot June night when a man who was neither living nor dead ran me off the road at the top of Sparrow Hill. My car went up in flames, my body went with it, and things like the itch of healing flesh ceased to be my problem. Try telling my back that. It's been itching for three weeks now, ever since the Queen of the North American Routewitches decided that dying in the 1950s shouldn't deny me the right to have a tramp stamp tattoo of my very own.

I squirm against the seat of the battered El Camino that's currently devouring miles along I-75 North, the highway that runs between Key West and Detroit. I'll hop out when we hit the Michigan state line, catch another ride, and make my way toward Buckley Township. Tommy passes through there every few weeks. He can give me a ride along the ghostroads to the Last Dance, where Emma can hopefully tell me what the hell the sore spot on my skin really means. Hopefully. Fifty years dead and gone, and I'm still no better at some aspects of this ghost shit than I was the night Bobby pushed me into the ravine.

I squirm again, attracting the attention of the man behind the wheel. I try to turn my squirm into a seductive wiggle, smiling at him from under coyly lowered lashes. I couldn't tell you his name if you paid me, but I've met his kind before. He'll keep me in the car as long as I don't make trouble, or until we hit the state line. Then he'll put his hand on my thigh and ask whether I want to make a few bucks to help me get wherever it is I'm going. I'll tell him the ride's worth more than the money, and things will proceed from there. Same dance, different partners.

I was a virgin when I died, and I lost my virginity shortly after. There's a sort of weird irony to that, because I really don't remember why I thought it was so important for me to stay "pure." I just wanted to be loved. I still do, I guess, but it isn't an option anymore, so I have sex with strangers in truck stop parking lots and rest stop bathrooms in exchange for the life they let me borrow and the rides they're willing to give me. It's not a living—not exactly—but it's the only thing I've got, and that makes it good enough for me.

The smile didn't do the trick. The man looks at me oddly, brow furrowed, like he's no longer sure what I'm doing in his car. I know that look, too. That's the look a man gives a girl when he picked her up hoping for sex without strings, and has suddenly realized that sex without strings isn't always a good idea. I don't normally get *that* look until after the fucking ends, when they decide that "a pretty girl like you" who does the things I'll do must be nothing but a whore. Styles change, music gets hard to listen to, and hemlines bounce up and down like kids on a trampoline, but hypocrisy is the one thing that never goes out of style.

"Where did you say you were going again?" he asks, sudden suspicion in his words.

I bite back a sigh before it can get away from me, trying one more smile as I reply, "Toward Detroit. I gotta get to my aunt's place before Sunday, or she'll call my folks and tell them I'm late. They'd be pissed if they found out I went to Florida for Spring Break, you know?" It helps that I'm sweet sixteen forever, a dewy-eyed peaches-and-cream girl, no matter what I do to myself. Death has its privileges.

But something about me is bothering the driver, and whatever I'm trying to sell, he's not buying. The car slows as he eases off the gas, navigating us toward the side of the road. "I misunderstood. I'm not going that way after all."

He's lying. I know he's lying, and he knows I know he's lying, and it doesn't matter, because there's not a damn thing I can do about it. He's the one with the car, and he knows I'm not carrying any weapons, because my outfit leaves me nowhere to hide them. Bikini top, cut-off shorts, rainbow-stripe socks: the picture of a party girl trying to get home before she's missed. He never asked what I was doing in Key West without a bag. They never do.

"Oh," I say, letting my smile slip away into confusion. "I—I'm sorry? Did I say something wrong? I'm just trying to get home." That's the hitcher's classic line, but it's too late for the classics; I can see it in his eyes.

The car drifts to a stop on the shoulder of the highway, and I step out before he can ask for his jacket back. Once I'm out of the car, he'll have to decide whether it's worth pursuing me. They almost never take that risk. He's like all the others, because he doesn't say a word as he leans across the seat, slams my door, and hits the gas, leaving me alone, too-warm and still healing, on the side of the road.

Sighing, I stick out my thumb and start walking. Another ride will come along eventually. Another ride always does.

The best thing about having a jacket is the way it makes me live again, at least until the sun comes up the next morning—dawn to dawn, that's the longest a borrowed life can last. The worst thing about having a jacket is the way it makes me live again, especially when it's the middle of the afternoon in the middle of Georgia, and the sun is beating down like it has a personal grudge to settle. The novelty of sweating wore off an hour ago. I wipe my forehead as I trudge along the median, giving serious thought to taking off the jacket and letting myself drop into the twilight, where I may be cold, and hungry, and itchy, but at least I won't be broiling.

The bottle-green Ford Taurus that just blazed past slows, hazard lights coming on as it pulls off to the side of the road. I tug up the collar of the jacket to make it look a little less ill-fitting and break into a jog.

It's a middle-aged car, with a dent in the passenger side door deep enough to use as a punch bowl. The man behind the wheel looks like he's in his late twenties, sandy hair, brown eyes behind wire-rimmed glasses. He lowers the window as I come jogging up, and asks the question that begins this ritual—a question that pre-dates cars, and highways, and even the United States of America:

"Where are you heading?"

Something about the honesty of his expression pulls the real answer out of me before I have time to consider: "Buckley Township, up in Michigan."

"I've never heard of it."

That's why honest answers are a bad idea. Name big cities, major thoroughfares—places people know. You're more likely to get a ride if the driver believes you're heading for a real place. "From here, you just drive toward Detroit." I muster a smile. "Please? I'll go as far as you'll take me." I don't tell him any stories, don't try to sell him any lies. I'm too tired and too hot for that. I just wait.

That seems to be the right approach, for once. After a moment, he nods, leaning over to unlock the door. "Hop in," he says. "I can get you a good chunk of the way there."

"Thanks," I say, hooking the door open and sliding into the smooth, well-worn embrace of the front seat. "Thanks a lot."

"Don't mention it," he says. The engine starts and we pull away. I allow myself to relax, trying to ignore the sweat trickling between my breasts and the constant itching on my back. Maybe this day won't be so bad after all. I've got a coat; I've got a ride; there's even the chance I'll be able to talk the driver into pulling off somewhere for a milkshake and a cheeseburger. You try being dead for fifty years and see if you can describe a better day.

So why do my nerves feel like they're on fire, and why do I feel like I'm missing something?

The driver stays silent until we're back in the flow of traffic, moving through the sea of station wagons, pickup trucks, and sport cars. Then he glances over, light glinting off his lenses, and asks, "So what's your name?"

His accent is familiar, all the flat plains and open spaces of Michigan tucked into his vowels and hidden in his consonants. He sounds like home. "Rose," I say—and since this is a day for honesty, I add, "Rose Marshall."

"Nice to meet you, Rose. I'm Chris." His smile is as quick and bright as the light that glinted from his glasses. "I'm heading for Detroit, so I guess I can get you most of the way to Buckley. You have family there?"

"I used to." My own accent is tissue-thin and faded from the road; I could be from any part of the country or every part of the country at the same time. I offer a smile of my own, and add, "I grew up there."

"Heading home?"

"Something like that." He's the kind of man I would have liked when I was alive. I can tell that already. He isn't looking at me like I'm an adventure he can have and brag to his friends about; he's looking at me like I'm a real person, just as alive and important as he is. He's wrong about at least part of that. It's still nice to see.

Chris nods. "Well, then, Rose, let's see if we can get you home."

It's a much nicer day when viewed through a car window, flashing by at a speed feet can never match—the speed my hitchhiker's heart tells me the world was meant to move at, miles turning into dust and memory behind us. The heat is no match for the air conditioning, which cools the sweat from my skin and leaves me grateful for the coat I'm wearing. I sort of wish I had some pants instead of my coquettish party girl cut-offs, but my clothes turned solid when I donned the coat, and taking it off would give me a whole new set of troubles.

My first impression of Chris turns out to be the right one. He's the kind of man who picks up a hitchhiker not because he wants something, but because he doesn't want to see a girl walking alone along the highways of America. He makes polite conversation and halfway funny jokes, the kind that get funnier the longer you think about them. I realize after we've been driving for about half an hour that I like him even though I didn't meet him while I was among the living. That's rare, these days, when hitchhikers are viewed as either predators or victims looking for a wolf to take them down.

"So what brings you this way?" asks Chris—a question with no good answer, since "I'm trying to reach a diner that's only accessible to the dead, so I can grill a *beán sidhe* friend of mine named Emma on what the hell is wrong with me" isn't likely to go over well.

"I was visiting friends," I say, as vaguely as I can. The idea of calling the Queen of the North American Routewitches a friend is ludicrous, but it's easier than telling the truth. "I'm just heading home."

"No car?"

"I don't have my license yet." That's a lie, although I'm sure my license technically expired when I did. Oh, I miss driving; miss the feeling of my own wheels burning down those miles, turning those roads into history and those horizons into possibilities . . . I shake myself out of it, saying, "I'll be able to get one this fall."

"Hitchhiking isn't exactly safe."

That's a line I've heard before. I flash him a smile that's more sincere than it might be, and ask, "What is, anymore?"

He laughs. He's still laughing when we go around a bend in the highway and I forget all humor; forget the sweet chill of the air conditioning, forget the itching in my back. All I can remember—all I can think about or know—is the taste of lilies and ashes, overwhelming the world of the living in a veil of mourning yet-to-be. It's too thick to be coming on this fast, like a hurricane blowing out of nowhere and turning a blue sky black with bruises. But here it is, heavy and hard and thick enough that, for a moment, I can't breathe.

There's only one thing in my world that can bring on the taste of inevitable tragedy like this, and it's the thing I'm not prepared to deal with. Not now, not here, not with the ink still drying underneath my skin and a man I like enough to save sitting in the driver's seat.

"What's wrong?" asks Chris, seeing the sudden tension in my face, the sudden whiteness of my complexion.

"N-nothing," I say, taking shallow breaths to filter out the cloying lily taste of the air. "Nothing at all."

The sky on the ghostroads is black with the shadow of an onrushing storm, and there's nothing I can do to get out of its path.

Bobby Cross is coming.

The Ghostroads, 1955.

I've been on the ghostroads for three years. I know how to take substance from a borrowed coat, how to beg a ride from a stranger, how to fall from the daylight into the twilight. I can't control my movement from the twilight to the daylight—it happens or it doesn't, according to some pattern of forces I don't understand yet—but the older hitchers promise me I'll learn, if I can keep to the roads long enough.

That's the big concern, the one shared by every hitcher I meet: the fear that I won't last long enough to learn the things I need to know. I'm dead. I should be nineteen years old, I should be burning rubber out of Buckley, heading for a future too big and wide to even imagine. But I'm not. I'm sweet sixteen and cold in the ground, and the last thing I should be worried about is dying. And still . . . I'm still afraid.

The man who ran me off the road is named Bobby Cross. He's not dead, but he runs the ghostroads like we do. They say he can cross between levels with a thought, burn rubber from the midnight to the daylight without making any of the usual stops or payments. They say he doesn't follow the rules of the living or the dead—and they say he eats ghosts, rips us out of the world and turns us into nothing but the scent of incense on the wind. That's why he ran me off the road to begin with. He was hungry, and he looked into my living heart and saw a meal that just needed preparation.

He has my scent, knows the shape of my soul and the nature of my death. I'm the ghost that got away, and he'll take me if he can. That's what the older hitchers tell me, and I believe them. I don't know who listens to the prayers of the dead—Hades or Persephone or some other screwed-up ghost god I didn't pay attention to in English class—but I pray a lot these days. O Lord who art probably not in Heaven, deliver me from men who've killed me once and would kill me again, if I gave them the chance. O Lady, hallowed be thy name, get me the hell out of here.

Please. Deliver me from evil and deliver me from darkness, and leave me on the ghostroads for a thousand years if that's what it takes to pay for my sins, but please. Deliver me from the arms of Bobby Cross.

Georgia, 2013.

The second shock of Bobby's approach comes hard on the heels of the first one, the smell of wormwood and gasoline laying itself across the lilies and ashes until it almost washes them away. My teeth snap shut, my back arching in a shocked, involuntary motion that makes my tattoo burn like fire. Bobby isn't just coming, he's here, he's *here*, he's within a mile of us, and the power of his presence is enough to blur the lines of the accident ahead—I can't see the shape of it, can't see whether there's a way for me to avoid it. He's too big and too loud, and too damn *strong*. Right now, I can't tell the victims from the bystanders, and the fact of my failure burns.

Chris practically radiates concern as he tries to watch me and the road at the same time, only a lifetime of good driving habits keeping him from veering onto the shoulder. Poor bastard. He tries to do a favor for a pretty girl on the highway, and what does he get? Some chick having what looks like a seizure in his passenger seat.

He can't know that I'm fighting my own urge to flee, to drop down to the deepest levels of the twilight and let him handle what's ahead of us alone. The coat I'm wearing gives me life until I choose to give that life away, and for his sake—because he was kind to me, because I have to stand and fight once in a while, or I'll forget how to do anything but run—I won't let go. Not until I know what Bobby's here for.

Not until I know whether Chris can be saved.

"Rose?" It isn't the first time Chris has said my name, but it's the first time I've *heard* it, and hearing is enough to snap me back into my own head. The lure of the ghostroads fades, becoming less urgent. "Rose, are you okay? Do we need to stop?"

We need to *run*, run so far and fast that Bobby Cross will never find us. But I can't say that. Running might be what brings the accident on. So I swallow the words, force myself to settle in my seat, and answer, "No. I mean no, I'm not okay, and no, I don't need you to stop.

Not yet. Maybe next time there's a rest area? I think I need some water." Some water, an exorcism kit, and a priest or two would be more like it. Too bad they don't sell those at the Gas-N-Go.

"Deal," says Chris—and he sounds like he means it, like he'll go inside with me instead of promising to wait in the car and then blazing out of the parking lot the second my back is turned. He's a nice guy. That just makes all this worse, and I find myself hoping, hoping *hard*, that Bobby is ahead because he, like any natural disaster, sometimes strikes without warning, and not because he's on my trail again.

The first shock is past; I'm beginning to feel my way into the accident ahead. It's a big one; eight cars, at the very least, and death enough to keep the *beán sidhe* busy and the doom-crows satiated for years. That must be why Bobby's here. An accident this large is like an all-you-can-eat buffet for him, and the menu will feature all the finest dishes. Not everyone who dies on the road leaves a ghost behind, but enough do . . . and enough of those ghosts are shaped by the road to make them his chosen fuel.

I take a breath and hold it until my lungs ache before letting it slowly out again. The whole time, I'm digging deeper into the accident ahead, trying to feel where it ends and we begin. We're five miles out, which is good. It's between us and the next exit, which isn't. If Chris were less of a nice guy, this is where I'd say something lewd, suggest he pull off and take me into the trees to pay for my passage—but I know his type well enough to know that sort of thing won't work. If I try it, he might leave me by the side of the road, which solves the question of how we're getting *me* away from Bobby, but leaves him undefended.

Chris won't stand a chance if he drives alone into what's ahead. He's a part of it, my nice guy; I can smell it now. The car is filled with the scent of lilies, too strong to be just a warning. They're a premonition. Maybe I can stop Chris from dying, and maybe I can't, but if I leave him here, nothing will protect him from Bobby. There won't be any rest stop; the accident is too close, and the taste of ashes is too strong.

"Could we maybe slow down a little?" I ask, doing my best to look sick but-not-that-sick, unsettled by the heat and the speed and the road, but not quite into the territory of serious illness. It's a difficult masquerade, and not one I have much familiarity with.

Maybe it helps that it's not entirely a lie; I really *am* feeling sick to my stomach, and the pain in my back is bad enough that it feels like my tattoo is trying to burrow all the way down to my spine. Chris nods, easing back on the gas. "Sure, Rose," he says. "Just let me know when you're feeling better, okay? Are you sure that we don't need to stop?"

"Not yet," I say, and smile wanly.

It's the smile that does it. Chris nods again, fully accepting what I'm telling him. I wish I didn't have to lie to him like this. While he's among the living, it's not like I have a choice.

He's still looking at me when we come around the bend, moving slower than we were, but not slow enough, and the taste of ashes and lilies takes everything away even before Chris starts swearing, hauling hard on the steering wheel, tires finding no traction on asphalt slick with oil and rough with bits of broken glass and broken futures. He's shouting, and the air stinks like burning rubber, and someone's screaming, and I think it's me—

And he's lost control of the car. He doesn't know it yet, but the car does. She's trying to help, tires straining for purchase, engine screaming with the effort of survival. She's too young, the bond between them too fragile, and in the end, she's just a machine, barely aware enough to know that she's about to—

And the smell of wormwood is heavy over everything, the *stink* of it, like a corpse unembalmed and left to rot by the side of the road, but that's what he is, isn't it? Just a corpse that won't lie still, a corpse that makes more corpses, zombie dragster, bastard son of the silver screen. Bobby Cross is here, Bobby Cross is *coming*—

And I'm wearing a coat, and I realize too late what that means, what the onrushing wall of twisted steel that used to be cars means if we hit it while I have this coat on—

—and we slam, hard, into the segmented body of the great black beast called "accident," and everything is blackness, and the smell of burning.

The Ghostroads, 1965.

I've been on the ghostroads for thirteen years. Long enough to see my classmates marry, start families of their own, put the yearbooks on the shelf and forget the girl who starred on her very own page in her Junior Year, the one titled "In Memoriam." Long enough to see my boyfriend graduate. He saw me once, when I was young and careless, and it broke something deep inside him, in the space where mourning lives.

Long enough to learn to slip between the twilight and the daylight like a bride slips between the sheets on her wedding night; long enough to learn what it means when I touch a trucker's hand and taste ashes, when I flag down a ride and smell lilies on the wind. Hitchers aren't death omens, but we're psychopomps, if we want to be. "It can make you crazy," says one of the older hitchers, a lanky man who goes by "Texas Bill," whose eyes contain a million miles of desert road. "All those lives, all those deaths—leave them, Rose. Find another ride, and keep your sanity."

Emma at the Last Dance (which is the Last Chance sometimes, they tell me, and those are the times where you need to be wary and beware) says something different. "By the time they hear me singing, it's too late," she says, and she sounds sadder than any living soul should sound—but she's not really a living soul, is she? The rules are different for the *beán sidhe*, and I don't know quite how they apply to her. She can see me like she belongs in the twilight. She can loan her coat like she belongs in the daylight. She is what she is. "You get an early warning. You get a chance. That's just this side of a miracle, Rose. You should treat it like one."

I listen to them both, but I've made up my mind, and not because of anything either of them said. No; what made up my mind was a white-haired old trucker who bought me a grilled cheese sandwich and showed me pictures of his sister, of her little house in Florida, the place he was going when he retired. Just four more cross-country runs, he said, and his skin smelled like lilies and ashes, and I knew, even if he didn't, that he was never going to see his sister's little house on the beach. And I didn't help him. I didn't even try. I told him I didn't feel good, ran for the bathroom, and fell back down to the ghostroads, where the dead are the dead, and the living don't look at us that way.

His truck crashed on I-5, blind curve, bad driving conditions, a perfect storm of bad luck and bad decisions. Word in the truck stops is that his body wasn't even recognizable when they pulled it from the cab. That doesn't bother me as much as it would have once—being dead for eight years has given me a very different outlook on death—but what came after is another story. One of the trainspotters was near the place where the crash happened, riding the rails from San Diego to Vancouver, and he came looking for me as soon as he figured out what rail line I was closest to. That's the trouble with trainspotters. They can see the future (sometimes, when they're looking in the right direction), but they're limited in more ways even than the hitchers.

"He came in the stink of wormwood and soured gasoline," said the trainspotter, grabbing my hands. I wasn't wearing a coat. He caught them anyway. Damn wizards. "He came like the wind out of the west, like a crow to the battlefield. He came on black wings of burning rubber and shadow, and he drove his victim as a wolf drives a fawn. He has claimed another soul, Rose Marshall, and you might have stopped him, had you cared enough to rouse yourself to action. Shame, shame on you, shame and a thousand nights of wandering lonely. Shame, and all the sorrows of the road."

"You're a little behind the curve on cursing me," I snapped, and I yanked my hands out of his. The trainspotter looked at me sadly, a thousand miles of broken hearts etched into the lines on his face. I shook my head. "I already have all the things you're wishing on me, and Bobby Cross is not my fault."

"No. He's not. That blame belongs to others. But he *is* your responsibility." And then he turned and walked away. His message had been delivered. I was no longer his concern.

But Bobby Cross was mine—my concern, my responsibility. So let Emma and Texas Bill make their recommendations—it doesn't matter. That man died because I wouldn't help him, and while I might not have saved his life, having me there could have saved him from something worse than death. Maybe Texas Bill is right; maybe trying to change the fates of the living will make me crazy. Right now, I don't care. Bobby Cross is not my fault. If anything, I'm his. That doesn't mean I can sit back and let him rule these roads.

Sometimes, all a dead girl can do is stand up and take responsibility for the things that gather in the shadows.

Georgia, 2013.

One nice thing about being dead: I bounce back a hell of a lot faster than the living do. I open my eyes to find myself sprawled on the asphalt, broken doll cast to the side of the road, with an aching head and skinned patches on my hands and knees. My tattoo is burning like a brand, the pain somehow focusing, rather than distracting me. I manage to lift my head, despite the ringing in my ears, and scan for Chris.

He wasn't as lucky as I was. He's also sprawled on the pavement . . . but he isn't moving. Maybe I'm not that lucky, either; maybe I'm only still moving because being dead makes me harder to kill. My legs won't answer my command to move, and the ringing in my ears is getting worse. It's with relief that I release my hold on flesh and bone, feel my borrowed coat drop through what had been the substance of my body only a moment before, and climb, finally, to my feet.

Things are different here on the edge of the twilight. Black clouds streak the sky like spilled ink, and the broken cars glitter with firefly brilliance in the process of slowly—so slowly!—fading into darkness. People stand near the broken bodies of their cars. Not that many, not one for every driver who must have died in the collision but . . . enough. Only one stands out to my eyes; the one to whom I owe assistance. Chris is standing by his own fallen body, a look of deep confusion on his face, like he can't quite understand. I've seen that look on too many faces, on too many roads. I should give him time to come to terms with what's happened. At the very least, I should give him time to recover from his shock. But the air tastes of wormwood, and there are many things here, on this borderland highway, but what there isn't is *time*.

My skirt rustles against my ankles as I start toward him, the green silk as clean and crisp as it was on the night I wore it for the first—and last—time. The prom gown is no surprise, not here, not with Bobby close enough to taint the shape of the world. The length of my hair is no surprise either, lemon-bleached curls loose against the sides of my neck. The wind that blows around us doesn't touch me. Nothing touches me but the consequences of my own motion. So it goes, when the dead come too close to the day.

"Chris," I say. "Come on. We need to get out of here."

His head comes up, confusion in his eyes. It only deepens as he sees the way I've changed. He picked up a scruffy hitchhiker in a coat two sizes too big for her, and now he's facing a prom princess from an era that ended before he was born. I've slid out of date one inch at a time, and there's nothing I can do about it. "Rose?"

"Yes." I walk faster now, all but running—but I mustn't run, I don't *dare* run. I can't pull him onto the ghostroads without his consent, not this soon after his death, and I definitely can't pull him any deeper into the twilight if he's fighting me. Run and I'll frighten him more than he already is, and if that happens . . . if that happens, he'll be lost forever. No afterlife for Bobby's victims. No second chances for the souls he claims. "Come with me, and I'll explain."

"What—what happened? I lost control of the car . . ." His eyes flick to the body on the asphalt, confusion starting to thin as terror takes its place. "Where did you get that dress? When did it get so dark? What's going *on*?"

I don't have any answers that I can offer to him; not without making things worse than they are right now, and that's saying something, given that he's standing over his own corpse and I'm waiting for the bogeyman to descend. I close the last few feet between us, reaching for his hand. "Please, Chris. We don't have time for this."

"I don't know, Rosie my girl," says the voice behind me. It's cool and crisp, California accent painted over something sweeter and slower, something out of the deep Southern states, where the summer nights are hot and wet, and wise men know the cost of a crossroads bargain. Maybe if he'd stayed at home, he would have known better. Maybe. "There's a case to be made for your having run shy of time some sixty years gone. Can't say I think much of granting you time on top of that just because you got all dressed up for me."

The graveyard chill that sleeps inside me when I cast my coats aside melts away, replaced by a tight, hot ball of fear. I take one more half step forward, until I'm almost touching Chris, and whisper, "Stay behind me. If you value your soul, *stay behind me*."

Chris doesn't say a word, nothing but terror in his eyes. I don't care. Let him be afraid of Bobby; let him be afraid of me. I have other matters to worry myself about. So I turn, squaring my shoulders.

"Hello, Bobby," I say.

And Bobby Cross—Diamond Bobby, Hollywood legend, gone but never, *never* forgotten—smiles.

This is Bobby Cross, has *been* Bobby Cross since that night in 1950 when he drove out of the daylight and into the dark:

Short by today's standards, five foot eight and compact. A dragster's build, the kind of man who makes hearts melt and panties dampen. Dark hair. He used to wear it sleeked and slicked and shaped to within an inch of its life, but not these days; unlike the ghosts he leaves in his wake, Bobby is among the living, and still allowed to *change*. Now it hangs loose and careless, that tousled style that's so popular with the kids I see at the races, or lounging on the beaches. He looks as young as they do, as effortlessly carefree and strong, and it's been long enough since his day that he doesn't even get the "hey, aren't you . . . ?" reactions anymore. I wonder if that stings, down in the blackened depths of the swamp he calls a soul.

It's his eyes that give him away. They aren't remarkable. They're pale brown—plain, even—but something about them makes people take a step back and give him a wide berth. The living aren't meant to see the things he's seen, or ride the roads he's ridden.

The smile that slides across his lips doesn't reach those eyes. He looks me up and down, and offers a cool, "Same old Rosie. You trying to play the hero on me? You should know better. All those years of running away, you're going to make your stand here and now? For *these* people?"

"Got a better idea?" Chris' hand is on my shoulder, and oh, I just met him, and oh, it doesn't matter; he's every driver I couldn't save, and if I don't at least try, I may as well give in right now, because if I don't try, Bobby already has my soul. "Why did you do this? These people didn't do anything to hurt you."

"Why do you take rides when people offer them to you? Why do you take their coats, drink their coffee, suck their cocks?" Bobby's smirk is painful to behold. "We're not so different, Rosie girl, except that I admit what I am—and you, I'm afraid, are about at the end of this road."

"Let them go." I take a step forward, watching Bobby all the while. I'm faster than he is. He's got powers I don't understand and weapons I can't touch, but I'm *faster.* If I can get the ghosts out of here, maybe I can drop into the twilight before he catches hold of me. Maybe. "They're all fresh ghosts. They can't be what you really want. I've got a lot of miles on me."

"What makes you think that makes you worth more, and not less? A lot of things call for virgins in place of whores."

"But the road treasures the things that have traveled the furthest." The thrift store fashion of the routewitches; the battered, duct-taped shoes of the ambulomancers. Distance is just about the only thing that's universally respected on the road.

Bobby's smile this time is slow, dark, and horrifying. Whatever it is he does to the dead, it can't be painless; not if he's looking at me like that. I stand my ground, the tattoo burning hot against my skin. Apple said the tattoo would protect me, that the Ocean Lady was allowing me to take it away because the routewitches feel responsible for Bobby's darkness. I have to believe her. There's no choice; not here, and not now.

"I've been tired of you for decades," he says. "I'll take you and let them go . . . but not, I think, in the order you're hoping for. First you give yourself to me, and then, once I'm sure you're not going to pull any little hitcher 'tricks,' I'll let them go."

The sky is getting darker. I want nothing more, right now, than I want to run. "Why should I believe you?"

"Because, Rosie, darling, you don't have any choice. You can rabbit-run the hell out of here and pray I'm not toying with you—I might be—since if I am, I'll just grab you and take every soul still standing as my due. Or you can surrender, admit that I've won, and wager that I'm a man of his word."

I don't want to. But he's right. I have nothing left to lose; not with Bobby Cross standing right there. "I accept your terms," I say, and hold out my hands. "I'm yours."

I have no coat, no borrowed life to wear, but it's somehow no surprise when Bobby's hand clamps down on mine. A man who feeds on the dead must be able to touch them. Chris says something I can't make out, finally realizing, I suppose, that something more important than his death is happening in front of him. Maybe that's a selfish way of thinking, but if there's proof of existence after dying, I'm it, and here I am, approaching my own ending.

I thought I knew what cold was. I was wrong. Bobby's fingers redefine cold, tell me that every frost and snowfall I've ever known was just the prelude to the main event. Winter radiates from his skin as he tightens his grip and yanks me into an embrace. My skirt tangles around my ankles; I all but fall into his arms.

"So eager," he says. "I always knew you would be." And Bobby folds me in his arms, and lowers his mouth onto mine.

The Ghostroads, 2013.

I've been on the ghostroads for sixty years. The girl I was, the girl Bobby killed, is barely a memory—*I* barely remember her, and I knew her better than anyone. Life was only the beginning. I've seen all the joys America has to offer, walked away from them, and come back to find them transformed to something glorious and new. I've met monsters and danced with gods. It's been a good time, and a bad time, and one hell of an adventure. And I still wish I hadn't died.

He's young, this Florida fry cook, so young that I must seem like some sort of fantasy, the beautiful girl who walks in and says she'll do anything he wants if he'll do her one little favor. Two, really—if he wants to do any of the things his eyes say he's thinking, he'll need to give me a coat. Right now, I think he'd give me a kidney if I asked for it.

"It's . . . it's like this red round ball, like an apple, and flowers all around it. I think lilies, and some sort of funky white flower. I mean, it's pretty, but it's sort of weird, y'know?" His tone turns apologetic. "Most folks get little things when they get tattooed drunk. Like, hearts and birds and the names of their moms. It's probably going to cost a lot to get that lasered off."

"Maybe I won't bother getting it removed." I look over my shoulder at him, smiling as coyly as I can with the itching in my back threatening to drive me crazy. "Is that all you have to say about it?"

"It's pretty," he repeats, like that's the secret password to my pants. "It's all flowers and fruit and shit, but it's pretty. I could take a picture with my phone if you wanted . . ."

"That's okay," I say hurriedly. I show up just fine on camera, and that's the problem: my face never changes, and I don't want to attract the wrong kind of attention. "Pretty" will have to be good enough, for now.

We have sex on the floor of the storeroom after he gives me his coat, and he's enough of a gentleman to let me be on top, and it almost distracts me from the burning in my back, for at least a little while. Time to head to the Last Dance. Maybe Emma knows what the gift the Old Atlantic Highway gave me means.

Maybe I'll ask her after a burger.

Georgia, 2013.

There's a pause. Bobby's hand clamps down on my neck, his arm all but spasming . . . and then he's shoving me away, that same hand going to his mouth. The anger in his eyes is easy to read, and it terrifies me. "You bitch!" he shouts. "What the fuck did you *do?* What the fuck are you trying to pull?"

The tattoo is burning hotter than ever, but it's a good heat, clearing the chill of Bobby's fingers from my skin. I straighten, glancing back to be sure Chris is still there. He is, seemingly rooted to the spot. I'll have to get him to the Last Dance soon, or Emma won't be able to help him get anywhere at all. "I'm not trying to pull anything, Bobby," I say, turning back to my oldest enemy. "I said you could have me. It's not my fault if I'm too much woman for you."

"You *did* something," he spits. "What did you do?"

"To be honest, I have no idea." I take a step forward, gambling everything one more time. It's a gambling sort of day. "Want to try again? I'm still willing."

Bobby snarls. For a moment, he looks like a beast, some monster out of a fairy story, come to drive me back into the dark. "I don't know what good you think this is going to do you. You can't bring these people back to life."

"No. But that doesn't mean that I have to let you have them." I tilt my chin up. A cornered snake is still a snake. "What's it going to be, Bobby? Walk away, or try to figure out just how far I can push this?" I don't even know what "this" is. Hopefully, neither does he.

He snarls again, and spits, "This isn't over." Turning on his heel, he stalks away—away from the accident, away from the shade of Chris, away from *me*.

Seconds trickle by like sentences of execution, and Bobby Cross—the man who killed me once, and would do it again, given half a chance—is gone.

"Deliver me from Bobby Cross," I whisper, and turn to face Chris, who is staring at me with confusion bordering on terror.

"I'm dead," he says.

"Yes," I agree. It seems like the safest option, just now.

"I'm *dead*."

"Yes." I gesture toward the wreckage of his car. "Bobby caused an accident, and you were in his way. I'm sorry."

"Is this your fault? Could you have stopped this?"

For once, I'm grateful to know the answer. "No," I say, and offer him my hands. "I couldn't have stopped it. All I could do was be here when the crash happened, so that I could be the one to get you home."

"Home? But I'm *dead*."

"There are a lot of kinds of home, Chris." I slip my hands into his. His skin is cool—the dead are always cool—but he lacks the chilling, killing cold of Bobby Cross. I suppose that gift is reserved for the men who've sold their souls. "Now come on. You ever hot-wired a car?"

"What? No."

"Good. Then we can begin your afterlife with a little education."

Only one car in the crash was loved enough to leave a ghost behind, a battered pickup truck that's healing by the second, the years wiping away like so much dust. Six more ghosts come out of the wreckage, all confused and shaken and uncertain of the rules that bind them now. I scan their faces, labeling them without really thinking about it—hitcher, homecomer, white lady. Emma can sort them out, help them decide who needs to move on and who wants to find a place in the endless arms of the midnight America.

I twist the wires until the truck gives a purring roar of acceptance, ready to drive us wherever we need to go. I give the crowd one last scan, and say, "I'm Rose Marshall. Some of you may have heard of me—they call me the Lady in the Diner." Murmurs, and shocked expressions. Sometimes it's good to have a reputation. "Now, you can come with me, or you can stay here. I have to warn you that the man who caused this accident may come back, and if you stay, you're on your own."

"Where are you taking us?" shouts one brave shade, hidden somewhere in the crowd.

I allow a smile, feeling the tattoo burn my skin. Chris stands by the passenger side door, ready to let me drive this time. "I'm taking you home," I answer, and that's the truth, that's all the truth they'll ever need. I'm taking them home.

They climb in one and two at a time, these new ghosts of the road. I slide behind the wheel, pat the dashboard for luck, and whisper, "O Lord, who art probably not in Heaven, hallowed be thy name. O Lady, deliver me from darkness, deliver me from evil, and deliver me from Bobby Cross."

"What?" asks Chris.

I shoot him a smile. "Nothing," I say. "Nothing at all."

The wheel fits easy in my hands, and we roll forward, out of the daylight, down into the dark.

2014
Prom Night Sweethearts

THE DEAD KEEP their own calendar. Every ghost is a sovereign nation, unbound by the laws of the living. We have our commonalities—Halloween is universal, for reasons which may seem obvious but aren't obvious at all, once you get below the surface—but on the whole, every one of us marks time in our own way, measuring by the dates that matter to us. Some of them we choose. Some of them we don't. All of them bind us, using our personal laws against us and forcing us to conform to whatever our deaths have made us.

There are holidays on the ghostroads, too. Forgotten holidays, holidays that have slipped between the cracks of the daylight world. The people in the twilight pray to dead gods, building temples to religions that were lost so long ago that no one really remembers what they were. Living faiths have no comfort to offer to the dead, so the dead go seeking comfort from their own. Saint Celia of the Open Hand, who keeps the phantom riders running true along their routes. Danny, God of Highways, whose given name has been forgotten, and who guards the gates between the twilight, the darkness, and the light. There are hundreds of ghost gods on the ghostroads, and their faiths are as faded and tangled as back country roads.

I've met a few of them. I still refuse to believe in their divinity, just as a matter of principle. It doesn't seem to matter, either way. Their worshippers keep their calendars, and the rest of us keep calendars of our own.

Always, of course, there is Hades, Lord of the Dead.

And even when he turns his face away, there is Persephone.

The Last Dance Diner, 2013.

"It's a mistletoe branch surrounded by white lilies and—I think that's white asphodel, actually, which makes a lot of sense, if you think about it." I'm not wearing a coat right now. I'm not wearing a shirt of any kind; it would cover my tattoo, which would defeat the whole purpose of this exercise. Emma's fingers trail beneath the surface of what should be my skin, sending cold shivers through me. I hate being touched by the living when I'm not solid. The fact that Emma isn't technically quite alive doesn't change that.

"Yeah, well, I'm thinking about it, and it doesn't make any fucking sense at all." I'm snapping at her. I know that, and I don't particularly care. "What the fuck is asphodel?"

"It's a flower." She pulls her hand away. "This isn't the kind of asphodel you'd find in a botany textbook. This is white asphodel. *Real* white asphodel, and that only grows in one place."

"Where's that?" I stand, rolling my shoulders and calling my clothes back into existence in the same motion. White tank top again, phantom recreation of the shirt I once borrowed from the only boy I had the chance to love before I died. Gary never wore this shirt, but it's a comfort all the same.

Being dead means never moving on—not all the way. Not until you pass that final exit, and move on from everything.

Emma walks back around the counter, eyes glinting a brief, feline green before she starts dishing up a slice of apple pie. "The Asphodel Meadows in the Greek Underworld. The land of the balanced dead. If you're not good, and not evil, you go there when you die."

"Great, so it's what, a moral judgment?"

"Of sorts." She turns, setting the plate of pie in front of me. "The center of the design is a pomegranate, sliced to show the seeds at the center. I can't be sure, but it looks like there are six seeds missing. It's Persephone's blessing. I think, anyway. It's not like the Lady of the Dead has me on her speed dial."

This is starting to sound like something too good to be true. I don't trust things that seem too good to be true. They never are. "Meaning what, exactly?"

Emma produces a button-down sweater from behind the counter and hands it to me. Coats are the traditional attire of the hitchhiking ghost, but any outerwear will do, providing it belongs to the living. Somehow, Emma manages to count. "Meaning Bobby Cross has no claim on your soul as long as Persephone is tasked with watching you. Not unless you do something monumentally stupid."

I shrug on the sweater before reaching for the pie. "Again, meaning what, exactly?"

"I'll be completely honest with you here, Rose. I'm an Irish death omen and collector of the unquiet dead. I was born when the Roman calendar still looked like a fad that couldn't possibly last. And I haven't got the slightest idea." Emma smiles brightly. "You want a malted before you hit the road?"

"Why the hell not?" I pick up my fork, driving it deep into the flaky piecrust. "Make it a double."

"On the house," says Emma, and her laugh is the sound of church bells ringing in the faraway cathedrals of the dead.

Buckley, Michigan, 2014.

Time runs differently when you're in the twilight. Sometimes, hours there can be minutes in the daylight, or days, or weeks. Once, I spent what felt like a weekend at the Last Dance, bussing tables and bumming cigarettes off one of the cooks, and when I stepped back into the lands of the living, two years had gone slithering by like snakes vanishing into high grass. So it isn't really a surprise when I shrug off the last traces of the ghostroads and find myself in a world where the summer has somehow run backward by more than a month. The trees are lush and green, and the fall that was threatening only hours ago is long, long gone.

I've lost the better part of a year to the twilight. I take a moment to glare at the world before taking another moment to figure out where I am.

It doesn't take long. I'm standing on a long country highway. There's a telephone pole nearby, and on it is a bright orange flyer. "BUY YOUR TICKETS TODAY TO GUARANTEE A WONDERFUL NIGHT!" it screams, in big block letters. Underneath that, smaller, is the legend, "Buckley High School Senior Prom." There's a price—more per ticket than I paid for my dress, once upon a couple of decades ago—and a date.

It wouldn't matter if the date wasn't there, just like it doesn't matter that I don't have a calendar. The dead have their own holy days, their own ways of marking the time that passes after they've passed on, and for me, the holiest of holies is the Buckley High School Senior Prom. It's like Easter. It moves around the calendar, always within a small range, always subject to its own rules . . . but it always comes as the school year is drawing to a close. One big formal dance for girls whose lives won't offer many opportunities for formal dancing; one beautiful night for spiking punch, losing virginities, and living out your dreams. Such big dreams. Real life almost never lives up to the dreams of a senior prom. It tries. It just can't compare.

I've attended thirty senior proms in the years since I died. Five of them were here in Buckley. They're . . . magnetic, I guess is the word. Once I get close, they draw me in, just like a moth being drawn to a bug zapper. Not the most flattering comparison. Too bad it's such an accurate one.

I sigh, leaning over and brushing my fingertips through the paper. Just to test, I try to reach for the ghostroads, and find nothing but shadows. I'm here until the last dance is over, the punch stains have been wiped off the gymnasium floor, and the drunken, giggling cheerleaders have been chased out of the janitor's closet.

"Bully for me," I mutter, before shoving my hands into the pockets of my jeans. It may be the day of the senior prom, but the dance itself is still far enough away that I can wear jeans if I want to, rather than being locked into a homecomer's endless, pointless struggle to get back to a place that isn't there anymore. One eye scanning the road for a ride, I turn and begin trudging my way down the sidewalk. No matter how inconvenient it might be, this is a holy night, and on holy nights, good girls—alive or dead—follow the rites of their religion.

I have one small advantage over the breathing girls of Buckley, the ones for whom tonight will be the first, last, and only senior prom. Unlike them, I don't have to worry about what I'm going to wear. I just have to worry about how many of them will be dead before morning.

On second thought, maybe they should be worrying about that, too.

Buckley Township: where the more things change, the more they stay the same. The town has grown since I lived here, slowly spilling out into the surrounding fields and farmlands. The forest is still mostly intact, the trees standing sentry against intrusion. The lake and the swamp are exactly as they've always been, dangerous, foreboding, and deadly to the unprepared. I used to wonder how many bodies were buried there. Now that I've met a few of the ghosts who haunt the waters of Buckley, I can say with authority that I don't want to know. The land around Buckley has never been tamed, not really, and it doesn't suffer fools lightly, if it suffers them at all.

The storefronts have altered as they strive to keep up with the times, but they still seem to lag behind the outside world, the towns and cities that aren't struggling to survive in the hand of the forest, that aren't trapped under the shade of the nearby hills. It's strange to walk these streets and see signs offering computer repair and cell phone services where the record store and the five-and-dime used to be. Time stops for no one, I guess. There's another Buckley nestled deep down in the twilight, one where it's still 1952, one where all the little details still match the little details hidden in my heart. That's a dead town, a place that only exists because I do—there are no other

Buckley ghosts from my generation still wandering the ghostroads. When I move on, *if* I move on, that dead little town will fade away. Maybe that's not such a bad thing, because this is the real Buckley, this changing, increasingly strange place, and it deserves to be fresher in my mind than its own time-locked reflection.

I'm lost deep enough in my own thoughts that I don't realize that I've managed to walk halfway to the school until the car pulls up next to me, blinker flashing in the brief staccato rhythm that means "You've got a ride" in the secret language of the road. I stop where I am and turn toward the car, a battered old Toyota in that shade of middle-class brown that hides the rust better than just about anything else. The passenger-side window creaks down, revealing a teenage girl with hair almost exactly the color of her car's paint job. I don't get many rides from girls. Something about me says "there but for the grace of God," and they keep their distance.

She has red-and-yellow ribbons in her hair—the Buckley High School colors—and flecks of coppery rust dot the middle-class brown of her eyes. "Get in," she says, with a small lift of her chin. It's more command than request, and I find myself obeying without stopping to think about it. "I'll fill you in on the way."

Prom night isn't like Halloween, when the dead live again, but it's something similar for me, anniversary of my death, pagan ritual in school colors. I can feel solidity falling into my bones like night falling on the forest, turning me physical from the inside out. I slide into the seat, almost taking comfort in the way my feet pass briefly through the floorboard before I pull them back—still dead, still free, at least for the moment. It's too late to run away, but it's too soon for the music to start. "Thanks for the ride," I say, old ritual, new target.

"I was going your way," she replies, with an equally ritual calm, and I realize that I never told her which way I was going. She hits the accelerator, eyes on the road as she adds, "There's a wrap for you in the back. I looked through some of the old yearbooks to make sure I had the right color." I hesitate, and she sighs heavily. "It's just a damn *coat*, okay? You need it if you don't intend to go walking through any walls in the next few hours. I feel more comfortable when I know my passengers are actually gaining some small measure of protection from their seat belts."

"I—wait—*what?*"

"Although I guess if you're dead already, the seat belt thing is sort of a moot point." She stops at the light on Pierce and Robinson—there wasn't a light there when I was alive, just one more sign of how the town has changed—before turning to look at me. "I'd feel better if you were corporeal in my car, okay? And since I'm the driver, I get to choose the radio station and dictate the physical state of my passengers."

The look in her eyes finally snaps into focus. I can't stop myself from frowning as I ask, "You're a routewitch, aren't you? What are you doing in Buckley?" *What are you doing here, on the night of the prom, the one night when I can't cross the city limits or get away? Why did you pick me up?*

What's going on here?

"I was born in Detroit. We moved to Buckley when I was five," she replies, attention going back to the road. "My grandfather was from Buckley, and when my dad died, Mom decided she'd come here to be close to his side of the family. Her side's nothing to write home about. Neither is his, really, but I live with them. I don't have to write."

"Oh." Even routewitches have to come from somewhere, I suppose. I've just never given much thought to where they belong when they aren't running the roads or going home to the arms of the Ocean Lady. I lean over the seat, looking into the back. A wispy strip of pale green silk lies puddled on the upholstery. That familiar jolt of solidity races up my fingers as I pick it up, noting the thin lines of silver embroidery that run through the fabric. It's beautiful, delicate, and a perfect complement to the prom gown I'll be wearing before the night is over.

I settle back into my seat and wind the wrap loosely around my shoulders, feeling gravity settle over me like a shroud. I fasten the seat belt before looking toward the routewitch behind the wheel. Her eyes are still locked on the street beyond the windscreen. I clear my throat, and say, "Um, thanks. For the coat. And the ride. My name's Rose."

She actually laughs at that, the sound easy and clear and eerily familiar. "Oh, I know. You're Rose Marshall, otherwise known as 'the Girl in the Diner,' or 'the Lady in Green.' Personally, I like the local name: 'the Spirit of Sparrow Hill Road.' You're here because this is the anniversary of your death, and whenever you're near Buckley during prom season, you wind up crashing the party."

"How did you—"

"You're here tonight, specifically, because I begged the road to send you. The signs and portents have been crazy ever since the start of the school year. Old lady Martin's cat had a whole litter of kittens with no eyes, and somehow, all the scripts for the senior play got replaced with *Macbeth*. Something seriously major league bad is coming. I wanted at least a little supernatural muscle on our side when things went south."

I blink. "What makes you think I can do anything to help?"

"It's prom night in Buckley, and you're a Marshall. Marshalls always come back to Buckley when they're needed. It's what makes us better than the Healys."

Only one word in that sentence really stands out to me, and I'm repeating it before I take the time to think, voice going a little shrill as I demand, *"Us?"*

"Us," she agrees, and slants a smile my way, a wicked gleam in her eye that I remember seeing, too many times, in the eyes of my big brother. "Hi, Aunt Rose. I'm Bethany. I'm your brother Arthur's granddaughter."

"Of course you are." I slump in my seat, feeling the prom coming closer by the second, while this girl who is blood of my blood drives us toward the high school.

Prom night in Buckley Township. Not exactly the most wonderful night of the year.

The high school hasn't changed nearly as much as the rest of the town. The squat brick buildings still seem to huddle like angry gods in the middle of their parking lots and athletic fields, glowering out over the students who dare to approach. Some people say schools are cathedrals to learning. Not Buckley High. Buckley High is a prison, and the only way to get parole is to keep your grades up, keep your head down, and pray.

Bethany pulls into a spot near the street, using the spreading leaves of the sycamore trees to conceal the car from casual view. "We have about two hours before the dance starts," she says, as she unclasps her seat belt. "I'm on the decorating committee, so I can get us inside now without raising suspicion."

"And the fact that nobody knows me won't be a problem because—?"

"I'll tell them you're my cousin from downstate, and that your folks made me bring you to the prom." She slants a half-amused glance in my direction. "It's not like it's totally a lie. We *are* related, and you *are* from downstate. It's just that you're coming from underground, not points south."

"Dead girl jokes. Oh, yeah, those are my favorite. Almost as much fun as being branded the pity date." I'm still grumbling as I climb out of the car, feeling the hot mugginess of the summer air settle across my skin. Michigan summers. I used to measure out my life in Michigan summers. Now I use them to measure out my death. "Then what? I help you hang streamers, pretend I'm not looking when somebody spikes the punch, and wait to see if some unnamed doom falls on the senior prom?"

"Something like that." Bethany starts walking across the parking lot, cocky little routewitch too young to know how hard the world can hit. I hurry to catch up. My sneakers aren't sneakers anymore; sometime during the ride they became green silk flats. Prom night is starting to exert its hold on me. "Whatever it is, it's going to be bad. I don't think we'll be able to miss it once it starts."

"You are way too vague to be a Marshall."

"And you're way too dead to criticize." She doesn't sound annoyed; more amused, like my complaints are meaningless. In a way, I guess they are. She's a routewitch, and this is her territory now, not mine. It's prom night in Buckley, which means running away isn't an option, and the fact that she's alive means the shots are hers to call. That doesn't mean I have to like it. So I glower at her as we walk across the sun-bleached blacktop, faded white lines that delineate one parking spot from the next crisscrossing like railway tracks under our feet. She thinks we have two hours before the start of prom. I could tell her things about time, the way it bends and twists around the holy moments in your life, but I won't. I don't have the words, and I don't think Bethany has the ears to listen.

"How is Arthur?" I ask, just to break the silence. I'm as solid as ever, but the hair that tickles the back of my neck is longer than it was when I got into the car. Prom night is rushing me on, and as all the other girls get ready, I'm getting ready, too. Whether I want to or not.

"Old. Crotchety. Mean as a snake when he thinks you've crossed him." Bethany's smile is sweet and distant. Maybe I could like her after all. "He took Mom and me in when nobody else wanted anything to do with us. I owe him a lot."

And he's still in Buckley, still breathing. That explains why she's here, little routewitch running a fixed route, like a hamster running in a wheel. She'll strike out on the open road one of these days, but even routewitches know the worth of family. She'll stay until my brother goes.

"Does he know . . . ?" I wave a hand, jade beads rattling against each other as the bracelet on my wrist slides a few inches down my forearm. I wonder what my clothes look like now, whether anyone who happens to be passing by will see a transparent dress sketched over T-shirt and jeans, or whether the reality is already turned the other way around.

"No." Bethany shakes her head, quick, decisive, with no pause for thought. "I tried to tell him once, but he wouldn't let himself hear me. He didn't want to know. I think . . . I think he knows, deep down, that if he listened when I told him about the way the road can sing, if he *believed*, he'd have to believe all those stories about the ghost of Sparrow Hill Road."

Believe that your granddaughter is some kind of witch, believe that your decades-gone little sister has never been allowed to rest.

That wasn't the sort of choice I'd have wanted to make. "Poor Art," I sigh.

"I deal," says Bethany, and then she's opening the door to the Buckley High School gymnasium—when did we finish crossing the parking lot? When did we pass the point of no return?—and stepping onward, into the dark. I hesitate, clinging to the illusion of choice for as long as I can. Bethany looks back at me, eyebrows raised in silent question, and with another sigh, I step forward, following her into the darkness.

Prom themes are the universe's way of getting us ready for the endless indignities it plans to heap on our heads, like fashion trends and bridesmaid dresses. No one ever seems to admit to being the one who thought that "Rain Forest Romance" or "A Dance on Mars" was a good idea. They just follow the mysterious sketches that tell them to put the streamers here, the crepe-paper flowers there, and the endless buckets of glitter everywhere that glitter shouldn't go.

Whoever chose this year's theme wasn't feeling particularly creative. The Buckley Buccaneers will be celebrating the magic of prom night in a gymnasium transformed into a bizarre combination of pirate ship and South Seas Island, complete with sand-covered, papier-mâché "dunes." The banners hanging to either side of the stage proclaim that tonight is a night for Adventure. Where? On the High Seas, naturally.

"This is the third pirate-themed prom I've been to at this school," I inform Bethany.

"Look at it this way: it's the third one you've attended, but you've managed to miss fifteen of them, so the numbers are still slanted in your favor." She smirks when she sees the horrified look on my face. "The drama department really enjoys recycling props. Why don't you go for a walk-around, and see if anything strikes you as off?"

Everything about this strikes me as off, from the lighting in the gym to the poster that greeted me when I stepped off of the ghostroads. The trouble is figuring out exactly where the problem lies.

Maybe it's just Bethany's doom-saying, but I'm starting to feel like she's right, and something dangerous is coming. I just have no idea what "something" may turn out to be.

"No problem," I say, and turn, skirts swishing around my ankles as I start my circuit of the gym. Counterclockwise, of course—the natural direction of the dead—and moving slow, trying not to miss anything.

No one could step into this gym and guess anything other than "senior prom." The decorations are perfect, that magical combination of cheese and class that somehow tears down social barriers, turning a fractured student body into one entity, at least until the last song ends. Crepe paper roses hang from the ceiling, the Buckley Buccaneer leering out of a hundred unexpected corners like some sort of comic pagan god. There's something wrong with some of the banners. At first, I assume it's just the differing levels of skill in the high school art classes coming through. Then I turn a corner, and find myself looking straight into the eyes of a life-sized, painted pirate. There isn't time to smother the shout of surprise that pushes past my lips.

The clothes are right, the silly hat and sillier parrot of the Buckley High mascot painted in loving detail. But the hat is in his hand, rather than being forced down over his perfect duck's-ass hair, and the look in his painted eyes is flat, judgmental, like the eyes of a snake somehow granted human form. Bobby Cross. I'm looking at a painting of Bobby Cross . . . and that's when I realize something I should have realized from the start:

I never made it to the prom on the night that I died. There were no pictures of me in my prom dress, because I *never made it to the prom.*

"Shit," I mutter, and take a step backward.

"That took you *way* longer than I thought it was going to," says Bethany from behind me. I turn toward the sound of her voice, mouth already starting to shape my first demands for information. Whatever question I was going to ask is forgotten at the sight of the tin cash box swinging toward my temple. Then it hits, sending jolts of pain all the way down into my toes, and the world goes black.

I don't even feel it when I hit the floor.

Sometimes, being alive really sucks.

Hitchers are a weird little offshoot of the ghost world: we mess up the rules, just by being what we are. We're dead and buried. Our bodies are rot and wormfood, if we have bodies at all, if we're not just ashes on the wind. We don't age, we don't sleep, we don't need to eat or drink when we're on the ghostroads, and we have the option—even if very few of us ever choose to take it—of moving on to whatever destination waits beyond the last freeway off-ramp. At the same time, give one of us a coat, and we're alive again, all the way through. A lot of ghosts turn solid on the anniversaries of their deaths, but only hitchers transition all the way back to the lands of the living. Combine that with a coat, and well . . .

There's a reason I'm not happy when I open my eyes to find myself tied to a chair, and it's not just because she didn't buy me dinner first.

Just on the off chance that it's past midnight, I try letting go of the strings tying me to the wrap Bethany so "charitably" provided. Nothing happens. It's still prom night in Buckley, and that means I'm anchored here, whether or not I want to be. "Fuck," I mutter.

"Language," says Bethany sweetly, stepping around the corner, into view. She's still wearing the T-shirt and jeans she had on when she picked me up. Why didn't that strike me as strange? Decorating committee or not, she should have at least had her foundation makeup on, should have done *something* with her hair. "This is a place of learning, Auntie Rose. Mind your tongue, or you'll wind up getting detention."

"When I was a student here, we knew enough to mind our elders," I snap. "Untie me right now and I might be able to write this off as a funny, funny prank."

"You're not my elder tonight, Aunt Rose. You were sixteen when you died, and I'm seventeen now. I'm an upperclassman." Her smile isn't nearly as chilling as the six girls who come walking up behind her, each of them carrying a candle in one hand and a silver carving knife in the other. "I'm disappointed in you. I really thought you'd be more of a challenge than this."

"Did someone contact all the crazy bitches of the world and say I was in the market for a good fucking-over?" I demand. "First Laura, now you—*God!* Can't you people leave me the hell alone?"

"To be fair, I got the idea when I heard what Miss Moorhead had managed to do. I mean, catching a hitcher? That's not easy, not even when you know the things that call them. Things like the story of their death . . . and the fact that they almost always have a thing for haunting family." Bethany reaches up and tugs one of the ribbons free of her hair. "You were so set on chasing the things that bind you that you didn't even notice that this wasn't a real dance."

"Like anybody decorates the *gym* anymore?" asks one of the other students, wrinkling her nose. "Ew. That's what the community center is for."

"Vicky?" says Bethany, in a voice like honey.

"Yeah?"

"Don't talk." Bethany keeps her eyes on me. "There's a bounty on your head, Auntie Rose, and the man who wants you—you have no idea how much he's willing to pay. I won't ever have to worry about anything again. Not me, not my mother, not even Grandpa. We'll all be set for life."

"And all you have to do is kill me," I say, bitterly. Maybe I didn't see that the prom was a decoy, but I was distracted, and I've never encountered anything like this before. "So what do the rest of them get out of the deal? Cash on the barrel? Bragging rights? What?"

"Don't be stupid. I can't *kill* you. You've been dead since before my father was born. All I'm doing is handing you over to someone who has a purpose for you. As for what my friends get . . . there's not much for any of us in this podunk little town. We're getting out."

"By making deals with Bobby Cross?" There it is: there's the name, hanging out in air between us like road kill, like something dead and rotten and stinking. "You should know better. Arthur should have taught you better."

"How? He never knew what happened to you. No one ever knew,

not until the night the asphalt up on Sparrow Hill started talking to me, started telling me all about it. I think I was supposed to sympathize with you, when all you did was go and get yourself killed over a boy. But Bobby . . ." Her eyes go distant, star-struck. "He knew what he wanted, and he found a way to get it. I respect that in a man."

I stare at her, disgusted and aghast. "Please tell me you're not hot for Bobby Cross." When she doesn't answer, I gag, only exaggerating a little. "He's a monster! He sold his soul!"

"But he got what he wanted, didn't he?" She smiles again, brightly. There's an edge of pure hammered crazy there that I probably should have seen earlier. Hindsight's a bitch. "And so will I. Bobby's on his way here now. He's coming to collect his payment, and then he'll take us all to the crossroads, and show us how to make his bargain."

"You can't just *go* to the crossroads. You need a guide. You need . . ." Apple said the King of the Routewitches went with Bobby to make his first bargain. If I'm what they stuff into the gas tank, and Bethany is in the car—blood of my blood, a powerful charm on the ghostroads—they might just make it all the way. "Bethany, you can't do this. Your Queen gave me Persephone's blessing."

"I heard about that." She reaches into her pocket, produces a Swiss army knife. It looks very sharp when she clicks it open. "Funny thing: Persephone's blessing can only protect you against people who are sworn to the dead. Living routewitches and high school students who haven't had a chance to make their bargains yet? We don't count."

She takes a step forward, raising the knife in her hand. The other students move to follow her. I'm sure they expect me to scream, to beg them to spare my pitiful imitation of a life. It's almost a shame to disappoint them. I can barely hold back the laughter as I say, "No, you don't count. And you *can't* count, either."

"What are you talking about?" she demands. She leans down to grab my shoulder, probably intending some small, ritual cut to begin the bloodletting. Her hand goes cleanly through what should have been solid flesh. She's still staring at me, surprise written large across her face, when I cast a glance toward the silk wrap—now lying on the floor, having fallen right through me—and offer her a smile.

"You needed to keep track of time, Bethany. It's midnight. That means you can't hold me here. Oh, and by the way, your Queen? Is going to be *pissed* when I tell her about this."

And, still smiling, I vanish.

I don't go far, just from the little room where they had me tied to the chair—we were in the old weight room, I realize now, the equipment put away, out of sight—to the hallway outside. I want to know what they'll do, how many of her companions will panic at the first sign of something that's truly unexplained. Talking about ghosts and selling souls is all well and good, but what do you do when the Devil actually comes to collect his dues?

Voices drift down the hall, some raised in panic, some in simple confusion. "—was *right here*, so where did she—" "—oh, God, you mean she was really a ghost? We really caught a ghost? I thought—" "—was the Phantom Prom Date, Bethany, I mean, that was the real thing. What if she comes back for us? What if—"

Bethany's voice cuts across the others, cold as ice and filled with commanding anger: "All of you, shut the fuck up. I can't hear myself think. She won't have gone far. Tracy, Minda, you get the salt and seal the edges of the gym. Keep her locked in here. Everybody else, stay alert. She's probably pissed."

"At least she's smart enough to figure that part out," I mutter, and vanish, moving through the space between me and the gym door faster than my niece's minions can hope to travel. Salt can bind a ghost, that's true, but it takes a special kind to catch a hitcher, and I doubt that Bethany's cronies have the skill to do it.

The night air is cool, and tastes like minutes wasted in a doctor's waiting rooms, precious seconds that you'll never get back again. One more prom night, come and gone. It doesn't really matter that I spent it at a decoy prom, tied to a chair by my grandniece. A prom night is a prom night, and this one is slipping into memory. The ghostroads will open soon, and then I can get the hell out of here.

I almost have to respect her, in a way. Sure, she's probably insane, but I understand what it is to want out of Buckley so badly that you ache with it, so badly that you're willing to do just about anything if that's what gets you an exit.

"Leaving so soon, Auntie Rose?" asks Bethany, from right behind me. I turn toward the sound of her voice, reflex as much as anything, and flinch back as the dried flower corsage she throws at me bounces off the center of my chest, long-dead flowers filling the air with sour-sweet perfume. Bethany's expression is triumphant. That worries me. Not as much as it worries me that the flowers actually made contact.

"Prom night's over, Bethany," I say, trying to keep the shock from showing on my face. How did she get out here so fast, and how in the hell did she hit me with that thing? I'm not wearing a coat. I don't have a body to *be* hit. "Give it up."

"Prom night's never over for you, Auntie Rose. That's why they call you the 'phantom prom date,' isn't it?" She smiles, pointing to the corsage that lies between us like a road-killed squirrel. "Gary Daniels bought this for you on what should have been the night of your senior prom. 'Course, you were long dead before he could give it to you, and they'd barely stopped blaming him for being the one who killed you when you were buried, so you never got it. It's yours. And that means you're not going anywhere."

My breath catches in my throat; until that moment, I hadn't really realized that I was breathing. I've heard of things like this, ghost-catchers, tokens that the living have held onto for too long, imbued with too many memories, but I've never seen one. It just figures that if there was going to be a ghost-catcher tuned to me, it would be in the hands of my crazy grandniece with the Bobby Cross fixation. I put my hands up, palms turned toward her.

"Come on, Bethany. Let's think about this, all right? You don't want to make a deal with Bobby Cross. He's . . ." A bastard, a madman, a murderer. ". . . he's not a very nice man, and he's not going to play fair just because you hold up your end of the bargain. I'm family. Doesn't that mean something?"

"Family didn't mean anything to you when you decided to go off and get yourself turned into road kill. Grandpa's been mourning you as long as I've been alive. He even wanted to name me 'Rose.' Don't you think it's time to rest?" Bethany starts toward me, the bug-zappers that spark and flash around the edges of the school roof sending glints of blue light off the knife in her left hand. "It doesn't have to be this hard. You've had *so* many years, and I'm sorry, Auntie Rose, but I have to do what I have to do. You, of all people, should understand. You remember what it's like to be trapped here."

The corsage smells like lilies and ashes, or maybe the smell of lilies and ashes is rising from the parking lot around us, routewitch facing off with road ghost fifteen minutes after midnight on prom night. This is the sort of thing that's rare enough to have power all its own, and in the far distance, I can hear the sound of an engine, screaming.

Bobby Cross is coming to collect what he's been promised.

I'm running out of time.

Bethany's friends—minions, whatever they are to her—are still inside the high school, probably sealing the exits with salt and watching through the windows, smart enough not to get involved now that the odds aren't in their favor. The ash-and-lily smell is getting choking, Bobby burning road between him and Buckley.

"Come on, Bethany," I urge. "The doors are closed. You haven't taken anything from him, you don't *owe* him anything. Go inside, and don't look back. This doesn't have to happen."

"That's where you're wrong, Auntie Rose. I took the corsage when he offered it to me, and this always has to happen." Bethany takes another step forward. She's taller than I am, more solidly built. She's probably on the track team, a sport where she doesn't have to count on anyone else to support her. Routewitches like things that let them cover distance. She looks utterly confident as she closes on me, and she should look confident, because I'm a slip of a girl in a confining silk dress, doe-eyed and breakable.

It's too bad she isn't really thinking this through. I'm a slip of a girl who's spent the last fifty years in and out of truck stops, riding with bikers and arguing with fry cooks on exactly how much they get to slap me around before I start slapping back. And I don't have to worry about getting hurt for keeps. She goes for my ribs, sharp stabbing motion, all her momentum behind it.

I go for her eyes, nails hooked into claws, and the fight is on.

There's nothing sexy about two girls really throwing down, especially not when they're in a parking lot in the middle of a summer night. Bethany shrieks when I scratch her and starts swinging wildly; the knife misses, but her elbow doesn't, and sends me rocking back a few feet. The gravel underfoot makes it hard to keep my balance. I scramble to get upright and charge forward, burying my shoulder in the pit of her stomach. The air goes out of her in a hard gust, and she lands on the pavement on her ass, gasping.

"*Stay* down," I snap, already half-winded. Bethany snarls, sounding more animal than human, and scrabbles to her feet, lunging for me again. I'm not prepared. Her hand catches my hair, and then she's whipping me around, sending me flying away from her. I land hard on the pavement, skidding to a stop at least six feet away.

I'm barely back to my feet when I hear the sound of two hands, clapping slowly. For the first time, I realize that I'm tasting wormwood, and I turn toward the sound, already sure of what I'll see.

Bobby Cross meets my eyes, and smirks. "Nothing like a good chick fight to start a night off the right way, is there, Rosie girl?" he drawls. Bethany is struggling to get her breath back, raking fingers through her hair, making herself presentable. The irony of Bobby Cross being her dream date hasn't escaped me. "You're a sight for sore eyes. Or maybe just a sight to make eyes sore. Tired of playing hard to get?"

"Come get me, and find out," I suggest. I'm not breathing hard. I'm not breathing at all. I look down and see the shredded petals littering the pavement around me, like the leavings of a flower girl at a funeral. It would have bound me here, kept me flesh and blood, but Bethany left it on the ground when we started fighting. One or both of us must have stepped on it, shredding it and destroying its power over me. Amateur mistake by an amateur routewitch.

It's the last one she's going to make. Bobby takes a step forward, one hand half-raised in my direction. Then he stops, face contorting in a snarl. "You were supposed to cut it off her," he says, turning toward Bethany. "I came here because you promised she'd be meat when I arrived. You swore you'd cut that warding off her body. You trying to welsh on me, girl?"

"No!" protests Bethany, eyes widening. For the first time, she seems to know that she's in danger . . . and it's too late for me to do a thing about it. "She fought back. I didn't realize that she'd be able to fight back."

"Fifty years on the road, you didn't think she'd have a trick or two?" His boot heels click as he closes the distance between them, fast, so fast it's like he barely moved at all. Bethany screams when he grabs her wrist, and screams again when he jerks her against him. "You're going to learn, girly. You can't break a deal with me."

"Aunt Rose!" She twists to look at me over Bobby's shoulder, and her eyes are the pleading eyes of a trapped animal. "Please, help me! Don't let him—"

"You're the one who said that family didn't mean anything, Bethany," I say. Her eyes widen, hope draining out of them. I feel like I'm going to be sick. But I can't save her from Bobby, not here, not now, not when she made the bargain of her own free will. The only thing I can do is offer myself in her place . . .

And she's not worth it.

Bethany screams as I walk out of the parking lot, out of Buckley, down into the twilight, where the ghostroads hold no surprises anymore. Even as the daylight fades around me, taking the smell of ashes and lilies with it, I think that I can still hear Bethany, screaming. I'll be hearing her for a while, I suppose. And I walk on.

2014
Do You Believe in Ghosts?

THE PREACHERS THAT WALK and talk and trade their snake oil sermons among the living talk about death like it's some sort of vacation. "Going to your eternal rest," that's a popular one. So's "laying down all worldly cares," or my personal favorite, "at peace in the fields of the Lord." I've seen more than a few fields since I went and joined the legions of the dead. Most of them didn't have any Lord to speak of, and the few that did were dark, twisted places, controlled by ghosts who'd gone mad and decided that they were gods. The real gods of the dead don't fuck around with fields. Just in case you wondered.

If there's some peaceful paradise waiting on the other side of the twilight, no one has ever been able to prove its existence—not in any way that I'm willing to accept, and this is my afterlife, right? I get to make requests every once in a while. I know the daylight exists, and I know the twilight exists, and if there's anything beyond that, I'd like to see a road map and a tourism brochure before I agree to go. The ghostroads aren't Heaven. They aren't Hell, either. They just are, eternal and eternally changing, and I've been here a lot longer than I was ever anywhere else.

The preachers that sell their snake oil to the dead don't preach about paradise. They preach about the sins of the living, and the silence of the grave, and the unfairness of our exile. But they never say what we've been exiled from, and if you're fool enough to ask, you won't be welcome in that church for very long.

Alive or dead, the world turns on faith, and on the idea that someday, somehow, we're going to get our just rewards, and the chance to finally rest. I didn't believe it when I was alive. I definitely don't believe it now. These days, I'm just happy if I have time to finish a cheeseburger before the shit starts hitting the fan.

The air conditioning is turned just a little too high, raising goose bumps on the half-naked tourists who walk, unprepared, out of the muggy Ohio summer. Most of them turn around and walk out again, unwilling to deal with this two-bit diner where the music's too loud and the air's too cold. They won't be missed. The folks who stay seem to know the deal they're getting when they come through the door, because they bring coats, and they all seat themselves. I fit right in. Best of all, one of the busboys is a routewitch, probably clearing tables to get his bus fare to the next stop on his private pilgrimage. He pegged me the second I walked in. The jacket I'm wearing is his, a Varsity prize from some high school I've never heard of, and every time he passes the counter, he slides another plate of fries my way. If I believed in Heaven, I'd be willing to write this dirty little diner down as a suburb.

This is definitely my kind of place.

The sound of the door opening doesn't even get my attention. I'm too busy sizing up the waitress on duty, trying to figure out how I can talk her into giving me a milkshake—of her own free will, of course, since it doesn't count otherwise. Someone takes the stool next to me.

"How's the pie?"

It's an innocent question, a way to strike up conversation with a stranger. I've heard it before. I still smile as I turn my head to the man beside me. "I wouldn't know. I'm just passing through, and I haven't had the pie yet."

One look is enough to let me take his measure—I've got some experience with this sort of situation. Mid-twenties, brown hair, eyes the color of hard-packed median dirt. He's cute enough to know it and be cocky, but not cute enough to be arrogant about it. There's a difference. I like it.

His smile travels half the distance to a smirk as he asks, “Well, then, how would you feel about letting a stranger buy you a piece of pie?”

“Only if he’s willing to stop being a stranger.” I offer my hand. “Rose.”

He takes it, shakes once, and lets go. “Jamie. So you’re not from around here?”

“Nope. I just rolled in from Michigan, and I’ll be heading out as soon as I find a car that’s going my way.” This is another familiar script; I could recite it in my sleep. “I’m taking some time to see the country, you know?”

“Yeah. That’s cool.” He pauses while he flags down the waitress and orders two slices of pie, one peach, one apple, both a la mode. She heads for the kitchen, and he looks to me, asking, “So is there any chance you have local friends? Relatives? Anything?”

“Sorry, but no. Why do you ask? Are you wondering if anyone will figure out where you dumped my body?”

He laughs. “Not quite. I’m in town with the rest of my crew, and this is the part where we fan out to talk to the locals about, you know, local legends, hauntings, that sort of thing. We’re from the Ohio State University.” He leans closer, lowers his voice, and says, conspiratorially, “We’re here to catch a ghost.”

For a moment, I just stare at him. He stares back. And then, in unison, we start laughing.

Oh, this is gonna be too good to miss.

Jamie wasn’t kidding; he’s here with four other students from the Ohio State University, and they’re planning to catch a ghost. Of the other students, two are physics majors; one is in folklore; one, for no apparent reason, is in physical education. I’m not sure what Jamie’s major is. I’m just sure he’s in charge, and that his little squad of junior Ghostbusters isn’t very happy that he came back from his scouting expedition with a date.

“You do understand this is a serious scientific expedition?” asks one of the physicists, for the sixth time. Their dialogue is practically interchangeable, a long checklist of questions that all boil down to "you are an intruder, you aren't supposed to be here, get out, get out." It's like trying to talk to a haunted house—a fact that doubtless wouldn't amuse them in the least. I'd probably be unable to tell them apart if it weren't for the fact that they look nothing alike, and one of them is a guy. Instead, I take a perverse pleasure in refusing to remember their names.

"We're staking out an abandoned diner somewhere off the highway in hopes of seeing a ghost," I say drily. "I'm not seeing the 'serious.'"

"But we're going to get something no one else has ever managed to get," says the folklore major. Angela, I think her name is. She looks like an Angela.

"What's that?" I ask. I love ghost-hunters. They're so hopeful, and so willing to walk wide-eyed into the places where angels—if not Angelas—should fear to tread.

"We're going to catch a ghost," says Physicist One.

I start to laugh, and stop as I realize that they're serious about this. "I—wait—*what?* You can't *catch* a ghost. I mean, nobody's even sure that they exist. How are you planning to pull this off?"

"We had a little help," admits Jamie. His tone says he doesn't want to tell me, and his face says he's been praying for this opening. People like to brag. I think it's an essential part of the human condition. "Marla, get the book."

The phys ed major blinks, her eyebrows knotting themselves together. "Are you sure that's a good idea? We just met this girl."

"I'm sure." Jamie looks at me, chin slightly tilted up, like he's trying to present his best profile. That's when I realize what he thinks my role in this little drama is going to be: I'm the wide-eyed Timmy to his mysterious Mr. Wizard, the adoring ingénue ready to be seduced by his showmanship and drama. I'm okay with that. I've played worse parts in my day. "We can trust her. Can't we, Rose?"

"Absolutely," I agree, nodding so vigorously that for a moment, it feels like my head is going to pop clean off. "I'm *really* interested. Like, *really*."

Marla still looks unconvinced, but she turns, rummaging through the big plastic storage bin that serves as the group's "ghost hunting supply chest" until she comes up with a battered brown journal that looks like something you'd find in a high school senior's backpack. She holds it reverently, and for a moment, it seems like she's going to run away from us rather than risk bringing a nonbeliever into the fold.

Finally, grudgingly, she says, "You'd better be right about her," and thrusts the book against Jamie's chest, hard enough that I can hear the impact. He takes it before it has a chance to fall, and she retreats, joining the sullen, glaring twosome of the physics majors. It's weird, but I'm actually starting to feel a little nervous. Why would she be reacting so badly if they didn't really have something? I understand people getting jealous—Jamie's good-looking, and the way she looks at him tells me she'd like to give him a little physical education on the side—but this isn't jealousy. This is something else.

"Professor Moorhead came to our club meeting, and brought us this," says Jamie. He flips the book open to a point about halfway through, holding it out toward me. He's showing it, not offering it; the distinction is in his hands, the way his fingers grip a little too tightly against the cover. That's okay. I couldn't hold it right now if I wanted to. I'm having enough trouble keeping myself from sitting down involuntarily, because it feels like the air has just left the room.

The newspaper clipping is old, a little yellow and curled around the edges. That doesn't make it any less painful. LOCAL TRUCKER DIES IN TRAGIC CRASH says the headline. *Larry Vibber, age 42 . . .* , that's how the article begins. There's a sidebar—there's always a sidebar—and that's what really makes my heart hammer against my ribs, like a raccoon kit caught in a snare and trying as hard as it can to work its way free. Suddenly, this little outing doesn't seem nearly as funny as it did a few minutes ago.

A GHOST STORY COMING TRUE? *The tale of the Girl in the Diner is a familiar one on these American highways, and some of Mr. Vibber's fellow truckers have reason to believe that it's true . . .*

And then: *Larry Vibber's body was the only one retrieved from the crash. So what, then, explains the woman's jacket in the seat next to his?*

Stupid *stupid* Rose; there's only so much evidence you can leave, only so many breadcrumbs you can scatter before the witch in the woods starts catching up with you. "Whoa," I say, hoping I don't sound as unsteady as I feel. "So you're hunting for the ghost of Larry Vibber?"

"Better," says Jamie. "We're hunting for the Girl in the Diner."

I nod slowly. "Of course you are."

It makes a certain sort of fucked-up sense. If you're going to catch a ghost, why not start big? Why not start with a ghost that everybody's heard of? I suppose I should be flattered that this little crew of collegiate ghost hunters wants to stuff me into a soul jar—or whatever it is the kids are using for their exorcisms these days—but mostly, I feel the serious need to run very far, very fast. There's just one problem with that little plan. If they're going the high-tech route, I'm fine. But if whoever gave them that book also gave them some more traditional routes for attracting the restless dead, this could be a bad night for everyone concerned.

"Who did you say gave this to you?" I ask, looking around the group. "I mean, 'cause wow. If I had the stuff to hunt a ghost, I'd probably want to hunt it myself, you know?"

"She can't," says Marla stiffly, looking offended by the very idea. "She's a professor. It wouldn't be appropriate."

"A professor? Of what? Ghostology?"

"The Ohio State University doesn't have a parapsychology department," says Physicist One. "If we did, we'd have better faculty support."

"Professor Moorhead teaches American History," says Jamie, and flips to the front of the book, where the face of a woman stares out at me from another, older newspaper clipping. The picture is black and white, but I know her hair is dirty blonde, and that the eyes behind her glasses are pale, and cold.

PROFESSOR LAURA MOORHEAD TO SPEAK ON THE LEGEND OF THE GIRL IN THE DINER, that's what the caption underneath says. I take a breath. Force a smile. And ask the one question that stands a shot at saving me:

"So what do we do first?"

It turns out that what we do first involves driving out to tonight's designated hunting ground, an abandoned diner in what was once a truck stop and is now a deserted patch of asphalt and gravel. The freeway redirected the traffic, the trucks stopped coming, and time moved on. I've seen it before, these little dead spots, and they break my heart a little more each time. I ride in the back with Angela and the Physicists, ceding the front seat to Marla in the vain hope that it will make her glare at me a little less. This night's going to be long enough as it is.

"So how long have you been into ghosts, Rose?" asks Angela. She's at least trying to make conversation. I appreciate that.

Answering "since I died" seems like a bad idea right now. I pretend to give her question serious thought before I say, "Oh, forever, I guess. It sure seems that way sometimes."

Angela nods, expression set in a look of absolute and total conviction as she says, "I started believing when I was eight. That's when my grandfather's ghost came to me and told me things were going to get better."

Scrooge was right about one thing: most spectral visitations are actually dreams or indigestion. I have to fight to keep my eyes wide and filled with belief. And if her grandfather really *did* come to visit her when she was a kid, why the hell does she think catching a ghost is a good way to spend a Friday night? If anyone was going to be live and let not-live about the dead, it should have been her.

"Have you ever experienced a genuine paranormal visitation?" asks Physicist Two. The question sounds more like a demand: *Prove it. Prove that you belong here.*

I'm still trying to figure out how to answer when the minivan pulls to a stop outside the broken-down old diner. "We're here!" announces Jamie, with near-maniac cheer. "Everybody out and to your stations. Rose, you're with me."

So much for getting Marla not to hate me. She shoots me a venomous look as I slide out of my seat and move to stand next to Jamie. He hands me a container of salt, ignoring her displeasure.

"Angela, Tom, you go west. Marla, take Katherine inside and start setting up the camera."

Marla may not be happy, but she doesn't argue. She moves quickly and efficiently. So does everyone else. In a matter of minutes, it's just me, Jamie, and the salt.

"Come on," he says. "Let's get started."

"I can't wait," I reply, and follow the crazy ghost-hunter into the night.

Their approach is a weird synthesis of traditional and technological. Cameras to catch any apparitions, gauges to catch any unexpected fluctuations in the local temperature . . . and spirit jars with honey and myrrh smeared around their mouths, to catch any wayward, wandering ghosts. Salt circles with just a single break in their outlines. Half-drawn Seals of Solomon on the broken asphalt. Even scattered patterns of rapeseed, fennel, and rye, guaranteed to attract any poltergeists who happen to be in the area. They aren't missing a trick. If I weren't already wearing a coat and hence protected from their little surprises, I'd be worried.

"So what are we hoping to achieve out here?" I ask Jamie, as we walk slowly around the edges of the old parking lot, throwing down torn carnival tickets and bits of broken glass. "This doesn't seem very, you know. Scientific."

"That's why we're going to succeed when nobody else ever has," he says. He sounds so damn *serious*. He really believes what he's telling me. "We're pursuing synergy between the spirit and material worlds."

"I have no idea what that means," I say. I sound serious, too. I have no damn clue what he's talking about.

Jamie smiles. "It means keep scattering those ticket stubs, and by morning, you're going to see something you'd never believe."

"Oh, I can believe that," I murmur, and keep scattering.

The sun's been down for a little more than an hour. Everyone seems sure that nothing exciting will happen until midnight—they insist on calling it "the witching hour," which is making me want to scream—so people are mostly just checking equipment and taking walks around the grounds, making sure everything has stayed in place. So far, the valiant ghost-hunters have managed to successfully attract two raccoons, a stray cat, and a hitchhiker who isn't quite as dead as I am.

"Spirit world, one, college kids with a high-tech Ouija board, zero," I say, sweeping my flashlight around the edges of the blacktop. They're letting me patrol on my own now, probably because they don't really think there's much I can do to disrupt things if I'm on the other side of the yard. Marla's probably hoping I'll see something mundane and scream, thus proving that she was right and Jamie was wrong.

I don't think she'll be getting her wish tonight.

When I actually *do* see something, it's not mundane at all. One of the spirit jars is closed, rocking gently back and forth with the weight of its pissed-off contents. I stop beside it, squatting down, and tap the glass. The rocking stops. "Yo," I say. That's about as much ceremony as I can muster at the moment.

There are no words—bottled ghosts don't really communicate in words, per se—but the spirit jar manages to communicate, clearly, that it would like to be opened. Right fucking now.

"That's nice," I say. "What'll you give me?"

Some of the suggestions the spirit jar makes are anatomically impossible, even for someone as flexible as I am. At least one of them would require my cutting off one or more limbs. Still, I have to be impressed at how articulate it manages to be, given its current lack of vocabulary.

"Nope, that won't be happening," I say. "How about we try this: I'll let you out, and you'll go far, far away, and not bother any of the nice, incredibly stupid people that are here with me. And in exchange, I won't hunt you down and shove you back into the jar. Deal?"

The jar mutters something sullen.

"Deal?"

Grudging assent this time. I reach out and remove the lid, ready to fight if I have to. I don't. Some innocent backwood haunt too new to know to avoid the scent of myrrh and honey blasts out of the open vessel, chilling the air around me for an instant before it vanishes, racing back into the twilight, where it will presumably be safer than it is out here.

"It's always nice to meet the neighbors," I say, returning the lid to its half-open state. With luck, they'll never guess the jar was tampered with. I retrieve my flashlight and resume walking.

By the time I finish my first circuit around the lot, I've freed two haunts, a spectral lady, a will-o'-the-wisp, a pelesit, and a very confused poltergeist that takes half the carnival tickets with it when it goes. It's like a weird naturalist's cross section of the ghosts of the American Midwest, and it would be a lot more interesting if I wasn't expecting one of the ghost-hunters to appear at any minute and demand to know what I was doing.

Instead, a high, horrified scream rises from the direction of the diner. It sounds like one of the Physicists. I stop where I am, turning toward the sound, and wince as the taste of ashes and empty rooms wafts, ever so slightly, across my tongue. "Oh, God, these idiots are going to get themselves killed," I say, and break into a run. The screaming escorts me all the way.

The ghost-hunters are backed into the far corner of the diner, packed into the space that still holds the shadowy ghost of a jukebox, playing songs I'm too far into the daylight to quite make out. The temptation to drop down and hear them would normally be a problem for me, but at the moment, it's easy to ignore the phantom jukebox. The massive spectral dog standing between me and the terrified college students seems likely to be a little more important.

"How the holy *fuck* did you people manage to attract a Maggy Dhu?" I blurt out the question before I have a chance to consider its ramifications—namely, that it betrays my knowing more than I've been letting on, and that shouting is likely to attract the attention of the Black Hound of the Dead.

Sure enough, the Maggy Dhu swings its head in my direction, lips drawn back to display teeth like daggers, eyes burning the smoky, angry orange of midnight jack-o'-lanterns and the sort of harvest fire that used to come with a side order of barbecued virgin sacrifice. I take a step back. "Uh, nice doggy. Good doggy. Don't eat me, doggy."

"I don't know *what* that thing is, but it is *not* Scooby-Doo!" wails Marla.

"Not Scooby-Doo, Maggy Dhu," I say, keeping my eyes on the dog. It's the only thing in this room that can hurt me. That means it gets my full attention. "It's a Black Dog of the Dead. It harvests souls. What did you people *do*?"

"N-nothing," says Jamie. He sounds like he's hanging onto his sanity by a thread. I guess when he said "ghost," he was picturing something nice, friendly, and human-looking, like, say, a hitchhiking dead girl from the 1950s. Not the afterlife equivalent of Cujo on a bad hair day. "We were just reading the incantations from the book, and then this . . . this thing . . ."

"It came out of nowhere," says Physicist Two. She doesn't sound as scared as the others, possibly because she sounds like she's talking in her sleep. We all have our own ways of coping. "It bit Tom. He's bleeding a lot. Can you make it go away?"

Shit. Well, at least that explains the screaming. I'd be screaming too, if a Maggy Dhu had just tried to take a chunk out of me. I don't remember whether they're venomous. I don't think so. There's a level at which things like venom cross into "overkill," and when you're a two-hundred-pound spectral hound, you're basically there. "I don't know," I say, with absolute honesty. The Maggy Dhu is still watching me. I think it's growling. That's just great. "I'm going to try something, okay? Nobody move."

Nobody's moving. I'm inclined to take this less as a sign of obedience and more as a sign of blind terror. Whatever. The end result is the same. I take another step back. The Maggy Dhu finishes its turn, growl becoming audible. It's been summoned from the ghostroads to this dead little diner, and it's pissed. I understand the feeling.

"Fuck me," I mutter, and take off running.

There is no possible way for me to outrun an angry Black Dog for more than a few panic-fueled yards. That's fine, because a few panic-filled yards is all I need. These kids may be amateurs and idiots, but they're amateurs and idiots who've been turning this place into a giant ghost trap since the sun went down. I have no idea what it takes to catch a Maggy Dhu—I don't deal much with the totally nonhuman inhabitants of the twilight—but if there's a standard mechanism, I'd bet my afterlife that it's somewhere here.

Actually, that's exactly what I'm doing. I should let go, drop down into the twilight, and let the Maggy Dhu teach these kids the last lesson they're ever going to learn. I should let it remind them that there's a reason the living don't dance with the dead. And I can't do it. Maybe it's because Laura would expect it of me; maybe it's just that everyone deserves to be dumb, at least once, and you don't really learn from the things that kill you. So I keep my grip on the borrowed life I'm wearing, and I run like hell.

The pelesit got snagged in one of the half-drawn Seals of Solomon, but there are still five of them untriggered, scattered around the edges of the lot like a weird version of home base in a game of tag. The first one is just ahead when I hear the Maggy Dhu's claws scraping against the gravel behind me. I put on a final burst of speed, feet easily clearing the lines of the unfinished circle. I feel like an Olympic sprinter. I feel like my lungs are going to explode. I don't think I like either feeling.

The sound of pursuit stops, and the Maggy Dhu starts to growl again. Now it sounds well and truly pissed. I stop running, bracing my hands on my knees and fighting for air as I twist to look back at the Black Dog.

It's pressed against the circle's edge, eyes glowing hellfire red and legs braced in the posture of a junkyard mutt getting ready to charge a trespasser. I've never seen an animal that angry. At least it hasn't realized yet that the circle's broken, or it would already be on my ass again. It'll figure it out eventually. Hopefully, I'll be breathing again by then.

"I don't suppose I could convince you to go home," I wheeze.

The Maggy Dhu barks furiously, trying to bite the barrier that keeps it from biting my ass instead.

"I'm going to take that as a 'no,'" I say, and let the Maggy Dhu bark while I finish getting my breath back. I don't age, and that also means that no matter how much shit I go through, I'll never be in better shape than I was in when I died. Back then, girls didn't go in that much for extracurricular running like their asses were on fire. Sometimes I really wish I'd picked a better era to die in. Like one where all high school students were capable of completing a three-minute mile.

The Maggy Dhu backs up, clearly intending to charge the barrier. Then its paws pass outside the open spot in the circle. The expression on its face is almost comic as it realizes that it isn't captive anymore. And then it's chasing me again, and laughter is the last thing on my mind.

I have to wonder what this looks like from inside the diner. If the ghost-hunters are being smart, they've surrounded themselves with salt and are staying as far from the windows as possible. Judging by the shadows I see in the glass as I run past, they're not being smart.

The Maggy Dhu, on the other hand, is remaining good and pissed. I would envy its single-minded devotion to its purpose, but since that purpose is eating me, I'm not in the mood to root for it just yet. It sidesteps the second Seal of Solomon—great, the demon dog has a learning curve—and keeps coming after me, gaining speed all the time.

One of the patches of rapeseed is right up ahead. Nothing I've ever heard has implied that Maggy Dhu are bothered by things like that, but hell, any port in a storm, right? I charge into the middle of it, stepping as high as I can to keep from scattering the seeds. If it doesn't work—

The Maggy Dhu stops at the edge of the field of rapeseed, nose dropping to the pavement. I don't know how good dogs are at math, but if it follows the same rules as every other ghost that can be stopped by scattering small objects, it has to count every seed before it can come after me again.

"Thank God for stupid folklore," I mutter, taking a deep breath before I walk, much more slowly now that there isn't a homicidal Maggy Dhu on my ass, toward the piled-up spirit jars.

Three of them haven't been visibly triggered yet. "And thank God for over-prepared college students," I say, picking up the largest of the jars and peering inside. It's definitely empty. It should work. Maybe. Possibly.

Okay, probably not. But lacking any alternative that doesn't result in the Maggy Dhu chowing down on Jamie and his little band of lunatics, it's the best chance I've got.

The Maggy Dhu is still sniffing the ground as I walk back to the rapeseed field. I whistle low, the way I used to whistle for the dog we had when I was little. The Maggy Dhu's head comes up, a growl vibrating from the depths of its chest. "Hi, puppy," I say. "Catch."

The spirit jar hits the Maggy Dhu in the middle of the chest. It yelps, a surprised look spreading across its face.

And then it's gone.

Jamie and the others are scattered around the diner, doing a frankly piss-poor job of hiding themselves under broken tables and behind the remains of the counter. Only one of them, Angela, is huddling in an unbroken circle of salt. The rest of them would be easy pickings for the Maggy Dhu if it were still running loose. Good thing for them the Maggy Dhu is currently having a nice nap in the spirit jar under my arm. I stop in the doorway, watching them watch the windows. Not one of them is bothering to watch the door. That's the sort of sloppy shortsightedness that can get a person killed, especially on a night like this. Placing two fingers in my mouth, I whistle.

The reaction in the diner is nothing short of electric. Physicist Two scrambles to position herself in front of the prone body of Physicist One. Angela crosses herself, muttering in frantic, high-pitched

Latin. Marla slams back against the wall, raising her handheld EMP device like the weapon it so clearly isn't. Jamie just stares.

"Hi," I say, amiably. "Having a nice night? It's a little warm for me, but hey, it takes all types, right? You're from Ohio, you must be used to it, right?"

Angela squeaks out something else in Latin before catching her breath and asking, "R-Rose? Are you . . . are you okay?"

"Winded and cranky, and I could really use a milkshake, but that weird dog didn't bite me, if that's what you're asking. It chased me around the parking lot a few times, and then it went running off down the road. Don't you people do any scouting before you start hunting for dead stuff?"

"I thought you said it was a . . . what did you call it, a Maggy Dhu?" Marla sounds uncertain. Good.

I shake my head. "I was wrong. I guess I got overexcited."

She slowly lowers her EMP device. "But I thought I saw . . . it ran away?"

Given a choice between the believable—a big black dog tried to eat us all and then ran away into the night—and the terrifying—a big black *ghost* dog tried to eat us all, until I managed to suck it into a clay jar from Pottery Barn—even the most enthusiastic ghost-hunter is going to go for the mundane explanation. It's a matter of self-preservation where their sanity is concerned. There are things the living aren't meant to deal with knowing.

"Gosh, Rose—I mean, you could have been seriously hurt." Jamie takes a step forward. He's starting to realize that he left me to face the Maggy Dhu alone, and even if his conscious mind is rejecting the reality of the Black Dog, part of him knows exactly what he did. "Are you all right? Did the dog hurt you?"

"Like I told Angela, I'm fine. How's Tom? Did you manage to stop the bleeding?"

Deflection is one of the most useful tools in my particular toolbox. "No," says Physicist Two—Katherine, she's Katherine; she's the one who's terrified but not currently in danger of dying. She steps aside, giving me my first clear look at her pale, shivering companion. "I keep thinking I have, and then he starts bleeding again. We need to get him to a hospital."

A hospital isn't going to help him; not at this point. I can see the shadows around him, gathering like a burial shroud. If Laura were here, I'd kill her. I don't care if she's Tommy's one true love, there's a *reason* the living don't interfere with the dead.

This is where I should walk away. And I can't. "Hold this and stay here," I say, thrusting the spirit jar into Jamie's hands. "Whatever you do, don't drop it. Angela, I need you to clean up as much of the salt as you can. Make sure there's nothing left that can be considered a circle."

"What are you going to do?" demands Marla.

I sigh. "I'm going to beg."

"I stand here open-handed and begging for your mercy, I stand here hopeful and contrite. I stand here ready for your judgment." I hate begging. It always feels so much like . . . well . . . like begging. I ball my hands into fists, plant them on my hips, and demand, "Well? You owe me. I let you out of that damn jar. Now get your spectral ass over here."

The air chills, fills with the scent of dried corn and harvest moons, and the haunt appears. She gathers herself out of the night, wrapping her translucent body in the semblance of a cotton nightgown. Her hair is long and glossy, stirred by a wind that I can't feel. She's on a level of the twilight that I'm not native to. For right now, that's fine by me. "Who *are* you?" she asks. I can barely hear her. That's fine, too.

"I'm Rose Marshall, I'm the one who let you out of the jar, and I'm the one you're about to do the favor for. We clear?"

Haunts aren't the smartest things on the ghostroads. Something about the transition between the living and the dead seems to burn out about half their brain cells. It makes them shitty company, but it also leaves them suggestible, which is a bonus from where I'm standing. She frowns, perplexed, and asks, "What favor?"

"There's a man inside the diner. He and his friends conjured a Maggy Dhu by mistake, and he got bitten. He's not supposed to die yet. He doesn't have the right smell. I need you to fix it."

I'm right about this haunt being new, because she just looks more confused. "Fix it?" she asks. "How?"

"He's dying." I shrug, gesturing toward the diner. "Kiss him."

A kiss from a haunt can kill the living or heal the dying. It's one of those nasty double-edged swords that the twilight is so fond of. Kiss the haunt too soon and it's good-bye, you silly mortal coil. Put it off too long, and all the kiss will do is guarantee that you'll be coming back as a haunt yourself. I'm gambling a little—Tom could be farther gone now than he was when I left him—but I don't think so. He was holding on pretty tightly when I came outside.

"No more jars?"

"No more jars," I promise, and just like that, the haunt's gone, soaring toward the diner. She vanishes through the window, and the screaming inside starts all over again.

This time, I don't bother hurrying as I walk toward the sound of screams. I'm done with good deeds for the night.

"It was amazing," Angela says, grabbing my hands for what feels like the seventy-third time. "This glowing figure came right through the wall and kissed him, and his arm just healed! Like it was never hurt in the first place! It's a miracle! Oh, Rose, you should have seen it!"

"Uh-huh," I agree. Katherine and Tom have the spirit jar that contains the Maggy Dhu. They've promised to seal it and drop it into the nearest lake without telling the others, and that's good enough for me. If they decide to play Pandora, well, they can't say I didn't warn them.

"And Jamie got the whole thing on film!"

No, he didn't. "Uh-huh."

"I'm sorry I was such a bitch before," says Marla, walking over to us. Jamie is half a step behind her. They both look shaken. Shaken enough not to do this sort of thing again? I guess only time will tell. By the time it does, I plan to be as far away as possible. "I thought you were just looking for cheap thrills. I didn't realize you knew more about this than we did."

"Uh-huh," I agree again. It's safer than any of the alternatives I can come up with, most of which involve laughing in her face.

"I wanted to say thank you," says Jamie. "I really don't know what would have happened if you hadn't been here to distract that dog. I'm just sorry you missed seeing the ghost. That was . . . it was amazing. It was life-changing. It almost made all this worth it."

"Only almost," adds Marla.

"No more ghost-chasing, right?" I ask, folding my arms. "This was a one-shot deal, it didn't work out, and now you're going to remember that your mothers taught you not to play with dead things?"

"But we *saw* a ghost, Rose," protests Angela. "It wasn't the one we were trying for, sure, but we can try again. We can find the Phantom Prom Date. We can—"

"It wasn't a stray dog."

Tom's announcement comes as a surprise to everyone but me. They turn to look at him. He's leaning on Katherine, still pale and shaky from blood loss. He'll live. That's all I promised him.

"What, you saw the owner?" asks Jamie.

"No," Tom says. "It wasn't a dog at all. It was some sort of warning, okay? We need to leave the dead alone. They don't like it when we mess with them, and we got lucky tonight. That thing could have killed us all. Maybe there's a reason nobody's ever caught a ghost. Maybe there's a reason Professor Moorhead wasn't willing to do this herself. You can keep messing around if you want, but I'm out, and so is Katherine."

"And so am I," says Marla. "I don't know if it was a . . . ghost dog . . . or what, but this is so not the sort of thing I want to get myself killed doing."

"What about the Girl in the Diner?" asks Jamie, almost frantically. "What about all the things *she's* done? Now that we know we can do this, don't we owe it to the world to—"

"To what?" I demand, my already frayed temper finally giving way. "To go messing with some poor, innocent ghost who's just trying to keep herself busy? If she was some kind of mass murderer, don't you think that would be in *every* version of the story, not just the ones you can trace back to some slumber party or other? I mean, jeez, people, do a little more research than 'oh, the professor says she's bad, let's go catch her, she's eeeeeevil.' "

Now they're all staring at me. Tom and Katherine don't look surprised; that's to their credit. Jamie and Marla still look confused as hell. And Angela . . .

Gold star to Angela, because she looks like she's just seen a ghost.

"You were here all along," she whispers. Jamie shoots her a startled look. Marla takes a step backward. Natural reactions, both of them, although I admit, I'd been hoping for better. At least a little scream or something.

"Yeah, well. I get bored sometimes." I look at Jamie. He's the leader of this little group. They'll listen to him. I hope. "Leave me alone, Jamie. Don't follow me, don't lay traps for me, don't try to track me down. Not because I'll hurt you—I'm not that kind of a girl—but because you have no idea how many things could have killed you tonight, and next time, I won't be here to make nice with them on your behalf. Do I make myself clear?"

He laughs nervously. "Rose? What are you talking about? I know it's been a kind of a weird night, but don't you think you're taking things a little bit too far?"

I sigh. "God save me from smart people and college students. You're all such fucking idiots." It only takes a second to shrug out of my coat, the cold rushing back into my bones like the tide flowing in to fill the harbor. I'm still solid, still alive . . . until I let go of the sleeve, and the coat falls to the pavement.

"Leave the dead alone," I say. Maybe it's the fact that I'm see-through and glowing, but this time, they listen; this time, the only sound is Angela hitting the ground in a dead faint. I'm pretty sure she landed on some of the broken glass we scattered earlier. "You're going to want to put some Bactine on that," I add, and disappear. Not the most memorable last words ever, but hey, infection is nothing to fuck around with.

The ghostroads flow back into place around me. I sigh, shake my head, and start walking. I want to put some miles between me and Ohio before I venture back into the daylight.

Wouldn't want a group of familiar faces offering me a ride.

2014
The Killing of Route 14

EVERYTHING THAT LIVES CAN DIE, and there are a lot of definitions of the word "life." Humans, and things that look like humans, tend to assume that our life is the only kind that counts: fast, hot, animal life, life that begins screaming and all-too-often ends the same way. We're very set in our ways, and that carries over even onto the ghostroads, where you'd think that we'd know better. You'd think that dying and waking up in a whole new kind of life would be enough to shake most of us out of those tired old patterns. You'd be wrong.

Before I died I believed humanity alone ruled the Earth, and that no other creature could ever hope to challenge our dominion. I learned pretty quickly that I was wrong, but it still took years and years and a lot of hard lessons for me to accept that sometimes, houses and cars and well-loved toys can have a life of their own, one capable of carrying over into the twilight. There are ghost planes in the sky, and ghost gold mines in the mountains. Ghost skyscrapers stand on the horizon, unyielding, even as the rest of the twilight changes around them. Ghost stories tell themselves over and over again, like secrets on the wind.

And then there are the highways. Those great arteries of travel, down which a million cars and a million souls will pass year by year. They live, just like people, or cars, or stories.

And everything that lives can die.

The Last Dance Diner, 2014

It takes longer than I would have preferred for me to hitch my way back to the Last Dance after dealing with those college idiots back in Ohio. The thing about the ghostroads is that nothing stays static for long—everything moves around and changes according to its own unknowable whims. The Last Dance is usually anchored somewhere near Michigan for me, but it can move, and when it does, I have to move with it. This time, the road leads me all the way to upstate New York before the feel of it changes. I smile at the man behind the wheel, and say, "This is as far as I go. Do you think you could let me off here?"

He blinks, confusion and honest desire warring in his expression. It's clear what he thought my payment for the ride would be. I chose well with this one: despite his expectations, he's gentleman enough to pull off to the side of the road and hit the button that unlocks my door. "You sure?" he asks. "We're only about thirty miles outside of Albany."

"I'm sure," I said, and slide out of the car. The air around him is clean, smelling of nothing more unusual than exhaust fumes and unwashed human skin. He'll make it home safely, assuming he doesn't stop for any more hitchhikers. I flash him a smile. "Be safe."

"You, too, Rose," he says, and he's gone, one more pair of taillights receding into the distance, one more life I didn't need to save. I shrug off the coat he gave me, feeling a sting of regret at giving up my borrowed life so easily, and drop down into the twilight. The glass-speckled ground of the highway shoulder changes under my feet, becoming the smooth tarmac of the Last Dance parking lot as the late afternoon sunlight mellows into early evening. The neon sign is lit, beating back the natural darkness that the twilight is heir to. I smile and start for the doors, glad to be back in what passes for home these days.

The bell over the door rings when I push it open—Emma prefers that even her less corporeal clientele not walk through the glass, as it tends to remind the ghost crows that sometimes gather in the parking lot that there's nothing actually keeping them outside. Emma herself is behind the counter, sliding a vanilla ice cream soda to the only other customer in the place. It's a woman, and I can't see anything of her but her hair. Her hair is enough. It's silver-white, the color of moonlight shining through corn silk. It's been a long time since I've seen a woman with hair that color. I'll never forget it.

I stop in the doorway. The bell rings again as the door swings shut behind me.

Emma looks up and smiles, but there's an apology there, sitting uneasy in the space behind her eyes. The woman in front of her picks up her ice cream soda, takes a sip through the straw, and turns, directing a smile of her own at me.

"Hi, Rose," she says. "It's been a long time."

The longer you're dead, the more people you'll meet. It's simple mathematics, really. I was never very good at math when I was in school, and "simple" doesn't mean "fun." "Hello, Mary," I say, walking to the counter and taking a stool some distance away from hers. "What are you doing here?"

"I wanted an ice cream soda, and this is the best place in the twilight to get one," says Mary. She's still smiling. That's not helping matters any. "Also, I wanted to talk to you, and everyone knows that if you hang around the Last Dance long enough, you'll run into Rose Marshall."

"Maybe I need to start hanging out somewhere new," I say. Emma sets a faded denim jacket on the counter in front of me. I take it, shrugging it on, and feel the flesh settling over my phantom bones. This is the only place in the twilight where I can be among the technically living, and it's worth it for the malted that follows the coat, the glass cool and smooth against my fingertips. "What do you want?"

Mary frowns a little. "That's no way to greet an old friend."

"In case you forgot, we're dead," I say, and push my straw aside as I lift the glass and take a gulp of sweet vanilla shake.

"What does dead have to do with it?"

I put down the glass. "Dead men tell no tales, and dead girls make no friends. I don't want to talk to you, Mary. Please leave me alone."

She sighs. "I was afraid it was going to be something like this." There's a soft hiss of vinyl springing back into shape as she slides off her stool and walks over to me, feet scuffing against the linoleum floor. They're small sounds, *living* sounds, and they have as little business here as she does. Mary Dunlavy is dead: that much is true. But she's not a ghost of the road, and only road ghosts belong in the Last Dance.

I don't want to look at her. I don't want to *see* her, with her cross-roads eyes and her hair like the moon reflecting off the silvery corn in the fields beside the highway. Mary Dunlavy and I go way, way back. We were both born in Buckley; we both died there. That's where the similarities end.

"Rose."

"Go away, Mary."

"Rose, I need you to look at me. Please." There's a note of raw pleading in her voice, as out of place as a penguin in the desert. "I know what you've been doing. I know that you've been taking the first steps toward finally stopping Bobby Cross. Dammit, Rose, I know you walked the Ocean Lady. Now please, for my sake, for the sake of Route 14, *look at me*."

Damn her anyway, for making me care. Slowly, I turn on my stool, the malt glass still cool in my hand. "What do you want, Mary?"

She looks at me, young and earnest with her eyes like a mile of empty road, and she says the last thing I would ever have expected: "I want to help you."

Daly, Maine, 1981

It's been a long, hot summer, and I've been lucky enough to bake my way through most of it, going from car to car and coast to coast while the days unspooled around me. I hooked up with a trucker in San Antonio who got me all the way to California, although only barely—the sun was coming up as we rolled across the state line. From there, I ran all the way up to Washington, into Vancouver, and hitched my way all the way back across the country. I didn't count the rides I got, or the drivers I smiled at. All that mattered was the road, and the need to keep on moving.

Only now I'm standing outside a gas station outside a little town called Daly in upstate Maine, and I have to wonder what I'm doing with my death. There hasn't been a car through here in hours, not since the harried mother of two who'd picked me up outside Bangor said she was very sorry, but this was as far as she could take me. My thumb is ready. There's no one here to show it to, and I don't like the way the station attendant keeps looking at me. He's either planning to call the cops or bury my body in the woods behind the building, and I honestly don't know which it's going to be.

"Fuck this," I mutter. Every hitcher knows that when you can't get a ride, there's only one option left, short of dropping down into the ghostroads and trying again later. I shove my hands down into the pockets of my jeans and start walking away. I hear a door slam behind me, presumably as the station attendant finally comes outside. I flipped him off over my shoulder and kept walking. That's one of the first rules you learn when you exist only on the roads: Never look back if you don't have to. Whichever way you're going, that's the right one.

The gas station parking lot yields to the paved road, which yields in turn to a gravel frontage road that may need to be downgraded to "hiking trail" if it gets much narrower. The need to keep moving is still with me, and so I scowl at the woods and walk on.

It's not until I turn off the frontage road and onto a deer trail that I realize I'm being led.

It's a subtle feeling, a soft tugging at the back of my mind, like a fishhook made of feathers, but it's there, and now that I've recognized it for what it is, I can't stop feeling it. I try to let go of the flesh and drop down into the twilight, but the compulsion won't let me. It wants me to keep going the way that I'm going. Maybe if I'd caught it earlier . . .

I didn't catch it earlier. That means there's nothing for it but to keep going. I mutter profanities to the trees, and I pull my hands out of my pockets long enough to draw my borrowed jacket a little tighter around me. If I'm not being allowed to descend into the twilight, I'm going to hold onto the semblance of humanity for as long as I possibly can. Maybe whoever rigged this idiotic compulsion will let it go when they see that I'm alive. There's virtually nothing in the world of the living or the worlds beyond that can recognize a hitcher as a ghost when we're wearing a human form.

Virtually nothing. I walk around a bend in the trail and there she is, white-haired and gray-eyed and still wearing her Buckley High School letter jacket, like that matters anymore, like that ever mattered in the first place. She's sitting on a fallen log, and she's clearly waiting for someone. She's clearly waiting for *me*, and I don't know what she is, I don't, and that isn't important, because everything about her screams *run now, run and don't look back*. She can't be more than seventeen on the outside, but on the inside . . .

Age among the dead has nothing to do with the shape of your skin, and everything to do with how many years your body has spent moldering in its grave. This girl, this slowly smiling girl, died before I did. I know it just as surely as I know her name, because there's only one other ghost who runs the East Coast roads in a Buckley High School jacket, and no one knows what she is, and no one ever gets close enough to ask her.

"Hi, Rose," says Mary Dunlavy, who died on Sparrow Hill Road in 1939, thirteen years before I would follow in her fatal footsteps. She stands, smiling easily, and offers me her hand. "I figured it was time we met."

I stare at her, mouth as dry as the dust beneath my feet, and I have no idea what to say.

The Last Dance Diner, 2014

Mary and I sit at opposite sides of the private booth at the back of the diner, me eyeing her mistrustfully, she sipping her ice cream soda with exquisite patience. She hasn't said a word since we sat down. It's clear that she's ready to wait all night, if that's what I need her to do. I want to outlast her, to bite my tongue and glare until she goes away, but being dead hasn't done a thing to make me patient. It's probably a miracle I've lasted this long. Her straw hits the bottom of her glass, making a slurping noise, and I finally snap.

"What do you mean, help me?" I demand. "What are you trying to do? We're not *friends*, Mary. We've never been friends."

"Only because you didn't want us to be." She shakes her head, pushing her empty glass aside. "I really hoped we could find some common ground between us. We're both Buckley girls. Shouldn't that count for something?"

"All I wanted when I was alive was to get the hell out of Buckley. Why would I be looking to make friends with someone from town now that I'm dead?"

"Because I understand where you come from in a way that nobody else is going to, that's why. I remember climbing Sparrow Hill and trying to see past the woods to the big city. I remember running past the old Healy place because maybe it was haunted. We have the same roots."

"Roots don't mean a damn thing after the tree's been cut down." I shake my head. "You have nothing to offer me, and I'm not going to kill anything else for you, so you can stop making nice. It isn't going to work."

"Rose . . . what kind of ghost do you think I *am*?"

"To be honest? I never spared you a moment's thought after we buried Route 14. So you tell me. Gather-grim? Reaper? Really *specialized* reaper? I didn't know you people got assigned to highways, but hell, you're a little out of my wheelhouse. I'm willing to believe just about anything."

"I'm not a psychopomp. If I were, I wouldn't have needed you."

I frown. "If you're not a psychopomp, then what the hell are you, and why are you here?"

Mary takes a deep breath, and it says something about how confused she has me that I don't know whether she needs it or not. Is this theater, the way that most ghosts will walk on floors rather than floating above them, even when they're not solid? Or is this a function of her nature, the way that I can bleed when I'm wearing a living person's jacket?

"Look, Rose . . ." Mary hesitates. "I've been wanting to tell you this for a really long time, believe it or not. And I know you're going to want to freak out on me, because that's the kind of person you are. Can you please just try to reserve judgment until I can finish explaining myself to you?"

I scowl at her for a moment before I yield, curiosity winning out over common sense, *again*. It's the story of my death. "I'll try," I say.

"Okay. Have you ever run into a group of ever-lasters?"

"Ugh." There's nothing false about my shudder. The ever-lasters are the ghosts of children who, for whatever reason, decided to keep going to school after they died. Most dead kids haunt their houses, or the places where they died, or find another group of the dead to belong to. Not the ever-lasters. They haunt schoolyards and playgrounds, playing four-square and double-dutch and watching over their alma maters. Some people say their jump rope songs and clapping games hold the wisdom of the twilight, if you stick around long enough to figure it out. I've never felt the urge. They're dead kids, and that's creepy as hell, if you ask me.

"You know that rhyme they have? The one that starts with 'homecomer, hitcher, phantom rider'?"

"Yeah," I say, with a small nod.

"How does it go?"

"Uh . . . 'homecomer, hitcher, phantom rider, white lady wants what's been denied her, gather-grim knows what you fear the most, but best . . . keep away . . .' " I stop, the words turning to ashes on my tongue, and stare at her. Mary, Buckley girl Mary, who once made me help her kill a highway. Pretty Mary Dunlavy with her crossroads eyes and her hair the color of moonlight on the corn.

"Gather-grim knows what you fear the most, but best keep away from the crossroads ghost," says Mary, and I know what she is, and I am so screwed.

Daly, Maine, 1981

"You're Mary Dunlavy." I try to take a step backward, but the compulsion that dragged me here won't allow it; moving away from my goal isn't the plan. Crap. "Uh. Look, I don't know why you dragged me here, but I promise you, you've got the wrong girl. No matter what it is you want, I can't help."

"Pretty sure you're wrong about that, Rose," she says. She sounds almost sorry.

"I'm a hitchhiker," I shoot back. "Unless you're looking for tips on flagging down a ride, I'm not your go-to ghost."

"You're a hitchhiker, but you're also a psychopomp, and I need a psychopomp. A strong one, one who's actually been doing her job, not just letting the dead figure things out on their own. Right now, in this part of the country, that's you. So congratulations, Rose Marshall: you've just been drafted."

I frown. She's starting to piss me off, which is actually a good thing, at least for me—I'd rather be angry than upset and confused. "Okay, *Mary*, I get that we're both from Buckley and that you're some kind of spooky urban legend and all that crap, but you don't have the authority to draft me. You don't look like a road ghost. Even if you were, that wouldn't put you in some position of power over me. I'm a hitcher. That means I cock my thumb and I am *gone*."

"Then why haven't you left already?" Mary shrugs. "I'm not the only one holding you here, although I admit, I did have something to do with getting you to come in the first place. Stop fighting with me, and listen to the road. Listen to what it's trying to tell you."

I glare at her for a moment, more for effect than anything else, before I close my eyes and try to figure out what the hell she's talking about. I can't drop down into the twilight, but I can feel the road beneath my feet, and I can feel the thousand other roads running under the living one. They're the ghosts of this place, of this time. Some of them are truly dead; some are lost; some are part of another America entirely. One by one, I filter them out, until only two roads remain. The one that I'm standing on, gravel and neglect and cool vitality . . .

and something else. Something sharp and sour and dark, a corpse that hasn't yet figured out that it needs to stop moving, that the time has come to be still. My eyes snap open of their own accord, and I'm staring at Mary Dunlavy like she's going to have the answers I need.

And maybe she is. "Route 14 is near here. It's an old stretch of highway, almost forgotten by the modern maps. They should probably rip it out, let the forest have the land back and replace it with a loop where fewer people die or disappear."

"So it's haunted?"

"No."

"But—"

"It's dead, Rose. It just doesn't know it yet." Mary shakes her head. "I need your help. We need to kill a highway."

The Last Dance Diner, 2014

"You can't be a crossroads ghost," I say, fighting the urge to go insubstantial and drop through this layer of reality. The midnight is below us, and I'm not a midnight ghost. Worse yet is the thought that maybe Mary *is*. No one knows what level the crossroads ghosts belong to. I could slide into the midnight and find her there, already waiting for me. "You *can't*. They don't really exist."

"The crossroads exists. You've been there."

"Yes, but—"

"And the crossroads guardians exist. You have to know that. You've seen a bargain being struck."

"So what?"

"So sometimes, someone wants to find a crossroads without finding a road ghost first. Sometimes someone needs a guide. And sometimes a bargain needs to be witnessed by a third party. Someone who isn't a crossroads guardian, and whose signature isn't being etched in the dirt." Mary shakes her head. "I am what I am because of the way that I died, just like you."

"How the hell do you die a crossroads death?"

She looks at me flatly, and her eyes are a hundred miles of bad road. "You die at the crossroads, begging for a second chance, that's how. It's no more or less likely than anything else; just rarer. So can we move on, and stop playing 'you're not real' games when there's serious business to discuss?"

"Serious business, right. Like how you want to 'help' me. Why the sudden urge, Mary?"

"You're going after Bobby Cross."

"Bobby Cross needs going after."

"If you've been to see Apple, you know how he became what he is."

I nod. "I won't say that Apple's a big fan of his, but she knew his basic story. Big star wants to be bigger, goes to the crossroads, buys himself eternal youth at the cost of a whole lot of innocent souls. I'm tired of him. I'm tired of being chased, and I'm tired of *running*. That means it's time for me to turn this bus around and ram him with it."

"Do you always talk in driving metaphors?"

"I'm a hitchhiking ghost. It was this, or talk in Disney metaphors."

Mary rolls her eyes before she sobers again, a smile I had barely even noticed fading from her lips. "A deal like Bobby's is . . . well, it's rare. It takes a lot of work on the part of the crossroads guardian who brokers it, and it takes two witnesses, one living, one dead. The living witness was the King of the North American Routewitches. He stepped down soon after that, and Apple was crowned the new Queen. The dead witness . . ." She hesitates, and I don't want her to say what she's going to say next, because I can read it on her face, and this isn't right, it isn't *fair*, she's just another girl from Buckley, and no matter what I may say about roots, I miss having them. But she speaks anyway. She was always going to.

"The dead witness was me, Rose. I'm sorry. I'm the crossroads ghost who witnessed Bobby's deal. I put my name on his contract. And I am so, so sorry."

Daly, Maine, 1981

This is a terrible idea. I would tell Mary that, but I've already told her several times, and I don't think she's actually listening to me anymore. She keeps ranging ahead through the forest, never far enough to let me out of her sight, but far enough to make it clear how impatient she is. I'm not clear on why she's in such a rush, and I don't want to ask. There's too much of a chance that she'd tell me. As to why I'm following her at all . . .

I'm curious. I've never felt anything like Route 14. It's a black gash across the ghostroads, and now that we're getting closer, I can smell it, a weird mixture of burning tires and antifreeze, like an accident that's simultaneously starting and burning out. It makes my head hurt a little. I could probably stop that by letting go of my coat and the flesh that it carries with it, but since the ghostroads are still outside my grasp, I want to save that particular parlor trick until I actually need it.

Mary stops walking when she reaches the edge of the trees. I hurry to catch up with her, and my breath catches in my throat as I see what she's looking at.

The edge of the forest is about six feet of sloping dirt and stone above the pavement. Whoever built this highway cut it straight through the middle of the landscape, not caring how badly they scarred the earth in the process. And that's what this is: it's a scar, it's something alive and dead at the same time, pulsing with a horrible vitality that makes my teeth itch and my skin crawl. The sky overhead keeps flickering between the bruised black of the twilight and the sunny blue of the living world. Someone who wasn't dead wouldn't see that flicker, but I can't imagine that anyone could possibly be comfortable here. Everything stinks, burning tires and antifreeze, yes, and worse—so much worse—the fading scent of ashes and lilies. There have been so many accidents here. I can't even begin to unsnarl them.

Some places turn bad because they're haunted. I've seen it happen to stretches of road before, usually after they've attracted a homecomer or a white lady. This is the first time I've seen a highway that was actually haunting *itself*.

"How is this possible?" My voice comes out in a hushed whisper, like I'm afraid that speaking too loudly will somehow attract the road's attention.

"Fucked if I know," says Mary with a shrug. "I just know that it happened, and it's killing people. I want it to stop."

"You knew I'd have to help you if you showed me this." The ghosts of impacts shudder in the air, distorting it until it creates the illusion of a heat-haze above the yellow dividing line. All those accidents that didn't have to happen, all those people who didn't have to die . . .

If I were actually alive, and not the temporarily incarnate ghost of a teenage girl who died in 1952, this is when I would toss my cookies all over the shoulder. I never thought I'd miss throwing up.

"I did," Mary admits. There's no apology in her tone. "I know this isn't your usual gig, but it's not mine either. It's not anyone's. It's just a mess that needs to be cleaned up. I'm hoping that between the two of us, we can figure out a way to do it."

I want to ask her what happens if we don't figure out a way. I don't say a word, because I know, damn her, I already know. Route 14 has been killing for years, and since there are no ghosts here, it doesn't set off the usual alarm bells in the living psyche. If we don't figure out a way to kill it, people will keep using it, maybe as a daily drive, maybe just as an occasional shortcut—and people will keep on dying here. They'll keep dying in accidents that never should have happened, in a haunted house with no walls or doors or exits. Mary's right; this has to end.

I stand on the bluff overlooking Route 14, and I wait for inspiration to strike.

The Last Dance Diner, 2014

"I don't know what's wrong with you, but that joke wasn't funny," I say—and my voice comes out in a whisper, like an echo of that day in 1981 when I stood in front of a self-haunting highway with a dead girl

I barely knew. "That's sick. How can you joke about something like that?"

"I'm not joking, Rose. I wish I were. I wish I'd refused to witness the contract, even though that would have made me subject to the castigation of the crossroads. I'm so sorry. I'm sorry for what he did to you, what he did to all of you, but I was still warm in my own grave, I didn't know—"

"You did this to me?" I'm not whispering anymore. "You're the reason that bastard ran me off the road? You're the reason that I *died?*"

"You would have been dead by now already," says Mary—and it's clear almost as soon as she's said the words that she knows she should never have let them pass her lips. Her eyes go wide, pupils dilating. She presses herself backward against the vinyl cushion of the booth behind her. She's fast, I'll give her that, but she's not a road ghost, and if there's one thing the road has given me, it's speed. I'm across the table with my hands locked around her throat before she can get out of range.

I am not a violent person, for the most part. But like everyone, I'm willing to make an exception, under the right circumstances.

"I was *sixteen!* I had my whole *life* ahead of me! You let him have me! *You did this to me!*" Emma is suddenly behind me, her hands on my shoulders, yanking me away from Mary. I fight her. I'll be ashamed of myself later, but here and now, I fight her, trying to squeeze for just a few seconds more, trying to make Mary understand the extent of her crime against me. It's a cliché to say that someone "ruined your life." By witnessing Bobby Cross' contract, Mary did more than ruin my life. She ended it.

"Rose!" Emma gives me one last yank, pulling me back across the table and shoving me down into my seat. I snarl and strain against her hands. Emma pushes me down even harder. The *beán sidhe* is surprisingly strong. Or maybe not surprisingly—she isn't a ghost, after all. The rules for her are different, and they always have been. "You know I don't tolerate fighting in my place. Really, Rose Marshall. I thought better of you."

"Blame her," I snarl, still glaring at Mary.

As for Mary . . . she's sitting where I left her, the outlines of my fingers standing out livid on the white skin of her throat. I should feel bad for hurting her like that. I don't. I *can't*. If that makes me a bad person, then so be it. At least I didn't kill her.

"I know what she did," says Emma. "She told me, when she asked if she could have this meeting here, in the Last Dance. She was hoping that being in a familiar place might make you listen before you tried to hurt her. I'm ashamed of you, Rose, I really am. I thought you believed in second chances."

"I didn't know," says Mary. My eyes narrow as my attention goes back to her. She sighs, and says, "I'd barely been dead long enough to know what a contract *was*, and the guardian kept saying it was fine, it was just fine, it was perfectly reasonable . . . crossroads ghosts are supposed to keep crossroads guardians from letting too much chaos out into the world. We're what limits their power. A guardian with a fresh ghost . . . I got taken advantage of, Rose, and you paid the price. I am so, so sorry."

"Is that true?" I look to Emma. "Is she telling me the truth?"

"The crossroads isn't evil, but it's not of this world," says Emma. "Not the way you are, or even the way that someone like me is. Crossroads guardians come from the crossroads. They want to help the crossroads get its way. Crossroads ghosts are a . . . a defense mechanism, if you will, the same way ghosts like you are a defense mechanism for the road. You help drivers make it home, one way or the other. Ghosts like Mary help people get what they're willing to pay for without hurting too many people in the process."

"Bobby Cross timed his bargain well," says Mary, and there's a coldness in her words that wasn't there a moment ago. "He waited to go to the routewitches until he knew there was a new crossroads ghost to appeal to. He asked for the crossroads nearest the place I was haunting. He played me, Rose, and you paid. Now you're hunting him . . . and I want to help."

I look at her, the girl who killed me, and I don't know what to say.

Daly, Maine, 1981

It's a road, and I'm a road ghost. Maybe that's the answer. I start forward, my feet sliding in the gravel of the shoulder, and in no time at all, I'm standing on that narrow strip of ground between the hillside and the pavement. Mary shouts for me to be careful—at least, I think that's what she does. She sounds like she's very far away.

I'm about to step forward onto the gleaming black surface of the road when I realize that there's something wrong. Mary shouldn't sound that far away, and me . . . I can be impulsive, but there's no way in hell I should be walking headlong into a haunted highway. I turn, eyes searching the shoulder for the pale silver of her hair.

I'm still looking when the tarry hands reach up through the road, grab my ankles, and pull me under. There's barely time for me to take a breath; then the whole world is blackness. They're yanking me down faster than I would have thought possible. Tar is clogging my ears, pressing against my lips, and the smell of it fills my nostrils. I could let go of my coat, abandon the flesh that's binding me here, but something about the whole situation tells me that this wouldn't be a good idea.

If the road can grab me like this while I'm alive, what's it going to do to me once it realizes I'm already dead? Most threats in the living world can't touch ghosts. This threat isn't *in* the living world. It's in both worlds, and that makes it a big, big problem.

I kick against the hands that hold my ankles, trying to force them to let me go. They respond by yanking harder. I give up on them and start grabbing at the tar around me, dragging myself upward. They're still pulling me down. I refuse to let them win.

Then hands are coming down through the darkness, fingers fumbling as they lace with mine, and I'm being hauled back up, into the light.

It felt like I was yanked down for miles. Mary is able to pull me back to the surface in seconds. We collapse onto the shoulder, me wiping tar from my eyes and mouth as I cough and choke, Mary scrubbing her tar-covered fingers hard against her pants.

When I'm sure I can talk without inhaling half of Route 14, I cough one last time and demand, "What the *fuck* was that?"

"Why do you keep expecting me to know?"

"Because you're the one who found this stupid thing!" I'm *covered* in tar. It coats my clothes, and I can feel it running down the small of my back, sending questing fingers toward the waistband of my jeans. This is disgusting. This may well be the most disgusting thing I've experienced since I died. I cast a glare toward the smooth black pavement. "It tried to kill me."

"Yes. It failed."

"Only because I'm already dead. I didn't even step on the stupid thing."

Mary's expression turns solemn. "That means it thinks we're a threat."

"Oh, fucking swell, the homicidal highway thinks I'm dangerous. That's just what I always wanted."

"You're pretty high-strung, aren't you?" Mary picks up a piece of rock from the shoulder, bouncing it thoughtfully in her hand before skipping it across the highway like she was skipping it across a pond. It doesn't sink. For the rock, the road is solid. "You should really think about switching to the undead equivalent of decaf."

"Gosh, you're funny. You're so funny I could just *die*." I wipe some more of the tar off my arm. I'm considering taking off my jacket and letting the tar fall through me when a new sound catches my attention—the sound of an engine in the distance, the steady burn of gasoline, the friction between rubber and road. I shouldn't be able to hear all those things from this far away, but I do, just like I shouldn't be able to smell the sudden mixture of rosemary and sugary perfume hanging in the air. My voice is a whisper: "Someone's coming."

Whoever it is, they're in danger. The road wants a sacrifice. And whoever it is, they can still be saved, if I can just figure out *how*.

The Last Dance Diner, 2014

"Bobby has weaknesses," says Mary. "Vanity. Pride."

"Tell me something I didn't know," I mumble. I can't meet her eyes. They all say that she has crossroads eyes. I thought that the first time that I saw her. How could I have been so *stupid*? How did I not see what she was?

"He's bound by the crossroads, same as the rest of us," says Mary. "He can chase you to the ends of the earth, because he raced you once, on Sparrow Hill Road, and you lost. He took the pink slip on your soul."

"What?" I stare at her. "I never agreed—"

"You didn't have to. You were alive and you were on the road. That meant you were in the race. That's part of the rules for him: he has to find an in. He can challenge drivers, and he can demand that routewitches race him, but he can't interfere with pedestrians. It's against the rules."

"So all I have to do is get people out of their cars and they're safe?" That can't be the answer. For one thing, I've seen him go after people on foot before. Amy, back in Wisconsin. She was on foot when Bobby Cross came for her. There has to be more to this than how you're traveling.

"Not quite," says Mary. "He'll cheat if he thinks he can—if there's no crossroads ghost or crossroads guardian nearby to remind him that he's not allowed to play dirty. And that's another thing. He has no power at the crossroads. Get there, and he can't touch you."

"But I might have to make a bargain if I want to stay, right?"

Mary looks away. Gotcha.

"All right, Mary. You're telling me stuff, but you're not telling me the one thing I really need to know. How do I stop him? How do I kill Bobby Cross?"

She sighs. In that moment, she sounds very small, and very sad, and very much like a lost girl from Buckley. "You don't," she says. "He can't be killed. But he can be weakened."

"All right," I say. "That's going to have to do. How do I weaken him?"

Mary looks back to me, eyes wide. Then, slowly, she smiles. "It's the car," she says. "Bobby has no power. It's all in his car. Go for the tires, the windshield, anything to weaken him—to slow him down. If you can get him off the road, he's stuck until the car repairs itself."

"The car runs on ghosts, right?"

"Right, but it's the miles that keep Bobby young. Ghosts go into the gas tank, the car keeps moving, Bobby Cross remains the man who never grows old. If he stops long enough, all those years will catch up with him."

"Good to know." It *is* good to know. I just don't know how much good it's going to do me. I can throw rocks. That's about the extent of my car-destroying powers.

"It's not much, I know. Still . . ."

"Every piece helps, Mary." I'm surprised to realize that I mean it. "Someday, we'll get that bastard off the ghostroads. At least now I understand why he's so set on catching up to me. Every time I slow him down, I hurt him." Maybe someday all those little delays will be enough to take him out for good. A girl can dream, can't she?

Mary smiles like the sun coming over the Buckley hills, and flags down Emma. "I think this calls for burgers," she says.

Daly, Maine, 1981

The surface of the road remains still and calm, but I can hear that car getting closer in the distance. Mary doesn't seem to hear it yet. Mary's not a road ghost.

"Okay," I say, mostly to myself. "There has to be an answer, there has to be . . ." Every ghost has its weaknesses. So do the undead. Their biggest weakness is usually the body, which is crumbling around the spirit it contains.

The body . . .

"Oh, I am going to regret this," I say, and back up until my shoulders are against the slope of the hill. Mary turns to me, eyes wide.

"Rose, what are you—"

She doesn't get to finish her question before I break into a run, sprinting as hard as I can toward that highway. When I hit the edge, I leap, and I dive, headfirst, into the smooth black pavement.

I'm still wearing the jacket. I should fetch up against the concrete, getting at minimum a bloody nose for my trouble. Instead, I break through the black like a swimmer breaks the surface of the water, and the hands rise out of the tarry dark, grabbing me and dragging me down.

This time, I don't fight them. If anything, I help, swimming farther and farther into the black. The hands have to be taking me *somewhere*; they have to be feeding something, or the road wouldn't bother with this blatant a display of power. It must think it's going to get a reward.

My lungs are burning, but I force myself to keep my jacket on as the hands yank me ever downward. This has to end soon. This has to stop. There has to be a bottom, because there's always a bottom, somewhere past the point of no return.

When my head slams into something solid, I know that I've reached it. The hands let go, but the tar remains, thick and black and cloying, pushing its way into my nostrils, my ears, every beaten, battered inch of me. I start feeling around blindly in the dark, searching the road bottom for anything that feels out of place, anything that would have been bad enough to kill this road and leave it living at the same time.

Just tar, and smooth stone, and blackness . . . and a skull. A human skull, old and frail and worn down smooth by the hot tar pouring over it. But he wasn't old, was he? He was young when they found him walking by the roadside, sun in his hair and a pack over his shoulder, heading from nowhere to no place at an easy amble. He never saw the danger in their eyes, never saw the way they eyed his meager belongings. He was too comfortable on the road, and when they came for him—

The memories in the bone are overwhelming. I clutch it close to my chest and perform the last parlor trick that I have in me, allowing my borrowed coat to fall away from my suddenly incorporeal body. The tar goes with it. I'm still underground, but what surrounds me is the normal earth that goes beneath poured pavement. The actual skull of the long-dead hitchhiker is somewhere in the dirt. I hold its ghost in my hands, and together, the ghost and I rise through Route 14, up into the light.

Mary is still standing there when I emerge, resplendent in the green dress I never got to wear to my prom. The ghostly skull comes with me as far as the road's surface, and then it's gone, replaced by the young man I saw walking in the long-buried past. He's squinting in the sun. He looks confused.

"Rose!" shouts Mary.

I turn just in time for the car I heard coming earlier to slam into us. I catch a glimpse of the terrified man behind the wheel, and then the car is gone, driving through us like we were nothing more than smoke. The taillights vanish around a bend in the road, leaving Route 14 to the dead.

"What happened?" asks the man.

"What's your name?" I counter.

"Dennis."

"Well, Dennis, you were brutally murdered, and then this highway"—I kick uselessly at the road; my toe passes through it—"used your unquiet spirit to fuel a murderous rampage. The road's dead now. You're free. You're welcome."

"You did it." Mary walks out onto the road—which is *just* a road now, and will be just a road for the rest of time—and moves to join us. "I didn't think . . ."

"I'll add 'highway killer' to my list of accomplishments." Route 14 is dead for real, now. It was already dying, and only Dennis was keeping it staggering along, like a battery shoved into a slot too small for it. The drivers who still remembered this road existed will forget it, one by one, until the forest takes it back. As for Dennis . . .

He was always meant to be a hitcher. I can see it in his eyes. Maybe now he'll get the chance.

"What do we do now?" he asks.

I smile. "There's a gas station near here. Let's go put our thumbs out, and see what we catch."

It's no real surprise that when we turn, Mary is gone. She didn't seem like the sort to stick around. I'm sure I'll see her again, and maybe it's the memory of tar filling my ears and nose, but I'm in no hurry for that to happen.

The Last Dance Diner, 2014

"Do you forgive me?" she asks.

We're standing outside, the glare of neon from the diner's sign casting strange lights on our hair. I can see Emma through the window, clearing away our dishes. I force myself to focus on Mary, as much as I can. "You didn't know that what you were doing would get me killed."

"No. But I knew it would get *somebody* killed. I think Bobby went back to Buckley because he knew it was my hometown. He wanted me to pay for refusing to sign the contract until the crossroads guardian wrote out the rules in full."

"Sucks to be you," I said. "Also sucks to be me. Sucks to be pretty much everyone, once shit like this starts going down."

"But do you forgive me?"

I think of Dennis, smiling shyly as his first ride slowed to pick him up. He's mostly in Canada these days, exploring all the places he never got to go when he was alive. I guess seventy years fueling an unquiet highway leaves a guy with a certain longing to see the world. He'd still be down there if not for Mary. People would still be dying there, and no one would know why.

"As much as I ever can," I say. Mary smiles sadly. Here and now, in the shadow of the Last Dance, it seems like that will have to be enough.

Book Four

True Stories

So when sunset shuts the doors of day, I start my car,
She's a coffin and a crypt away, and that's too far.
When I pull up beside her and say, "Wanna ride?"
Well, I know it doesn't matter that my baby died.
Here's a bit of advice, boy, take it as you will:
You just might find you've met the love of your life at night on Dead Man's Hill.

I don't put much stock in sunlight or in what folks say,
It doesn't matter if my ghost-girl's just a myth by day.
My baby's never gone to Heaven, wouldn't if she could,
She likes to mix her nice with naughty, likes to shake it good.
Here's a bit of advice, boy, take it as you will:
You just might find you've met the love of your life at night on Dead Man's Hill.

She was a little too bad for Heaven, she was a little too good for Hell.
They wouldn't light the "Vacancy" sign for any of the things that were hers to sell.
Well, if the afterlife won't have her, she can still be an angel to me,
She'll be my after-midnight graveyard girl for all eternity.

—excerpt from "Dead Man's Hill," by Johnny Sutton and the Sanders.

There is a tendency when looking at stories to ask, "What does this story *mean*? What does this story *symbolize*?" Endless arguments have centered on the symbolism of the Phantom Prom Date's hair color and the style of her dress. Others ask whether her legend might be two ghost stories blended into one—the girl in the green silk gown, whose stories are usually negative, filled with blood and vengeance, and the girl begging for a ride by the side of the road, whose very presence allows the drivers who pick her up to avoid fatal accidents.

Several real figures have been proposed as the origins of the Phantom Prom Date. Three girls of the right approximate age and coloration died in Buckley Township, Michigan, over a twenty-year period. Their deaths were all ruled as misadventures, although some scholars have put forth the idea that the story of the Phantom Prom Date may have arisen to hide a darker tale, one of human sacrifice and attempts to raise the Devil. Whatever the case, and whatever the story's origin, it has spread, until her pleas for a ride may be heard anywhere in North America. The Phantom Prom Date may never make it home, but she has certainly managed to make it everywhere else . . .

—*On the Trail of the Phantom Prom Date*,
Professor Laura Moorhead, University of Colorado.

2015
Crossroads Bargains

THERE'S ONE THING every haunt, spirit, and shade on the twilight side of the ghostroads learns early and well, and it's this: your word is sometimes the only currency you have, and those are the times when breaking it can leave you vulnerable to the kind of consequences that you don't recover from. The Kindly Ones watch for oathbreakers. Certain types of shadow only manifest in the path of liars, and they can cling and catch like tar dredged up from the bottom of a vengeful highway. If you want to survive in the twilight, you tell the truth—at least on the ghostroads. Lying to the living that don't belong in the twilight spaces doesn't come with any consequences. The living don't count. Lying to your fellow dead, on the other hand, or, God forbid, lying to the routewitches or the ambulomancers . . .

That's playing the sort of roulette that the house always, always wins. Never make a promise that you don't intend to keep. Never incur a debt that you don't intend to pay. Never double-cross a routewitch. We may not have much of a life here among the dead, but what we do have is too precious to gamble on a hand that can't possibly be won. Exorcism would be kinder than some of the tools the routewitches have at their disposal.

I was pretty honest before I died. A good girl. I'm not as good as I used to be, but I'm a lot more honest, because the stakes are a lot higher than getting grounded or missing a school dance. The stakes are death and worse-than-death, and I like my current state of being.

But that's just me. Some people still make bargains they can't keep; some people still make promises that they don't intend to honor. Some people still let the bills get higher than they ever meant to pay. And some of them, Persephone give me strength . . .

Some of them are my own flesh and blood. Such as it is.

This particular stretch of Indiana highway is familiar. I've walked it before, and I'll probably walk it again, the world being what it is, and people being a little reluctant to stop in the middle of a cornfield to pick up an unfamiliar teenage girl. Thanks for that one, Stephen King. You and your goddamn children of the corn can go piss up a rope for all the walking that you've made me do over the course of the last twenty years.

Still, it's a beautiful evening, with that sort of purple-bruised sky that only the American Midwest ever manages to conjure. It's almost the sort of sky we had when I was alive, before pollution gilded the world's sunsets in all the pretty shades of poison. There are even fireflies dancing above the corn like tiny falling stars, and the whole world smells like green and good growing things. A night like this, I almost don't mind walking. Besides, my last ride was recent enough that I still have a coat to keep me warm, anchoring me in this world for as long as I choose to stay or until that setting sun comes up again tomorrow morning, whichever comes first.

I'm so busy walking through the growing dark that I don't hear the engine behind me, the crunch of wheels on roadside gravel, the rattle of the truck's back gate, a battered old thing held up by rope and bailing wire as much as by the memory of what it used to be. I'm lost in my own little world, right up until strong arms grab me around the chest, hoisting me up and off the ground almost before I can squeak. Then I'm in the hay-and-corn-husk–filled bed of the truck, and we're accelerating away from the place where I was grabbed, and all I can think is that we're about eight seconds away from someone getting slapped.

Common sense wins out for once, and I decide to forgo slapping in favor of the more sensible option: letting go and dropping back down into the twilight. So I release my hold on the coat that binds me to the mortal world, and it falls through the memory of my flesh to land with a rustle in the chaff surrounding us. Then *I* let go, and *I* fall . . .

. . . right into the bed of a clapped-out old junker of a pickup truck, the bed filled with hay and corn husks. The man who grabbed me is watching with obvious amusement, not making an effort to hide it. Slapping still sounds like a good option, but if these people can drive straight from the daylight to the twilight that might not be the best idea.

I straighten, trying to look like I'm not scared enough to bolt for the deepest, darkest hole I can find. These people could probably follow me there. "Okay, you fuckers, I'm warning you, I'm a bad person to abduct. I have friends."

My abductor laughs at that—actually laughs, like I just said something unbelievably funny. There's an answering chuckle from behind me, and I glance over my shoulder to see the first man's virtual twin. They're both sturdy blond Minnesota-looking farm boys, so clichéd that they could have walked out of the pages of a L'il Abner funnybook adventure forty years ago. "Miss Rose, I think you don't quite understand what's going on here," he says, accent confirming my guess as to his heritage.

"Yeah, well, I'm dead, not psychic, so when you want me to know something, you need to *tell* me." It's getting easier to suppress fear in favor of anger. There's not much I hate more than I hate to be laughed at. "Why did you grab me? Where are we going? *How* are we going?"

There isn't much of a vocabulary to bridge the worlds of the dead and the living. When you're living, you don't need it, and once you're dead, you have better things to worry about. The farm boy who grabbed me seems to understand, which is something of a relief; he nods, once, and says, "Well, Miss Rose, I grabbed you because if we stop this ol' truck, she's not likely to start up again until after the solstice, which seemed a bit long to wait when we're wanted tonight. We're heading to the Rest Stop"—I can *hear* the capital letters, like he's talking about the only rest stop in the world—"and we're traveling by magic, I suppose. Magic, and combustion engine."

"Okay, *why* are we traveling to 'the Rest Stop' via magic and combustion engine?"

"Now there's a good question." He smiles, and there's a glint in his eye that whispers "routewitch." I would have seen it before, if I hadn't been so annoyed. "We're going to see the Queen."

The tattoo on my back hasn't burned since I left the Last Dance, but with his words, it starts burning again. The Queen of the Routewitches has summoned me, and that means my debt to her is coming due. This is a lot sooner than I thought it was going to be.

I hope like hell that I'm truly prepared to pay, and the truck drives deeper and deeper down into the twilight, away from the lands of the living.

The transition between layers of the twilight is silken-smooth, like peeling the nylons from a hooker's legs. The drop from the twilight onto the asphalt shores of the Ocean Lady is something else altogether. The truck jerks and shudders like it's hitting the world's biggest pothole, and the sudden pressure in my chest tells me that I've been slapped back into solidity, back—temporarily—among the living once again. I pick myself up from the bed of the truck, dusting straw off my arms and glaring at the routewitch thugs surrounding me. "You know, I think I've spent more time incarnate in the last year than I have in the last *decade*."

"Congratulations," says one of the routewitches.

I focus my glare in his direction, wishing I'd lived long enough to reach an age where my glares could be considered more cutting than cute. "That wasn't intended as a happy statement."

Now it's time for the routewitch to glare. He's not cute, exactly, but his L'il Abner haircut and bib overalls render the expression impotent, robbing it of menace. "You've been invited to the Ocean Lady, Miss Rose. That's an honor most ghosts never get."

"And me without my party dress." The words are out before I realize how true they are: I'm *not* in my party dress. My coat is discarded in the chaff, but I'm still wearing the clothes I conjured for a day on the Indiana road, blue jeans and an old workman's shirt with Gary's name stitched in black on the breast pocket. I'm incarnate, back among the living whether I want to be or not, but I'm still in ghost's array. I don't know whether that's a good thing or not, and I don't have time to know, because here comes the Rest Stop on the Ocean Lady, blossoming in front of us like the last neon oasis in the desert of the dead.

If the Last Dance Diner is every diner that's ever been or ever will be, the Rest Stop is something more, something bigger and more profound. It's every roadside dive, every truck stop, every place where a weary traveler has ever had cause to stop and lay their head. I didn't see it clearly the last time I was here; the Ocean Lady didn't know me yet, and didn't yet speak the language of my heart. She does now, after a fashion, and the structure ahead of us is every good thing about every good place the road has ever offered me. It's the diner where Gary kissed me for the first time, nervous teenage affection that tasted like chocolate soda and tomorrow. It's the truck stop where Larry bought me a burger and let me show him the way he had to go. It's a thousand places, a thousand moments, and it hurts my heart, makes it skip a beat it shouldn't be taking. Looking at the Rest Stop, I understand why the routewitches don't encourage the dead to come here. In its own strange way, the truth of the Ocean Lady's soul might kill us.

L'il Abner the first scoots up behind me, warm and solid in the slightly unreal twilight dark, and says, "We're almost here, Miss Rose. You might want to get yourself ready."

"Are you going to tell me what I'm getting ready *for*?"

"That's for the Queen to do, Miss. All we know is that she sent us to find you, and that it was very important that when we found you, we found you in the corn."

It doesn't take a genius to know that doesn't sound good. I clutch the edge of the pickup bed, the heartbeat I shouldn't have hammering in my chest, and I let the Ocean Lady open her arms and welcome her wayward children home.

The Queen of the Routewitches doesn't need to justify herself to dead girls, which explains the way she had me collected, but she's a reasonable person, for the most part, and she doesn't make me wait for my reception. She's standing on the blacktop when the truck pulls up, an old green-painted picnic table with an honest-to-God picnic basket on it behind her. There's an older routewitch seated there, a woman I don't know, with ribbons tangled in her oddly girlish ponytail.

The truck rocks and rumbles to a stop, and I hear the driver's-side door slam before the previously unseen driver himself is there to open the back of the truck, offering me his hands. I could balk, but it's better to pick your battles when you can. I let him help me down. The feeling of solid ground beneath my feet is a comforting thing. My type of ghost exists because of rides freely given, not because of rides we never agreed to take. The L'il Abners climb down after me, bowing deeply to the whisper-thin Japanese teen now walking toward us. Apple. Queen of the North American Routewitches. She's older than she looks.

"Thank you so much for coming," she says, like I had a choice. Her gaze flicks past me to her subjects. "Thank you for bringing her. You're free to go. The Lady's hospitalities are open to you all."

Whatever that means, it must be good, because the routewitches are gone almost before she's finished speaking, offering quick apologies and good-byes as they hustle toward the building. In a matter of seconds, the three of us—me, the Queen, and the routewitch I don't know—are alone. I fold my arms, trying to look defiant. It helps that she looks so young. Apple and I stopped aging at approximately the same point, although I did it by dying, while all she did was leave the living world behind.

"You could have called."

"You don't have a phone," counters the Queen. "He still hasn't taken you."

"Not for lack of trying." I sigh. I owe her, and so I should probably stop glaring. That doesn't make it easy. "I'm guessing you didn't ask me here for dinner. What's going on?"

"Dinner is a part of things. I asked you for a favor, and you promised to grant it to me. Will you keep your word, here on the back of the Ocean Lady?"

"Do I look like an idiot? Of course I will."

"Then come, sit down, and eat with us. I'll explain what has to happen tonight." The Queen gestures to the picnic table. I'm smart enough to recognize an order when I see one, and so I walk past her to the picnic table and sit down across from the older routewitch. The Queen follows, sitting next to me.

"Who's your friend?" I ask.

The older routewitch raises her head and looks at me. That's all she has to do, because her eyes are familiar, even though they're filled with shadows, and with screams. There's a thousand years of agony in those eyes. Some small, bitter part of me isn't quite convinced that that's enough.

"Oh," I say. "Hello, Bethany."

"Hello, Aunt Rose," she says, in a quivering voice that's just as old as the rest of her.

The Queen of the Routewitches is laying out a picnic spread fit for, ironically, a queen. As always seems to be the case when I'm in her company, I don't have any appetite at all. "And this started out as such a *good* night," I say, plaintively.

Thankfully, both Bethany and the Queen have the grace not to reply.

"When Bobby Cross carried Bethany into the dark, I'm sure he meant to kill her and render her soul for fuel," says the Queen matter-of-factly, as she spreads mustard on a slice of white bread. "Unfortunately, he hadn't reckoned on her belonging to your bloodline—which is ironic, given that it was her relation to you that enabled her to trap you in the first place."

Something neither of them has apologized for, by the way. I frown. "What does that have to do with anything?"

"You're protected from him. As blood of your blood, so is Bethany, if not quite as . . . directly. He was able to take her into the twilight. He was able to steal her youth, her innocence, and her hope. But he couldn't take her soul. In your own way, you stopped him." The Queen's gaze is level as she turns it on Bethany. For the first time, I hear disapproval of my niece's actions in her voice as she says, "Amusing, given the situation."

"I could die laughing," I say, deadpan. Bethany reddens, looking down at her untouched sandwich. "So why am I here? It sounds to me like things are in balance. She tried to fuck me over, and she got fucked instead. Case closed."

"Those books are balanced," the Queen agrees. "But as a routewitch, she has the right to ask the Ocean Lady for aid, and the Lady answered her. It wasn't my decision; I wouldn't have called you if she'd come to me alone. As you say, some punishments, we earn."

The routewitch relationship with the Ocean Lady—ghost of the oldest true highway in America—is complicated. They treat Her half as a place, half as a person, and all as a goddess. I've been learning a lot about routewitch religion lately, and believe me when I say that I am not qualified to even begin to explain. "So the Lady said she'd help. Meaning what, exactly?"

"Meaning you have to take me to the crossroads before the stroke of midnight," says Bethany. It's the first time she's spoken since we acknowledged each other.

I stare at her. "You're kidding."

The Queen of the Routewitches sighs, deep and tired. "Sadly, she's not. That's how you'll pay your debt to me, Rose Marshall: by taking my subject, your niece, to the crossroads to barter for her future."

"Fucking swell," I mutter, and the twilight all around us seems to agree.

"Have another sandwich," the Queen suggests. "You're going to need it."

At least there's pie.

Going to the crossroads, the quick and dirty version: as long as there have been people, there have been roads, places where the footsteps of a hundred strangers have worn a groove in the world and changed it in a way that might seem superficial, but goes all the way down into the root of things. As long as there have been roads, the places where those roads met have held a power entirely their own. Towns spring up in the places where roads meet. Fairs are held. Goods are exchanged. And sometimes, if you're desperate, or stupid, or just feel like you have nothing left to lose, bargains are made. I don't know who made the first crossroads bargain, and I don't need to know, because that groove, too, has been worn into the root of things. Go to the crossroads at midnight when you need to make a deal. Everyone knows that's how it works.

What the proverbial "everyone" *doesn't* know is how to get to the crossroads, because there's only so much magic to go around these days, and not just any old intersection will do. You need the right combination of place and time, madness and longing, and you need to get there by the stroke of midnight, because that's the way it has to go. I've never gone to the crossroads for myself. In the decades since I died, I've only ever gone for other people, and even then, only when they begged, only when there was no other choice.

"What makes you think I can even find the crossroads?" I ask, vainly hoping the Queen will recognize what a lousy idea this is and get her piece of deceased masonry to call off the trip. "It's been a long time since I had to go there."

"Twenty-six years," Apple agrees. "It was in Coney Island that time, wasn't it?"

"Yeah. It was." The girl I led there was eleven years old and was born almost a hundred years before I was, and when she found me, she had no shadow. I took her to the crossroads because I didn't know any other way to get a shadow back, and I guess it worked, because after she stood at that roadside for half an hour, she ran over and hugged me, shadow chasing her heels. Then she kicked her feet away from the ground and flew into the sky like a kite without a string, and I never saw her again.

"It won't be this time."

"This is a bad idea," I say.

"I know," says the Queen wearily.

"Can we just go?" asks Bethany.

Apple's hand flashes out like a striking snake, and the sound of her palm meeting Bethany's cheek is louder than it has any right to be. Bethany stares at her, eyes young and hurt amidst their nest of wrinkles. The Queen glares back, her own eyes briefly betraying her own greater age. "You will not speak to your family with anything less than courtesy," she commands. "I am asking your aunt to do this because the Lady bids it; were it left to me, I would call this a just punishment for your actions. Do you understand me?"

"Yes," whispers Bethany.

"Good. Remember: you are here because you are a routewitch, and I cannot bar you without just cause. *She* is here because she's welcome."

That seems to be my cue. I sigh, standing. "Come on, Bethany. Let's go spend the night doing something stupid and suicidal."

I don't wait to see if she'll follow me. I just start walking.

Bethany follows; of course Bethany follows. I'm her only chance at getting her youth back, and as a routewitch, she can expect to be old for a long, long time. We walk down the drive to the Rest Stop gates. The road beyond ripples slightly, unreal and undefined; it is all roads, it is no roads, and it is, at least potentially, the road to where we're going. "Take my hand," I order. She isn't worthy of a "please."

"Why?" asks Bethany, suspiciously.

"One, because *you* asked *me* for help, so it's not like I'm trying to walk you into a trap, which, two, you've already done to me once, but mostly because three, I'm going to go from the Ocean Lady to the ghostroads to the daylight, and if you don't hold onto me, you're likely to get lost somewhere along the way." I offer her a thin smile. "Unless you want to spend a few days wandering one of the twilight layers without an escort?"

Bethany takes my hand. I'm almost disappointed.

"Good call," I say, and step through the open gate to the shimmering road beyond.

For me, now, after being dead so long, moving between the layers is an automatic thing most of the time, almost as easy as flexing the fingers of my hand. Not so with Bethany hanging onto me, mortal deadweight that understands, on some profound, unaware level, that living flesh was never meant to do this sort of thing. Bethany screams as reality flickers around us like a broken strip of film, endless past and present roads tangling together. I keep pulling, keep rising upward through the twilight, back toward the day. We're not going *all* the way, not quite—the crossroads exists in a place just below the surface of full daylight, in a place where things become possible because no one's ever told them that they can't be.

We're almost there when I realize that we're about to have another problem. Bethany is still alive, and I, by definition almost, am not. Which wouldn't be a problem if I had a coat, but my most recent coat is lying discarded in the bed of a pickup truck a lot of layers of reality away from here. "Shit," I mutter.

"Shit?" demands Bethany. "What do you mean, shit?"

My fingers are already turning hazy in hers. She'd have noticed already, if she wasn't so busy freaking out. "Just hold on!" I command, and try to pull us through the layers even faster, anything to build up enough momentum that Bethany will be carried with me when holding on ceases to be possible.

I've never tried anything like this before. I guess I shouldn't be surprised when there's a blinding burst of light and everything goes away, replaced by darkness. Darkness, and the distinct feeling that I've just screwed something up. "Shit," I mutter again . . . and the world is gone.

I come to slowly. I'm sprawled in a nest of crushed corn stalks, scenting the air all around me with the rich green perfume of harvest coming.

That's the first thing. The second is that I'm deeply—disturbingly—solid. I shouldn't have been able to crush the corn. I sit up, and only an instinctive grab at the fabric sliding down my chest keeps Bethany's coat from tumbling to the ground beside me.

"Are you awake *yet?*" Bethany demands. I turn, still clutching the coat, to see her standing next to me. "This cold is killing my joints."

"I hadn't noticed." I shrug into the coat as I stand, tugging it tight around me. The feeling of solidity tightens with it. Back among the living once again. I'm starting to feel like a ping-pong ball. "How long was I out?"

"Too long. I don't remember giving you permission to pass out."

"Well, since I don't remember giving you permission to ransom me to Bobby Cross, I guess we're essentially even. Come on. We're burning moonlight." I turn once to get my bearings—it's easier to get lost in a cornfield than it is to get lost almost anywhere else in the world—and start walking briskly across the uneven ground. At least we don't need to hold hands anymore. That's more family togetherness than I'm in the mood for.

Bethany swears and sputters as she stumbles after me. For all that she grew up in Michigan, same as I did, she doesn't seem to have done much walking in cornfields. Or maybe it's just her abruptly advanced age. It must be hard to grow old gracefully when you do it overnight. "Slow down!"

"Speed up!" I shout back. "We're on a pretty tight schedule here."

"Why?" She's panting as she staggers to my side. I take pity and slow down slightly. My debt to the Queen probably won't count as paid if Bethany drops dead before I can get her to the crossroads. Too bad. "I want this taken care of more than you do, but doesn't midnight happen every night? If we miss it tonight, can't we just try again tomorrow?"

"Nope." I can see from her expression that she doesn't understand. This seems to be my night for taking pity. I sigh, and explain, "Once you start looking for the crossroads, you're *on* one of the crossing roads. It's some sort of symbolic metaphysical thing, since you still need to find the roads in a physical sense, and I don't really understand it, but them's the rules. My friend Mary could probably explain it. Anyway, she's not here, and we have until midnight."

"Or what?"

"We wait a year."

Bethany's eyes widen in undisguised alarm. "What? I can't spend a *year* like this!"

"That's true. You may not *have* a year like this." I'm being nasty—Bethany doesn't look *that* old—but it's difficult to really care. This isn't how I planned to spend my evening. Or any evening. Ever. "So you'd better keep up."

"Bitch," Bethany mutters, picking up her pace a little more in order to draw a step ahead of me.

"Guess it runs in the family," I say, and keep on walking.

The cornfield extends for what feels like miles. We eventually come out on a wide dirt semi-road beaten into the corn, worn by years of farmers' footsteps as they checked their harvests. I know the road as soon as I step onto it, feel the electric tingle in the soles of my feet; I've never been here before, and I've been here dozens and dozens of times, because this is the initial spoke on the crossroads wheel. If it isn't the first road, it's the road that will lead us to the first road. The first road will lead to the second road—they have to cross, after all—and then Bethany can make her bargain. Whatever that bargain might be.

Bethany steps onto the road behind me, and stops, letting out a deep sigh of relief. "Oh, thank God. This is the right road."

"This is part of the right road. Don't get too excited."

She shoots me a glare that reminds me that of the two of us, I'm the one who looks like a teenager, but she's the one who actually *is* a teenager. "Why are you like that?"

"Like what?"

"A spoiler. Spoiling things. This is the right road. Why won't you just let it be the right road?"

"Because maybe it's the *wrong* road. Maybe it's the road that leads to the road that leads to the right road, which doesn't mean *this* is the right road. Maybe I'm walking through a cornfield in the middle of the night with the niece who tried to hand me to my personal devil, and maybe that's not the sort of thing that puts me in a good mood. Maybe being dead for the better part of a century has made me a realist. Or maybe I just don't like you. Did you consider that?" I look steadfastly ahead, and keep on walking. "Next time, try asking one of the other routewitches."

"I did. They all turned me down." There's a wistful edge to Bethany's voice that makes me stop and turn to look at her. "They said . . . they said I got what I deserved. That I shouldn't have been messing around with things that I didn't understand. That I shouldn't have been messing around with you."

"Routewitches and road ghosts have an arrangement. You don't mess with us, we don't mess with you." I start walking again. Bethany follows. "Most routewitches wind up road ghosts when they die. I guess they view treating us with respect as an investment in their own afterlife."

"Were you a routewitch?"

The question silences me for a moment. I think about it as I walk, and finally answer, "I think I might have been. Maybe. But I never had the opportunity to travel, and it's supposed to be travel that makes a routewitch understand what the roads are saying." I'd *wanted* to travel. Gary and I used to talk about it all the time. It never happened, and then I was dead, and travel became a fact of—for lack of a better word—life.

"You could ask for that. At the crossroads."

"Ask for what?"

"The chance to be a routewitch."

I wheel around to face her, stopping in my tracks. "You mean the chance to be alive again? Is that it? I could go to the crossroads and ask whatever . . . whatever fucked-up horror movie version of a fairy godmother it is that makes bargains there to bring me back from the dead?" I can tell from her face that she means exactly that. She's trying to make me *want* to go to the crossroads, like that will somehow transform this from a chore into the world's most bizarre family outing. "I should leave you, I should leave you right here and let you find your way without me."

Bethany's eyes widen in alarm. "Don't do that! I just . . . I just thought . . ."

"You thought I'd want to be alive again. Right. See, there *was* a time when I wanted to be alive again. There was a time when I would have sold my soul for the chance to be alive again. But that time passed. My world got old and moved on, and I kept on being sixteen years old. The phantom prom date, the girl who never grew up, Wendy without a Peter Pan. My mother died, my brothers got married, my classmates graduated and got lives, and I was still sixteen, and I was still on the road. If you'd explained the crossroads to me when I was a year, five years, even ten years dead, I would have jumped at the chance to get my world back. My world isn't there anymore, Bethany. It's never going to be there again. So asking me if I want to be alive again isn't just insulting, isn't just superficial, it's *mean*. Now shut the fuck up and just keep walking."

"I'm sorry," Bethany whispers.

"Yeah. So am I." I turn and started to walk again. The cornfields and the smell of the green surround us on all sides. And we just keep going.

The cornfield road gives way to a slightly larger road. This one comes with bonus haystacks, and the unending magnetic pull of the crossroads somewhere in the distance ahead. It knows we're coming. It's waiting for us. I just hope it understands that only one of us is actually coming to deal.

Bethany's having trouble keeping up. The walk is taking its toll on her, but I don't dare slow down. There's only so much distance between here and midnight at the crossroads, and if we miss the deadline . . . Bethany's going to have a lot more nights of achy joints and trouble breathing ahead of her. She's stupid. She's stupid, and short-sighted, and stubborn, and most of all, she's *young*. She's the kind of young I never had the chance to be. And yet a part of me understands her. She got into this mess because she wanted to get out of Buckley so badly she was willing to ransom someone else's soul in order to do it. There was a time when I wanted out of Buckley just as bad. Admittedly, I was going to do it by marrying Gary and moving someplace big and exotic, like Ann Arbor, but hell. Who understands kids these days?

"Are we almost there?" she asks, wheezing.

"Maybe. Probably not. I have no idea. It's a beautiful night. Enjoy it."

"Easy for you to say. You're never going to get old."

"I'm also never going to get married, have children, or go to Europe. Think of this as a preview."

"Oh, wow. Great pep talk, Aunt Rose."

"Cheering you up isn't my job. Getting you there is. So shut up and keep on walking."

Bethany mutters and keeps on walking. That's all I want at this point. The road is humming more and more strongly under my feet, and the distant taste of copper is beginning to cling to the back of my throat. We're getting closer. If we just keep moving, we've got a good chance of making it.

The road curves, bending back into the cornfield. Then it splits, the wider, smoother avenue continuing in one direction, while a narrow dirt trail branches off to the right. The ground is pitted and broken, making the first dirt road we walked down seem like a boulevard. Of course, that's the way we have to go. I actually slow down a little to let Bethany catch up. The increasing pull of the crossroads tells me that this is probably the first road—a conviction that only grows when I set foot on it. If the previous two roads were electric, this is like grabbing hold of a live wire. Bethany feels it, too, even more than I do. She gasps when she steps onto the broken ground. Then she starts walking faster, rapidly outpacing me. I let her. This is her journey, not mine.

She walks faster and faster, the corn closing around us like a series of green and growing curtains. I feel the second road almost before I can see it up ahead of us, a clean slash through the cornfield. This must be why the Queen wanted me taken from a place with corn. The spot where I left the daylight would determine where I'd tumble back into it, and if she knew the crossroads was going to be in a cornfield, doing it this way saved us a lot of time.

"We're here!" Bethany almost shouts, and breaks into a run, old woman racing through the corn. I'm half-afraid she's going to fall and break her neck. I still don't try to stop her. The crossroads has her now. If she dies in the process of getting to her goal, my part of the deal is still done.

Then Bethany steps from one road onto the other, standing at the point where the two roads cross. Too late to turn back now. She's committed.

"I am come to the crossroads with empty hands and a hopeful heart," chants Bethany, with the faintly desperate singsong of a schoolgirl reciting a lesson she's memorized but hasn't really learned. "I am come to the crossroads to bargain with all I have and all I am. I am come to the crossroads with nothing to refuse. Please, please, please, hear me, heed me, and give me the chance to pay for what I need."

Silence falls around her, blocking out all sound from the crossroads. I don't see anyone come to join her, but there is a sudden increase in the shadows clinging to the corn. Whatever happens between Bethany and the crossroads is going to be a private thing. No voyeurs allowed, living or dead.

Someone steps up next to me. I didn't hear him coming; I don't think he was there to hear. He feels like an absence in the cornfield next to me, a space that happens to be shaped like a man. A man who, when I look at him from the corner of my eye, seems vaguely familiar, like he could have been one of the younger teachers at my high school, but who, when I look at him directly, isn't there to see. I keep my eyes turned resolutely forward, watching Bethany talking to the open air.

The crossroads have to be guarded. Crossroads ghosts, like Mary, were alive once, like Bethany, like me. They're still a little human, deep down. Crossroads guardians . . . aren't. They never lived. All they care about is the deal.

"Hello, Rose," says the crossroads guardian. His voice is plummy and warm, and I forget what it sounds like almost as quickly as I hear it. "It's been a while."

"True," I say. "I wish it had been longer. I haven't had cause to come."

"Everyone has cause to come."

"That's a matter of opinion."

"Oh, Rose, Rose, Rose. You know that's not true. You needed help just recently, didn't you? You went to the routewitches. You could have come to us."

"To help me against Bobby Cross? Isn't it your fault that he's on the loose to begin with?"

There's a momentary silence, made deeper by the absolute still of the cornfield around us. Even the wind seems to have gone into hiding. Finally, chidingly, he says, "That isn't fair. He asked, we gave. That's the nature of commerce."

"Uh-huh."

"If he should have been limited further, the crossroads ghost who argued for the twilight should have put those limits down."

"Sure."

"We would have been glad to grant you aid."

"And charge me what, exactly?" Bethany is still waving her hands at the air, a look of naked desperation on her face. Whatever they're asking, whatever she's offering, I can't shake the feeling that she's fighting for her life right in front of me. This is all her fault. I shouldn't feel sorry for her. But I do. I guess Marshall girls just have a way of getting themselves into trouble.

"Ah. Now that's the question. Your bill would have been . . . exotic."

"Kinda figured." I shake my head, the man-shaped hole in the world flickering around the edges every time he comes almost into view. "I know it's your job to sell. Well, sorry. I'm not buying."

"That will change," he says, and he's gone, taking the feeling of gnawing, alien absence with him.

"Hope not," I reply to the empty air, and stand alone in the silence, waiting for Bethany to finish making her deal with the crossroads, and whatever angel, demon, or worse waits there for people like us. If I'm lucky, and the ghostroads are kind, I'll never have a reason to find out which one it is.

Midnight comes and midnight goes; that's what midnight does. Bethany stops gesturing, her hands falling to her sides as she slumps, defeated. She nods, just once. Sound returns to the cornfield, crickets chirping, an owl hooting in the middle distance, a train whistle sounding somewhere further out. The crossroads time is ending. I can even, for just a moment, hear Bethany breathing.

And then she falls, facedown on that old dirt road, and doesn't move.

"Bethany?" I ask, just once, before I start running toward the crossroads. "Bethany, are you—" But the question dies, because she's not okay, she's *not*, she *can't* be okay, because as I run, I feel my solidity drop away, and her coat, powerless now, slips through me and drifts to the ground. Only the living can grant life to the dead. If Bethany's coat has stopped working, that means . . . that means . . .

"Behind you, Aunt Rose." Her voice is young as springtime, young as a bell ringing on the first day of the school year. I stop running, my eyes still on the body she's discarded like I discarded my coat. Then I look away, and I turn, and I look into the eyes of my no-longer-living niece.

Bethany is herself again, all teenage cockiness, ribbons in her hair now natural, and not decades out of place. But oh, her eyes. Her eyes are a cold mile of road in the desert, and the crossroads that beckons. She used to have my brother's eyes. Now she has Mary's eyes, crossroads eyes, and she'll never be a human girl again.

She smiles a little, shame and cockiness and joy all mixed together in her expression, and says, "They couldn't give me back my life, so they gave me back my death, instead."

She had life, and she threw it away. A shorter life than she might have had, sure, but it was still life, and it was still hers. I want to shake her. I want to slap her. Now that she's on my side of the ghostroads, I could do it. Instead, I swallow, and ask her, "Why?"

"Because it was good enough for you."

I never said that, *I never said that*, but if that's what she chose to hear, it's too late now. For either of us. "You're not a road ghost. What are you?" *Do you know what you are?*

Now she looks uncomfortable, if only for a moment. "Crossroads ghost," she says. "I'm going to watch the bargains that get made here to make sure they stay fair."

I have to laugh. "You know they won't be."

"I know. But someone has to try. Even if I fail almost every time, it's still better than nothing."

No, Bethany, no; *life* was better than nothing. "If you say so." I look around the dark cornfield, listen to the train whistle blowing in the distance. "I should go."

She looks relieved as she nods. "Yes, you probably should. Midnight's over, and you didn't come to make a deal."

"Be sure you send someone to tell the Queen that I did my job."

"She already knows," Bethany says, and smiles, just a little, an expression of joy poisoned with grief. "The Lady makes sure that she knows whenever a routewitch dies."

The words hang between us for a moment, heavier than they should be. I take a step back. "Great," I say. "Enjoy your afterlife, Bethany."

"Be careful, Aunt Rose," she replies.

I drop deeper down into the twilight and she's gone, taking the crossroads and the cornfield and the train whistle with her. All that remains is the road, stretching out forever, with a thousand crossings and dangers waiting for an unwary haunt. This was the last favor I'm going to do for her; Bethany will have to find the dangers on her own.

I hope she learns faster than I did.

2015

True Love Never Dies

LOVE—TRUE LOVE—never dies.

Sometimes it just goes to sleep for a while.

Her name was Rose. She sat in the second row in Ms. Buchanan's third grade class. She had hair the color of the cornfields in September, and big brown doe's eyes that made me want to grab her hand and promise her that everything was going to be okay forever—double-pinky-swear. I'd known her since kindergarten, but on the second day of third grade, when she and I got picked to hand out the mimeo sheets for the teacher, walking down the aisles shoulder to shoulder . . . that was when I realized that I loved her. That I was never going to want to be with anybody but her.

I wasn't always nice to her the way I should have been. But I didn't join the other kids when they made fun of the patches on her sleeves or the way her skirts got shorter and shorter, eaten alive by their own mended hems. I didn't call her "Second Hand Rose" or "poor girl" like the other boys did, and if I never asked her to the school dances, I never asked anybody else, either. I was faithful to her before I knew what faithful really meant.

If I've committed any real sin in my life, it's that it took me so long to ask her if she wanted to go out with me. I fell in love when I was nine, but she didn't wear my jacket until I was fifteen, didn't smile at me with that mouth, didn't look at me with those big doe eyes of hers. I let six years slip through my fingers when I could have grabbed tight hold of every single day, and the penance for my sin is knowing I committed it. Knowing what we lost.

Her name was Rose. She was the only girl I ever loved—the only girl I guess I could have ever loved, the only one that I was designed for loving. She wasn't perfect. Nobody's perfect. But she was close enough for a small town boy who dreamed of one day touching something greater. I guess she felt the same way about me. She came back to me, after all, even if it was only once, even if I didn't know that she was already gone.

I've spent my whole life trying, but I never fell in love again—not the way I fell in love with her, when the world was young and innocent, and silly teenage boys believed their girlfriends were immortal.

Her name was Rose.

I'm making my way toward Ann Arbor when I feel the undeniable urge to turn south. It's like someone is tying strings around my wrists and ankles, trying to use them to pull me the way they think I ought to go. I stop where I am, feet sinking down into the dead dry grass by the side of the road, and try to tell myself that I'm not feeling what I'm feeling. I don't want this. I didn't want this the first time that it happened, and I don't want it now.

The teasing, tugging sensation doesn't stop. If anything, it gets worse, small tugs turning quickly into outright pulling, like the whole world has decided that it has nothing better to do than get me to turn around. I close my eyes, trying to feel my way across the twilight to the source of the feeling. Whoever it is, they don't know what they're doing. This is a summons without a "return to sender" attached, which can only mean one thing:

Someone tied to the few short years that I spent among the living is getting ready to join me among the dead, and the universe wants me to play psychopomp for their departure.

Thanks for that, universe. Thanks a *lot*.

The calls don't come as often as they used to. There was a time when I was making my way back to Buckley almost every year to pull some poor ghost away from the body they'd abandoned and help them find their way to the ghostroads. Irony is a bitter mistress: the fact that these people had me called to lead them to their afterlives didn't make them road ghosts, and none of them showed any inclination to stay for longer than it took to process the fact of their own death. One by one, I helped them deal with reality, and one by one, they left me. I was allowed to invite them to the party, but I wasn't allowed to go with them, or ask them if they wanted to dance.

Sometimes being dead sucks. The parts of it that involve finding the people I used to love and losing them all over again . . . those parts suck more than most.

The pull to the south is still growing in strength and urgency. I know from past experience that if I try to hitch a ride in this state, no cars will stop for me unless they're going the right way. Even if I can get my hands on a coat, I won't fully incarnate; not unless I give in and obey the strange, malleable rules of the road.

"It's not like I was doing anything with my night, right?" I mutter, and shove my hands into the pockets of my jeans, using the motion to thrust myself down through reality's walls, moving smoothly from the daylight to the top of the twilight. The sky flickers, going bad-special-effect black, and the stars become frozen diamonds, not flickering, not doing anything but shining. There's no wind here to ruffle the corn. Just the fields, and the sky, and the black serpent highway sliding smoothly off into the distance.

I step out of the grass, back onto the road, and start walking. Giving in to the tugging this easily feels a little like defeat. Frankly, I don't care. The sooner I can get this over with, the sooner I can get on with my death.

Like it or not, I'm heading back to Buckley.

The nurses don't think I hear them talking outside my room. They would, if they thought twice about it—everything else about this old body may be breaking down on me, and me without a manufacturer's warranty to my name—but my hearing's as good as ever. They don't think I'm going to make it to Christmas. That's a bit of a relief, if you ask me; I've been here without my Rose for long enough now. I'm tired. I'm ready to be done.

There's just one more thing that needs to be done. I've observed the rituals as much as I can, here in this sterile place where old men go to wait out the last lonely hours of their existence. I've poured the glasses of wine, I've kept her picture close to me—I've even bribed a couple of the orderlies to burn incense outside the building, where the smell won't attract that busybody of a nurse who keeps the ward. If I've missed a step, I don't know it. I guess I won't know it until I die.

I've never in my life been a gambler, Rose, but I'm gambling now. I'm gambling on you remembering me, and you caring enough to come. Please, Rose. Please.

Have mercy on a dying man. Remember that once, you loved me. Remember that once . . .

Once, I got you home.

Travel on the ghostroads is difficult to predict. Something that takes a day in the daylight can take a year in the twilight; something that takes a year in the daylight can be over in minutes in the twilight. It's all down to what the road thinks you need, and how capricious reality is feeling at any given moment.

Either reality is trying to be helpful, or I've somehow pissed it off, and this is how it punishes me. I've barely been walking for an hour when the tugging becomes strong enough to yank me clean off the ghostroads, and I find myself standing on the wide green lawn in front of a blocky white building. It takes a moment for me to get my bearings. This part of Buckley didn't exist in the 1950s. It's part of the endless expansion of the township, the slow encroachment on the forest that used to keep us from the world. *Sparrow Hill Senior Facility* says the sign mounted near the small, businesslike front door. That explains the feel of the place, like the whole thing is holding its breath, waiting to see who'll win—life, death, or none of the above.

I take a breath I don't really need, changing my clothes as I start walking toward the door. The basic nurses' uniform hasn't changed much since I died. Wear basic white and sensible shoes, and people will almost always assume you know what you're doing.

There's no one to notice as I walk through the wood of the front door and into the entry hall. The place is practically deserted, nothing but the night shift skeleton crew and the inmates locked in their individual cells. I walk a little quicker, following the feeling of being pulled. I'm rarely glad to have died. I can't really say I miss the chance to get old enough for a place like this one.

I still don't know who I've been called here to escort. My brother's the only living relative I have left, and I'd feel it if it were him. All the other blood kin close enough to call me back died years ago, and I never had that many friends. I wasn't exactly a social butterfly; coming from the poor side of town was bad enough, but my unladylike ways and fascination with cars really put the nails in my reputation's coffin. Not many people cared enough to look past the judgments and make their own decisions about what kind of girl I was. That was fine, because for the most part, I didn't want them to.

I had my dreams and my cars and my brothers. I had my shot at a better life. I had Gary.

The tugging leads me to a specific door, in a specific hall. I hesitate for a moment, unable to shake the feeling that I'm missing something—something I'll be sorry about later. I can't figure out what it is, and so I step through the wood, just one more ghost in a building that should be dripping with them.

The man in the bed in front of me is so old and worn that he's practically a ghost himself, barely anchored by the prison of his own skin. But his eyes are open, and his smile is warm as he watches me slip into the room. I should know him. He's the one who called me here, with his need and his dying, and I should know him.

The framed picture on the nightstand next to his pillow is of me, junior year, lemon-bleached hair rendered gray by the black-and-white film, forever young, forever a shadow of a shade. There's only one man who'd still be displaying that picture like this. There's only one man who ever loved me enough to care.

"Hello, Rose," says Gary. "It's been a long time."

She came. Oh, God, she actually came. It wasn't just a story. I wasn't out of my mind. She still looks as young as she did the night she died. I've missed her so much. I wonder if she even remembers who I am.

I can't believe she actually came.

I freeze in place, too stunned to speak, too stunned to do anything but stare at this worn-out mockery of the only boy I ever fell in love with, the only boy I ever kissed with living lips. I've kissed a lot of boys since the summer that I turned sweet sixteen, but his was always and forever the only kiss that counted. Now that I'm looking, *really* looking, my eyes refuse to lie to me; this is Gary Daniels, this is the boy who picked me up when I was newly dead and shivering by the side of the road on Sparrow Hill. This is one of the last men on earth with the power to call me back to Buckley, and the one that I least want to see right now. This is *Gary*.

This is Gary, and he's dying.

Even the smile on his face looks like it pains him, like the joy of seeing me again is too heavy for his aged shoulders to support. "You look . . . God, Rose, you look amazing." Confusion flickers in his eyes—his eyes. I should have known him the second I saw him, if only by his eyes. "What have you done to your hair?"

The question is so completely, perfectly *wrong* that it crosses the line into completely, perfectly *right*. I laugh out loud, shaking my head. "That's the first thing you have to say to me, after more than sixty years? 'Hello, you look great, what have you done to your hair'? Gee, Gary, you'd think you might start out with 'it's nice to see you,' or even a 'how've you been.'"

"I've missed you so damn much, Rosie." Gary settles deeper into his nest of pillows, joy mellowing into something sweeter: pure contentment. "I was hoping you'd come for me, when the time got close, but I couldn't really be sure. It's gotten so you can't tell the real routewitches from the charlatans, and it's not like I could go comparison shopping."

I blink, staying where I am for the moment, just inside the door, ready to run if I have to. "What do you know about the routewitches?"

"Not nearly enough," he says, earnestly. "I was a ghost-chaser for a lot of years, Rosie. I'm not proud of it, but that's what I was, because I was hoping that if I chased long enough, I might catch up to you. I met this redhead little piece of a girl just across the Minnesota line—I suppose 'met' might be too generous a word. I got found by her, and she told me that you were a road ghost, and that I had to let you be." His smile turns wry before smoothing back into serenity. "She told me you were real. That the night we had was real. That was all I really needed to hear."

"Was her name Emma, by any chance?"

Gary nods, once. "It was. She said you were doing as well as could be expected, and that I couldn't help you."

I can almost picture it, Gary, still young, if not as young as he was when we were together, sitting across the table from one of my only real friends in the twilight while Emma sipped over-sweetened coffee and avoided answering as many questions as she could twist herself away from. She did it to protect me. She did it to give Gary his life back. But part of my heart is still aching, and wishing she'd left things alone long enough for him to catch up to me . . . long enough for him to catch me.

"Oh," I whisper.

"She also told me how to find the routewitches . . . and that, if I asked them nicely enough, they'd tell me how to send a message to you."

"You mean they'd tell you how to call me back here when it was time for you to die." I can't keep the bitterness out of my voice, and so I don't even try. First Bethany selling herself to the crossroads for the illusion of youth renewed, and now my first and only love, dying old and alone in a room that smells of bleach and ashes and age. No one ever told me life would be easy, but no one ever told me death would be this hard.

"Yes." Gary starts to say something else, and stops as a cough forces itself past his lips. It's deep, bone-shaking, and it drives home what his age couldn't: that I'm here, in this room, tonight, because Gary Daniels is getting ready to die.

I take an involuntary step backward, shoulders passing through the surface of the door behind me. "I can't do this," I say. "I'm sorry, Gary, I'm so sorry, but I can't do this. I just *can't*."

He coughs one more time before getting his breath back and saying the worst thing he could possibly have said.

"Please."

There's still a moment in which I almost turn and flee the room; a moment when I almost give in to the need to run. The moment passes. "I guess I still owe you for picking me up on prom night," I say, and step forward, moving closer to the bed—moving into the field of his need, penitent begging for the attentions of a psychopomp. One step and my hair brushes my shoulders in heavy lemon-scented curls, sun-dyed the color of drying straw. A second step and the green silk skirt swirls around my ankles, fabric dancing with every move I make.

A third step and I'm standing next to his bed, and mine is the last hand he'll ever have the chance to hold.

Gary smiles, still wheezing slightly as he whispers, "Maybe I'm old-fashioned, but I like your hair better like this, Rosie." He raises one frail hand, moving as if to touch my hair. His hand passes right through me. Gary's eyes widen, and he holds his hand there for a few seconds before letting it fall back to his side. "I should've expected that."

"It's okay." I perch myself on the edge of the bed, putting my hands over his. He can't feel me there, not yet, but even the illusion can be a comfort for some people. "I've missed you."

"Oh, Rosie." He sighs, deep and long as the last breath of winter. "It's been so hard. You can't even begin to know . . . they all thought I was crazy. For a while, they even thought I killed you. It was *so* hard . . ."

I want to be angry with him, I really do; he was alive, at least, and had the chance to change things. I can't quite find the strength. This is Gary. This is the only man besides my brothers who really mourned for me. How can I be mad at him over that? "I'm sorry," I say.

"Don't be." He puts his free hand over mine, holding it just above the point where my phantom skin begins. I can feel him surrounding my fingers, and I can't help it; I start to cry. "Don't cry, Rosie. I loved you then, and I love you now, and I need you to do something for me."

"Don't worry, Gary. I know my job. I'll get you to wherever it is you're going, I promise." He's not dying on the road; he can't stay with me. He'll have to move on, and break my heart all over again.

"I don't mean that." His expression is grave. "I need you to go to Dearborn, to Carl's Garage. He knows you're coming. He's waiting for you. Just tell him that I've passed on, and he'll know what to do from there. Can you do that for me?"

"Gary, I don't—"

"Please, Rose? Can you do just this one thing for me?"

I worry my lip between my teeth before finally, inevitably, nodding. "I can do that."

"Thank you." Gary tightens his hands around mine as he sits up in the bed and kisses me deeply, kisses me with all the longing of sixty years spent apart. He takes me by surprise, and I don't realize what's just happened until I feel his lips smoothing under mine, his hands growing young and strong and sure again. He—the essential Gary, the one that fell in love with a girl from the wrong side of town—sat up to kiss me. The body he spent all those years wearing . . .

. . . didn't. It's still lying on the bed, like a coat that isn't needed anymore.

Gary pulls back, smiling that old devil-may-care smile, and says, "Remember, Rosie. You promised."

Then he's gone, winking out like a candle flame, and I'm the only ghost in the room. Just me, sitting alone with a slowly cooling corpse that no one has any use for anymore. I stay where I am for a moment more, and then fall back into the twilight, sinking down until there's no hand under mine, until I'm just a ghost among ghosts once more.

Please, Rosie. Please, keep your word . . .

I don't head straight for Dearborn.

Let me rephrase that: I *can't* head straight for Dearborn. If Gary wants me interacting with something in the world of the living, I have to follow the rules in getting there. It takes me three days and five coats to hitchhike my way from Buckley to the Dearborn city limits. Once I'm past them, I can walk the rest of the way, and so that's what I do, ignoring the catcalls and the shouts from passing vehicles. As long as none of them offers me a ride, I can go where I need to go.

None of them offers me a ride. After an hour of walking down increasingly broken and glass-spattered sidewalks, I find myself in front of a rusty converted warehouse with a sign in the window that reads, simply, *CARL'S*. This has to be the place.

The coat I'm wearing gives me the substance necessary to open the door and step into the cramped office, which smells like motor oil and stale beer. "Hello?" I call. "Is anyone here?"

I'm beginning to think this errand ends with me standing in an empty room forever when a man with a handlebar mustache of impressive size—almost as impressive as the beer belly that strains against his coveralls—emerges from the door behind the counter, jaws busily working a wad of incongruously pink gum. "Yeah?"

"Um." I blink once, and then ask, "Are you Carl?"

"Who wants ta know?"

"Rose." His face remains blank, not a trace of recognition in his eyes. I try adding a little more information: "Gary sent me?"

"Aw, shit." True regret wipes away the blankness as he shakes his head, one hand coming up to tweak at the end of his mustache. "Old bastard finally died on us, huh? And you must be the dead little girlfriend. Guess you got his messages after all. Good for him. I mean, he coulda done better in the rack department, but hey, who am I to judge? The course of true love never did run smooth, and alla that shit. I guess you'd better come with me."

"I . . . wait . . . what?" The rapid-fire delivery of so many different sentiments leaves me reeling, although I'm pretty sure that I was just insulted. "Come with you *where?*"

Now Carl smiles, although the regret remains, tucked around the edges. "He didn't tell you, huh? Ain't that just like him? Wanted to surprise his girl. Guess I can't blame him for that after all this time. Come on, girlie. It's not my place to say, but I'm the only one who can show you."

I frown, but in the end, we both know that I'm going to give in. It's not like he can hurt me, after all, and Gary sent me here. "Okay," I say, and follow Carl out of the office, into the garage.

The garage is connected to a small junkyard—not all that surprising, really. It's a good place for old cars to go to die. There's even a crusher, big enough for most single-family vehicles. A car sits next to it, shrouded in a plain gray canvas.

Carl starts talking as soon as we're outside. "I just want you ta know that this goes against everything I stand for as a mechanic," he says, jaws still working at the gum. "But it makes sense to everything I stand for as a routewitch, so I guess I'm doin' the right thing whether I do it or not. You better appreciate this, girlie, that's all I have to say."

"Appreciate *what*?" I ask.

Carl gives me a withering look and walks over to the shrouded car. When he yanks the cover away, I gasp. I can't stop myself.

The unshrouded car is a cherry 1952 Ford Crestline Sunliner, painted a deep sea green that looks just as good on a car as it did, once upon a time, on a prom dress. The sunlight caresses the paint like a lover. I understand the impulse. This is a car to be courted.

"He rolled off the assembly the day you died," says Carl, dumping the cover to one side. "Color's a custom job. So's the engine. There's a piece of the car you got run off the road in worked in there, and some mandrake root—some other things, too. He's a real special guy."

"She's beautiful," I whisper. Then I pause, realizing that one of us has the pronoun wrong. "Wait—did you just call this car 'he'?"

And then Carl fires up the crusher.

It's hard to describe the sound of a car that's been loved—really and truly *loved*—being murdered. Because that's what this is; murder, pure and simple, metal and rubber compacted into a single contiguous piece of lifeless slag. I shriek wordless dismay and run to the crusher's controls, like pushing the "stop" button might somehow undo what's just been done in front of me. "You can't do this! Why would you do this?!"

"Your boy asked me to," Carl replies, easily fending me off. I'm too small to shove him out of the way, and anyway, the smashing sounds are getting softer; all the major structural damage is already done, and what remains is simply reducing rubble into ash. "He said you'd come if he called for you. I didn't quite believe him, even after I heard about you stirring things up on the Lady."

"Is this—is this some sort of punishment? He made you do this to punish me?" The sound of metal being torn continues, but the screaming is over. The car is dead, beautiful thing that it—that he—was.

To my surprise, Carl laughs. "Punish you? *Punish* you? You really are dense, aren't you? Does that come with the dead thing?" He produces a set of keys from his pocket, holding them up for me to see. Sunlight glints off the keychain, the grinning cartoon face of the Buckley High School Buccaneer leering at me from somewhere not quite the past, not quite the present. "You know, he really loved you. A man would have to really love a woman to do this just to be with her."

He tosses the keys, keychain and all, into the still-grinding teeth of the crusher. They vanish almost instantly, blending into the remains of the car. Carl turns and looks at me, expectantly.

"What?" I cross my arms and scowl at him, trying not to look as confused as I feel.

"Look in your pocket," says Carl, and I follow his orders before I stop to think about them, uncrossing my arms and sticking my right hand into the pocket of my borrowed coat. There's nothing there but lint and a crumpled toll receipt. "Your other pocket," says Carl.

Blinking, I stick my hand into the pocket of my jeans . . . and find a set of car keys. I pull them out and stare at them. The light glints off the face of the Buckley Buccaneer, just like it did before Carl threw him into the crusher.

". . . how?" I ask.

Carl, meanwhile, grins like he's just won the lottery to end all lotteries. Clapping meaty hands against his knees, he all but shouts, "It worked! Damn if I'm not going to drink on this for the next ten years. Girl, you just saw a goddamn *miracle*, and I am the *miracle worker*."

"Okay, I'm confused. Can you please explain what the fuck is going on here?"

"Take off the coat," he suggests. His grin gentles, fading into something sadder and more sincere. "He really was a damn good man. I hope you deserved him."

"I tried to," I say, and slip out of my borrowed jacket. When a routewitch says to strip, it's generally best to do it. The junkyard jumps a bit as the fabric hits the ground, shadows turning sharper, bits of old metal lighting up around the edges with ghostlight memories. "Now what?" I ask, and my voice is as transparent as the rest of me.

"Drop down to the ghostroads, and say hello," says Carl. "It was nice meeting you."

"Nice meeting you, too," I say, still not sure whether I mean it, and let go of the daylight, falling down into the sweet dim dark of the twilight, and the ghostroads. The shadow of the junkyard remains, the parts of it that are old enough and enduring enough to have spirits of their own.

And parked in front of me, in the same place it sat when I saw it for the first time, is a cherry 1952 Ford Crestline Sunliner. Waiting.

I approach the car with something between curiosity and awe. I don't have a heartbeat, but it still feels like my heart is frozen in my chest. The paint job has changed colors, going from the green of my dress to a soft, misty gray, like a ghost seen from the corner of your eye and gone before it quite takes form.

"Gary?" I whisper.

The car doesn't answer, exactly—not with words, anyway. But the door is unlocked when I try the handle, and the upholstery is warm when I slide into the driver's seat. I rest my hands against the wheel, still trying to make sense of what I'm seeing, what Gary and Carl have somehow managed to *do.* Here, on the ghostroads, this car is as solid a thing as I am, a ghost among ghosts.

My hand is shaking as I let go of the wheel and slide the key into the ignition. The engine rumbles to life, all but purring as it wakes, and the radio, unsurprisingly at this point, turns itself on. The sound of Bing Crosby's voice flows into the cabin, sweet and strong and perfect, singing a song I haven't heard in years. "You'll never know how many dreams I've dreamed about you, or just how empty they all seemed without you," he sings, and there are tears in my eyes, and I don't bother wiping them away. "So kiss me once, then kiss me twice, then kiss me once again. It's been a long, long time . . ."

"Oh, my God, you crazy bastard." I lean my head back against the seat and laugh, and laugh, and wonder how many years he spent planning this: how many days he spent with the car, just sitting in the driver's seat, letting himself sink into it. Letting himself imbue it. Cars can leave ghosts behind, when they're loved enough, but that wasn't what he was doing; he was trying something much stranger, and much more difficult.

And somehow, through some insane bend in the rules, it worked.

"I missed you so much," I whisper, and lean forward, resting my head against the wheel. This isn't an embrace, not really, not as such, but then, when you're dead, you learn the art of the compromise. You learn that sometimes "almost" is the best option of them all. And maybe, if you're very lucky, you get the chance to learn that nothing is forever—not even saying good-bye.

The radio station changes, abandoning the year I died for something a lot more recent: Journey, singing about how loving a music man ain't always what it's supposed to be. I'm laughing through my tears, and somehow, that's exactly right.

I sit up, wipe my eyes, and put my hands back on the wheel. Gary's engine is still purring, a sweet bass line beneath the radio's crooning. "All right, you crazy bastard," I say. "Let's drive."

"Can I talk to you for a minute?"

She turns around, all suspicion and wariness, those big doe eyes of hers shadowed with the fear that I'm here to make fun of her, to join the list of boys who've thought that "poor" means the same thing as "easy." "Sure," she says, and clutches her books a little tighter.

"Do you have . . . I mean, I was wondering . . . would you like to go to the Spring Hop with me?"

She studies my face like it's an exam question, fear fading in the face of pure amazement. When she realizes I mean it . . . I think I'd do almost anything to make her give me that look again. How did I let this wait so long?

"I would love to," she says, and it's 1950, and we're going to live forever, and I'm going to marry her someday.

Just you wait and see.

A wise man told me once that love—true love—never dies. It's just that sometimes, we can't see it clearly. Sometimes, it goes to sleep for a little while. As Gary and I blaze down the ghostroads, a gray streak in the twilight that never ends . . . for the first time, I think I can believe that he was right.

2015
Thunder Road

THERE'S ONE THING every journey—and every story—has in common. Then again, stories and journeys are the same thing, aren't they? Every one of them begins somewhere, trembling and frightened, like a green-clad ghost-girl who doesn't even realize yet that she's left her body in the burning wreck behind her. Every one of them moves onward from that point, little ghosts growing up to become full-fledged urban legends, letting their legs and their longings carry them from one side of the American ghostroads to the other. Every one of them gets more complicated as it goes, harder to predict, harder to understand unless you've been there since the very beginning.

Every one of them eventually ends. Whether you want them to or not.

Sometimes we're excited, eager, yammering "Are we there yet?" and demanding that the driver hit the gas a little harder, begging the storyteller to feed us the hints and tastes of what's to come a little faster. Sometimes we're reluctant, like children on the way to see an adult they already know they don't like visiting; we drag our feet, we whimper and cajole, we do everything we can to stretch things out a little farther. Whichever way we go, we know there's no real point to it; we know that we can't change anything. Journeys end. Stories end. Everything ends.

The only thing you can do when the ending looms is roll down the windows, let the wind blow back your hair, and drive your hell-bent, hell-bound ass to where it needs to go. Everything ends. So suck it up and face it with a little dignity already.

Gary's engine hums contentedly as we blast down the ghostroads, his radio playing a succession of Top 40 Billboard Hits from the year that I died. Maybe we're in the honeymoon period right now, both of us trying to be worthy of the other, but I honestly don't give a crap. I spent more than sixty years dead without him, and he spent just as much time living without me. If we want to be sappy and stupidly in love for a little while, that's our business.

I do have to wonder whether Gary really understands what he's managed to get himself into. Having a car is wonderful, but it doesn't change my nature. I'm still a hitcher, still have that need for flesh and contact worked deep into the ghosts of my bones. Eventually, I'll have to drop from the twilight into the daylight, find someone who smells like ashes and empty rooms, and convince him to give me a ride to where he thinks I need to go. I can skip the joyrides, the embodiments just for the sake of cadging a cheeseburger or kissing a stranger, but there are always going to be times when the living world calls me and I have to go. It's what I am. I can't change it, and I don't think I would even if I knew how. The girl who was willing to change everything about herself for love died a long time ago. I still look like her, sweet sixteen forever, but let's face it: I grew up.

Then again, maybe Gary did some growing up, too. He did get old, after all, which usually requires a certain measure of maturity, and he did figure out how to get his soul re-smelted into something that could stay with me. I don't know whether turning yourself into your first girlfriend's car is romantic or creepy, but since we're both dead, I also don't know whether the distinction between those things actually matters.

"Just call me Morticia," I say, hitting the gas a little harder. The radio dial spins without any help from me, and as the theme from *The*

Addams Family blasts through the cabin, I swear it's undercut by the sound of my first, last, and only boyfriend, laughing.

We pull into the parking lot of the Last Dance as the eternally twilit sky is fading into another false gloaming, taunting the dead with the thought that, someday, the sun might actually rise. There are whole cults devoted to measuring the gloamings, like every little scrap of light has meaning. Personally, I think it just happens because whoever or whatever is in charge of the ghostroads likes fucking with us.

"I'm going to go talk to Emma," I say, getting out of the car and tucking the keys into my pocket. They feel solid there, almost as real as a coat. I've already experimented with changing my clothes, remolding myself to suit my environment. No matter what I do or how I change, the keys travel with me, sometimes in a pocket, sometimes on an elastic band strapped to my wrist, sometimes tucked into the front of my bra. Again, romantic, and marginally creepy.

Gary flashes his headlights once, which I interpret as a gesture of understanding. I mean, I have to interpret it as *something*, and "Sure, Rose, go take care of your business" is as good an interpretation as any. He doesn't turn himself back on or go all Christine in order to stop me, and so I walk across the parking lot, hearing the gravel crunch beneath my feet. The Last Dance is pretty damn real, no matter *what* level you're standing on.

I'm almost to the door when the sign flickers, neon shadows shifting from green and gold to a bloody sunrise red. I stop where I am, feeling like the world stops with me. For a moment, everything is frozen in the gloaming, silent except for the soft, insectile buzzing of the neon sign illuminating our night that never ends. I take a step back, tilting my head upward, and look.

Last Chance Diner says the sign, in that familiar looping cursive. The letters blaze crimson, almost violent in the way they split the darkness. Last chance. Everybody out. The tattoo on my back is abruptly burning like a brand, until it feels like it should set my clothes on fire, burn them right off me, spontaneous after-death combustion.

I don't know what the fuck is going on here, but I do know one thing: whatever this is, there's not a chance in hell that it's good.

"Emma?" There's no one visible in the dining room, which is subtly changed, shifted ever so slightly away from the place where I've spent so many hours over the last sixty years. I couldn't tell you what the changes were if you held a gun to my head—which would probably be a waste of time anyway—but I can tell you that the upholstery is ripped in the wrong places, and the scuffs on the counter spell out a new set of unreadable runes. The jukebox in the corner croons softly to itself, some generic love song from the 1970s. It doesn't matter which one. "Emma, are you here?"

She doesn't answer me. I didn't really expect her to.

My steps are cautious as I make my way across the unfamiliar floor, watching all the while for signs of a trap. I've always known about the Last Chance. Hell, Emma sells postcards with pictures of the place, and the tacky legend "I made the right call at the Last Chance!" That doesn't mean I've ever been here . . . or that I ever wanted to visit.

The Last Chance is the place you go when everything goes wrong.

Once again, I'm almost to the door, this time the swinging door between the dining room and the kitchen, when something changes. The air suddenly tastes like ashes and empty rooms, like lilies and the sour tears of a hundred weeping parents who can't understand how something like this could happen to their precious little high school football star. I stagger, catching myself on the edge of the counter before my knees can quite finish buckling under me, and fight the almost irresistible urge to puke.

That's another thing I never thought would happen in the afterlife. If there was any real justice in the world, being dead would mean freedom from tossing your goddamn cookies.

It's while I'm hanging there, keeping myself on my feet solely by clinging to the counter, that I realize what's so terribly wrong. Because Emma's apron is lying on the floor, where I never would have seen it if I hadn't been overwhelmed by the taste of someone close to me preparing to die . . . and there's blood on the white lace edging. I'm pretty sure she didn't decide to play with raw hamburger for fun. I'm not normally called to the death of cows.

The taste of ashes keeps getting stronger as I force myself to straighten up, using the counter's edge to all but pull myself along. The kitchen door swings open under my hand.

What feels like only seconds later, I'm running across the parking lot with Emma's bloody apron in one hand and a half-torn note in the other, shouting, "Gary! Start your engine! We gotta *go*!"

The driver's door is open by the time I reach it, and I fling myself into Gary's seat, grabbing his wheel in both hands. He slams the door behind me, and I hit the gas, sending us roaring off in a spray of gravel.

Oh Lord, who art probably not in Heaven, hallowed be thy name. Oh Lady, deliver me from darkness, deliver me from evil, and please, please, let us not be too late.

Please.

"Emma's the redhead you met in Minnesota," I say tightly, as Gary roars down the ghostroad, letting me guide us toward the distant taste of ashes. It's getting stronger; we're going the right way. "She's a *beán sidhe*. Not quite living, not quite dead. I mean, to be entirely honest, I've never been sure *what* she was. Not really."

My laughter sounds almost hysterical in the confines of the car. Gary's radio flicks on, playing the Doors—"People Are Strange."

I manage to stop laughing, and reply to the implicit question, saying, "We're all strange here, and it never really mattered, you know? She was my friend. Is. She *is* my friend. I just . . . this is bad, Gary. Emma runs the Last Dance. She's supposed to be off-limits."

The radio dial spins, and Jim Morrison is replaced by an old folk song asking me if I know the way to where I'm going.

"Yeah, I do. A really bad man's got Emma, and that means we're in serious trouble." I take a breath. I don't want to do this; I don't want to explain, because if Gary's the only man I've ever loved, then Bobby

Cross is the only man who's ever made me feel like this, cold as clay and burning up all at the same time. I always feel like a dead girl. Bobby Cross makes me feel like I'm damned. "I need to tell you how I really died, Gary. It's going to be hard. So just listen, okay?"

The radio dial spins again, and the music clicks off. Gary's silence is all the answer I need. I force the words out one by one as I begin, "Robert Cross loved to drive. He loved the speed, and the thrill of the chase, even when all he chased was the wind. He chased that wind all the way to Hollywood . . ."

Gary holds his silence until I stop speaking. Then the radio clicks on, spinning once through the stations in question. I nod.

"We're going to get her, and bring her back." I brace my hands against the wheel, trying to ignore the burning, letting go of the thin threads that hold me to the daylight levels high above. "He left directions. Come on, honey. Let's hit the midnight."

I don't know anything about Heaven or Hell. I usually figure that they wait beyond those final exits that the drivers I guide sometimes take, but I've never seen them, or talked to anyone who's been there and back again. I do know the ghostroads. There are a thousand highways cutting through the afterlife, ranging from the daylight all the way down to the midnight. My natural habitat is the twilight, where the living are close enough to be remembered and distant enough to be safely ignored. Most road ghosts seem to live there, remembering life, celebrating death. When I can't stay in the twilight, I usually ascend to the daylight, where I can catch a ride, bum a meal, and earn enough credit in the eyes of the gods of the dead to pay the fare for descending.

What I don't do is descend past the lowest, murkiest levels of the twilight, the places where the dead have been dead so long that I might as well be the living to them. The places where life is a lie, and no one ever reaches the last exit on the ghostroads. I'm not comfortable going even that low; I avoid it if I possibly can. Which is why it feels so wrong to be guiding Gary deeper with every turn we take, the layers of reality ripping away around us. We're going all the way down.

The radio dial spins, and some modern folk singer offers to let me sleep while she drives. I shake my head once, sharply. "It's not safe," I say. "You haven't been dead long enough to drive these roads alone." The things some of the creatures in the midnight can do to an innocent ghost are enough to give me nightmares. And I don't technically sleep.

He doesn't have an answer for that. I take a breath, hold it, and shift down one more time.

The transition between layers of twilight is usually seamless, like walking down a gentle slope. Going from the twilight into the midnight is nothing of the kind. Gary's wheels actually lose contact with the road, and we drop about five feet before hitting the pavement with a bone-rattling thud. My teeth snap shut on my tongue, and phantom blood fills my mouth for a moment before my body remembers that it's already dead, it can't bleed anymore. My tattoo is on fire, a burning brand pressed against the small of my back. That's almost certainly not a good sign.

Then again, neither is the fact that when Gary rolls to a stunned stop, we're on the road outside of Buckley. Not the road of today, with its bright new signs and its expensive billboards; the road of 1952, the way it looked on that last long, hot summer, when we spent the longest nights racing like we thought we had a chance of beating the Devil.

There are cars parked in the distance, their lights burning like candles through this impossibly black, long-ended night. I glance up through the window. There are no stars.

"Looks like this is where we're going," I murmur, patting the dashboard once, as much for my comfort as for Gary's. "Let's roll."

His headlights flick on, slicing the dark like knives, and we roll forward, moving toward the circle of light cast by those unfamiliar headlights. We're halfway there when the taste of ashes and wormwood fills my mouth. I shudder. Bobby Cross. Some devils never die.

The man himself is standing just inside the circle of headlights, his feet spread in a classic Hollywood tough-guy stance, one hand in the back pocket of his jeans, the other holding a cigarette. He looks like a still frame from the movies of my childhood, a fallen angel who hit the bottom and kept on falling.

"Hello, Rosie girl," he says, in a voice as sweet as poisoned candy. He's speaking softly. His words still carry through Gary's closed windows, past the sound of his rumbling engine. "Why don't you get out of that dead boy, and come have a little chat with me?"

Gary's engine snarls. I lay a hand gently on the wheel.

"Trust me, baby," I say. "I have to go."

There's a long moment where I'm afraid Gary won't unlock the door, that he'll just turn and roar away down the road, rather than risking me with Bobby. Then his engine settles, turning off with what sounds like a sigh, and his door swings slowly open.

"Thank you," I say, and slide out of the seat, going to meet the man who killed me.

It doesn't really surprise me when my feet hit the pavement wearing green silk flats, the skirt of the matching dress tangling around my ankles. If I'd known I'd be wearing this prom dress for the rest of eternity, I might have been a little more careful to make sure it was something I could run in. Still, at least I'm used to it; I've learned to work with it, over the years. I square my shoulders, lift my chin, and walk calmly toward Bobby, trying not to grimace at the increasing burn from my tattoo.

"I always knew you hitchers were kinky, but dating a *car*, Rosie girl?" Bobby clucks his tongue, shaking his head in mock disapproval. "If I'd known you were that hard up, I might have offered to take you for a ride or two. You know. Before I took what was mine."

"I'm pretty sure no woman in the history of the world has ever been *that* hard up, Bobby," I say.

He smiles maliciously. "I don't know about that. Your little niece seemed to think I was a good enough way to kill an evening."

"And look how well that turned out for her. It's a nice offer, Bobby, but no thank you." I stop just outside the circle of light, folding my arms across my chest. This close, I can see that only one of the cars is real; the rest are smoke and mirrors, special effects from his Hollywood days. "You have a friend of mine. I'd like her back, if you don't mind."

"Why, Rose. I have no idea what it is you mean."

I grit my teeth. "Emma. The *beán sidhe* who runs the Last Dance."

"Oh!" Bobby snaps his fingers. "Well, shoot, she just slipped my mind. Probably because she's been so quiet since I went ahead and gagged her. Never let a *beán sidhe* speak her mind if you can help it. Those bitches have tongues that can leave a man bleeding, if you let them run."

"Give her back."

"Wasn't aware that she was yours in the first place."

He's toying with me; he'd never have taken her if he didn't know I'd come after him. He's been toying with me since Bethany, and maybe before that. I force myself not to lunge for him, and say, as calmly as I can, "She's my friend. I want her returned, safely. Now."

Bobby smiles. It's that same sweet, seductive expression that once won him a million hearts and dampened almost as many pairs of panties, but there's something sour underneath it, something that taints and twists whatever appeal he might once have had. This apple's rotten, through and through. "It doesn't work that way. You know it doesn't work that way."

"What do you want, Bobby?"

"What do I ever want?"

"Didn't we just do this? It won't work. Persephone's blessing says hands off to creepy boys who bargain with the crossroads and want to hurt me."

"Maybe so, but Hades outranks her." Bobby reaches inside his shirt, pulling out a chain. The charm dangling from its end makes my stomach twist itself into a knot and makes my tattoo burn hotter than ever. "You put this on of your own free will and the Lady of the Dead won't give one good goddamn what I do to that pretty little soul of yours."

Gary's engine snarls in the darkness behind me. I want to turn and run to him, throw myself into the driver's seat and get the hell out of here, but I can't. Emma needs me. I was a soft touch when I was alive, and Persephone help me, I may be a softer touch now that I'm dead. "So you expect me to just give myself up? I don't think so."

"And neither do I." Neither of us expected to hear Bethany's voice. That's clear from the way Bobby's head whips around, expression a mask of pure fury. I turn more slowly, somehow resigned to the sight of my recently dead niece walking toward us through the midnight. The darkness doesn't quite touch her; it skates off her skin like water off a duck's back. She may be dead, but she's not the sort of dead girl who belongs to the ghostroads. They can't touch her. "There are rules for engagements of this kind, Bobby. You know that."

"What kind of tricky shit is this?" he demands, in the voice of a petulant child. "You can't be here, you dumb bitch. You're too used up to dig your way this deep."

"That was a different time, and the past is another country," says Bethany, and her voice is the rustle of crows in the corn, the sound of the wind blowing down empty highways. "You're trying to break the rules, Bobby. You've interfered with people who never touched the crossroads, nor made any bargains there. That can't be allowed, I'm afraid."

He stabs his finger in my direction, snapping, "*She* isn't protected. Not from me. Not from this."

"That's true; she has no protections against you that haven't been given to her on her journeys. You killed her, and that grants you a claim over her soul. But the *beán sidhe* wasn't yours to touch. You never killed her, and she never made a deal." Bethany's smile is sweet, and no kinder than a rattlesnake's. "You can make a wager. You can issue a challenge. But you can't make an exchange."

"What the fuck are you trying to say?"

"She's saying you can make me fight you for Emma, but you can't just trade one for one," I say, finally getting the gist of what Bethany's trying to tell us. "I guess you don't have that kind of authority."

"Who's to say she does?" Bobby looks truly angry now, fury distorting that eternally youthful face in ways that aren't attractive in the slightest. "Why does that dumb little bitch get to tell me what I can or can't do?"

"Because that 'dumb little bitch' is speaking for the crossroads." I glance toward Bethany, seeing the miles stretching out to forever in her eyes. "Isn't that right?"

"Got it in one, Aunt Rose," says Bethany. She smiles, and for a moment—just a moment—she's a normal teenage girl, unchanged, innocent. The girl she might have been, if she'd never fallen prey to Bobby Cross. The moment passes, and the eyes she turns on Bobby are filled with shadows too deep and too dark to have ever been human. "I am here because you are ours, and your actions here endanger more than you have the right to damage. Because we were . . . acquainted . . . while I lived, I get to be the one to judge whatever you decide is fair."

"I killed her, I should get to eat her," snarls Bobby. "That's what's fair."

"But she got away from you. She walked the Ocean Lady and won Persephone's favor. She found the crossroads, more than once, and was tempted, but made no deals. She's passed outside your ownership, and if you want her, you have to win her." Bethany folds her arms, smiling sweetly. "You have to pay if you want to play. So find a fee that suits you."

Emma is here, somewhere. Bobby's not going to let me walk away without a fight, and I won't go without Emma. "A race," I say abruptly, taking a step forward. "Him and me, there and back. Winner takes all."

"Done and done," says Bethany, before Bobby can object. "You each have something you can wager."

"I won't cede my claim to her," says Bobby.

"No one can make you. But if she beats you here, today, she takes the *beán sidhe* and leaves unhindered. If you win . . ." Bethany glances my way, looking almost regretful. I brace myself for what comes next. "You get her pink slip. The boy's soul is yours."

"What?" The word bursts forth unbidden. "Gary isn't part of this!"

"He is now," says Bethany. "What you do after losing is up to you. Do you accept my terms, Bobby Cross, Rose Marshall?"

I want to refuse them. Bobby must see that in my face, because he smiles, slow and poisonous, and says, "I do."

"Rose?"

I close my eyes, unable to shake the feeling that this, all of this, is nothing more than wrong. "I do," I whisper, and silence falls.

"I'm sorry, I'm so sorry," I whisper for what feels like the thousandth time, resting my cheek against the warm leather of Gary's steering wheel. "I didn't know what else to do. I'm so, so sorry."

The radio spins, flicking through half a dozen songs from our brief earthly time together before stopping on a song I don't recognize, one that entreats me to "gamble everything for love." The volume stays low, soothing, not blaring in my ear.

I sigh, closing my eyes. "I'm still sorry. This isn't what you signed up for."

The music goes briefly silent before clicking over to a modern station, where the song informs me that losing me is like living in a world with no air.

"Okay." I have to laugh at that, just a little, and laughing even a little makes me feel enough better that I can sit up, wiping the phantom tears from my cheeks. "Maybe this *is* what you signed up for after all. Come on, baby. Let's go kick a dead guy's ass."

The engine turns over, and then we're rolling through the midnight, heading for the night's designated drag strip . . . heading for the future. Whatever that future is going to be.

I set the challenge, so Bobby chose the raceway. It shouldn't be a surprise when we follow the markers to the makeshift starting line and find ourselves idling at the base of Sparrow Hill, where the road winds its way into the even deeper dark beneath the trees. Bobby is already there, standing next to his car. So is Bethany, standing off to one side with a checkered starter flag in her hand. We're really going to do this.

It's hard to strut confidently in a green silk prom dress, but I've had years to practice, and I almost manage it as I get out of the car and cross the dusty pavement to where Bobby stands. "Emma," I say. "Where is she?"

"You'll get her if you win," replies Bobby. "You won't win."

"My hostage is present," I say, indicating Gary with a wave of my hand. "Now show me yours, or this doesn't happen."

"The terms are fair," says Bethany.

Bobby scowls like a storm rolling in, and stalks around to the back of his car, where he unlocks the trunk and hauls a rumpled, bound, and gagged Emma into the questionable light. Her eyes are closed and her head is lolling forward, but she's breathing. I don't know how hard it is to kill a *beán sidhe*. Hopefully, tonight is not the night when I find out. "Happy now?" he demands.

"Not by a long shot," I say. "Leave her here."

"Why would I do a silly thing like that?" He runs a fingertip lecherously down the curve of Emma's cheek, smirking at me. "Your hostage is going on the race with you. So's mine."

"The terms are fair," says Bethany again, sadly this time, like she'd rather be saying something else. "But you can't keep her in the trunk. If your hostage is damaged, the entire contest is invalidated."

"Fine," snaps Bobby. He wrenches open the passenger-side door and all but tosses Emma inside, slamming the door behind her. "Now can we get started?"

Bethany nods. "You are to cross the hill and return. First one here wins. If you cheat, I'll know, and you will be penalized. Is everyone in agreement?"

"Yes," says Bobby, and "Yes," I say, and then we're walking back to our respective cars, Gary's engine already live and running, Bobby's own dark machine roaring into bitter wakefulness. I have to wonder if Bobby's car is self-aware; I have to wonder if it understands what it does, or what its driver is doing.

There isn't time for lengthy contemplation. Bethany is standing at our ad hoc starting line, the starter flag in one hand—and there's no point in wondering where she got it, she's a crossroads ghost now, and I guess that comes with a few party tricks of its own. She watches with calm, sad eyes as we roll up to either side of her, our idling engines like dragons in the quiet midnight. Then the flag comes down and there's nothing to do but drive.

I haven't been on Sparrow Hill since the night I died there. I used to drive it all the time, but that was decades ago, and even ghosts can forget the little things, like how sharp the first curve is, or how fast the trees block out all the light. Even during the middle of the day, it's always dark on certain parts of the road, and this is a long way from the middle of the day.

The little things only distract me for a few seconds. A few seconds is all that it takes for Bobby to snare the lead, his taillights burning bloody through the darkness. I swear and slam my foot down on the gas, sending Gary leaping forward. The gap between us is still narrow, and we haven't lost this yet.

Bobby's car has a better engine, but my car has a better soul, and that can count for a lot once you're on the ghostroads. Gary and I slide through the gap between Bobby and the side of the hill, tires chewing dirt for a few seconds before we're back on solid pavement and blasting our way through the night. Now it's Bobby's turn to come racing up behind me. I hit the gas a little harder, hauling on the steering wheel, not allowing him to pass. Everything depends on this. I can't lose.

We're the first ones over the hill, the first ones to hit the marker that says it's time to turn around again. Gary takes the turn smoothly, and we pass Bobby as we drive back into the shadows of the hill.

The pass is easy. That should bother me, but I'm too focused on the road ahead, too focused on winning—for Emma's sake, for Gary's sake, for the sake of my own soul. I don't realize just how wrong it was for Bobby to let me pass him like that until his car comes blazing out of the darkness behind us like some dark avenging angel, and his bumper slams into mine.

The impact is hard enough to send me rocking forward into the steering wheel, Gary going briefly out of my control. He wobbles on the road, and I swear, scrambling to get us back on track. Bobby slams into us again and again, making it impossible for me to do anything but hang on. I've been here before. Terror is racing through my veins like a drug, because I have *been here before*, and I didn't survive it last time, either.

He hits us one more time, and this time, I can't keep control of the wheel, and Gary's tires can't keep their contact with the road, and we go tumbling down, down, down into the dark, falling into the endless shadows on the side of Sparrow Hill.

The first time I took this fall, I was alive, and the trauma of it knocked me out. This time, I'm dead, and so is my car. That makes a bit of a difference. So does the fact that this is the Sparrow Hill of the past—the one where my first car has already gone over the edge. I grab the wheel, shouting, "Trust me!" and steer us through the wreckage created by my crash. It's hard. The ground is broken and filled with dangers, and my teeth rattle with every impact. Gary's bearing the worst of it, and he doesn't complain, although his radio flickers wildly, a dozen songs in a second, none lasting more than a single note.

There, up ahead of us: there's the light of the road, dim by any other measure, but a beacon when viewed from the absolute darkness of the trees. We burst through the last barrier, and we're out, tires screeching as we skid to a stop just past the finish line. Panting, I slump back in my seat. "You okay, honey?"

Gary's radio spins; "Back in Black" blasts briefly through the cabin.

"Oh, good." I sigh deeply, unfastening my belt. "I'll be back. I hope."

Gary doesn't have an answer for that. The radio clicks off just before I shut the door.

Bobby Cross is pulling up as I walk back over to Bethany. His car has barely stopped before he's out, striding toward us, grinning to beat the band. "Hand over that pink slip, honey-girl, and then we'll see about what you can do for me to get it back," he says.

"No," says Bethany.

"No?" echoes Bobby, disbelieving. I share his sentiment, but don't say anything; I just turn to her, and stare.

"No, she won't be giving you her pink slip, but you'll be giving her your hostage." This time, Bethany's smile is cold and cruel. "You lose."

"Now, hold on one damn moment, missy," he snaps. "She didn't finish the race."

"Yes, she did. Distance was never stated. Only cross the hill and back again. She finished the race. She just took an alternate route to the finish line." Bethany points to the shattered underbrush marking the scene of my first crash. "Rose Marshall is today's victor. Return the *beán sidhe*, and go."

"You little—"

"I speak for the crossroads, Bobby," says Bethany. Her voice is soft, and louder than thunder, all at the same time. "Do you truly wish to argue with us? We did not forbid you to drive her off the road, but neither did we forbid her to survive being driven. If you break this bargain with us, you break them all. Are you willing to live with the consequences of that choice?"

A look of utter terror flashes over Bobby's face. He's been in the dark for a long time, and all to stay young and beautiful forever. "No," he says, hurriedly.

"Then return the *beán sidhe*, and do not test our patience in this way again. You can still claim the girl, if you can catch her fairly. You will not take her tonight."

Still ashen, Bobby pulls Emma from his car and drops her to the pavement. He doesn't look back as he climbs into the driver's seat and blasts away, leaving the four of us alone.

Make that the three of us. When I turn to thank Bethany, she's gone. I look at the place where she'd been for a moment. Then I nod, and make my way to Emma.

She's still gagged, her hands tied behind her back, but her eyes are open, and focus on me as I kneel to pull the gag away. She coughs, weakly. "You didn't have to do this," she whispers.

"Hush," I reply, and start working on the rope that binds her wrists. "You're my friend. Besides, I couldn't let you die before you got the chance to see my boyfriend again."

"Boyfriend?" asks Emma, blinking.

"He's the hot guy behind me. The one with the smokin' wheels."

Emma's eyes flick past me, and widen as she sees Gary—the only possible "hot guy with smokin' wheels" on the road. Then she starts to laugh, punctuating her amusement with more coughs. "You have to be kidding me."

"Nope. I am working hard to redefine weird." I straighten, helping her to her feet. "I'm getting a malted for this, right?"

"You're getting all the malteds you can drink, forever," she says, fiercely, and pulls me into a hug. "Thank you."

"What are friends for?" I pat her back with one hand and turn to smile at Gary. He flashes his headlights at me. My smile widens. "Let's go home."

Last Dance Diner, says the neon sign, glowing through the darkness like a lighthouse guiding us safely into port. The lights are on, and there are people inside, being waited on by Emma's staff. After the midnight, this level of the twilight seems almost bright enough to be the day.

We slide into the parking lot, and Emma pats Gary's dashboard, saying, "I'll send Dinah out with some fresh oil. Thanks again. For everything."

His radio spins, and the Beatles tell her that they get by with a little help from their friends.

"Don't we all?" Emma turns her smile toward me, only the weariness at the corner of her mouth betraying what she's been through tonight. "You coming?"

"Yeah," I say, and kiss Gary's steering wheel before sliding out of my seat. He closes the door behind me, and my feet crunch in the gravel as I follow Emma toward the warm and welcoming light of home.

I won't tell you this is how it ends. I won't tell you this is where it ended. Those things would be lies. But I'll tell you this: the road is as long as you want it to be, and every accident can be a blessing, if you're willing to look past the bad parts and find the good ones, like the friends who wait for you on the other side. I won't tell you this is my whole story, but it's as much as I'm going to share right now.

If you ever need me, I'll be there to get you home. And in all the Americas, from midnight to noon and in-between, the truckers roll out, and the diners stand like cathedrals of the road, and the beat . . . the beat goes on.

The Price Family Field Guide to the Twilight of North America Ghostroad Edition

THE LIVING

Ambulomancers. Characterized by their extreme reluctance to trust themselves to any form of vehicular transit, these born wanderers are eternally on the move, gathering strength and power from the distance they have traveled. A novice ambulomancer will be able to control the road in small ways, finding food, shelter, and protection even within the harshest environments. An advanced ambulomancer will actually be able to interpret the language of the road itself, using this information to predict the future and manipulate coming events. Ambulomancers can be of any species, human or nonhuman, although humans and canines are the most common.

Routewitches. These children of the moving road gather strength from travel, much as the ambulomancers do, but the resemblance stops there. Rather than controlling the road, routewitches choose to work with it, borrowing its strength and using it to make bargains with entities both living and dead. The routewitches of North America are currently based out of the old Ocean Highway, which "died" in 1926, and are organized by their Queen, Apple, a young woman of Japanese-American descent who matches the description of a teenage girl who mysteriously disappeared from Manzanar during World War II. The exact capabilities of the routewitches remain unclear, although they seem to have a close relationship with the crossroads.

Trainspotters. Very little is known. They have been called "the routewitches of the rails," but no direct information has yet been collected.

Umbramancers. These fortune-tellers and soothsayers are loosely tied to the twilight, but the magic they practice is more general than the road-magic of the routewitches and the ambulomancers. It's unclear exactly what relationship the umbramancers have to the twilight. They have been seen visiting the crossroads; there are no known bargains involving an umbramancer.

THE DEAD

Beán sidhe. The *beán sidhe* are alive and dead at the same time, which makes them difficult to classify, but as they prefer the company of the dead, we are listing them here. These Irish spirits are associated with a single family until that family dies out, and will watch their charges from a distance, mourning them when they die. They regard this as a valuable service. We are not certain why.

Bela da meia-noite. The bela da meia-noite, or "midnight beauty," is an exclusively female type of ghost, capable of appearing only between sunset and midnight. They enjoy trendy clubs and one-night stands. They're generally harmless, and some have proven very helpful in exorcising hostile spirits, since they'd prefer that no one get hurt.

Crossroads ghosts. Marked by their eyes, which all sightings have described as "containing miles," these ghosts speak for the crossroads, a metaphysical construct where those who are connected to the afterlife in some way are able to go and make bargains, the nature of which we still do not fully understand. The best known crossroads ghost is Mary Dunlavy, who tends to answer questions with "I'll tell you when you're dead."

Crossroads guardians. The flipside of the crossroads ghost is the crossroads guardian, a being which was never alive in the traditional sense, but which now represents the interests of the crossroads in all things. When asked about crossroads guardians, Mary Dunlavy's response consisted of a single word: "Run."

Deogen. Also known as "the Eyes," the deogen are noncorporeal, foglike, and often hostile. They will lead travelers astray if given the chance, and have been known to form alliances with other unfriendly spirits. A deogen/homecomer team-up is to be feared.

Einherjar. These dead heroes are supposed to stay in Valhalla, if it exists, so we don't know why they sometimes crop up in the living world. They become solid in the presence of alcohol or violence, and they very much enjoy professional wrestling.

Gather-grims. Next to nothing is known about this class of psychopomp; we're not honestly sure that they exist. We have heard them mentioned by other ghosts, but they are leery to answer questions, and will generally change the subject. Investigate with caution.

Goryo. These powerful ghosts are most often of wealthy backgrounds, and are commonly of Japanese descent. All known goryo were martyred, or believe themselves to have been martyred, leading to their undying rage. They can control the weather, which is exactly the kind of capability that you don't want in an angry spirit fueled by the desire for vengeance.

Haunts. All haunts lost love at some point during their lives, although it may have been decades before they actually passed away. Their kiss can cure all known ailments. It can also kill. Which it does seems to be fairly arbitrary, and based on how close the person being kissed is to death. As haunts are not terribly bright as a class, they often misjudge their affections. Try not to encourage them.

Hitchhiking ghosts. Often referred to as "hitchers," these commonly sighted road ghosts are generally the spirits of those who died in particularly isolated automobile accidents. They are capable of taking on flesh for a night by borrowing a coat, sweater, or other piece of outerwear from a living person. Temperament varies from hitcher to hitcher; they cannot be regarded as universally safe.

Homecoming ghosts. Called "homecomers," these close relatives of the hitchhiking ghosts want one thing only: to go home. They are typically peaceful for the first few years following their deaths, when their homes are still recognizable. The trouble begins once those homes begin to change. Homecomers whose homes are gone will become violent, and in their rage, they have been known to kill the people who offer to drive them home.

Maggy Dhu. Black ghost dogs capable of taking on physical form. They can weigh over two hundred pounds, and their bite is deadly to the living. The Maggy Dhu are somewhat smarter than living canines, but they are still animals, and are often vicious. Interestingly, all types of dog can become Maggy Dhu after death; many are believed to have been Chihuahuas in life. They are believed to harvest souls.

Pelesit. Ghosts bound to living masters through an unknown ritual. They appear normal in the twilight, but have trouble manifesting fully in the living world unless they are at or near the scene of a recent murder.

Reapers. These dark-cloaked ghosts seem to exist only to guide the spirits of the recently deceased onto the next stage of their existence. We don't know why. They do not speak to the living, and none of us has ever been willing to commit suicide for the sake of an interview.

Strigoi. The strigoi are an interesting case: the dead use the name to refer to a specific type of angry ghost, capable of becoming fully corporeal when it revisits the site of its death. These ghosts have no truly vampiric qualities, and seem to be unrelated to the cryptids of the same name.

Toyol. The toyol are sorcerously bound spirits of infants who died before or shortly after birth. The less said about them, the better.

White ladies. These spirits of abandoned or betrayed women can be of any age, united only by the tragedies that killed them. They are not technically road ghosts, but are often mistaken for hitchers, and have been recorded seeking rides as a cover for their violent revenge. White ladies are extremely dangerous, and should be avoided.

Playlist

"Weep For Us Little Stars"	Guggenheim Grotto
"Mercy of thc Fallen"	Dar Williams
"Lollipop"	Ben Kweller
"The Living Dead"	Phantom Planet
"Earth Angel"	Death Cab for Cutie
"Barton Hollow"	The Civil Wars
"Arizona 160"	Amy Speace
"El Viento del Diablo"	Bruce Holmes
"Dance in the Graveyards"	Delta Rae
"Heads Will Roll"	Yeah Yeah Yeahs
"By Way of Sorrow"	Julie Miller
"Shadows of Evangeline"	Tracy Grammer
"Life is a Highway"	Tom Cochrane
"Thunder Road"	Bruce Springsteen

SONGS

As I mentioned at the front of the book, Rose's story really began in song form. Here in print for the first time are some of those songs for your enjoyment.

PRETTY LITTLE DEAD GIRL

This is the "filthy libel" version of Rose Marshall's story, and was the title track of my first album. Rose hates it.

It's a very sad story, it's a very sad tale,
All about what can happen when your brake lines fail.
It's the tale of Rose Marshall—the sweetest sixteen—
And why you shouldn't race at Sidewinder Ravine . . .

Let me tell you about Rose Marshall,
The sweetest girl that you'd ever see.
They always say that the good die young,
Well, she died back in fifty-three,
Kept her prom night date with the cemetery.

They used to call her 'her Daddy's darling';
The people said she'd go pretty far.

She had the love of friends and family,
But little Rosie loved her car—
Used to fly through the night like a shooting star.

> Now she's a pretty little dead girl in a coup de ville,
> And she's looking for a drag race up on Dead Man's Hill,
> And if you've got a brain, boy, you'd better drive on by.
> Because she looks real sweet and she smiles real nice,
> But you'd better take some well-meant good advice:
> If you race with Rose, then you're probably gonna die.

No one's really quite sure what happened;
None of the folks involved survived.
Three hours to prom and Rose got restless,
Said she was going for a drive.
It was the last time they saw her alive.

The sheriff said she'd been doing ninety
Along the edge of the ravine;
Two sets of tracks—but here's the strange thing—
The other car was never seen.
Whoever clipped Rose, well, they got away clean.

> Now she's a pretty little dead girl in a coup de ville,
> And she's looking for a drag race up on Dead Man's Hill,
> And if you want to live, boy, you'd better drive on by.
> Because she doesn't play by no natural laws—
> Sure she's a pretty little kitty, but this cat's got claws,
> And if you race with Rose, then you're probably gonna die.

'bout three years later the stories started;
They say she's out there on the hill.
They say she's looking for a prom date.
So long dead and she's sixteen still.
She never grew up and she never will.

Some people say that she's just a legend;
Some people say that she's something more.
Here's what I know: when Rose gets restless,
She still puts the pedal through the floor,
And her boyfriends don't come home no more—

SPOKEN (Rosette #1):
Sam Harris was a good man. Real sweet. Real compassionate. A genuine boy scout of the highest order. That's why he was coming to pick me up from the diner that night. Guess he was real worried about me, because he took that shortcut up along Sidewinder, even though I'd told him not to, even though I told him I didn't mind a little wait . . . Sam Harris was a good man. And now he's a dead one.

If you get in her way then she'll ask you to race her,
It's like a shot of 'dumb idea' with a 'bad plan' chaser,
'Cause she's a bat out of hell wearing patent leather shoes.

SPOKEN (Rosette #2):
When you got right down to it, Jimmy was always, without a doubt . . . Jimmy. A little sweet, a little stubborn, and a whole lot sure that he knew what was good for him. 'Don't mess with the crazy ghost-girl up on Dead Man's Hill', I said, and sure enough, the very next night . . . well. I guess a long fall off a steep cliff taught him to listen to his girlfriend. Until he hit the bottom, anyway.

She's not looking for a savior, she's not looking for a ride,
And you shouldn't go look for her if you're not a suicide,
'Cause it's been fifty years and nobody's seen her lose.

SPOKEN (Rosette #3):
I guess Thomas got lucky. He went up to the hill looking for answers, and when he found them, he managed to get away with his life. Yeah. Real lucky. He hasn't left the house for almost fifteen years. Keeps saying he knows too much. If that ghost talked to women, I'd tell her a thing or two. With a shotgun.

If you beat her in a race, well, she'll give you her pink slip,
But if she beats you to the curve, then you're in for a long
trip,

'Cause she's looking for a boyfriend who can dance the whole night through.

SPOKEN (Rosette #4):
Harry . . . was an idiot.

She's a little out of date but she's never out of style,
And she'll lead you to your fate with a shimmy and a smile,
So if you feel like living, don't let Rosie race with you.

Let me tell you about Rose Marshall—
Might be the last thing you'll ever see.
They say some stories will never die,
Well, she died back in fifty-three,
Kept her prom night date with the cemetery.
She died back in fifty-three,
Kept her prom night date with the cemetery . . .

Pretty dead girl, pretty little dead girl.
Pretty dead girl, pretty little dead girl.
Pretty dead girl, pretty little dead girl.
Pretty little dead girl in a coup de ville.

GRAVEYARD ROSE

If "Pretty Little Dead Girl" is the filthy libel version, this is the almost over-idealized version. The truth is somewhere in the middle.

Well, I pulled into the truck stop lookin' for a cup of joe;
It was sometime after midnight, with five hundred miles to go.
I'm a loner by my nature, and a trucker by my trade;
It's a lucky man can do the things he loves and still get paid.

It was just another diner, nothing special, nothing strange,
Just the sort of spot a man can stop when home is out of range.
Just a wide patch on the highway, neon, diesel, glass and chrome.
Not the sort of spectral port of call a good ghost should call home.

> But she's never been a good ghost, not for one day in her death;
> She stopped playing by the rules the day that she gave up on breath.
> She's the angel of the truck stops; it's the afterlife she chose.
> She's the flower of the graveyard, she's our ageless roadside Rose.

She was standing in the shadows, neon highlights in her hair,
And I almost walked right by her, never knowing she was there.
She was laughing as she said, "Hey, Mister, help a girl in need?"
And I don't know why she chose me, nor the reason I agreed.

And the neon traveled with her as she moved to take a seat,
Like a sailor coming home the day his journey is complete.
Don McLean was on the jukebox, belting out his great good-bye;
When I asked her what she'd like, she smiled and said, "I'll have the pie."

> And she's never been a good ghost, not for one day in her death . . .

I don't know just when I knew her, but I knew her all the same,
Because truckers have our legends, and our ghosts have got their fame.
She asked, "So have you guessed my name?"—I answered, "I suppose."
Then I offered her my hand, and said, "It's nice to meet you, Rose."

Well, she didn't seem a bit surprised as she reached for my hand,
And she didn't have a heartbeat, and she said, "Please understand,
I'm not here to cause you trouble, and this isn't what you think.
I'm not here to hurt or haunt you. I'm just looking for a drink."

I said "I heard you were a killer"; she said "lies, all lies,
Though it's true I'm often with a driver, on the night he dies.
For men can sometimes get confused on a road that they don't know;
They need someone who knows the way to tell them where to go.
They need someone to steer them straight to where they're meant to be . . .
They need a hand to hold the map, and that's why they need me.

And I've never been a good ghost, not for one day in my death,
I gave up on playing by the rules when I gave up on breath.
I'll rove these roads forever—it's the afterlife I chose—
But I'll help you if I get the chance . . ." and I said, "Thank you, Rose."

Well, I drove her to the limits of a town not far away,
And she vanished like a fable at the breaking of the day.
As she slipped away, she kissed my cheek and said, "We'll meet again . . ."
And I find that I'm not worried 'bout the how, or 'bout the when.

For there's beauty on the open road a man can learn to find;
Flowers blossom on the median, and fate is sometimes kind.
When it's time to make the final drive, I won't be scared at all,
Rose will be right here beside me, all along that final haul.

And she's never been a good ghost, not for one day in her death;
She stopped playing by the rules the day that she gave up on breath.
She's the angel of the truck stops; it's the afterlife she chose.
She's the flower of the graveyard, she's our ageless roadside Rose.

She's the blossom of the median; she's the place a lost man goes.
She's the flower of the graveyard, she's our ageless roadside Rose.

WAXEN WINGS

Given the opportunity, I would probably have become a country singer. I didn't have it, so I write things like this.

I needed something more than sitting here and counting down
The minutes of a life lived in the margins of redemption.
I needed something more than just a footnote in a sleepy town—
"She lived and died according to the currents of convention."

Icarus had waxen wings and if he fell, well, he still flew;
He tried to reach the heavens and they slipped right through his fingers.
If someone gave me waxen wings, I'd reach out for the heavens too,
And leave behind these alleys where the ghost of hope still lingers.

I needed something more than anyone could ever give me;
I needed something I could understand.

I tried to spread my wings, I prayed the heavens would
forgive me,
And if I fell, I prayed that they would leave me where I land.

I needed something more than sitting here and counting cards
The coffee spoons and cigarettes that measure endless days.
I needed something more than dead-eyed lovers, more than
dead-grass yards—
The shadow girls and phantom boys who never found their
ways.

Icarus had waxen wings and took a chance on something more;
I wonder if he laughed out loud when gravity embraced him.
They say that luck's a lady, but I think that fate is just a whore,
She keeps chasing all the pretty boys until one lets her taste him.

I needed something more than anyone could ever give me;
I needed something I could understand.
I tried to spread my wings, I prayed the heavens would
forgive me,
And if I fell, I prayed that they would leave me where I land.

Ain't no wings for little girls who ought to know their places;
Ain't no wings for baby-dolls who try to join the races.
You've known a thousand girls like me—you can't recall their
faces.
We live inside our own regrets. We fill the empty spaces.

I needed something more than sitting here and killing time
The wasted hours that blew away like ashes in the wind.
I needed something I could face, some mountain I could climb,
A pair of waxen wings to bear me to my happy end.

Icarus had waxen wings and yes it's true, he ended badly,
But I like to think the ending that he had was what he chose.

I'd rather choose to grab for glory; if I fall, then I'll fall gladly.
The only ones who get to fall are the ones who risked, and rose.

HANGING TREE

Rose's road has not always been a happy one.

Meet me in the shadow of the hanging tree,
Where the skeletons of mercy dangle still.
Love is like a shadow hanging over me;
I always say I won't. I always will.

And love is like the mountain,
And it doesn't care
That my stillborn heart beats naked in my hand.
Love is like the winter,
And it isn't fair . . .
But the hanging tree's been hurt. It understands.

See the pretty maidens in their summer gowns,
With hollyhocks and lilies in their hair.
Counting off the petals as they shower down—
He loves me not. He loves me. He'll be there.

And hope is like a promise
I can never keep,
A tangled maze of tragedy and blame.
I lay me down each night,
And still I never sleep,
But the hanging tree forgives me, all the same.

So lay me down where the tangled roots
Of the past hold tightly to the land;

I've been here before, I know the way.
So lay me down in the gentle arms
Of the only one who understands;
The hanging tree's the only love I've ever had
Who ever said that I could rest, that I could stay . . .

Leave me in the shadow of the hanging tree,
Where the sins of past transgressions sing and sigh.
Love is like a story never meant to be;
I always say I won't. I always lie.

And faith is like the shadow
Of the hanging tree,
It's rooted deep in everything we are.
It catches us in chains
Until we're never free,
But the hanging tree forgives my every scar.

Meet me in the shadow of the hanging tree;
Bring your shattered heart like rubies in your hand.
Maybe love was never really meant to be,
But the hanging tree keeps faith. It understands.

SPARROW HILL ROAD

And I leave you, for now, with the true side of the story, however much it stings.

Good girls only make the news one way.
Special reports when the kids are asleep
And the ghouls come out to play.
Good girls make their marks and fade away,
People say their prayers and they shake their heads
And they bury them anyway,

And they'll tell you "she was lovely,"
Though they all forget the names
Of the ones who pay the good girl's fee
Down the rocky road to fame—

So when the crossroads call and your faith is thin
And you're afraid you might explode,
Go and talk to the girl in the green silk gown
Who walks on Sparrow Hill Road.

Good girls never really seem to last.
They shine so bright and they shine so brief
And we leave them in the past.
Good girls always pass us by so fast,
And the people say that it's such a shame
When the die's already cast,

And they'll tell you that they're sorry
As they move on down the road.
It's just someone else's story,
One more debt that wasn't owed,

Now when the shadows seem to know your name
And your dreams have all plateaued,
Go and talk to the girl in the green silk gown
Who walks on Sparrow Hill Road.

And she'll say she was a good girl,
Did the things that she was told,
And she'll say that she was frightened
Of the things the night might hold,
And she'll say they used to call her "Rose"
Before she paid their price,
When she died to live forever
Through the good girl's sacrifice—

And when the night hails down and you're afraid
That you'll never get what you're owed,
Go and talk to the girl in the green silk gown
Who died on Sparrow Hill Road.

And when you see her face in the truck-stop light,
When the final cock has crowed,
Then you'll go with the girl in the green silk gown
Who died on Sparrow Hill Road.

Acknowledgments

If you've made it this far, you've been to Buckley Township, and to the Last Dance Diner; you've driven the Ocean Lady, and all for the sake of winding up here, on *Sparrow Hill Road*. Thank you so much. Rose's story has been a long and winding one, with at least three distinct points of origin. Those of you who know my music may have met her first in the song "Pretty Little Dead Girl," which is a filthy, filthy lie, and those of you who follow my short fiction may have encountered her on *The Edge of Propinquity*, where I was a 2010 universe author. Wherever you first met Rose, it's because of you, and people like you, that my little hitchhiking ghost has managed to travel this far. Words are not enough to express my appreciation.

Thanks to Sheila Gilbert at DAW for taking a chance on my ghost girl, and to Jennifer Brozek at *The Edge of Propinquity* for saying, "I'd like to know more about Rose." Thanks to all my original Rosettes, Michelle Dockrey, Amy McNally, Erica Neely, and Meg Heydt, as well as Alisa Garcia, who joined our girl group for the recording of *Stars Fall Home*. Aly Fell brought Rose to something resembling life with his incredible cover; I am so lucky to have him. As always, thanks to Christopher Mangum and Tara O'Shea for website design and maintenance, to Kate Secor for admin duties, and to Michelle Dockrey for endless editorial.

My soundtrack while writing *Sparrow Hill Road* consisted mostly of a lot of classic rock and modern country, including Little Big Town, Christian Kane, and Miranda Lambert. Any errors in this book are entirely my own. The errors that aren't here are the ones that all these people helped me fix.

Going my way?